I0586409

Amanda Minnie Douglas

**The children at Sherburne house**

Amanda Minnie Douglas

**The children at Sherburne house**

ISBN/EAN: 9783337215675

Printed in Europe, USA, Canada, Australia, Japan

Cover: Foto ©Andreas Hilbeck / pixelio.de

More available books at **www.hansebooks.com**

# SHERBURNE HOUSE

BY

AMANDA M. DOUGLAS

AUTHOR OF "THE LITTLE GIRL IN OLD NEW YORK," ETC.

———————

NEW YORK

DODD, MEAD & COMPANY

1897

TO

# Grace Virginia Halsey

A FRIENDSHIP IS LIKE THE UNFOLDING OF A FLOWER. THERE ARE
BLOSSOMS OF A DAY RARE AND FRAGRANT, THERE ARE OTHERS THAT HAVE
SEASONS OF BLOOM, AND SOME COME TO US YEAR AFTER YEAR WITH THEIR
IMPERISHABLE SWEETNESS.

A. M. D.

NEWARK, 1897.

# CONTENTS.

# THE CHILDREN AT SHERBURNE HOUSE.

## CHAPTER I.

### A GLANCE AT THE PAST.

"EVERYTHING in the world has come to Dell Sherburne. She seems to have a double portion."

Fanny Beaumanoir sat on the step of the great porch at Sherburne House. Her sister-in-law was in a pretty wicker rocking-chair, doing some exquisite lace-work. Beside her, on a soft rug, the baby of the household laughed and crowed, and three little ones were tumbling about on the grass, with a small colored maid to see that no harm befell them.

A lovely summer afternoon, with the scent of the morning's shower in the air, and a sky still broken with some fleecy, drifting clouds, tempering the sunshine. All the air was sweet with fragrance.

The eight years of Tessy Beaumanoir's married life and the cares of motherhood had not worn her or brought any dissatisfactions. There had been very few sorrows and many joys. Her life might have seemed narrow to some women, but she said to her husband it reached to the ends of the earth. Like her own mother, she had an inexhaustible fund of love for her children, but she had also many glimpses of the wider world, and her husband was fond of having her keep in touch with the topics of the day.

"Yes," in answer to Fanny. "But certainly she deserves it all. I was a little afraid at one time that she—that both of them would be so engrossed with the lives of others that they would forget to have anything of their very own. And now they have had two lovely years. They will be home this autumn. Oh, I do want to see her and the babies!"

"Millicent is quite wild about it also." Then Fanny gave a little sigh.

"I am glad there have been no changes," said Tessy softly—"no vacant places."

"No, only new places," with a short laugh. "She must have enjoyed that German episode and seeing her old lover a happy husband and father. And Bertram liked him so much. Oh dear, who could have dreamed of so many splendid things when she first came here! We all walked over her like a triumphant march of fiends. How we did hate to think of her reigning here! And *now*——"

"Now that she has a little boy of her own it almost seems to me as if she had deprived him of his birthright."

"Nonsense!" declared Fanny. "Don't you and Len get to having conscientious scruples."

"We talked it over last night. No, we have not exactly conscientious scruples," with a faint smile. "They will go back to New York—you could not imagine Bertram Carew contenting himself in a place like this. Even Leonard, proud as he is of the old estate, does enjoy a wider sphere."

"And you are perfectly happy," Fanny said after a long pause.

" Because I have all that I care for. I love a home
and children—yes, and old people in it. And when the
children grow up I shall have another life in theirs."

" You and Dell are fortunate people."

There was a touch of sharpness in Fanny's tone—regret rather than envy.

How strangely sweet the children's laughing voices
sounded ! All the world was bright and happy, except
some few people who had missed their vocation. What
was a woman's vocation—marriage ? Well, surely she
had found opportunities ; let that satisfy her.

Everything was so tranquil over here—two old ladies
who had grown into an almost poetical harmony ; two
really old maids nearing fourscore. Both had had years
full of a certain kind of duty. Aunt Aurelia's life had
been very full and pleasant until Lyndell had been pro-
jected across it by some curious fate. How they had all
protested inwardly ! And one of the strange consequences seemed to be her part in bringing about the very
conclusions they had planned, or at least hoped for without her. She had touched all their lives, even hers.
Did she wish this had not been ? It was one of the
things she could never quite answer to herself. It had
made a difference to her.

When Fanny dropped into these silent, retrospective
moods there was small use in arguing with her or trying
to comfort her. Perhaps one reason why she liked her
brother's wife so well was because she did not try. So
Tessy felt free to follow out her own thoughts, and they
flew with the swiftness of birds to Dell Carew, who had
always been the dearest of sisters without kindred blood.

And the two years had been so replete with delight.
Everybody wondered how the old doctor and Miss Carew

had been persuaded, at their time of life, to make the grand tour. But the doctor really wanted to go, and the children had been so exigent. However, he would not stir a step without Miss Neale. And a young clergyman, recently come to Ardmore with a mother and sister, would be delighted to take the old house and care for Miss Neale's dependents until he could suit himself with some habitation, or, as some of his more appreciative hearers surmised, until he had a better call elsewhere.

" It does seem as if brother ought to have this dream of a long and arduous life satisfied," Miss Carew said, as if in extenuation of such a frivolity at her time of life. " And he insists that he will not stir a step without me."

" Of course I should go," declared Miss Sherburne. " Nothing would give Lyndell greater delight. And Laura and Mr. Beaumanoir will see that nothing goes wrong with the house."

Dr. Carew had cordially commended his new compeer. For the last two years he had been turning new calls over to him. And some of the old families he had taken a lifelong interest in had dropped out one by one or sought new homes. There never had been a time when he could be so well spared.

Ah, what a grand satisfaction it had proved ! They did not run around like the young people. There were so many things Dell was eager to show her husband. Trenholme Court opened wide its hospitable doors. The three older girls were married and gone, but some new ones were young women. Sir Purvis and Lady Trenholme never tired of the California Ranch, the Osbornes, and Colonel and Lady Ashton. There was London, with its storied piles ; and Miss Ashton, quite past middle life now, and with snowy hair, still devoted to art, though she railed good humoredly at the new methods ; and then Scotland and Ireland.

" At this rate it will take us seven years," said Dr. Carew. He had half a mind to consider his journey finished and return.

" But you know you promised Millicent to go to Germany. And what if it should take us a little longer ! Bertram is picking up new ideas all the time, and may write another book."

Lyndell was quite irresistible.

Then there was queer old Luckenwalde, with its mountain fastnesses. The old baroness was gone, and Baron Waldemar and his wife. Ulrike had retired to a convent, and the other sister lived in solitary state, enlivened now and then by a flying visit from her brother Franz and his wife.

Baron Zahn was sole master now at Trachenburg. His pretty German wife and golden-haired children quite delighted Dell. He surely had not broken his heart over his first love, though he said, " I have never quite forgotten thee, Mignonne, and was glad to hear of thy happiness. And I often think of Emil's sweet wife and her little girl. I hope they will come over some day. We will make them most welcome."

Then there had been journeying about storied places, and galleries, and churches, and hospitals. They had found Anita Garcia quite a famous singer, and engaged to a Russian nobleman. They went to hear her at Vienna, and certainly she sang in a most exquisite manner. She was a little shy of Dr. Carew at first, but charming in her gratitude to Lyndell.

"I did not think I should ever marry," she said to Dell ; "so many singers have unfortunate lives. And I could tell so little about my mother, my own family. So, two years ago, when he first asked me, I told him 'No.' And when he persisted, I related to him all my sad little story and your goodness, and he has watched over me and followed me from place to place until I have come to love him. I shall not give up singing—it is a part of my life—and he is extravagantly fond of music. So I shall be very happy."

And then they go on again.

"Yes," said Lyndell, "it would take seven years to see it all, and we cannot spend so many golden years out of our lives for pure pleasure."

They rambled about storied Greece, and in the Greek capital they erected household gods for a brief while. Bertram met some friends deeply interested in archæological discoveries. Miss Carew was delighted with a chance for a little home life. And here the second great joy of Lyndell's life came to her in a double portion, as Fanny had said, in the birth of a son and a daughter.

Miss Carew was delighted with the boy, but the doctor held the little girl to his heart with a great throb of thanksgiving. All these years he had waited with a silent prayer that this greatest blessing of all should be granted to the children he loved so dearly.

The babies throve finely. The elder doctor kept watch and ward that they should be left largely to nature's methods. They slept for hours undisturbed. It was well for Bertram that he had found an outside interest, for when he was in the house he could only hover about his wife and babies in a kind of speechless ecstasy.

When he was away he wondered if it was not some radiant dream rather than reality.

It had been a kind of new beginning. Not that the few years of their married life had proved unsatisfactory —far from it. There were many things one must needs learn by experience—the richness of real living, which was different from dreams. For in dreams one had no positive concern; in the living there must be a continual effort for higher things.

Once he had spoken of Dell's gift to her cousin.

"I wonder," he said with a softened inflection, "if you will ever desire Sherburne House for your own boy?"

Lyndell glanced up out of clear eyes.

"I think you will have something better than that for him," she returned gravely. "No, there has never been a moment in which I have thought of it with any longing."

He bent over and kissed her. He thought now that in his lover's pride he had asked a great sacrifice of her. But he was jealous of his own name and his father's, and how could he endure to have his own son relinquish it? And it had seemed a kind of poetical justice to have it come back to Leonard Beaumanoir, to be in some sense his wife's portion as well as his own.

Fanny's thoughts had strayed still farther back, yet they could hardly be disconnected from Tessy either. She recalled the first time she had seen Lyndell Sherburne. Had they exaggerated the stout figure, the child's complexion burned with sun and wind, the rough hair—red they all decided to call it—the brusque, ungracious manner? What a contrast she made with the others! She had heard a good deal of neighborhood talk about the Sherburne beauty. It was a conceded point. Millicent had it as well as Leonard. And Violet was a handsome woman, had been a lovely young girl. True, Ned was only up to the average. And she had been disappointed in every respect. At fourteen she bid fair to be as tall as her sisters, and her hair was hardly losing its gold. But she had not reached the mark of her ambition. Her hair had grown steadily darker. Her complexion was very well, fine and soft, but rather pale. When she stood before the glass she had to admit that she was only an ordinary girl. To be sure, she had a certain youthfulness, but she *was* six-and-twenty, and—unmarried.

There were so many single women in the cities; but here the girls she had danced and frolicked with six or eight years ago were mothers or settled into defined lines of spinsterdom. Oh, how she had hated the thought of not being married then! How queer it was that she should be the only single girl in the family! Of course she might have been married—comforting remembrance. Was it only two years ago that she had that lovely golden summer and autumn in California, and had proffered her the one thing she really coveted? No, not the real thing, not the pure gold. Even *she* had detected the false ring. Oh, why had she been so wise, so exigent? If she could have accepted in a careless, worldly manner, if she could have brought herself to the creed of her cousin, Ethel Longworth! And it was queer, too, when she was not a really fine and noble woman. Millicent, Violet, Alice, Dell, and Tessy were miles beyond her. Only she *did* see, she had glimpses of that truer life, and in her spasm of conscientiousness she felt she had no right to bring this other soul down to arid levels when it might reach heights. Of course, if he had pro-

tested—a man in love would have, surely—but there had
been a certain element of duty in it, as if he was salving
his conscience ; and she wanted love, not mere duty.
Then she had returned, and they had all joined in sending Millicent away for a long holiday. She had been
devoted to home since that tragic, early widowhood.
To be sure, there was a compensation in her genius, but
even that needed fresh pastures occasionally. It had
been the one heroic effort of Fanny's life, and it had
brought forth no fruit at all. Reese Drayton had seen
Millicent long enough to fall in love with her, and he
had made a sort of ideal of her when she had been in
New York taking care of Dell. Yet she had come
home with knowledge and richness stored up for stories,
with a certain brilliancy of description, a new charm, a
lovely color, and splendid health, a kind of rejuvenating
influence that made her seem almost a girl again, but no
engagement. There was much to talk about. Grandon
Park, where miles of wilderness were being made to
blossom like a rose, and business and civilization went
hand in hand. But Bevis Osborne was wonderfully interested in the sanitarium, though it was to be called
Carew House and wear a home-like aspect. An experienced missionary had gone out from New York on Dr.
Carew's recommendation—a Mr. Moore, and a physician
of Drayton's choosing. Little cottages were springing
up, and families sent out to fill them, people to whom
the great city was fraught with temptations innumer-
able, and employment at the best irregular. Had Millicent and Reese Drayton seen no point of sympathetic
response through all this time ? Perhaps Millicent had
some objection. She had been admired a good deal ;
but Fanny recalled the fact that she had never allowed

any friend to cross the line that would have made him a lover. Perhaps her heroism had been useless. Men and women had learned to love after the bond had been perfected by the marriage ceremony. Her course had not brought her the high content, the sense of well-doing that she expected. Of course, if Millicent *had* returned engaged, that would have been the end of it. But now they were all coming home to welcome the Carews, for Mr. Drayton was especially anxious to meet Dr. Carew. And Mr. Drayton had such a strong desire to see Sherburne House. There might be a delicate way of showing him she had learned her mistake. Men were caught by that flattering knowledge.

Princess—they called Tessy's eldest girl that, though she was named for Aunt Aurelia—ran up the steps and flung herself in Aunt Fanny's arms, breaking her reverie, and the consciousness brought a bright color to her cheek, a curious, hesitating expression to her eyes.

" Somebody is coming, Aunt Fan—guess."

She tried to put her small, dimpled hands over Aunt Fanny's eyes. A ridiculous thought flashed through the mind of the elder—was it a presentiment as well—she would be the old maid aunt of the family.

" Prinny, dear," entreated the soft voice of her mother.

Miss Armitage and her brother came up the path. Fanny rose blushing and laughing, the child still clinging to her. Mrs. Beaumanoir held out her hand with a cordial welcome. They seemed in a huddle for an instant, a charming bit of confusion. Then Tessy picked up her baby and pushed forward the willow chairs, begging her guests to be seated.

Fanny smoothed her ruffled plumes. What was the

expression in the young clergyman's face? It looked mightily like admiration.

"I am essaying the rôle I expect to practise many a year," she exclaimed with a kind of bravado—"that of old maid aunt. Let me see; I have eight nieces and nephews. Isn't that enough to make one feel venerable and frisky at the same time?"

"I think you are to be envied, Miss Beaumanoir, in the matter of having so many brothers and sisters," returned Miss Armitage. "I have all my life wished there were more of us. And it must be really delightful to think of the weddings and the family interest. I have been quite charmed with the large families hereabout."

"Mrs. Beaumanoir can appreciate that also. We are not niggardly in family relations," said Fanny.

Princess ran down to the children again, but Fanny kept her seat on the step.

"We have heard some news—I do not know exactly what adjective to use in describing it, joyful it must be to you—that the Carews are coming back," said Mr. Armitage.

"Yes," replied Tessy. "Oh, you were thinking about the house? Why, it is odd, Fanny, but the doctor never mentioned it. Oh, you will be notified of course."

"I am afraid I do not want to be notified," declared the young clergyman with a smile. "I have become so attached to the place and the people, the quiet, delightful life, that, since my flock are not tired of me, I have quite resolved to go on. I have regained my health entirely, and mother is charmed with the climate. The winters are so different from the long, bleak Vermont winters that she thinks she has almost fallen on Paradise. We have enjoyed the old house so much that I should be loth to leave it. But I suppose Dr. Carew's attachment is stronger than mine. His old patients are never weary of longing for him."

"They will all come to Sherburne House," said Tessy, "and I have a feeling that Dr. Carew will not care to gather up his old practice again. He gave a good share of it up to Dr. Underwood before he went away."

"He is getting to be quite an old man," commented Fanny. "Oh dear, if people did not need to grow old!"

"Still there is something gracious and beautiful in serene old age," returned the clergyman, "and a life well used."

"Dr. Carew's has been more than well used. It has been a splendid, earnest life."

"I can readily believe that. He ministered to souls sometimes. I think a good, conscientious physician has a wider scope than a clergyman. He gains access to human hearts more readily."

"I don't see how they can ever give up Bertram again. And the old doctor was so fond of Dell. I am almost sure they will never separate. And Miss Neale has such a big, motherly heart for babies. I suppose the world hereabout thought it couldn't live without Dr. Carew, but it has survived two years. And Dr. Bertram wouldn't live out of New York."

Fanny glanced up triumphantly, as if she had settled the matter with her collective arguments.

"Miss Beaumanoir, you inspire me with hope," said Mr. Armitage ; "and yet I ought not be selfish in the matter. But there is something so restful about the old home. Perhaps it was because I had been so worn out with my city work and was longing for a real home, where I could have my mother and sister and some one to care for me. Mother needed a more genial climate as well. I think she has gone back at least five years."

"You and Mrs. Carew ought to compare notes," said Fanny with sudden vivacity. "When she was a little girl and first came here she was quite ill for a long time ; at least, she was not getting well, and Sherburne House was full of cousins and aunts and everybody ; so Dr. Carew took her home. And she made Pilgrim's Progress out of it all, like a veritable fairy story. The old doctor has been in love with her ever since. I almost wonder he let Bertram have her. But I do not believe he would have allowed any one else to marry her."

"It must have been a case of very fervent love. I remember her saying of one room, ' And the name of that chamber was Peace.' I only saw her twice, and shall be glad to renew my acquaintance with her. When do you expect them ?"

"Early in September. They have been taking a rather leisurely journey homeward. And, Mr. Armitage, you will have an opportunity to see the whole Sherburne clan. They expect to gather from near and from far."

"We shall be glad to meet them, I am sure. Mrs. Kirby delights in talking them over, from old Mr. Sherburne down. And Miss Sherburne and Miss Carrick— I hope they are well ?"

Fanny sprang up and begged Tessy to keep her seat. She set two more chairs in the circle and then ran upstairs. The old ladies often sat and talked awhile after their nap, and did not get down until nearly supper-time.

Miss Aurelia had a very delicate look, though her general health was comparatively good. She had never been so vigorous since her illness. But Miss Carrick certainly improved. She always declared Sherburne House was a foretaste of heaven. In all her life she had never known such utter freedom from care.

Miss Armitage went out on the lawn and talked to the children. They were all such bright, eager little things, so full of merriment. Tessy used to think of her own childhood as she watched them. Miss Aurelia declared there never had been any such sweet children, and their father thought them perfection. They were a little trying sometimes to their mother, but she kept them a good deal in the wide, beautiful out of doors. Often on the long summer days her heart ached for the myriads in the tenement-houses of the crowded city.

Both old ladies were fond of the young clergyman. But now they talked a good deal about the home-coming of the stray members of the family. There would be quite a reunion.

Presently Miss Armitage said they must go. They had a long walk before them, and were quite rested.

"But I am going back to Beaumanoir presently and will drive you home," said Fanny. "It is quite too far to walk both ways."

Tessy had disappeared with her baby, but she returned now with a servant, who set out a dainty tea-table with thin-cut bread and butter, cake and fruit, iced tea, and some bubbling hot in the curious, old silver kettle. Miss Carrick declared she was quite spoiled by her afternoon cup of tea. They had a pleasant chat over it. Tessy had so many charming ways that always fitted in with the occasion.

Then the carriage came around, and Mr. Armi-

tage expressed his sense of obligation as he took his
leave.

"Do you know, you have quite comforted me, Miss
Beaumanoir," he said as they were driving along.
"Somehow I found myself unwilling to leave the old
house. I had hardly thought to get so interested in the
people and the work. I had a curious feeling that when
I was strong again I ought not loiter in pleasant places.
I wonder if we do not sometimes think there is an absolute virtue in wearing ourselves out, and despise the
work that may be a little easier? Still the children in
the wilderness found many compensations."

"I think you can find work enough to do here," she
made answer, "and another house to live in; only I
have a strong presentiment that Bertram Carew will
never part with his father again."

"Family ties are so strong with you here. I enjoy it
so much. I like the respect paid to parents. There is
a charm in most of the elderly people I have seen. It is
like living a pastoral. I occasionally wonder if I have
come to the land where it is 'always afternoon,' and
shall presently feel the lotus influence."

"Oh, you keep too busy. You have too many Northern ways. No, there is not the slightest danger," and
she gave a bright, airy smile.

"I shall accept your verdict." He bowed gravely and
thanked her again as they paused before the old house.

# CHAPTER II.

THE Osbornes were in Washington, and would be down in a day or two was the word Leonard Beaumanoir brought home one evening. And the Carews had sailed. Mr. Drayton would meet them in New York.

" Alice is handsomer and younger than Ethel. Her children are extremely pretty. Violet will have to look to her laurels. But they cannot outshine us," he remarked proudly.

Violet and Mr. Amory had settled themselves in Washington, rather in the suburbs, though the capital, like all modern cities, was stretching out and growing more beautiful. With the birth of her second child Violet had a longing for a permanent home. It was a question for some time just where it should be. New York had many fascinations. Everything in art and science came to it. The Carews were sure to settle there.

" Still," began Violet, " we want a real home for ourselves, if there is any true living left. I have my doubts until I go to Beaumanoir. Then all the freshness of feeling returns, the fervor and faith and earnest endeavor, as if life had some aim. Perhaps that isn't art," and she gave a vague smile.

" No, it isn't. It's an awful heresy. But you must remember that I've never been very art mad. Perhaps I am not a real genius, after all."

"But you do paint splendid portraits, you must admit," she answered with fervent admiration.

"And I'm not sure but soul portraits are going out of fashion as well. My genius seems to lie in the direction of supplying a soul where there is none—guessing at it. And if you guess on the flattering side you please your patron, provided your price is high enough. Everybody likes to be rated at his or her best. The time has gone by when one could paint a truly great picture. Or else there are so many people doing well that it takes an immense effort to distance them. And you know I recognized my limitations long ago, and chose happiness, like any other weak man."

"I don't know why unhappiness should be considered heroic when it is of one's own making. That seems rather like Gifford. Bearing the inevitable bravely and trying to surmount it holds the elements of true heroism according to my thinking. I don't care if it is old-fashioned. And now, which is most heroic or convenient?"

"The choice is yours," said Paul Amory.

"Then I shall be nearer the home folks in Washington. We are going to live somewhat for ourselves."

"Until Lyndell comes home and stirs you up with impossible theories," he returned laughingly. "But remember Mrs. Longworth will rout us out every little while, and we will have to be upon exhibition. Can you start an ideal home in the midst of society?"

"Oh, my dear, we shall be quite on the outskirts. We will be rural with a 'little patch of ground.' And in the rush and turmoil people may forget us."

So they chose their house and arranged it to their fancy, with a studio in an L part. For with the advent of her boy Violet began to long for some permanent place where she might take root. She had quite enough of wandering. She wanted a little quiet to enjoy the memories of what she had seen and heard, and to rear her children properly. Motherhood had assumed a new sacredness in her eyes.

It was delightful to be so near that her mother or Millicent or Fanny could run up every little while. Edward had settled himself in Baltimore. Cecil was deep in a course of architecture. There were no children in the first generation any more.

She made her house pretty and attractive, and though Ethel declared they might as well be buried alive as in the far end of an almost unknown street, Paul Amory's friends seemed to find him without any difficulty, and invitations piled up in the pretty receiver.

Mrs. Longworth still kept her place in society. She ran over to Europe in the summer, had a bit of the London season and a glimpse of Paris, just enough to meet the latest celebrities and order a few gowns. She had a week or two at Berkshire and Tuxedo, and then set her house in order for a winter campaign. Mr. Longworth was fortunate in all his ventures. Mrs. Lepage from fancied invalidism had fallen into a real decline, and sent rather peremptorily for Gifford and Alice. Lieutenant Harry would be home at midwinter from a three years' cruise.

Ethel provided her mother with a nurse, who was well paid to endure her whims and tempers. She was not so poorly but that she could occasionally take a drive on pleasant days and receive in her own beautiful sitting-room. But she knew her reign was over, though she still insisted on being " made up," and was interested in the latest styles. Mrs. Beaumanoir looked years younger.

Alice Osborne came with her husband and her two children, a fine, sturdy boy past six, and a dainty, golden-haired girl of four. Mrs. Lepage had fretted about them.

"Of course they have run wild in that heathenish country," she said. She had not yet become convinced that there could be civilization on a ranch, hardly in a Western city. "Your house will be torn to pieces with such wild Arabs. Really, Ethel, you should have let them go to a hotel."

She almost wished she had when she saw the attraction the child held for her husband. He was bright and intelligent, ready to talk, though not forward, the picture of health and boyish grace, tall for his age, and full of protecting love for his little sister, who seemed rather shy among strangers. Yet for any unusual noise one would hardly have dreamed there were strangers in the house.

Alice was really shocked at the change in her mother. She had been used to the growing old gracefully in Lady Ashton's case; the soft, fine skin getting a little wrinkled, but retaining its peachy bloom, the silvery tint softening the hair, the pretty ways of interest and affection, the keeping in touch with the topics of the day. And her mother was not really old—a little past fifty. But the wearing demands of society in the earlier years, the continual fretting over misfortunes for which she might justly have blamed herself in part—but she never did—the stifling rooms and lack of exercise or interest later on had done its work. She was thin now and much wrinkled, and though she would have scouted the suspicion of dyeing her hair, it was "dressed" frequently and made much darker than its natural color, and brought out the sallow paleness distressfully when she was not "made up." When she insisted on being rouged now and then the contrast was painful.

"She looks very ill," Alice said to her sister.

Mrs. Longworth shrugged her shoulders and gave her lips a little curl as of doubt.

"It is her fancy," she answered. "If you had to live with her, Alice, you would give her her own way in everything. There really is nothing left for her but invalidism, you see. She had the good sense to relinquish society when she began to go off, which is more than some women display. She has her circle of friends, now one kind, now another, who take up the different fads concerning diseases and run through them all without having had one in real earnest. She is not well, of course—who could be under such a regimen?—but since it suits her and is less annoying than some other course to me, it is well enough," nodding her head in a satisfied manner.

"Hasn't she cared to go anywhere—to Beaumanoir or Sherburne House?" asked Alice with concern.

"Oh, she would be bored to death at either place. Len has deteriorated awfully—the result of his marriage with that silly little thing, who will no doubt have a baker's dozen of babies, and who calls on the whole household to admire them. It is enough to disgust one. Really, we must admit that mamma shows good sense in keeping away. And Len could be one of the leaders here if he had a wife with any ambition. He is a fine speaker, and has already been talked of for some public position. It is a shame he should have thrown himself away."

Alice sighed.

"Ned did better. He has quite a stylish wife, and Cecil is a fine young fellow. I should have taken Len in hand if I had not thought he would marry Lyndell."

"But he has Sherburne House."

"Still I am not sure it was a good thing, except for the prestige. He ought to be living right along here in Washington, going out to the men's dinners and keeping himself in the forefront. But you really can't do anything with him. Then he won't accept invitations, you see, with the freedom that he might if he was living here."

"But has Tessy given up all society ? It does not seem wise."

"What can she do with so many babies ? She was up awhile last year in the early winter, and they went about a little. I just called on her, for I had some engagements in New York I couldn't afford to miss. Otherwise I must have given a dinner or something for them. She'll make a queer little old woman presently."

"And Fanny is not married yet ?"

"Oh, she'll be the Sherburne old maid. There has to be one in every family, I believe. And the twins have gone to Dell. I shall be quite curious to know if her foreign tour improved her any. The idea of trotting two old people all over ! I really would not have thought it of Miss Carew. But Dell has a fancy for the devotional and all that. She poses most effectively."

Alice was pained by the tone as well as the captious criticisms.

"We enjoyed Fanny extremely," she said. "I never realized that she was so bright and humorous. And she did have a good deal of admiration."

" Fanny's straining after wit spoils her. It passes at sixteen, but is in bad taste at six-and-twenty. She could have married quite well, since we must admit that Fanny is no beauty. And to marry very well nowadays one must have beauty or a fortune."

Alice soon found that, heartless as her sister's verdict seemed in regard to their mother, it had a great deal of truth. She tried to rouse her to some interest beyond her narrow life ; but Mrs. Lepage was either cross or upbraided Alice with heartlessness in calling up the old troubles and sorrows, or talking of people in whom she had not the slightest interest. She considered herself badly used that Gifford did not visit her every year, and that the government should have sent Harry on such a long cruise. Florence's husband had an appointment abroad, and she had a baby, and she knew she should never live to see any of them again.

" But Gifford *is* coming presently. He had planned to accompany Millicent, but some very important business prevented. You will be proud of him, mamma. He is not so thin, and really fine-looking. You know he was quite unfortunate with a bad investment, but now he is prospering again."

" I dare say he will be like his father for luck. It seems very hard that your father should have let everything slip through his fingers, and I have nothing left for my advancing years. If I should live as long as Aunt Aurelia has I would have to go to the poor-house in the end, I know. But I shall not live. No one understands how weak and miserable I am. Ethel is very good ; of course she has plenty, but I don't see anything of her. It's luncheons, and teas, and dinners, and balls, and New York, and Baltimore, and Europe. I was alone in this house two months last summer, and anything might have happened to me."

"Was Mr. Longworth away?" asked Alice with a touch of anxiety.

"Well, he had to go off somewhere for a fortnight. But a man is not of much account in sickness. If I had a fortune it would be quite different. No one could show me devotion enough then."

"O mamma, you haven't a child who would allow you to want for the slightest thing," cried Alice tenderly.

"But it isn't like having of your very own. And I had always been used to it. I hold that the Sherburne fortune ought to have been divided. The coal and iron mines are bringing in no end of money, and Dell and her husband are running all over Europe spending it on everybody. And since poor Edward never could have a penny of it, it ought to have been divided."

Was this really her mother? Alice asked herself, with a great pang at her heart—this inconsequent, querulous woman, who was coming to want at one moment, and the next dying neglected and alone? Ah, what a sad travesty! It seemed wicked to have her own heart turn with such a warm, exquisite thrill to Lady Ashton, who seemed a truer mother without the vital ownership.

When Leonard came in she was agreeably surprised. Certainly he had not deteriorated in looks or in the joyous vigor that had been a noted attribute of his. He had the air and manner of intelligent and well-used prosperity, and his greeting of the children touched her motherly heart.

"But we have double your number," he said joyously. "Dell's wish for Sherburne House will be gratified. It seems an age since she went away, and we are all wild to see her. Heaven's best gift has not been denied her. And Bertram, it seems, has not been wasting his time wholly in riotous living. I have seen several fine articles from his pen. He has a well-trained, masterly mind. Of course you are going down to Sherburne ! And you must see Violet in her home, which is certainly ' fulfilled of all beauty and pleasaunce.' I've been planning with Osborne—can you go on Saturday ?"

" Oh, no, no. We are to make a long stay, so there need be no especial hurry. It is so long since I have seen mamma."

" But you know we have a very near claim on you. Tessy looks upon you quite as a sister. And I am impatient for us all to be in the old home once more. . You can't think, Alice, what it has been to me," and a shade of tender emotion crossed his face. " I am trying to live up to the gift and the giver. Yet we are not quite sure but that it ought to have been the birthright of Dell's boy."

" Oh, no," returned Alice. " Dell was wise as well as generous. It never could be as dear to any one as to you."

Leonard laughed. " I always look upon it as Tessy's wedding gift. I shall spare you the rhapsodies until you are fairly under my roof and must perforce listen to them. And we are all delighted that Gif is succeeding so well. In fact, I begin to think the Sherburne guerdon is prosperity."

" Gifford has reached a true conception of manhood now, I trust," Alice said tenderly.

" I am curious to see that wonderful Reese Drayton, who has fascinated you all. Milly and Fan quite went down to him."

" You may not like him so well on first acquaintance," said Alice, with a quick smile, " but on second acquaintance you will find him very charming. He and Bevis are like brothers."

" Yes, Osborne is very enthusiastic."

" We owe him a great deal," and there was a depth of emotion in her tone that struck Leonard as having some unusual undercurrent.

Until Sunday Alice felt that she had scarcely seen Ethel. There had been so much planning and comparing to do. There was the carriage and driver at her service, and she went out to the Amorys' one morning, when Violet insisted that she should remain all day. How utterly delightful it seemed with such a charming hostess, who had not only a half hour but a whole day for conversation, and who had some interest beyond the rush and whirl of society !

Would Ethel live her mother's life over again ? There had been the care and interest of children. And, as she remembered, her mother had been very fond of baby Florence, and proud of them all, though society's demands had been reckoned irresistible.

Pearl was still beautiful, and her father posed her for cherubs. There were multitudes of " thoughts" and " studies," a few finished scenes, and several portraits. An hour before noon a lady came to sit, and they repaired to Violet's room that adjoined the nursery, and now their talk was delightful with motherly satisfactions. Of course it had to turn on Tessy.

" She is just delightful," declared Violet. " It is Beaumanoir over again ; and Leonard grows like papa, except that I think the babies must be better. We *did* quarrel. Milly was always the peacemaker, I remember.

And I've a queer feeling about Milly now. I begin to wish she would marry again. She is so sweet and gracious that she ought to be set in a home of her own. And she ought to be more in society, have more real appreciation. You would laugh to see mamma. She is the most foolish and delightful grandmother in the world. Did she care so much for little Nora ? I have really forgotten. There was the awful sorrow. We might be jealous about Len's children, but she spoils mine and gives me no end of good advice ; and Ned's little boy is petted to the uttermost. But the world itself is hardly good enough for Edward Sherburne."

"Does Tessy give up everything for her children ?"

"Oh, dear, no. I don't know how she finds the time ; but when Len goes down they drive, or walk, or read, or sing, and she keeps herself up in the knowledge of the day. I was a little afraid at first. You see, Len had always been made much of by women, and he is made much of now. It isn't like coming home every night to the bosom of your family. A woman *can* drop down so easily, and babies are a good deal of bother. Out in your simple living you can hardly understand the demands made upon men by society women. Fascination is a fine art to-day. It puzzles you sometimes to know where the boundary ought to be set. But Len is as proud and as fond of her to-day as he was in the beginning. And when she can she goes up to some fine dinner or a concert or a house debate, and she keeps her youthful prettiness. Then, you know, her brother is getting to be a wonderful man. He has been out to Africa. Last winter he lectured in Washington on Japan, and had a crowded house, and no end of dinners afterward."

Alice smiled inwardly at the contrast of opinion. Then she said : " Didn't Ethel used to be fond of capturing lions ?"

Violet gave a pretty, doubting gesture. " I think Ethel has gone over to the hard, bright—I was about to say the showy—side of money. She attends the grandest functions ; she has the most exquisite gowns, and jewels galore ; she gives extravagant entertainments, at which only the elect are admitted. Mr. Longworth invites his business friends—a coal or iron or railroad magnate—to a man's dinner, and they have the house to themselves. They go their separate ways without a tint of scandal. She is fascinating in certain lines, and does somehow keep herself well informed. She meets the poets and painters and novelists worthy of note abroad ; she has entertained several of them at her house, but she does not appear to aspire to any especial intellectuality. It is as if she said continually, ' Money is the god of this world. See what money can do.' And then she rises loftily above money."

" If there had been some children," suggested Alice. " I noticed that Mr. Longworth seemed to take great pains to attract little Bevis, who made up with him at once. Bevis is very fond of men, perhaps because he sees more of them. But he simply adores Grandmamma Ashton."

" Is she never coming East again ? I thought her such a charming woman."

" It is rather difficult now for Colonel Ashton to get about. The hardships of his military life begin to tell upon him. And they are so serenely happy. Another year the Trenholmes are almost sure to come out. Five of Lady Trenholme's children are really settled, and that makes her family much smaller. They were so delighted with Lyndell's visit. But our old people are just charming. I don't know how we could live without them. Oh, I wish mamma——"

"You see, it would be quite impossible," subjoined Violet in a tone at once tender yet with a decisive, common-sense accent. "I thought at first that Ethel was rather hard and indifferent. I tried to mend matters a little, but I found it really was of no use. Aunt Edith has all the things she cares for in any great degree. She certainly would be embarrassing in society. Whether she had the sense to see this, or whether Ethel placed it forcibly before her I cannot tell ; but Aunt Edith never could accept second places, you know. She was much more the family authority than mamma."

Violet glanced up with a soft smile that carried comfort on an uncomfortable subject.

Alice knew this too well. Aunt Aurelia had been the only one who ever could make a stand against Mrs. Lepage. Alice remembered how near she had come to yielding to her own mother on the subject of marriage, and no doubt ruining her future. Aunt Aurelia had taken the proposal of Mr. Osborne in hand and made the way smooth for her. Yet her mother had never cordially accepted her life ; and the lover of the earlier approval was to-day a dissipated and well-nigh penniless gambler, separated from the wife he had married. There were many points on which, looking at it now, her mother had lacked judgment. Yet it was pitiful to see her thrust aside by the world she had worshipped so entirely.

Had she not, after all, reaped as she had sown ?

"If I could feel that she was not seriously ill," said Alice, in a tender, longing tone.

" But she has every comfort. Mrs. Ditmars is indulgent and patient. It would be useless to try to change anything, and we must accept the facts. No human being could improve under such circumstances, so we must not look for that. I think she does not suffer. There may be a good deal of discomfort when reasonable nature is thwarted on every side ; but when you cannot make people do what is best you have to yield. One cannot be disputing all the time."

It was very true. And Mrs. Lepage was still extremely fond of the news of the gay world. Mrs. Ditmars read aloud every morning the account of what had taken place the evening before, the description of the gowns, the decorations, and the feast. The poor invalid criticised sharply, had her revenge in unearthing the past of some society leader when she was low down in the social scale, recalled this or that tint of scandal, but it was powerless for harm. Then she pleased herself with the thought that if she still had money she would stand at the head, even as Ethel was doing.

To the sweet, wholesome, unspoiled sense of living this seemed terrible. And yet Alice Osborne understood that life with her would not be as endurable for her mother as it was here.

" I am so glad Harry comes home this winter," she exclaimed, dismissing the sombre thoughts. She had learned that there was no wisdom in brooding over troubles that could not be mended.

The sitter went away. There was luncheon and much art talk, then a drive to some of the finest points, but which looked tame, Paul Amory declared, when compared to the wonders of the West.

They had barely reached home when Osborne joined

them, having driven out in the Longworth carriage.

"I do not call this a visit," complained Violet. "I want whole days together. For when you once get to Sherburne you will not be allowed to stray beyond its fascinating precincts."

"But you will be there yourself. Leonard is to have a grand family party to greet and welcome Dell."

"Children and children's children," laughed Alice as she gathered her little ones beside her.

"I am glad love hasn't gone quite out of date," declared Bevis Osborne, smiling over at his wife. "I was afraid we had grown hopelessly old fashioned. We have had a bad example before us all these years."

# CHAPTER III.

IT was worthy of whatever discomfort there had been in Lyndell Sherburne's life to have the welcome to her father's house that awaited Lyndell Carew. For it would always be connected with her father, as if it had been his gift as well, since she had the happy consciousness that he would have approved of it. And she contrasted it with the home-coming of the unwelcome little girl whose hand was against everybody, and met the hands against her in the spirit of defiance. It seemed like something in another life ; perhaps it was. The last year had given her a sweet, blessed new life.

Leonard had driven on with the two elder people, who were to be his guests until plans were settled. Bertram Carew laughed over this—as if he had not settled everything already quite to his own liking.

She went straight to Aunt Aurelia first. Did she kiss amid some fond tears ?

No one had gone out of the circle. She was grateful for that. Additions had been made, that was all the difference. They laughed in the tremulous manner people do under the stress of deep emotion, there were broken sentences, they all talked together, and then the confusion was stilled because the voices failed.

But out of it all came order presently. Tessy had arranged her guests with delightful perspicacity. Miss

Carew's room opened into Dell's, and as she sat there with a baby in her arms it seemed as if she must always have been a part of the house as well. Everything was the same ; fashion and new styles had found no footing. The furniture suited the house, and Tessy's taste was too harmonious to disturb it.

"Dear Aunt Neale," Dell began laughingly, "you will have to open a *crèche*. Where have all the babies come from ? It makes one feel like being relegated to the older generation. The newer one will soon be growing up about us. Think of Millicent's tall girl. She has the oddly foreign look of her father with all that light hair."

"Millicent had several years the start of the others," returned Miss Carew. "If I could not remember her wedding so perfectly, I should feel tempted to deny that it had ever been."

"She is just the same noble Madonna girl as she was years ago, when she came and brought me my pretty gown, and I was so unthankful."

They both smiled as their eyes met ; but Dell colored warmly.

When they came in to supper, Tessy would not even alter this, though they were often high teas. The smaller table was arranged for the children just as it had been at that Christmas visit when she had been one of the children—Leonard's little son and daughter, Ned's boy, Violet's daughter, and the two Osbornes, with tall, fair Honora von Lindorm at the head. The babies were in the care of the nurses, most of them asleep. What a pretty picture it made !

"And Aunt Julia is coming with little Ray," said Tessy. "She is the picture of Archie, and Aunt Julia is the happiest woman alive, I do believe. As for Uncle Dick—well, if the child was not extraordinarily sweet she would be spoiled beyond redemption with his indulgence."

"We heard of the sisters at some German baths," remarked Dell. "Mrs. Trainor had quite a court of admirers. And it was said she had an offer of marriage from a Roman nobleman, who hastened to withdraw when he found her fortune was only an income that ended with her life."

Alice glanced up at Dell with a swift, odd expression. They both thought of Ethel's titled admirer.

"I suppose it will stand in the way of her marrying again," said Leonard, "though even an impecunious title seems sought after. And though I do not think Mrs. Stanwood's divorce has any legality, I could find it in my heart to wish that she might marry and thus take her entirely out of Archie's life. But if Mrs. Trainor should decide some time that her income would support a husband—and it is a generous one. I believe—I dread to think of what might happen. Still we won't borrow trouble."

"And the boys have grown so," said Millicent to Dell. "You know what a kind of gravely sweet boy Floyd has always been. He has just entered the theological seminary, and will be a clergyman. You can hardly imagine him in any other profession. Aunt Jue is delighted. Win is all for business, and is at Cornell. The little girl comes in as a special gift of Providence."

"The one treasure out of the wreck," interposed Violet.

Lyndell could see the change in Aunt Aurelia—the air of delicacy and frailness. But Miss Carrick was bright and cheery, and certainly had renewed her youth. She was invaluable to the household.

Maum Dinah had given up the kitchen to younger hands, though she still supervised. Cassy remained true to her mistress, though she had received several importunate proffers of marriage. She had so long been used to the refinements of a higher life, that to accept one with her own people was no temptation.

Miss Aurelia had felt rather troubled about one admirer. When it was decided she said : " You have been very faithful and kind to me, Cassy. I could never fill your place. I should like to feel that you would remain with me to the very last ; but if any excellent opportunity should come to you I could not be selfish enough to desire you to refuse it. If you should stay, you will find in the end that I know how to reward one who has so faithfully studied my interest."

" You may depend upon me, Miss 'Relia," returned Cassy in a tone of emotion.

It hardly seemed as if so many changes could take place in such a brief while. They had begun before, though Lyndell had hardly remarked them. Several marriages of the young people, the brides going to other towns or cities. Some new people had come in, semi-invalids in search of less rigorous winters. Two factories had been established at Ardmore. The colored population had drifted about. Many of the more enterprising young men had gone to Washington or Baltimore for servants or coachmen. But the older ones clung to Sherburne House and Mas'r Leonard, who was proving his affection for the place in the care he took of it.

Dell was delighted when she went around with him the next morning. New shrubbery had been set out and a few new paths made that added to the picturesque aspect. At the southern end, where the sun in the winter had a long sweep, he had built a pretty conservatory, that they filled in autumn with the more delicate plants.

"Tessy won't have much alteration made in Aunt Aurelia's time," he said with a proud smile. "There's not much to make anyhow; but we may modernize a little when our own children are growing up. Are they not a pretty lot, Dell? How the years fly! Why, it seems but such a little while ago that we had our feud." He reached over and took her hand and pressed it to his lips. "My best things have come through you," he added in a voice strongly moved with emotion. "But it would have been a sorrow indeed to me if you and Bertram had never known the exquisite joy of a child of your own. And it's queer you haven't named the boy."

"We decided upon Millicent long ago. But we are afraid we shall weight the boy down, Spanish fashion, with too many names if we make the attempt," she answered laughingly.

"There are two Edward Sherburnes already. We call our boy Ned, pure and simple. Of course I shall presently take the name of Sherburne legally. Dell, shall you never regret——"

She placed her hand over Leonard's mouth. "Don't say it!" she cried. "Never think of such a thing. Bertram will return to New York and gather up some of his olden practice, or get a new one, though he intends to confine himself largely to surgery. And our children will grow up there; but I shall like them to keep a warm interest in Sherburne House. And we have almost won over Papa Carew to cast in his lot with us. Bertram wants them both, and they want the children," glancing up with a humorous sweetness.

"If ever any one earned the sort of enjoyment that

rounds out an earnest, devoted life, Dr. Carew ought to have it. We missed him so much at first—and Miss Neale. But you can't think how Miss Armitage has stepped into her place. And another curious coincidence about it is, you know Aunt Neale lost the lover of her youth, and Miss Armitage, it seems, lost hers by a sad accident. She is a very sweet, refined, but sensible person, and a great favorite with young and old—almost like a clergyman's wife.''

'' And Dr. Underwood ?'' queried Dell.

'' He has succeeded well and is much liked. So many of the doctor's older patients are dead—and you know he did not take on many new ones at the last. We felt lost when he first went away, and shall miss him, for he is one of the old landmarks. But he does adore Bertram.''

'' They are such splendid friends ! Bertram has almost made a young man of him.''

'' And I do not see how he ever can give you up again.''

Dell's eyes were lustrous with emotion.

They came back to find the twins in their best attire, holding a reception. Miss Neale had the nameless baby, and the pretty, wholesome German nurse, who had lost both husband and baby, was devoted to little Millicent. It was too early to predict whether they would inherit the beauty of their Grecian birthplace ; but they were fine, healthy babies, and their father thought them daily miracles. If he had longed for and desired the blessing of fatherhood, it had been only in secret prayer. If it was not bestowed he had Lyndell, the wife of his soul. They had grown so together in the first year of their pleasant journeying about, so many mysteries had been unveiled to them. They saw where they had occasionally missed the divine accord, but not from any lack of love.

It is not all interpreted with the key of youthful ardor. There were heights and depths that came with experience and a clearer understanding of human needs. They would go on now watching the ripening harvest, and perhaps at the last, gathering up the sheaves of joy and content in their old age. And sometimes Bertram wondered how his father had lived through all these years with the light of his holiest love gone out in darkness, been brave and manful and tender.

Violet had gone over to Beaumanoir, but the Osbornes remained at Sherburne House. There would be so many old friends to meet. Tessy thought they ought to have a real neighborhood gathering. She had assimilated so delightfully with her neighbors and made Sherburne House a centre of interest to the elderly people, as well as to the younger married ones who had not allowed their range of thought to stray far outside of their husbands and babies. Miss Sherburne would have felt any slight to them, and yet she sometimes found them a little tiresome ; but Miss Carrick had that general interest without the trained discrimination that comes from a wider life. Mr. Beaumanoir often experienced a sense of wonder at the real wisdom of his son's choice ; and sometimes, when they came over to meet Millicent's circle, Tessy was not behind in her knowledge of the great world, neither did she let Leonard degenerate, as a woman who considered self first might easily have done. He was taking a great interest in the wider political aspects of the day, and it pleased his father very much.

Since there were no young people to dance, and so many babies to compare, a dinner was decided to be the most fitting. A day's visiting had not gone out of date in these regions. Everybody approved of the plan, and Millicent, who had just driven over, offered to help Tessy with the invitations.

Bertram and his father gladly accepted the proffer of the carriage to drive in to Ardmore and view the old place. The town had stretched out amazingly, and in the direction of the Carew home. Instead of the one winding road there were 'two broad, straight streets, though the old road had not been disturbed except in one place, that gave it a pleasant vista. A large saw-mill had been erected, since the material in the vicinity was almost exhaustless. Yes, there had been a great many changes in the two years.

The grounds at the Carew place looked a little more trim. Some of the old, half dead shrubbery had been cut out and replaced by a younger growth. Within there had not been many alterations, but the indescribable at-mosphere of different living permeated everything. It had almost a shock for Dr. Carew, an impression of sac-rilege. Then he smiled slightly with an inward half pain, half regret, and the sub-consciousness that change was inevitable when other hands guided the helm. Mrs. Armitage was older than Aunt Neale, Miss Armi-tage much younger. Their lives were laid on different lines.

They passed Dr. Underwood in his rather shabby buggy, that somehow went to the doctor's heart. They stopped for a little chat, pleasant, cordial, and with a touch of welcome from the younger practitioner that was extremely grateful to the elder.

Yes, Ardmore had changed. There was an air of thrift about it, a certain tidiness and improvement that

comes with prosperity and energy. There were several
new stores, there was a kind of city air creeping in.
Some of it had doubtless started before : but Dr. Carew
noted it with eyes that had not watched the progress of
two years.

Mr. Whittingham had taken the last long journey.
Spencer Kirby had endeavored to fill his place, and had
developed into a courteous, somewhat stirring young fellow much interested in improvements and real estate, and
quite ready to take suggestions from Leonard Beaumanoir. Mrs. Kirby had aged a good deal, but she was
placidly happy with her daughter-in-law and her grandchild.

" I see plainly that I have been crowded out while I
have been off careering round the world in search of
pleasure," said the doctor to his son with a touch of
humorous regret as they wound up the avenue. " People can get along very well without me. Perhaps they
wouldn't have faith in me after all this dissipation. I'm
an old man without a place."

" But the new place has opened," replied his son.
" You know it was an old dream that we should be together, and the little break of your absence has paved
the way. The younger people have grown up, new ones
have come in, and it would be in a certain sense beginning again. Besides, I want you, need you. And Dell
has set her heart upon it. You and Aunt Neale must
be grandparents to a houseful of children."

They had talked it over in their journeyings, though
the doctor had been obstinately non-committal. How
could he relinquish his lifelong home ? He had invested
it with hundreds of tender remembrances. And yet he
felt now the memories would be his wherever he went.

And was not his son and this sweet, noble girl woman that he had always coveted dearer to him than aught else? And the children he had counted on during his first dream of wedded bliss, so suddenly gone out in sorrow, might they not be added in this harvest time of old age?

As they entered the sitting-room at Sherburne House Miss Carew sat talking to the two elder women, the little group reinforced by Mrs. Beaumanoir. She had one of the babies in her arms. Had she the secret of eternal youth in her mother-love that had overflowed continually with the mysterious outgiving implanted by the wise Dispenser of all good gifts? What a mother she would have made! How young and charming she looked! To be sure, she was a decade younger than Miss Sherburne; but had not something been added in this long holiday? Well, it *was* good to get out of the ruts and wander in the wide, open country of the greater world.

Bertram was right. He and his sister belonged to them. Even if the new life came a little hard at first there would be absorbing compensations. He felt young and strong and vigorous, and his horizon had widened so much. He would have Neale go about and note the changes; it would be a more convincing argument than any words.

Lyndell and Millicent had a long drive in the glowing afternoon. The months of delight in California, the splendor of the new vision, the friends she had made, the work she had done, the experiment going on at Carew House, the great schemes of philanthropy that were broadening the world, were enthusiastically discussed.

" And you saw a good deal of Reese Drayton," she

said. " I am curious to know what effect the two years'
work has had on him. Bertram thinks him very much
in earnest."

" He is very much in earnest with his money ; but
he admits that it seems hardly his since it cost him no
effort at all. How curious that so much should come to
any one who has no real desire for it, no ambition to be
boundlessly wealthy. On certain lines he is an ideal
character, but there is nothing visionary about him ; he
is so simple in most of his tastes ; and what puzzles me
greatly is his stern uprightness in many points, the kind
of faith you come to have in him. He has had a great
influence over Gifford Lepage."

" Poor Gifford ! Alice is so encouraged about him
now. I wonder—there was that second lapse——" and
Dell raised her eyes questioningly.

" Gifford has a very weak strand in his character.
He needs some steady, restraining influence. He never
could have a better friend than Bevis Osborne. I think
he begins to understand that now. And it is curious
that rather weak natures have such a strand of obstinacy.
He made the bad investment of his little savings against
Osborne's counsel and advice, and when it was swept
away, I think he must have gone almost out of his mind.
A physician—a queer, scholarly, speculative German,
forty or thereabouts—picked him up and nursed him
through a long illness when Osborne had made futile
efforts to find him. He has taken charge of Carew
House with this Mr. Moore. Of course you know it is
for the reclamation of some of the weakest phases of in-
temperance—the men who have a conscientious desire
for reformation, yet feel unable to withstand the temptation. You would be interested in this Dr. Wolff at once."

"But I thought—there is a settlement——"

"There will be a town some time. Improvements have been made, and land is cheap. Mr. Moore has sent for several families from New York, with hosts of children, and they are in homes where their work will bring them the comforts of civilized life. There is space, freedom, cleanliness, both moral and physical. Bertram is right ; this is to be the benificence of the future."

"But the real foundation belongs to Mr. Drayton."

"He had the land, to be sure. Bertram roused him to some aims in the matter. And Dr. Wolff is just the man for the place. He and Mr. Drayton met in Germany long ago ; he was doing some sort of hospital work."

"Mr. Drayton had a hand in saving Gifford."

"So I surmised. But the credit is given to the doctor. Indeed, I think no one but the doctor knows the whole story. And you were his good angel in that earlier unfortunate episode. Dear Dell, curiously enough we are our brother's keeper. And the kindliest aspect in all this matter is the total forgetfulness that every one evinces. Gifford is taken in with such a trust and heartiness. And he is doing very well again. But he is the kind of man to have a family interest. There is a hunger all the time for something of his very own."

"I wonder if it would be wise ?"

Dell remembered this longing, this desire to appropriate some one supremely. It had been herself on two occasions. And he could make himself miserably jealous.

"That is a question difficult to answer. I think I have seen women who would bring out the best there was in him. Dell, did you ever think there are people who really cannot stand alone ? They must always have something to lean upon. Ethel is tremendously self-centred. If Gifford could have shared part of her strength."

" Isn't Ethel's a sort of obstinacy as well ? When Gifford began to make money at first he was determined to be a rich man. He had dreams of coming East and astonishing every one. He could see nothing else. And at first Ethel was resolved to have a title, you know, then money. It was a one idea and nothing beyond. But what I can't understand, if there is anything in heredity, is why Aunt Lepage should have been so different from your mother and Aunt Julia."

" It is environment as well ; and O Lyndell, it is a good deal aim, resolve. You know we did not use to think Leonard ambitious—and he made some sad mistakes. When he resolved to render himself worthy of you, it seemed as if the keynote of his character had been struck with a guiding finger. Yet it was not really love, not the divine regard. And we were all a little afraid, though papa would not have allowed you to be sacrificed. Life *is* a development, a living out of some things and going up to finer heights, if we have the strength and the true aim. And now you must go in and see Nannie Henry and her baby. I am so glad Spencer married. He was such a shy sort of fellow. But they had always been so friendly with the Henrys."

Mrs. Kirby put her arms around Dell's neck and cried a little.

" He would have been so glad to see you," she exclaimed with a little break in her voice ; and Dell knew for whom the pronoun stood. " One of your bright letters came just a week before he left us, and he was so delighted. I had to read it over and over. My dear, he was very fond of you."

" I shall never forget how good he was to me the first time I saw him, when I was such a miserable little girl. I have so many delightful remembrances. You were all so kindly."

" And you have made such a splendid-looking woman." Mrs. Kirby held her off a little and studied her. " There's the best of the Sherburne in you. And to think that you have two babies ! Spencer's little boy is the sweetest and dearest thing, and Nannie is just an own daughter. I am a very happy old lady," and she smiled through her tears.

Young Mrs. Kirby came in for her share of the call. She was a good-natured, every-day body with an assured faith that no one could have a better husband or a sweeter baby, hardly a more delightful life. It was charming to find so much content in a world of strenuous endeavor.

At first Mrs. Kirby thought she could not possibly come over to the dinner. She was quite feeble, and she seldom went out for more than a drive, or perhaps a call or two ; but Nannie joined her persuasion, and said she knew Spencer would be delighted to have his mother make the effort. The baby did his cunningest tricks for them, and went to Dell with a charming readiness.

There were several more calls, and then they drove home to find a houseful. Friendliness had not gone out of date, evidently. The little negro children stood around in groups, staring out of round, wondering eyes. Now and then Dell caught sight of a familiar face, and smiled with cordial remembrance.

" Will you write and invite Mr. Drayton down to the dinner ?" Dell said that evening to her husband. " He used to long for a sight of Sherburne House ; and he will be simply overwhelmed with Virginian hospitality."

" Yes ; he expects to make some stay in Washington. I do not think he will go back this winter, though I can't see that he has really taken root on the Western coast. I wish he might marry. Strange how we prescribe matrimony for all our friends."

Did Millicent care for him ? She had been very elusive all the afternoon when his name had come up in the conversation.

" If he marries rightly," Dell said with a breathless sort of pain. " And yet I never met a person who wearies so little of a single life."

Fanny had not won him, then ; that was some consolation ; yet why should the old feeling return ? Fanny was curiously changed in some ways. Why was Mr. Drayton's happiness dearer to her than that of her cousin ?

There was a continual coming and going at Sherburne House.

" I wonder if we shall wear you out ?" said Dell to Aunt Aurelia. " We keep everything in a turmoil."

" A very pleasant turmoil," smiling kindly up to the solicitous face. " We have counted so much on this home-coming. It is so pleasant to have you all together once more ; and it reminds me of the time when the others were young, and made a gay household at Sherburne."

Dell bent over and pressed her lips to the white forehead.

" You have been very happy, dear." It was more an assertion than a question.

" Yes. The older I grow the richer and more blessed life seems."

" You will have Aunt Neale.  Long ago, when you made your visit at the doctor's, I was jealous of her—yes, very jealous.  I thought love was the duty you owed Sherburne House, and in those dark days I felt your soul ought to be centred here.  And now I am glad for you to have the love and for her to know the continual delight of the broader family life."

" And if we take her away——"

" It will not need any compulsion."  Aunt Aurelia smiled.  " It would be dreary for them to go back to the old house ; and now that she has had you for two years she could not give you up without a heartbreak. And the babies !  They are a new life to her, Dell ; it is the one blessing I have steadily desired for you.  We are still old-fashioned enough to consider children a delight, not only in their babyhood, but in all the future— as young people, as brides and husbands, making new centres.  And though this joy has never been my very own, I have come nearer to it than many women.  I find the baby voices very sweet again ; and sometimes I sit and dream how the old life will be lived over when I am gone.  Leonard is like a son to me.  Eliza and I have had the best of all given to us.  And so I am glad you are to have Miss Neale and the doctor.  We thought at first we could not get along without him ; but he will not be so far away in the time to come as he has been these two years, and the Lord has kept us from harm."

Lyndell could not reply.  Bertram was coming up the walk, and she went out to him.  He took both hands.

" You have won over your father and Aunt Neale."

" Circumstances and changes have helped.  Yes, we shall make one happy family, I trust."

# CHAPTER IV.

"THE festive days at Sherburne are all days of splendor," said Millicent—" wedding days, birthdays,
and all."

Yes. How beautiful they had all been ! There was
a serene sky and golden sun, the whole little corner of
the world made fragrant by yesterday's rain. The house
seemed to overflow, and yet guests kept coming. One
of the arrivals of last night had been Major and Mrs.
Stanwood and Archie's little girl, now past four years
old, grown prettier than her babyhood had prefigured,
a sunny, merry child, made so, perhaps, by her grandmother's overwhelming love and tenderness. Her hair
was light and had not lost its tint of red gold ; the eyes
were a deep gray, in some lights almost black—the effect
produced by the long, dark lashes and well-defined eye-
brows. They had called her simply Ray—she had proved
such a sunbeam—and Aunt Julia felt she could not use
the mother's name.

Millicent and Dell were receiving guests in the spacious hall, while the maids convoyed them to their re-
spective rooms. The big Beaumanoir barouche came up,
and Mrs. Longworth was handed out in state by her
cousin Leonard, then a tall, somewhat thin young man ;
and last of all a fine, stately figure, rather stouter than

when Lyndell had seen him last, but looking hardly a day older.

"O Gifford!" she cried in surprise. "We were bewailing the fact that you could not come in time for the family reunion."

Reese Drayton had taken Millicent's hands in a strong, assertive clasp, and Dell had caught the sudden flush that went up to the very edge of the soft, dark hair.

"I did not think it possible; but Alice wrote a moving letter, and I found I could be spared, so I did not take long to consider. Dear, dear Dell!"

He still looked young for his thirty years, but there was an air of decision about him quite in contrast with the boyish irresolution she remembered.

One or two others pressed forward for a greeting, so several moments elapsed before Mr. Drayton presented himself. She had barely seen him in New York, her time had been so occupied and so brief. Was that last evening in some other life?

Neither of them spoke. The pressure of the hand was unuttered friendship. And then Fanny pressed forward with a curiously bright eagerness that made her daringly pretty for the moment, and an air of possessorship that amazed Dell. The next instant some one had swept by them, claiming her attention.

Presently the guests had all arrived. The babies and children were gathered in the old school-room, but the visitors went out in a throng to see the sight. Not all of them belonged to Sherburne, of course. Some of the younger mothers had brought the little ones they did not like to leave at home or were proud to exhibit. Happy young wives they were, even if they dwelt in cir-

cumscribed spheres and were not interested in the questions agitating the greater world.

Dell found Mr. Drayton amid the crowd.

"Will you take my cousin, Mrs. von Lindorm, in to
dinner?" she asked. "You ought to be excellent
friends."

"Mrs. von Lindorm is engaged. I heard her tell your
husband so a moment ago."

Leonard touched his arm lightly.

"Let us make Mr. Drayton do duty," he said smilingly to Dell. "Ethel seems to be the grand dame of
the occasion, and it won't do to give her a plain country
body. I was amazed, for I fancied at the last moment
there would be some convenient happening that would
prevent her coming."

Drayton bowed assentingly.

Both tables were full. Ethel had Paul Amory on her
other side, and was pleased at being so well placed. She
had some curiosity to see Mr. Drayton, Fanny had talked
so much about him.

Miss Fanny was over opposite. Ethel was rather surprised at her brightness and *verve*. And really she had
not gone off as much as one might expect. She looked
unusually young to-day. Why had she not captured
Mr. Drayton? There had been the winter in New
York. Perhaps he was *not* a marrying man. But when
she found he should spend some time in Washington and
considered himself warm friends with the Amorys, she
resolved to add him to her society list.

It was a mixed company, with some old-fashioned people sprinkled here and there, and some elderly people
who had been to feasts in old Mr. Sherburne's time,
who really enjoyed the knowledge that everything had

come around right ; yet they still had a vague feeling
that Lyndell Sherburne should have married her cousin.
Not that any one grudged the dainty little lady who had
Mr. Beaumanoir on one side and Bertram Carew on the
other, while Leonard had Aunt Aurelia and Lyndell.

There was much to be said, indeed sometimes a confusion of tongues.  Bits of wit and gayety went floating
round, reminiscences, the chat of the day, the stride in
knowledges, even the world of fashion was not left out.
They had some after-dinner speeches, and Dell colored
at finding herself almost as much of a heroine as on her
birthday.  They drank toasts, and gave good wishes,
and sang "Auld Lang Syne" standing when they rose
to disperse.

Truly Leonard Beaumanoir was a fine and gracious
master for Sherburne House.

"I do suppose Bertram Carew envies you just a little," Ethel exclaimed with her impressive air.  She was
fond of saying uncomfortable things to Leonard.

"No ; it was his wish for her, you remember," he
answered decisively.

" But now that he has children.  Len, in your experience of life, you don't find people living on the heroic
plane."

" Yes, some people live up to it—more than you
would think."

" Not but that I considered it the proper thing to do.
Dell never quite seemed one of us.  Whoever supposed
she would be so distinguished-looking.  Her two years
abroad have rubbed out the crudenesses.  Why hasn't
Fanny captured that Mr. Drayton with her many opportunities ?  Or is she really booked for spinsterhood ?"

" Aunt Aurelia has set her a good example," and he

gave a short, forced laugh. "What a pity your mother could not have come down! Sherburne health is a proverb in the neighborhood; and she——"

"The exception proves the rule, you know. Mamma really has nothing else to do but play invalid. She has married off her daughters to her satisfaction, and sons sometimes prove difficult and intractable. Still we must use our best efforts for Gifford and see that he doesn't get led into a trap *à la* Archie. Does anybody hear anything of that wretched creature?"

"She had a divorce, you know," Leonard replied with dignity.

"That would not keep her from coming back and throwing herself upon his sympathy. He is making money rapidly. They have had an offer from an English syndicate."

"So he wrote me."

"I hope he won't be soft-hearted enough to let her take him in a second time." She looked at her watch, which gave a dazzle of diamonds. "Can some one take me to the train? I must look up Gif; I can't have him philandering round with these country girls," with a rather satiric inflection.

"I believe there are only two *girls* here, and Miss Floyd is engaged. Yes, I will order the carriage. But must you return to-night?"

"I have a function to-morrow noon, and I want to look my best, so no morning journey for me," tossing her head airily.

She found Gifford in a centre of cousins, all talking eagerly and planning a drive for the next day. There was an immediate protest.

"I told mamma I would be sure to bring you back.

She has scarcely seen you after these years of absence. And I must have an attendant."

Gifford had a sudden mind to refuse, but he checked himself in time. "I shall see you all again. Dell, you remain here for some time?"

"Yes, though Bertram is to go up to New York, and I am to spend a few days with Violet, even if the season has not begun," she said with a little air that amused them, it so nearly imitated Ethel.

There were several others going to the train, and some of the carriages were ordered. There were many expressions of the warmest satisfaction at Dell's return, and cordial invitations given if she could find time for visiting.

"It has been delightful," said Mrs. Kirby. "I hardly expected to be so gay at my time of life. I don't understand what you have done to Miss Carew; she seems to have gone back full ten years. And those lovely babies, Lyndell. I don't wonder the young doctor looks so happy. But I have my nice daughter and little grandson. I only wish brother could have been here. But when you want to give me a treat, come over to our quiet home, where I can really talk to you."

It was pretty enough to see Spencer so attentive to his mother and his wife.

"There is nothing left to wish *you*," he said to Dell. "I've been thinking of the long-ago Christmas party, when you were a little girl in a short frock, and what pleasant times we had. I wonder if our children will have such heartfelt pleasures?"

Our children! How strange it sounded! Yes, she had stood in this very hall while Spencer was trying to persuade her to dance, and she had been so afraid of Aunt Aurelia.

The good-bys were longer than the greetings. Aunt Aurelia was so tired she went upstairs to her room, and Miss Carrick said the last good-bys for her. The Amorys went back to Beaumanoir, but Alice and her husband and Mr. Drayton remained. The latter demurred a little in view of the other guests ; but Leonard overruled all scruples.

"And you would not find a decent hotel in Ardmore," he said laughingly. "You Westerners have not pre-empted all the hospitality."

When order was a little restored the men strolled out on the lawn for a smoke. Dell ran up to Aunt Aurelia.

"Don't feel anxious about me," she said in a tender tone. "I do not dissipate much nowadays, and we seldom have such large companies. But I am glad there could be such a reunion once more in the old house, and that the good Father has brought us all together again. Dell, you have added a great deal of joy, even if we began in sorrow."

"O Aunt Aurelia, that was all forgotten long ago."

"You have your father's generous nature, child. If one could go back and have it different ! It was a sad mistake ; and he should have been made happy. It will not be a great while before I shall go to him and the others. But I want you always to remember that you have given me a great deal of happiness."

Dell kissed her fondly.

"Now go find Aunt Julia. How she has counted on your return ! And I am too tired to say another word. Send Cassy up with a cup of tea."

Aunt Julia was putting her baby to bed. She had run about so much she was almost asleep in her grandmother's arms.

They talked of Archie, who was prospering far beyond his dreams. He had been South in the early spring.

"I think he longs very much for a real home," said Aunt Julia. "Their book-keeper has a sweet, young wife who understands the art of home-making, and he goes once a week to spend the evening with them, and takes his Sunday dinner. He writes so much about them, and I can gather from many sentences how well he would enjoy a centre of his very own. Oh, why should such a misfortune happen to him?"

Dell sighed at the unanswerable question.

"I am never quite at ease. If Mrs. Trainor should marry and Helena find herself homeless, or if they should return to America, and she demand the child! Archie will never give her up; and the heartless manner in which she deserted it would go against her if she should make any effort to recover it. But the talk and scandal would be hard to bear. And what we must tell baby presently—poor little, innocent lamb!"

"If *she* would marry," said Dell. "But there are not many opportunities for women who have neither youth, nor money, nor beauty. And she hasn't the style for a regular adventuress. Mrs. Trainor, I think, must spend all her income, for they are at some of the most extravagant resorts."

"She could marry abroad, I suppose. Indeed, people marry on such divorces here. Leonard thinks Archie ought to get a divorce for desertion, as a kind of protection from any sudden demand. But that would not give him the liberty of conscience to contract another marriage. Still, Archie is a great comfort to me now; and he is taking a warm interest in his brothers. Floyd is such a fine, upright fellow."

" And Archie was one of the most honest-hearted of young men. Oh, I do sincerely hope nothing worse will happen. He has had trouble enough. When I think of that morning's interview and Helena's utter heartlessness, I feel as if I had been dreaming."

Then Dell bethought herself of her own babies. " I have forgotten myself, and been Dell Sherburne to-day," she declared laughingly. " Aunt Neale and much jaunting about have quite spoiled me. Then Freda is so trusty ; I wonder if one can have so much that it would beget carelessness ?"

" I am glad to see you so light-hearted and so happy, my dear darling," and Aunt Julia kissed her.

Dell found her babies asleep, and Freda sitting by the improvised crib. Miss Carrick and Aunt Neale were in the next room talking over old times. Alice she found in Tessy's nursery, and the three mothers, girls themselves only a little while ago, were in the tide of eager talk. How queer and unreal it seemed ! For somehow the festive day had carried them all back to the past.

" Your hero is quite magnificent, Dell," Tessy said in a little pause.

" My hero ?"

" Mr. Drayton."

" Oh, I think he is everybody's hero," with a bright flush she was glad the twilight hid. " Alice liked him ; didn't you, Alice ? and Fanny."

" I was almost sure he would marry Fanny," returned Alice. " And yet she doesn't seem quite the wife for him. He has changed a great deal, though his outward manner remains much the same. He has developed into a really splendid man. That adjective savors of extreme youth, but it is applicable all the same. There is one person I would be rejoiced to see him marry."

"Millicent!"

Dell uttered it almost under her breath, and felt as if she had betrayed a precious secret.

"Yes, Millicent. I do not think any one is quite worthy of her, yet I am not at all sure she desires perfection. She likes to work for and with people; and when one makes a real improvement no one is more ready to appreciate it than she. I have a feeling she ought to fill some wider sphere with her talents, and she will always be beautiful."

"She has a wide sphere," said Tessy softly. "No one can realize what she is to her parents, to all of us, to the friends—nay, even the strangers she corresponds with. You should see some of the letters she receives. People ask her advice on every point almost. What I want for her is that beautiful, sympathetic life of her own that is rich and deep and full, that is answered with a glance of the eye and a touch of the hand. I don't know whether she thinks she has had it all and must be content through the future years——"

"It must seem like a dream to her, as it does to all of us. Perhaps she never can put any one in that place," remarked Dell with tender gravity, as Tessy made a pause.

"Another love would be different, of course," said Alice. "And we do know that different loves are possible. Our views and desires change. If the love of youth grows and changes and ripens the result is happiness. Through the unfolding of pleasant things, the deep things grow up to the light, if the true seeds have been planted. It is taking advantage of the sunshine and the soft winds and the dews of heaven, as the better growth was meant to do. We might all be so much happier, we might keep out of the track of storms with a little wisdom. And if you can go hand in hand with this richer experience, find a shelter from tempests and a shade when the arid sun beats too fiercely. But no one seems to know it just at first, in youth ; and that is why after life is more complete. Millicent's seems as if the blossom stalk had been sharply wrenched out. It doesn't kill the plant, you know. It grows again and hides the wound with bright, lovely foliage. I think it might blossom anew with a fragrance and richness it really did not understand in the beginning."

"Millicent has had a good many admirers," said Tessy. "And she is devoted to Nora. Still we happy women do believe marriage a higher estate. I wonder— if we were not happy——"

"I do not think Ethel comes up to the finest, yet she is satisfied apparently ; and I know she would be miserable in a single life. Yet Ethel had a gift for art. Dell, we both used to envy her. And she has a genius for certain kinds of organization. I used to think she would gather people around her something in the fashion of the old *salons*. But she seems to have dropped that desire. Now it is to outshine some one in jewels or attire, or an elegant little feast ; crowds are vulgar in her estimation. And there is poor mamma, whose ambition has ended in invalidism. Well, there are marriages of every kind and degree."

Tessy heard herself called, and leaned out of the window.

"Aren't you women most tired of comparing your babies ? Do come down. The out of doors is too lovely to miss."

Tessy colored with conscious gratification. It was delightful to be wanted.

"Yes, in a moment," she answered, and went to make a few changes in her toilette, and take a look at the elderly people. Aunt Julia joined them. One of the Floyd cousins, nearing middle life, had remained. The men were still disposed of on the short, dry grass in various kinds of easy-chairs, and had been discussing the political aspect.

"We haven't quarrelled, though we didn't all agree," said Osborne. "That speaks well for our tempers. But you ladies are not so much interested in the weighty matters of constitutional lore."

"I am not so sure," said Dell. "Mrs. Beaumanoir has it all mapped out—a representative, a judgeship, a senator, and then perhaps minister abroad. Leonard, you will have no chance to grow stout and lazy."

"There is nothing like being kept up to the mark," said Bertram Carew with a cordial laugh of approval. And he wondered how this small, unaggressive woman, with so many girlish graces still hanging about her, could have influenced without ruffling, could have appreciated this rival in her husband's soul and not have been crowded out herself. Leonard was ambitious. His father's inmost thought took pleasure in him. Having him in this place and with such a wife had brought out the very best in him. Ned Beaumanoir was a nice, honorable, rather conventional business man who would never attain any great heights, but Cecil would make his mark. Could a man do better than give such hostages to the world?

The talk fell into a lighter strain, jest and good-humored badinage, reminiscent as well. Reese Dray-

ton was touched in the finer social sense. The dry air
was filled with wafts of fragrance from the wealth of
bloom in summer ripening, and the wind stirring the
evergreens, that shook out a mysterious melody with
their stiff, rustling branches. Overhead a faultless sky
in soft, clear blue pricked through with myriads of
stars.

The lights in the house defined the group of women.
He wished there was another among them with her Madonna face. He had heard the episode of Sherburne
House in a fragmentary, entertaining fashion ; he knew
Millicent's tragic story that she had overlived. Mrs.
Osborne had been in the midst of so many things, yet
the sweet tranquillity of her life had not changed. Was
it in the race or circumstances that had given them happiness and prosperity ? It was not a large allowance
that one out of all this number should go astray with the
unreason of youth and obstinacy. If half the world
was bent on saving the other half——

Tessy had given orders for a late, light supper, since
the feast had been so prolonged. Now they were summoned within, where candles and shaded lamps made a
softened glow over the fruits and plates of delicate re-
freshment. How like a pastoral it was ! One might be
in another world. Certainly it was ideal living. Yet
there was nothing extraordinary about these people beyond the fact that each one had an aim and was not content to merely drift through life.

As they were breaking up, Drayton paused a moment
by the side of Mrs. Carew.

"It is a longing gratified," and his tone touched
her. "I am glad to come to do honor to your return
and to wish you—what shall I wish you ? You seem to

have all the good things of life—their continuance, perhaps. What a holiday you have had !"

He glanced into happy, soulful eyes.

" It was perfect in that I had those nearest and dearest to me. Yes, I have had many blessings ; and yet I can recall sitting on this porch the most miserable little girl in existence. It is good to have had sharp contrasts. And—I am very glad you could come, that you *would* come." And there was a gleam in her eyes that indicated there had been room for doubt.

Fine and harmoniously developed as she was on purely human lines, he did not envy her to-night. True accord was the work of a lifetime ; but she and Dr. Carew were on the sure path.

" I wonder if I shall sink in your estimation if I confess to a double motive ? Sincerity ought to be the corner-stone of friendship ; but I want you to know—let us walk down the path. Mrs. Osborne said people came to you with confidences."

" Gifford !" a little startled.

" It is not the young man. I think he has come to the reign of common sense," and she felt rather than saw the smile, as it was in the tone. " He is not a bad fellow by any means, and has some excellent business abilities. He wouldn't have made a good lawyer ; and though there is a sentimentally religious side to his nature, he would have been a failure as a clergyman. I suppose it is not an easy thing to accept a life that runs counter to our ideals—and youth believes itself capable of everything. It is your one idea that brings success, not your many ideals."

" I have often wondered—— Oh, I want to thank

you for all you did that winter," and she put her hand in his with the fervor of gratitude.

"I think the winter was beneficial to us as well. It touched me at some of the dormant boundaries. It gave me a friend in your husband, whom I shall always honor. You may resent this, but I had begun by under-valuing him. As for the other matter, let us dismiss that forever. There are only two people who know it wholly—Dr. Wolff and his patient, whom he restored to his right mind. I hope Gifford Lepage will marry some tender, domestic woman who will adore him, intelligent enough to keep him from dropping down, and who will never soar above him. Are there any such left ?" with a humorous accent to his tone.

"You think he might——" Her mind reverted to some of her husband's theories.

"There are cases where marriage is a saving ordi-nance ; this would be one. Sooner or later love domi-nates a man with the desire of possessorship—his own wife, his own home. But I should be sorry to have him choose unwisely. I should like to choose for him, even if it is against the canons of free grace. And now—have you no curiosity to know my remaining motives ? I in-dicated that it was something beyond the pleasure of swelling your crowd of admirers."

Lyndell stopped suddenly and gave her companion a quick, searching glance. How brilliant Fanny had been ! He was to go over to the Beaumanoirs' to luncheon to-morrow.

"After having prescribed matrimony for others, I have no notion of being a castaway myself if an earnest purpose will win my cause. Will you take me for a cousin, Mrs. Carew, and wish me Godspeed ?"

"Fanny!" There was a passionate protest in her voice. It gave him a curious thrill.

"I asked your Cousin Fanny to marry me while we were out there at the Osbornes'. Lyndell Carew, you give people an ultra-conscientiousness. I thought myself quite hardened to the opinion of others; but there was a vulnerable point like a pin prick. I had paid her a good deal of attention that winter in New York. I wanted a clear conscience. See what your ultra-spirituality does," half complainingly.

"And then?" She drew a long breath, hoping against hope.

"She declined," in a quiet, unemotional tone.

"And if she had accepted you? I do not understand Fanny truly. Or are you full of subtleties?"

She studied him with a throbbing earnestness.

"If she had accepted me I should have, like your famous old Greek, 'paid back in turn.'"

She remembered the end of the sentence, that a feeling of honor would not allow him to repeat.

"I want you to believe I should have used my best efforts for her happiness," he continued. "But I had seen a possibility. I do not know if your cousin, Mrs. von Lindorm, is to be won, but if she is it will go hard indeed with me if I do not succeed. I wanted you to know."

"And I *do* wish you Godspeed."

The tone of her voice was so eager, so exultant that he suddenly felt certain of the end.

They walked slowly back. As she passed in Leonard took possession of him. Bertram was awaiting her in the hall, and with a tender good-night to the others they went upstairs.

" You look as if you had seen a vision." Bertram turned his wife around, though she tried to evade his smiling eyes.

" It is not wholly my secret," she said in a tone of entreaty.

" It was half mine before. I can guess. Some day you will be asked to receive Reese Drayton as a cousin. I told you once that when he had seen Millicent——"

" But he asked Fanny to marry him. I cannot imagine her refusing him. She has no ideal sentiment of love—and she liked him."

Had she not shown her preference to-day? Drayton had been on his guard. Dell could see that now ; but her satisfaction in the greater delight swept away the half pity.

# CHAPTER V.

WITH the dinner the visiting really began. Invitations came almost hourly. The Carews discussed the prospect of a removal. Miss Neale declared she had been so demoralized by the continual jaunting about that she was at home wherever the rest were. As to giving up Dell and the babies—and Bertram had grown into a nearer sonship than even in his youth. Even Miss Aurelia, with her deep-rooted affection for Sherburne House, gave her voice on Dell's side.

"I can't help thinking, as we grow older, that the young people are a great deal to us and keep us in touch with the tender humanities of life. There have always been so many here that vacant places would sadden the atmosphere. And presently, Cornelia, you will begin to need care, and the little watchfulness here and there is so grateful. I am ten years farther on in the march of life, to be sure; but you and the doctor will find it rather lonely. You see, our own friends keep dropping out, and we do not make others so readily. Why should not the younger generation give us a little of their abundance? And why should we be too proud to take it?"

The two doctors went up to New York. Bertram's house had been vacant for two months or more, and was now undergoing a thorough renovating. He had decided to have an office elsewhere, and the basement was to be transformed into a handsome dining-room. His father did not exactly assent, but he made no strenuous objections.

Bertram found a warm welcome among his compeers. His researches while abroad into the best foreign methods had added to his skill, and his literary work had placed him in the front rank. It would not be long before he caught up with the full tide.

"You will be such an assistance and pleasure to me," Bertram said in his persuasive tone, so hard for the father to resist.

"An old-fashioned country doctor!" rather disdainfully.

"Not so very old-fashioned, with your two years abroad. And, as I remember, you never were famous for falling behind. After this long time of sympathy and reciprocation I do not believe either could do without the other."

His secret soul had cried out for his only son, for the dear daughter of his love, for the children growing up in the household, for the delightful family life that would be such a blessedness to him and his sister. And as the break had been started, and it would take some time to slip back into the old place—— He knew he should consent, but he liked these little skirmishes with himself. And to give up his old friends too easily would be heartless.

At Sherburne House they were full of gayety and delight. Mr. Armitage and his sister were drawn into the circle, and Dr. Underwood was a good deal interested while the question of Dr. Carew's taking up his old practice was in abeyance. The absence had given him a good start, to be sure. And the outlying patients would be too great a drain on the elder man. Right in town he had been very successful.

Leonard had arranged his business to remain over several days. The four men found plenty of amusement. Gifford came down again. Ethel was off to a house party, and visiting with his mother was anything but a pleasure. Indeed, she soon tired of him, even when he listened most patiently to her complainings. If it had not been for the relief of Mr. Longworth, he could hardly have endured it at all.

What a curious married life when contrasted with that of Alice! It was something like this in his mother's time, Gifford remembered—his father always at business making money, his mother going hither and thither. And there was his father's long illness at Sherburne. He was glad now that he had been able to give him the kindly care. Yet as he reviewed the past he despised himself more than ever for the weakness that had led to the almost fatal missteps. And what friends had rallied to his assistance! It would be deepest ingratitude to subject them to any misgivings even in the future.

They had all gone over to the Beaumanoir luncheon, but Dell had been a little puzzled. Fanny certainly assumed her most attractive demeanor, and Dell had to admit there were numerous fascinations in it. Millicent was simply unapproachable where Mr. Drayton was concerned. No one seemed to remark it but herself—perhaps no one held the key. Did she understand, and did she mean to refuse in her high and fine manner to save him the pain of a rejection? And if this was so he would inevitably swing back to Fanny. She remembered him once appealing to Alice in a humorous manner for some footing of relationship.

" You will come over for a whole long day," she said
to Milly with her good-by. " I don't feel as if I had seen
a bit of you except the stately company side. Do you
know, you have grown quite grand and distant. I am
almost afraid of you."

" O Dell ! I am sure I have not meant to be grand to
you. I have counted so much on your return, and I
have rejoiced over the advent of the babies. Yes, I
will come when the crowd thins out a little. Violet
and Paul are going on Monday. It is so delightful to
have them really settled in Washington. Mamma is
captivated with the children, and Violet doesn't mean
that she shall love Len's best if she can help it. Papa
is so very fond of little Edward, and Princess we all hug
to our hearts. You will think me foolish, but I can't
bear to have Nora grow so fast. I am hungry for babies,
and I waste days over at Sherburne House. You must
not be jealous."

" I never have been jealous of Tessy." Dell looked
out of beautiful, honest eyes.

" No, dear," and Milly kissed her.

" Mr. Drayton will think we have a household mania.
However, Alice is touched with the same complaint. We
are a family of homes," and Dell smiled brightly. " You
saw a good deal of him when you were out on the ranch ?"

" Yes, I admire him very much. He has been a
splendid friend to Gifford in a business way. I think
he was interested in seeing us all at home in our common daily life. Only so far it has been rather uncommon. We are not always in such a whirl. He and
Leonard seem greatly taken with each other."

There was no stint or withdrawal in this. Dell felt
puzzled.

There were several delightful days with the heat quite endurable even at midday. But the days were full, and the evenings spent in a sort of family party. Then came Sunday, and they were all gathered in the old church with reverent attention. On Monday separations. Violet and Mr. Amory, nurse and two children, Leonard and Mr. Drayton, went up to Washington, Major Stanwood returned to Fortress Monroe, but Aunt Julia stayed to finish out her visit. Gifford and the Osbornes were now the only guests. The latter were going up presently to spend some time with Violet and Ethel.

Millicent came for her day. Nora was extremely fascinated with Auntie Dell, and the twins were a source of wonderment to her, though as yet they could not do much entertaining, and babies were not exactly a rarity.

They talked of the two years abroad, of the old haunts Dell had revisited, of the changes, of the strides made everywhere, of what artists and authors and scientists were doing, of the great unrest that threatened to precipitate a religious upheaval, of the friends Millicent had made, of the noted people both had seen. She did not show any embarrassment when Dell quoted Mr. Drayton; she mentioned his name without the slightest sign that he was more than any other friend. Was she really unsuspecting? Then why had she kept him at bay?

Dell found a very real improvement in Gifford—a cheerfulness and ambition that betokened a wider reach of manliness, a content with daily life. There was no longer the desire to lean on some one. The really good qualities seemed to have leave to expand. His laugh rang truer.

Ah, how the time slipped away! Mr. Drayton came

down for a few more days ; he was going up to New York on some business.

Yes, it was evident Fanny Beaumanoir had reconsidered, perhaps repented. What had made her refuse Reese Drayton when she had the opportunity of accepting him ? Did she really love him ?

Lyndell Carew was startled at this thought, and objections of every kind rose up in her mind. Yet could any one move a finger ? Could she order and arrange ?

If Millicent would give some sign. If Dell had known her less thoroughly, if she had not understood Mr. Drayton so well. He and Fanny would talk in unknown languages all their lives together.

But what if Fanny was capable of being ennobled by the divine power of love ?

She could not put her thought into words. It was hardly a thought, more an insight, a sub-consciousness. These two people would go along not disagreeing, for he would give Fanny her way. It would make little difference what her way was, that was the pity of it. If she chose fashion and show, he would take the more intellectual side, the philanthropic side, in which he was getting strongly interested. So many husbands and wives without any evil intent just drifted apart. Fanny *did* care for a certain kind of admiration. She enjoyed wresting it from people because it was not paid to beauty or superior fascination. She was not any more likely to make a scandal than Ethel, but men would feel her individuality, while Ethel belonged to a class. Ethel could bar out any one she chose by a kind of stony, dignified unconsciousness. Fanny would sting them by some sarcasm, and perhaps make an open enemy.

When the elder Dr. Carew returned to Sherburne the

matter of a removal was really settled. He had succumbed to the pressure on one hand and the fascination
of the fresh, stirring life on the other. If he had not
gone abroad the wrench would have been too much ;
but the tie was partly broken. He felt so well and renewed in strength—there might be years of usefulness
before him, and years of delight with these children of
his love.

" We will not dismantle the old house," he said to his
sister. " We may like to come back now and then, only
I suppose Sherburne will always open its gates wide to
Dell," and the soft smile seemed a cheerful acceptance
of the fact. " We are old people to make a new beginning, but I do believe we have been getting ready for it
ever since we stole a march on Miss Aurelia and carried
off Dell. And now we must pay the penalty of our
escapade," with the old humorous glint in his eyes.

" If you are content. Miss Aurelia has given up her
own life and really lives in that of the others. It is a
preparation for the greater change that comes to us all.
She is serenely happy and is ripening to a sweetness that
is at once appealing and admirable, entering into the
younger experiences by that sure touch of sympathy.
Yet what a curious discipline it has been, and now all
things have been added. So I think we can trust——"

They were old people, but Dr. Carew bent over and
kissed the companion who had been so much to him.

" We must go down and look up a few things. I am
glad the Armitages desire to remain. I shouldn't like
to think of the old house going to ruin while we were
frisking about."

It was a rather sorrowful task, but Miss Neale undertook it bravely. One morning Lyndell went with her.

Miss Neale's room had not been disturbed : it greeted them with all its old-fashioned quaintness. The bedstead, with its slim, high, turned posts, its white tester cover and fringed curtains and valance ; the dressing-table, with its white ruffled cover and little ornaments ; the nameless fragrances that had blown in the windows, of rose, honeysuckle, jasmine, and now all sweet, pungent, ripening odors. And here was the little room where Dell had come a worn and tempest-tossed pilgrim and found the Chamber of Peace. The tears filled her eyes at the remembrance.

"But I could not give you up," and she clasped her arms around Aunt Neale's neck. "You have been my second mother. You and Aunt Julia have filled the position by turns. And the children must have their grandmother—the sweetest grandmother in all the world."

Miss Neale flushed a delicate pink. Was this good thing to be added also—children's children ? Was it true that she need never again have the secret ache and longing of the women who have been denied ? To share Bertram's children ! To drop into old age with clinging arms about her and the sweet voices of childhood making the music her soul had hungered for ! She could never have asked for it ; she was deeply touched to have it so generously given.

The Armitages had taken good care of the house and the old pensioners as long as they had needed it. But the younger man, trained to newer methods, had already begun to teach the young generation to rely more upon themselves. The doctor had slipped into the habit of lavish giving by degrees, both of himself and his means. Dr. Underwood had worked in a friendly fashion with the clergyman. Miss Neale's Sunday class had been merged into a regular school. A young colored girl was assistant teacher. The doctor occupied a friendly and important place with the Beaumanoirs, and was a most welcome guest when business allowed.

Miss Carew could see the changed conditions everywhere. The old systems were vanishing. The hand of improvement was visible in the town. To be truly useful both she and the doctor would have to work on new lines. Would it not be quite as well to do the work elsewhere, surrounded by the best that love could give ? And had not they outgrown some of the old methods, some of the old beliefs, perhaps? Would there not be a little, even if unspoken, sense of rivalry between the two doctors ?

They were to make a short stay in Washington. Violet insisted upon this, and Ethel had been cordial in her invitation as well: Millicent was to come up as soon as they were settled. Dell had not seen much of her during Mr. Drayton's visit. He had gone to Washington now. There was a new railroad to be pushed through and kept out of the hands of a syndicate. Osborne had interested Mr. Longworth already.

It was true that Millicent von Lindorm had evaded Mr. Drayton. Her visit to California had been one of the delightful episodes of her life, a reawakening of energies and purposes that somehow in the every-day round had lapsed a little. Fanny was so often away ; her sister-in-law at Baltimore, a rather quiet person, always enjoyed the stir and life she brought, the people coming and going, and the invitations that poured in upon them. There had been a school friend in Chicago delightfully married ; indeed, Fanny had no end of ac-

quaintances. She had found it very stupid without
Millicent. Her mother's interest lay chiefly at Sherburne House, and there was but little companionship
between the mother and her youngest daughter.

When Millicent returned she slipped readily into the
olden place. Honora's education occupied her mornings, and there was frequently a pile of letters to go over.
Leonard had relieved her of many business cares, and
she was glad that he and his father had become such
thorough companions. Yet she did miss that larger,
delightful liberty, and the talks that had inspirited her.

"I should soon be spoiled in an atmosphere where I
was ministered to continually," she mused. "I should
become too fond of outside appreciation. Since mine is
a quiet life, I must not indulge in vain longings."

She had speculated upon Fanny and Mr. Drayton.
Now that she knew him better, she understood that their
natures would not harmonize in any grand accord or touch
the lines of true development. Then Mr. Drayton enjoyed his liberty of movement and his own desultory life.
He was the kind of man to be a sincere friend, and Millicent relaxed her habitual carefulness. She had felt
shocked and cruelly hurt at the first proposal of marriage she had received in her widowhood. Then her
good sense came to her relief. Men did not look at her
from her own standpoint, but with their more or less
romantic imaginings.

She had left the Osbornes a little suddenly at the last.
Aunt Aurelia had been quite ill, and various other family
matters seemed to render it necessary. So she had not
seen Mr. Drayton to say any final good-by, though he had
sent her a note of regrets some time afterward. It did
not really need a reply, and she waited so long in a state

of indecision that it appeared rather embarrassing to answer it.

Something in Fanny's eagerness to see him again quite startled her. And the day of the dinner her half suspicion was confirmed with a curious certainty. Fanny had been very changeable and captious of late, and only the prospect of the family reunion kept her at home. But now she was bright and good-humored, ready to run back and forth, and in some indescribable manner seemed to establish a prior claim.

Why should she, Millicent, object? The protesting mood surprised her. In every way it would be an excellent marriage for Fanny. For though the younger sister laughed about being in the ranks of spinsterhood, and called certain obstinate opinions " old-maidish ways," she would never make a contented single woman. She had no pursuit or even fancy to fall back upon. If the right occasion came she might rise to the heroic ; but there was so much more every-day living, the truest comprehensions of human life were drawn from common humanity she found, just as there were always stars in the sky, but only rarely a full moon of silver splendor ; so the ideal occasions seldom came to one's hand. Would this be one?

Millicent von Lindorm said to herself at first that she could not stand by, as she must in a marriage of this kind, and see this soul reaching after better sustenance fed on husks. With a woman like Dell or Alice or Violet he would not deteriorate. After all, why was she more solicitous for his welfare than for her sister's? It might mean the salvation of Fanny. There was a hot scarlet in her cheek, a sensation of faintness in her heart, a blinding light about her as of some unexpected revelation, a thing that had been so impossible apparently that she had not even suspected it. In that dazzling glare the possibilities of her own soul had been revealed. She shrank with a certain horror, then she was drawn with a sense of resistless fascination to look at this mysterious delight that throbbed and thrilled until the whole air seemed sentient with it. There were glances and half sentences that she did not know until this moment that she had remembered.

In the silence of the night she took herself to task. There were other duties for her—her little girl growing up to womanhood; her parents ageing year by year; yes, and her literary work that had been such a delight and solace. And there was the other memory.

It was like a dream, a strain of music one follows in the brain, but cannot bring to absolute sound, not forgotten, but impossible of realization. Had she lived through that life? Why could she not summon the pain and the sorrow and abase herself in it? Why could she not bring back the pang of separation, the nights of agonizing loneliness? Had she written her whole soul away in imaginary lives and sorrows?

Fanny certainly cared for Mr. Drayton. Under the badinage there was a vein of earnestness, an almost charming lure, so delicately was it done. She had studied this art in women when it was not flirtation.

She remembered in her early friendship with Bertram Carew, when he had insisted upon her trying a flight into that magical atmosphere of romance, she had been almost blind to her cousin's regard, in her own absorption. She would not fall into a second mistake. She would stand quite aside. For her own peace of mind and womanly self-respect, she must do this. And if

Fanny could win happiness, satisfaction, she would be content.

She had understood he was going up to Washington in the morning with Leonard. There were some new business arrangements to be taken over to Sherburne for Dell's consideration.

"Write a note and send by Hector," said Fanny. She was out of humor that last night's leave-taking had been so little sentimental. To be sure Mr. Drayton had said they would see enough of him the coming winter to be quite tired of him and wish him back in California.

"I will go," Millicent said. "I want to see Dell."

But Lyndell had gone in town with Miss Carew, and they would call at Beaumanoir.

"I hope it will be about luncheon time then," she said smilingly to Tessy. "I will take a look at the babies and Aunt Aurelia and then return."

"And you may have Mr. Drayton."

"I thought he was to go this morning!" in surprise.

"He did start," laughingly. "Leonard forgot an important paper, and he obligingly offered to turn back for it and go up at two. I have an idea you will find him at your house, for he would not be driven over to Ardmore again, though I invited him to remain to an old folks' luncheon." Tessy gave an arch look that might mean a great deal or nothing.

Millicent colored as she sprang down from her horse.

"How we shall miss them all!" Tessy said in a graver tone. "It has been so delightful."

"But I am a fixture," Millicent returned, "though I am not capable of filling the place of so many charming people."

Aunt Julia and Miss Eliza were in Aunt Aurelia's room. Millicent had a chatty little call, and then turned homeward, loitering a little by the way, hoping Mr. Drayton would have an hour or so with Fanny.

The man who an hour earlier had stepped aside and disappeared in a thicket of young pines, feeling that for once fate had played into his hands, threw himself down on the soft, fragrant, needle-covered turf, resolved to await her return. Fortunately there was but one road if a diversity of paths. He had picked up last evening's paper at the station, and he took it out now, feeling a second time that Leonard's package was safe.

The air had a drowsy, ripened breath like coming autumn, and there was a low-spread, brooding tenderness in the pine branches and feathery hemlocks and spruce ; a hazy sort of sky, through which the sun shone lazily ; a day to dream of joys to come, quite possible in this golden atmosphere.

He did not know whether there was any news worth reading. The moments seemed alike swift and tardy, and he half longed, half feared. But he had something to say to Millicent von Lindorm to be the very beginning of a new acquaintanceship. She had not held herself aloof out of any dislike ; he experienced a secret assurance of that.

Oh, there were the horse's hoofs falling gently on the sandy road ! He sprang up, brushed off the clinging leaf fragments, and strode out through another opening. She would turn just here. She did not look on that side of the road ; a fire-bird up in a tree preening his brilliant plumage caught her eye. What a fine, sweet, clear-cut face—a woman's face, full grown and informed with a sort of peerless maturity that one could trust always.

" Oh !" as she moved her head, and a sudden pleasurable light shone in her eyes, " I heard—I thought——" She stopped, blushing and confused, and unconsciously tightened her rein. Prince halted. Then the exquisite bloom of her face faded and the lines lost their fascinating softness ; even the eyes grew cold.

" An unexpected incident gave me this pleasure. I heard the ladies would be at Beaumanoir for luncheon. I thought I would invite myself over for another good-by." There was a delicate movement of the lines of his face, that with less serious intent might have been a smile. " I saw you cantering along the road to Sherburne and I waited. Come, Prince, not too fast a gait, however."

The horse nodded assentingly. Millicent felt helpless. It did not need a word to enlighten her. What she had vaguely dreamed of, wholly denied with a woman's inconsequence, resolved to crush out by indifference, had grown nevertheless. Yet men and women both had outlived a hopeless love. The man's face was set straightforward, looking at the stretch of road. She had learned over on the Western coast that it had lines of latent strength and steadfastness of purpose with all its gay indifference and indolence. And as the steps went steadily on, Prince arching his neck and giving an occasional flirt to his mane, her courage decreased, her secret knowledge was more certain and stood in her way.

" There was something besides business and pleasure that brought me East," he began in a low, resolute tone. " I dreamed over it for months. I saw the objections you could bring, would bring in all probability. But I resolved to win my cause in the end. I shall do it if it takes years."

" Oh, do not, I beseech you," she entreated ; " for it would be useless."

" It may seem quite impossible to you now"—his tone was singularly devoid of haste or passion—" but in time you will come to look at it in a different light. The very consciousness that a man's strong. abiding love is there for you to take when you will, even in times of sorrow, or, as it sometimes happens, the loneliness of middle life, will at least persuade you. I shall wait. Meanwhile, let us be friends. Let us study each other and learn whether there are any absolute irremediable points of discord. It would not do for either of us to make a mistake."

She was silent from sheer inability to advance any cogent refusal. Not to be friends would make a painful break and bring out the truth. Fanny—had she any right to take what her sister desired ? Even if it never came to her, she would suffer less than to have her loss continually flaunted before her in another's happiness. What she, Millicent, needed was time, and this proffer suggested it without the pain of argument. She had discussed other points with Mr. Drayton ; why should she feel so helpless here ?

" I have known men who fell in love with whole families, when, like myself, they had no ties. You, with your wide-spreading household relations, can hardly realize the consciousness of belonging to no one. I suppose I should have begun earlier ; I find myself quite envying your brother and Dr. Carew, with their large interest in life and their home ties. Perhaps in the end I shall bore you all ; but if you could understand the satisfaction, the harmony, and sympathy these visions give a man who has come to the time of life when he has a longing for the divineness of human affection, you would be lenient. So I shall keep anchored to you until you really shake me off."

"No one will do that"—she must make some sort of reply—"and we are all curiously indebted to you——"

"No, it is I who am indebted for some sensible methods of spending money, for a new interest in my kind, when I was beginning to think Solomon uttered the whole of wisdom in his tirade. To be sure, he was much older, and had had everything. Isn't that an argument against great fortunes, great prosperity, and indolent habits? Solomon should have had a prime minister like Dr. Carew. He would have colonized the world. I dare say there were some poor wretches in his time. He might have touched his prose of selfish complaint with the higher poetry of love to his neighbor. We seem to be a long while learning the real truths."

They went on then in silence, though the long, shrill whirr of the locust and the complaint or joyful note of myriad insects in the wood kept up a concert of sound that prevented embarrassment. Presently they made a turn up the avenue.

Drayton paused and took her disengaged hand. "I will say good-by here. I shall see you either in Washington or New York. I shall be with you in thought daily and hourly. You know now the nature of the regard proffered for your acceptance. I might once have fallen in love with your cousin if she had been free ; but I had not known you then. You are the only two women who have roused a desire of ownership in my soul. There can never be another. You are free until you give yourself to me. I am your loyal lover for the rest of my life."

He compelled her to meet his eyes. Hers were lustrous with emotion, his steady and shining. "Good-by," he said softly, and turned away with a pressure of the hand that was almost cruel in its intensity, leaving her amazed at her own silence, which was half acceptance.

# CHAPTER VI.

## WHAT DOES THIS MEAN?

PRINCE walked slowly up to the stepping-stone. Fanny was there and caught her arm as she dismounted.

"Was that Mr. Drayton?" she cried angrily. "He was coming to luncheon—he told Lyndell. And you are so late. What have you been doing? I could have gone half a dozen times; and, as it happened, there was no need of your going at all. Yes, why did he not come in?"

"It must have been my fault. I—I did not ask him," making a great effort at indifference.

"And you've been quarrelling!"

Fanny knew this was not true, but she trusted to get the truth from the unwarranted accusation.

"On the contrary, we parted in a friendly fashion." She was glad she could say it. "I was very remiss, but I did not think—if he had meant to come," she paused in embarrassment. "I will go and change my habit. Don't wait for me."

Something had happened between these two. Fanny Beaumanoir experienced a pang of maddening jealousy. But Millicent could not, would not accept him, she said over to herself a dozen of times before she reached the dining-room.

Mr. Beaumanoir and Miss Carew were in the full tide

of reasons why it was best to make the impending change.   Mr. Beaumanoir accepted the facts, but he did regret parting with his lifelong friends.

" We do expect to come back occasionally as visitors," said Miss Carew, " and in our extreme old age we may want a refuge from the pleasures and dissipations of the world.   And I know brother would leave everything and come to an old friend who wanted him."

Dell and Nora were planning a Christmas visit.   Nora was to have a good long release from study.   There would be pictures to visit, exhibitions and fairs and concerts.   They might even go to an opera.

Fanny's announcement, therefore, made a very slight stir.   Dell wondered a little, and then went on with her list of pleasures.

Millicent took off her hat and habit as if she were strangling.   She caught a glimpse of her flushed face and threw herself on her knees beside the bed, burying her face in her hands, and endeavoring to keep back the passion of tears that would have relieved her.   How weak and foolish she had been !   Why had she not told the whole truth ?   Ah, could she tell all of it ?   The heat in her face flashed up in a kind of indignant passion.

Yes, she had really been afraid to meet Reese Drayton on any ground.   She had kept silence even from good words—brave words.   With a wild rush the dozens of things she might have said swept through her mind. If she could have been noble enough to thrust self aside, to say this love should by rights go to another, and that she had had her cup of bliss.   What a sweet, simple, joyous love that was, with its blessed benison of sunny youth !   And it came to her then with something of a shock to wonder if they two met now for the first time.

O Heaven, that was disloyal! So far had the poison crept. She must uproot it if it took all the strength of her soul.

She bathed her face and went downstairs with all the tranquillity she could command. "No, she had not met Mr. Drayton at Sherburne. He had insisted upon walking in town, and she had overtaken him a little the other side of the drive. In her surprise she was afraid she *had* been inhospitable; but she fancied she might be late——"

"The idea of his walking in town when there are so many horses and servants," said Dell with a short, bright laugh. "I suppose he thought it would be ridiculous to say the good-bys over again. He doesn't assume that

> "'Parting is such sweet sorrow
> That he could say good-night till it were morrow.'"

"Mamma," began Nora, "I have made up my mind just what I want for Christmas—a splendid long visit at Auntie Dell's. I will practise my music every day, and talk German, and read French, and you won't have anything to bother, so you can write stories and stories."

"What will *I* do for a girl?" asked grandpapa.

"Why, you'll have to get Princess over here. She sings like a lark—doesn't she, Auntie Dell?—or a mocking-bird, for she sings everything. And she is very wise and cunning. And Ned Sherburne—Aunt Tessy would have two children left. I'd like a lovely long visit in New York."

"Christmas is a good way off," remarked her grandmother. "And you would leave mamma a long while?" with a suggestion of reproach in her voice.

Nora colored. " She could write every day for a fort-night and then come herself. We wouldn't have done all the things, would we, Auntie Dell ? I've been to Washington so many times. Don't you think I could go, mamma ?" pleadingly.

" We will consider, dear."

Millicent was thankful for the diversion. Then they let Mr. Drayton drop out of the talk, though Millicent could not help flushing when Fanny turned her sharp eyes in her direction.

When they had all gone—for Fanny went over to Sherburne, and grandpapa took Nora out driving with him—Millicent went to her room. She must settle this point with herself. Certainly Fanny *was* unusually interested in Mr. Drayton ; perhaps it might be the great incentive to a finer development, higher aims. She must stand aside and not mar this opportunity by any pretence of friendship. Even if there were no ques-tion of her sister's happiness, she could not accept his love. Let her keep firmly to this idea. When God gave her back to this home, He meant that she should respect her experiences and live for others. The heroism of life had seemed easy and natural, and now this atmosphere had been swept away. It was changed, hard, something to give up, but duty still, and she must keep to it. She must uproot this desire for a separate happiness, this bewildering revelation that she was loved and might love in return. She must not dally in that enchanted land of second youth.

She sat down at her desk and drew out a sheet of paper. She would write to Mr. Drayton and tell the truths she had so weakly let slip this morn-ing. Why, a girl of sixteen would have had more

courage and presence of mind.   It had taken her so by
surprise.

Was not that another evasion ?   With her strongest
efforts she could not extinguish the certain thrill at the
knowledge that he loved her.   She tried to make it
seem unnatural, but it was like a splendid gleam of
truth that could not be pushed aside.   Disguise it as
she might, insist that it shamed her womanhood, still
she could not shut out the radiant knowledge that she
was capable of loving again.   But she must not, she absolutely must not.

She made several copies.   No article for the eyes of
the world had ever been subjected to such a rigorous
scrutiny and revision.   She tried to put her personal
feeling out of the question.   This was a heroine who
saw the straight line of duty and would follow it.   There
were her parents, growing older every year ; there was
her child, to whom she owed a double duty ; there was
her work, in which she took an interest so earnest and
complete that it would naturally defraud any other.
She had laid out her plan of life, and she must not allow
any passing probability to interfere.

She folded, sealed it, and sent it to the office.   She
would not trust herself with the temptation of added
wisdom or cooler judgment on the morrow.   She was
uplifted with a sense of sacrifice.   Then she went to her
mother's room ; she did not really want to be alone with
herself.

"Dear me," said Mrs. Beaumanoir, "how quiet it
is !  I am really sorry all you children have grown
up and are, in a certain way, settled.   There was a
great pleasure in thinking about your future.   I'm
thankful enough there is so much interest at Sher-

burne House and that Aunt Aurelia will never be lonesome."

"We shall have Nora," ventured Nora's mother.

"Oh, yes. I do not know that I was thinking about myself altogether—scarcely at all," and she smiled. "I was considering how very pleasant and sensible it was that Neale Carew could look at the family change in the light she does. We shall all miss her and the doctor, but we have not had them now for the past two years. And Dell's children will seem like her very own grandchildren. I don't think I could have felt satisfied if there had been no babies. Dell's life would have been incomplete. What a delight she has been to us all, even if the beginning was not propitious! And there are no two happier people in the world than the old doctor and his sister, unless it is your own father and myself."

She glanced up with a mirthful light in her eyes. And then it died slowly out. Milly ought to be the centre of a happy household. To be sure, matrimony was rather flouted and disdained nowadays, but it was God's holy ordinance, nevertheless. And perhaps it was old-fashioned to believe in God.

"Oh, there are the Armitages! Let us go down, Millicent," glancing at the two figures coming up the walk.

Miss Armitage and her brother preferred to sit on the hospitable porch, which was shady and looked inviting, with easy-chairs, a table or two with books and magazines, and the hammock across the end.

They were delighted to have the question of the house settled so agreeably.

"My health has improved immeasurably," said Mr. Armitage. "And the old house suits us so completely. Only I sometimes feel as if I was taking life too easy;

but mother could not have stood the harsh Northern climate another year. Life is not so complex; there is more leisure, and one's nerves get into harmonious accord. What a fine old man Dr. Carew is, and quite learned enough for a professor."

"He has always kept up with the best. And his house was a sort of hospital, with Miss Carew as a Sister of Charity."

"He is fortunate, too, in having such a son. Mrs. Carew is charming. I should like to add them to my congregation, though we do increase a little in numbers, and the friendly spirit is encouraging. Miss Fanny is so bright and helpful. I am sorry to miss her," and he glanced about with a sense of disappointment, Millicent thought.

She recalled the bright, half-disputatious talks with Fanny. They were so used to having Fanny appropriate the chief interest; but was there another side to it? Oh, surely Fanny could not be in earnest. What if her preferences for Mr. Drayton had no truer foundation. A quick thrill of relief surged through Millicent.

The servant brought out some cake and fruit. They discussed one or two notable magazine articles. Mr. Beaumanoir returned without Fanny. They rose to go, but he insisted upon driving them home.

There was a very quiet evening, but Millicent felt strangely restless.

There was enough to do for the next few days. Lyndell was to go up to Washington for a visit with nurse and babies. Alice begged Fanny and Millicent to come also, as for the next fortnight she should be mistress of her sister's house. Ethel had gone off with a fashionable set on a round of pleasure. Washington was deserted, every one declared, and houses were shut up ; but somehow business went on and people were going to and fro, clerks and officials and military men, who were glad of Washington at any season. Then there were beautiful residences and grounds a little way out, and no one could take away the magnificent drives nor the spacious porches, with that delightful evening air that made everything restful, and the large, cool rooms full of comfort.

"I think I had better not go," Millicent said. "I may be needed for little matters here. If there is any special occasion I could run up for a day and a night."

Fanny made no demur. Millicent often stayed at home. She had made one great, generous proffer when she insisted upon her going out to Alice. Nothing had come of it. She was quite free to recall her regretted refusal. Only—if she knew what had happened that day—but Millicent had only been a little graver than usual, preoccupied. Perhaps it was some knotty point in story writing.

Hector came up with a handful of letters. Fanny caught at them, and two fell to the floor. Both girls stooped. Fanny picked up one, the other had a publisher's address in the corner.

"It is from Mr. Drayton." Fanny's eyes were hard, questioning, as she reluctantly handed it to her sister. "Perhaps you will reconsider when you know *his* wishes," she said with scornful insistence.

"Mr. Drayton's wishes cannot affect me." Millicent made a great effort to keep her face unmoved, and opened her letter. There was but one line.

"Sincerely your friend.

"REESE DRAYTON."

Millicent held it with a studied carelessness, that Fanny might see its brevity.

"I asked him"—what should she say?—" to undertake a little commission for me, and he has done it."

"Milly!"—she grasped her sister's arm—"tell me, tell me truly ; are you engaged to Mr. Drayton?"

"I am not. He has not asked such a thing of me."

She could say it in the strict letter. There was a touch of indignation in her voice, but Fanny fortunately translated it wrongly.

"Well, then, I will tell *you*. He asked me to marry him out there," nodding her head, " at the Osbornes'. I was foolish enough to refuse him. I suppose a woman *can* change her mind in love matters. I like him better than any one I have ever met. I—I mean to win him back if I can. I was horribly jealous the other day. I don't like all this superabundant endeavor and philanthropy and generosity run mad ; but he has plenty of money. Perhaps he would enjoy one of the high lights better, but I can play at it. It is one of the fads that come up now and then and runs its course, and he will tire of it and turn the whole business over to Gifford and that Dr. Wolff, and we will be trotting over the other Continent. Of course you would hardly think of marrying again ; and he is not earnest enough to suit you. I wasn't quite sure," with a rather awkward laugh, " but that you were in the running. And now I have a clear field. Milly, dear, that is what has made me so queer lately. But now the signs are propitious, and you may be glad to have me off your hands."

She gave her a hasty kiss and disappeared the next moment.

He had asked Fanny to marry him ! He had said to

her there had only been two women who had roused even
the thought of lasting regard in his soul. Yes, she had
been saved from a great mistake. She would not blame
him unduly, but he had not been frank or honest. A
quick pang rent her soul. To be deceived in him ; was
not Lyndell mistaken as well ? Yes, he belonged to the
less scrupulous class ; she could not quite abhor it, for
he was not the only one, let her remember. Was her
standard ideally high ?

She drew a long breath of relief. The matter was settled beyond a peradventure. Had there really been anything to settle ? She had slipped into the place of the
home daughter, and surely she had enough to make her
life happy. There would be Leonard's children growing up, Violet's and Lyndell's house would be like that
of another sister. Yes, it would be rich and pleasant,
far-reaching in its interests.

Yet she could not deny that she had seen a possibility.
And this other prospect stirred a sense of repulsion that
she vainly tried to dismiss. What if some untoward circumstances had forced, as it were, an unsuitable marriage upon Leonard, growing out of the mistake of
his youth ? They had all followed Anita Garcia's fortunes with a deep interest. Her marriage had not
quenched her desire for the world's appreciation. Mistakes were made continually. Perhaps the discipline
was needed, and she sighed.

Then she put the matter out of her mind with the
gentle acquiescence a generous soul gives. She was
too busy to brood over things she could not help or
hinder.

Dr. Underwood came up to Sherburne House to take tea
with the Carews. He was not so narrow but that he could

have welcomed his old *confrère* back—the man who had held out a cordial hand to him on his first advent in the place. There would still be plenty for him to do, but he would not be sole authority of course. He liked this semi-Southern life ; the people had been a new type, and suited him better than the frontier crudeness or the squalor of cities. He was of the higher intellectual type, but he considered his own enjoyment rather than fame— and so few won that.

And then followed the partings, less keen, perhaps, for the many recent changes. Aunt Julia was to go up to New York with them and take little Ray, as Archie was to come as a witness in an important lawsuit and must return the moment it was through.

Lyndell made merry over her caravan, as she termed it. They were so near now that it could hardly be termed a separation. She and Millicent had some tender confidences.

"And I shall look for a good long visit in the winter," she said. "It seems as if I really was beginning my married life over again and those early years had been merely courtship, when we were trying to aim at high things outside of home life—as if we had not really known what marriage was for ! Perhaps one cannot in the early years. It *is* children that make the true centre, that ease up the restless longings. It gives one a continual joy and hope for the future."

She was very happy and satisfied. It shone in her eyes, it deepened and softened her voice, but it did not narrow any aim or true purpose or friendship. All the sweetness and richness she had gathered in would be given out again. It was not to know any lack.

She came into her own home leaning on her husband's

arm, and as they stepped over the threshold he bent and kissed her.

" It *is* a new life," she said softly. " One is not married all at once——"

" For one's whole life, ' as long as ye both do live,' " he repeated solemnly. " The book has many pages in it, and we have turned only a few. If there is the sweetness of hope fulfilled, there is also the sweetness of experience, when truths develop and you come to their real meaning. There are new beginnings all along."

She ran through the rooms with a girl's eager delight. It was all changed and new save the pictures and a little of the furnishing. Three pretty apartments opening into each other, the farthest back to be used for the family sitting-room. And upstairs the nursery between her and Aunt Neale, and the babies smiling in their wide crib, looking as much at home as if they had not come from the other side of the world.

Still up on the next floor was the " Den," to be devoted to any leisure hours at home. There was the big sofa and the round table from the old Carew house, and some easy-chairs. This one she remembered well ; she had sobbed out her girlish sorrows on the doctor's shoulder sitting here with his arm around her.

" Oh, I do wonder if you will feel really at home, dear, dear papa ! It is such a great change to ask of any one."

He folded her in his arms, much moved.

" When I have a longing for solitude I can go back," he answered with the little gruffness that rises in deep emotion. " Oh, you cunning woman ! it was one of your deep-laid schemes to take us all over the world and give us no rest for the sole of our foot simply that we might not be able to resist the promise of the home held out so temptingly. And the love of children——"

"It ought to comfort age," she exclaimed in the pause. "The saddest old age must be that when children have grown indifferent or estranged. It would break my heart to have mine forget me when they were men and women."

He recalled with a sense of unalloyed joy that Lyndell never had evinced any petty jealousy through the years of her married life. He had hesitated a little whether this were a wise step. Yet was not all human love at its best to be a type of the divine? And if a man loved not his human brother, how hardly should he love that divine Elder Brother?

They were some time in getting fitted and settled. Dell felt at first that she would be almost a stranger again but for the Murrays. Mrs. Murray was a little older, but the same sweet, tender mother. Two more sons were married. Baby Densie was growing up into shy, sweet girlhood; Morna had babies of her own in her Scotch home, and Mrs. Murray had been induced to visit her there. She was occupied and interested in her own children and grandchildren, and though her heart was open to charity, she had not the gift for active, concerted work, even if she could have found the time.

"She is not narrow, either," declared Dell, when they were discussing her one day, "only she seems to live in a charming little world of her own, with no desire to stray outside of her fences."

"She has done a fine work in the world when you think of her sons and her daughters. If such success were given to every mother there would be little crime or sin. None of the boys have gone astray. It is a family to be proud of, brought up amid the temptations of the city," declared Bertram.

Laddie, the youngest boy, the baby in Dell's time, had been gifted with unusual musical abilities. He and Con were the family geniuses—Con, who was still on the whirl to the ends of the earth gathering up curious knowledges for newspapers, and going on exploring expeditions. Every time he came home his mother hoped he would marry and settle down, but nothing was farther from his thoughts.

Lyndell Carew soon found she had not been forgotten by the world of society in which she had once taken an active part. Cards and invitations piled up. Yes, it was the same restless, busy, exciting world, full of schemes and plans, one crowding another, each one sure it had the only true panacea for all ills.

She was wiser now. She had a sacred duty within the walls of home, a love, too, that filled every pulse of her being. Yet it would not decrease any true sympathy. Only, she had found her place. Instead of restlessness there had come a divine peace. She had not taken the vows of wifehood and accepted the duties of motherhood to throw them aside at the bidding of any new prophet, crying, " Lo here ! or lo there !"

" But you are not to narrow your life," Bertram said decisively.

" I have a habit of going to extremes," and Dell laughed, " but I doubt if I lose my fondness for knowing what the great world is about. And I seem to have a good deal of something suspiciously like leisure. Freda is so trusty, and Aunt Neale so grandmotherly that, in sheer lack of employment, I expect I shall take up some forlorn hope and do battle valiantly. You will not need to fear."

# CHAPTER VII.

## A WASTED LIFE.

ARCHIE STANWOOD had changed greatly in barely three years, Dell decided, when she held out the hand of cousinly welcome. He had kept his aspect of boyishness a long while, then he had suddenly merged into manhood, strong and rather stern. This was partly due to his business demands, and the rest to the solitary, inward life he was leading.

Aunt Julia had been visiting a friend while Lyndell was setting her house in order, a Mrs. Westwood and her daughter, who had come to New York nearly six months before to join in a suit for some property bequeathed to different heirs, yet vigorously contested by some of the nearest kin, who grudged that even a dollar should be diverted from what they considered their just dues. There had been numerous delays and appeals. The daughter, a fine musician, had been well patronized in Washington, but, coming in the early summer, she had found few patrons. The autumn had been a little better; and now Mrs. Carew was using her influence to establish one who had always been a favorite of Aunt Julia's, whom the mother love would gladly have welcomed if Archie's fancy had run that way.

"I envy the men who have homes," he said to Dell as he sat with his little girl on his knee. "In a few years I do hope to have one of my own. There are times when

I hunger for a fireside and my child ; but I could not take her to that ungenial climate even if mother was not so fond of her. At present I could not part them. You know now—you have babies of your own. But I must not depress you with my complaints. I have nothing to complain of, really, since I have chosen this lot for what it will bring me.''

'' And you are successful ?''

'' Yes ; a few years more will end my self-appointed exile. I shall have enough to make a nice start elsewhere. And when father gets retired on half pay we will have a pretty home together. Perhaps Winthrop will cast in his lot with us. Floyd, I hear, after the fashion of theological students, has engaged himself, though his choice is much wiser than mine, and he will no doubt be very happy. I suppose love *is* tempting to youth.''

'' Yes,'' returned Dell smilingly. '' A clergyman's daughter ought to make a good clergyman's wife. It will be a rather long engagement ; but if they tire of each other they will find that out. We are being married off, and almost before we are aware of it there will be another generation. Milly's daughter is growing fast. Really there will be another host.''

'' And Harry Lepage is due in a few weeks, I hear. He is to have quite a long furlough.''

'' Yes. Alice is to stay until after that. She has two charming children.''

'' When you are all together I must try to get away on a real vacation. I have been pretty well tied. But when I was once established it seemed the wildest of folly to throw it up when the business promised success. And I knew I had exiled myself.''

Archie Stanwood sighed. All his life to be wrenched out of its hopes and ambitions for a sacrifice that had no permanent good !

It was like old times to see Miss Neale and Dr. Carew. How happy every one seemed ! Bertram tendered Archie the friendliest of greetings.

He could hardly bear to be a moment away from his little daughter. She was rather shy at first, but grand-mamma had not allowed her to forget ; and the personal charm soon reasserted itself. Of her mother no one ever spoke, and happily the child had no consciousness of the tie. The explanation must be put off as long as possible.

Then Archie had to say good-by, and Aunt Julia prepared to return.

" O Dell, dear," she said, " I wish you might find a little time for Miss Westwood, she is such a sweet and noble girl. I can't see why some good fortune has not come to her ; and now, if this fails," pausing sympathetically, " I am afraid it will have an unfortunate effect upon the mother. She seems far from well."

" I will do my uttermost," promised Dell. " I do like her very much. And now I have resolved to bestow a good deal of my interest on really worthy people rather than schemes."

" Harry's vessel is in," announced Bertram a few days later. They had kept Aunt Julia on one pretence and another, mostly to comfort her, for sweet as the interviews were with Archie, they left hours of intense sadness. " At the Boooklyn yard. I shall go over to-morrow morning and see our fine lieutenant. Dell, you ought to have a bosom friend to capture this young hero. But when he gets to Washington they will swarm about him like bees."

The next day at noon he brought him up to luncheon. A fine, distinguished-looking man, changed almost out of recollection, Dell declared. She had missed him on his other visit ; and, owing to his having been once transferred abroad, he had not been home in several years. How they talked of the changes, of the old times, the summer when they were children on Long Island, Milly's marriage—the first among the cousins !

"I shall remain in port now long enough to get acquainted all around." Harry declared. "To-morrow afternoon I shall get off to Washington. How fortunate they are all there !"

Bertram, as usual, had to excuse himself for some hospital work, and the elder doctor to attend to the office calls. But there were the babies to see, who were growing in intelligence ; and little Ray, who inquired why Cousin Harry did not bring back her papa.

Aunt Julia would be glad of his escort to-morrow, and proud of bringing home such an addition to the family circle.

"You ought to be in their midst," Bertram said to his wife when he came home the next evening and found her alone.

"And run away from my own household ? I have a double chain to keep me a devoted wife," glancing up smilingly.

"As if you needed that," with sweet reproach.

"We do need the babies. I wonder now how we lived without them."

"We were learning lessons to fit us for this time," he returned gravely. "When I glance back over those years——"

"They were happy years," with a sort of jealous insistence. "I do not know now that I would take any one of them back—not a month or a week."

"Thank you," kissing her. "But I remember a time when I was absorbed in a certain book—Dell, how lovely you were, how heroic to make no complaint! And now that we have father, I am afraid I shall put a double portion of drudgery upon him while I play the lover. Come, let us have a song."

They were still singing when Dr. Carew entered. Their happiness was a continual source of joy to him.

Miss Neale had insisted that she should be left to her own entertainment. Already she had found some poor, or, rather, the doctor had brought them to her notice, and she had been spending the evening cutting out garments. One of the little girls had run a sewing machine in a factory until her cough had grown so severe she was compelled to remain at home. The mother went out washing. There were three children younger than the girl.

It was such a cozy room. Miss Neale never picked up magazines or papers until bedtime, lest her brother might happen in. She liked the old-time atmosphere, and she did not want him to miss it more than was necessary. Indeed, it was quite wonderful how easily he adapted himself to the new life. There was so much of wide interest in it. He was more than proud to see the esteem in which his son was held.

Washington was filling up rapidly. Some important measures were to come before Congress, and social life was all astir. Mrs. Osborne was still her sister's guest, making visits to Violet frequently, and really enjoying the advantages. Gifford found his hands full at first with Fanny's demands, and the delight he took in Amory's studio. When the news of Harry's return reached them all parties decided to remain until after the holidays. Mrs. Lepage suddenly considered herself quite important, and insisted on sundry additions to her wardrobe.

"She had been foolish to give up society," she declared. "She must make an effort for her children's sake."

Reese Drayton was quite fascinated with the panorama of the capital. He had found some old friends; he was much interested in Leonard Beaumanoir, and he kept a sort of watchful eye over Gifford; but that young man seemed to be putting forth his best efforts.

With Harry's advent Mrs. Longworth's handsome house had its doors opened wide to society. Three marriageable men were an undeniable card, for she adroitly drew Drayton within her circle. What had Fanny been about all this while that she had not captured this very eligible *parti?*

Mrs. Lepage made a great effort to join in the gayeties. Attired in her best, with all the art she could call to her aid, she came down on the occasion of the first "tea" of the season. The rooms were crowded, of course, and the air close and heavy with the odor of flowers and the concourse of people. And the poor woman suffered agonies of mortification when she found that even being the mother of an attractive young lieutenant just returned from a long cruise could not restore her olden prestige. Young women stared at her; older women had half forgotten her. There were so many strange faces that she shrank in dismay and anger—she who should really be at the head of these sons and daughters, for whom she had done her best, and who now saw her sit neglected and forlorn.

Alice made several efforts to get over to her; but there was one introduction, and another, and she seemed borne farther away.

"What a crush!" Reese Drayton was at her elbow at that instant. "Are these the amenities of civilized life? We do better out on the ranch. There is more room."

"And Ethel rarely does a thing like this. It is in the lieutenant's honor. Part of the crush is to see him."

Drayton laughed. "It is well to see it once in a lifetime, I suppose. But really, I haven't much fancy for such things."

There was a stir in the adjoining room, a half note of alarm. Some one had fainted.

Alice thought of her mother. She had left her comfortably ensconced on the sofa.

Fanny was making her way through the crowd.

"Isn't it awful! I don't believe half the people were invited. Who fainted? Oh, there is Gif! Why, it must be Aunt Lepage. She did looked wretched ten minutes ago."

"You can get through this door more easily." Drayton took Mrs. Osborne's arm and made a way through to the hall. Gifford was carrying his mother to the rear stairway, and one of the waiters helped him up to the next landing. Alice followed.

"I hope it is nothing serious," he said with some solicitude.

"Mamma was really not able to stand it. Thank you," and she flew up to her mother.

The nurse was stripping off her finery. The poor face looked frightful with its pink cheeks and red lips amid the ghastly pallor.

"She would have her gown just so tight, and she's thin enough, goodness knows. She isn't used to such things. I think she is very poorly."

After the faint succeeded a hysterical attack, and the doctor was summoned. The crowd began to thin out a little, as many of them were due elsewhere. Mrs. Longworth appeared serene and untroubled, and evinced no sign of fatigue. When she went upstairs Mrs. Lepage was quite tranquil. The nurse made a gesture and she paused at the door. Alice came out.

"I am to chaperone a theatre party after a little dinner at the Copelands'. Their aunt never goes anywhere. I'm to take Harry and Gifford. Mamma was silly to do anything more than just come down. When the rooms began to be so crowded it was frightfully hot. If I had not been the hostess I should have fainted away myself. I seem to have opened the season with a host of attractions. What numbers of men came in! I am afraid we shall be a wreck to-morrow. Don't worry about mother, Alice, she's used to fainting turns; and she is so little accustomed to any exertion the least thing overcomes her. Poor mamma! She can't accept the fact that her day has gone by and yield gracefully."

Harry came also. "It does not seem quite the thing to leave you alone," he began with evident solicitude. "How very poorly mother is! Do you suppose there is any real danger? I was positively shocked when I saw her first. Why, she looks quite an old lady compared to Aunt Beaumanoir."

"There is no immediate danger, I believe. Still I think she looks worse than she did a month ago."

"Some one ought to remain with you."

"There is Mr. Osborne"—she gave a kind of reassuring smile—"and Fanny. No, do not feel really anxious, Harry."

"I am glad she has *one* devoted daughter. What a tremendous crush it was! I could not help wondering what real sense or enjoyment there was in it. But I do want to see the play to-night——"

"Go with an easy conscience. It is late. Do not keep Ethel waiting."

But Alice waylaid the doctor and questioned him closely.

"She has a very weak heart," he said. "Fashionable women wear themselves out before their time. A few days' quiet will restore her. Do not argue with her and avoid exciting topics."

Gifford offered to remain at home, but Alice dismissed him with the same assurance.

The anodyne began to take effect. The dinner bell sounded, and she went down to the small family party— in great contrast to the crowd of an hour ago—Fanny and Mr. Longworth, herself and her husband and her little boy, who had become a great favorite with her brother-in-law, who insisted the child should come to the table when there was no company. His place was beside his uncle, and his pleasant chatter interested the busy man extremely.

Mr. Longworth was beginning to wonder now what he should do with his millions. He had a vague idea that in marrying a young woman there would be children. He had no especial fondness for babies, and thought the adoration of partial parents simply nauseating. But a son like this manly little fellow, a pretty girl like that of Paul Amory's or Alice's stirred in his soul a curious longing. He had been much engrossed in business—as

much for the real love of it as well as the money-making
side—and he had prospered beyond his aims. He had
made a will shortly after his marriage, when the possibility of children had been natural. If there never should
be any of his own lineage, Ethel was young and attractive, and would no doubt marry again if he should not
attain old age.

A curious pang rent his worldly heart. He remembered how Mrs. Lepage and Ethel had bewailed the marriage of Alice. Her husband was a fine man in every
respect, prospering as well, and they were not only
happy, but an unusually attractive couple. Alice looked
as if she might be five years younger than Ethel instead
of her twin. She was really beautiful, of that higher
spiritual type. And there was Mrs. Amory and Mrs.
von Lindorm, who charmed the more intellectual circles.
Why, at first Ethel had attracted just such people.

To-night he felt solitary with all his money. It could
buy a great many things, it could even draw strong and
true friends to him, but there was a new longing that he
could not understand himself, the desire that sometimes
comes to begin life over again and have it different.

Alice went upstairs with the junior Bevis. Mr. Osborne and Mr. Longworth retired to the smoking-room.
Fanny took one of the luxurious chairs, and as no one
came in indulged in a rather pettish frame of mind.
She was too really well bred and womanly to throw herself at Reese Drayton, but there were dozens of little society arts one could use that might mean much or mere
piquant entertainment. They had all failed, she admitted to herself with a sense of chagrin.

Why had he asked her to marry him? Did he consider it a duty after that winter in New York, when he

had been devoted in an indolent, fascinating manner, that she sometimes half suspected had been due to the desire to bask in the sunshine of her cousin's atmosphere? He had not been lover-like in California, and his proposal savored more of duty than the urgent need of love. This was why she had rejected it with a certain scorn. He was capable of loving ; she would have no perfunctory professions.

Yet if she had accepted him, would not the love have followed ? She could certainly have trusted him to do his whole duty. To be sure, he had no yearning after fashionable life, and would not years of all these complex social questions bore her ? She had no real missionary spirit, but she was wearying of the same round of pleasure year after year. No one said anything new and fresh. It might seem that to the young men, and the older beaux kept it as current coin to offer to the " buds" every season ; but she had heard the compliments and small witticisms and pretty speeches until they bored her. She was not an intellectual woman, not a diffuse woman. Her delights must always centre about herself. There was no especial outflowing to her nature. Millicent and Dell had these large ideas, these plans for others, this desire to uplift the world.

Millicent ! Why had not Reese fallen in love with her in that golden atmosphere, when there was no outside influence to sway either ? Would Millicent marry again ? She had always assumed the contrary. And in spite of a wilful pretence of blindness she could understand that these two people would make a complete whole, a marriage as happy and satisfying as Dell's or Violet's or that of Alice. Reese Drayton would be a better, broader, finer man if he married Millicent than if he succumbed to her blandishments. He would *love* Millicent. He would like and tolerate her. Not flattering, to be sure.

Of course she could marry, if not quite to her fancy. What made her so fastidious ? She felt honestly to-night that a life like Ethel's would weary her to death. She would want to make Mr. Longworth adore her, instead of merely admiring her. Yes, she desired to be loved with one of those fervent, daring, all-conquering passions that swept one off her feet. Were there any such men left? The very young ones were given to certain heroics ; she liked the strength of the next decade better.

But she did admit to herself there was no chance of an honorable conquest over Reese Drayton, and she would not descend to questionable arts. Perhaps he *did* love Millicent. But *she* had asked something of him, and he had answered. It could not be in the line of love-making. Millicent would not raise her finger to woo any man.

" I may as well go to bed and get some beauty sleep," she said presently with a yawn. She stopped and chatted a few moments with Alice. Aunt Lepage was sleeping peacefully.

Mrs. Longworth found herself the centre of attraction. The stylish young lieutenant and Gifford, who seemed roused to new life by his brother's return, beside the sort of half claim upon Mr. Drayton, who always came at her call, made her the kind of person society mammas struggled for. She enjoyed the sense of power. Her table was heaped with invitations. She gave an elegant little dinner, at which only the most desirable buds of the season were invited, and the band came later on for two hours' dancing. She had a new aim ; she would marry both of these young men to her own satisfaction.

Alice and her husband felt they must return, though Colonel Ashton insisted he was really better than usual. Grandmamma was pining for the children.

"I think you had better stay and be my little boy," Mr. Longworth said to Bevis, who had become his companion in drives and the leisure hours of his evenings.

Bevis looked at his mother. "There's grandpapa," he answered slowly. "He would miss me a good deal. If you could send for him I would like to stay. But I am almost afraid he couldn't come, he is so lame."

Mr. Longworth was touched by the tender consideration for the grandpapa who was no real kin. If there was such a love to cheer his declining years!

In the midst of the gayety the blow fell almost without warning. Mrs. Lepage had been so nervous and exacting and so full of plans one could hardly judge of her real state. There had been some fainting spells, and then she had rallied and sat up and talked of coming downstairs to her Christmas dinner, begging Ethel to make it a real family gathering.

"I do not believe she could stand the excitement," Alice said; "the least thing tires her out. Fond and proud as she is of Harry, she sends him away in a few moments."

The nurse said the same thing. The doctor pressed his lips together in a half doubtful fashion, and instructed the nurse to watch her closely and keep her from all excitement. There were so many engagements, that one and another just looked in and greeted her cheerfully.

"We will wait until after the new year," said Alice Osborne when her husband spoke of returning.

Alice used to wonder in a strange awe when the spirit flared up with a sudden strength and the voice for a moment lost its fretful sound. But it always dropped down again. Did she realize anything of this great change coming upon her?

The anodyne soothed the restless nerves and dulled the warning pains. She had accustomed herself to them for so long a time one could only go on in the same way.

The end came quite peacefully. Mrs. Lepage had been very uneasy through the night. Several times she had asked if her sons had come in. Toward morning she had fallen asleep, and when the light of the winter dawn came Mrs. Ditmars knew well what the gray pallor and faint, infrequent breathing meant. She despatched the maid for Mrs. Longworth, judging rightly enough that the scene would affect her less than Mrs. Osborne. She waited and watched. There was a flutter in the throat, a vague movement with the hands. Long afterward it seemed to her the soft sweep of a trailing wrapper sounded through the hall.

"She never even roused," said Mrs. Ditmars. "I did not think it would be so soon. But she did not suffer."

Ethel shuddered. She had a horrible shrinking from death, and turned ghastly pale. Of course the end came to everybody some time.

"I must tell Mr. Longworth," and she hurried away. There had been little sympathy between herself and her mother. It would have been quite impossible for the most tender love to awaken a response in this soul, that had quenched so long ago the sense of spiritual life. She could be proud of her children's successes, but she felt crowded out of it all because she had passed unlovely middle life and was going down the hated hill to old age. What use was life if she could not keep her olden place and still be a power in society !

The curious hush of death pervaded the house. They all spoke in low tones, as if some unguarded sound might disturb her. There were messages to be sent, consultations to be held.

" It is fortunate that I really did not make any plans for Christmas. The Creightons are to give a splendid ball, and Mamie Creighton wanted the boys so much. She came in yesterday and really coaxed. She would be such a splendid catch for Harry. But it *is* dreadful to have it happen just at this time, when the season is beginning. I have three gowns coming in the next steamer. I had counted on such a gay winter. And now everything must be stopped."

" I am thankful we stayed ;" Mrs. Osborne's voice had a tremble in it.

" Yes ; it is an excellent thing that you should all be here. Poor mamma ! She has been no comfort to any one this last year. She aged terribly. She seemed to drop down after Florence was married. Well, she had the consolation of knowing we were all nicely married. Gif seems on the road to success. Now, if he only marries sensibly—and we might have had such a splendid winter. It was so when papa died. Alice, we must be thinking about some mourning. I must send to Madame Lemke. O dear ! I hate mourning, and to be dropped out of everything, or have to drop yourself out."

The boys, it seemed to Alice, were much affected. They had known the pleasantest side of their mother ; but Alice had a shuddering dread that forbade her to hope just yet. What had happened in that dread instant when two worlds met and the soul stood before God ?

The family all gathered at the funeral. Dell and Bertram came for the few hours. Millicent and Nora—indeed, all the Beaumanoir family were present.

" Can I come for my Christmas visit, Auntie Dell ?" said Nora wistfully. " I have been thinking so much about it, and the babies."

" Why, yes. Milly, let us take her home with us. You can come up later on. I suppose they will want you at Sherburne House on Christmas Day ; but you can spare Nora ; and Alice is coming up for a farewell visit, so there will be the children to entertain her. But you wouldn't be homesick, Nora ?"

" Not with you, Auntie Dell," and the child smiled radiantly.

Milly seemed overborne. She knew she had been rather dull of late, and Nora felt the change from the throng of aunts and cousins. She had not taken Nora to the city in a long while.

Alice was to rejoin them almost at once. The boys were to remain until Ethel had formulated some plans.

" Though I have half a mind to go abroad," Mrs. Longworth said. " It is so stupid to be out of society ; and on the Continent there are galleries and studios and museums, where you are sure of meeting some one you know."

# CHAPTER VIII

THE Osbornes had gone down to Sherburne House for Christmas, and at the last moment Ethel had joined them. And just at the end of the old year they had come up to New York for a brief farewell. Nora welcomed them warmly. She had a passionate longing for children. Dell remembered her own love for association with those of her own years, though Nora and Aunt Neale fraternized delightfully, and she was quite fascinated with Uncle Bertram.

Ethel had decided to go abroad.

"I do not understand her at all," declared Alice. "Being twins, there should be some occult sympathy between us; but we always were dissimilar. I am not sure but Milly had a great influence on me, and then yourself, my dear Dell. Have I any mind of my own?" and she glanced up with some of the old archness.

"You have shown your strength in many ways that have made for peace and happiness."

"I did not suppose I could ever feel sorry for a self-sufficient, worldly man like Mr. Longworth; but I do. He has come to the time when domesticity would be so much to him. I really hated to bring away little Bevis, he had grown so fond of him. How proud he would be of a son of his own! And what a curious married life it is! Ethel doesn't consult him about scarcely anything. She has no especial interest in anything he is doing. She is always well bred and ladylike ; she never gives any derogatory little flings about him, as some married women do. Is she going to repeat poor mamma's life ?"

" It looks very like it."

" She wants Harry to go with her. He has five months. But he has been abroad so much that he declares he wants a good long time at Sherburne and in New York. He was charmed with Tessy and the children."

" And Gifford ?"

" Gifford wants a visit with you. They may come out together. I hope they will. Gifford is developing a fine kind of strength. Bevis is really proud of him. I am glad Ethel will not have the opportunity to persuade him to marry some society girl. And," smiling a little, " he begins to think of a home of his very own. He has such an excellent opportunity that it would be a positive sin to throw it up ; and somehow I do not think him quite the man for a struggle with a great city. A few years of home life would settle any wayward tendencies. If there are people wrecked by marriage there are also people saved by it."

" So sacred a bond ought always to be the salvation of humanity. One sentence in the marriage service often recurs to my mind—' not to be entered into unadvisedly or lightly, but reverently, discreetly, advisedly, and soberly and in the fear of God.' Thank Heaven there are a few such marriages. But when you see the poor, ignorant creatures rushing into it with the merest momentary impulse you do wish there was some law to restrain them."

"No one is really educated for marriage," and Alice sighed. "Perhaps in the new order of things——"

"Training in useful methods and independence will help," exclaimed Dell decisively.

"If the young men do not come to consider merely selfish comfort with no responsibility. It is one of the great problems of the world now. And marriage *is* best, even when there has to be some effort at making it the best."

They were not to have an unalloyed visit. Yet the beginnings of things are often a great way back, like the seed in the dark earth.

A messenger came early one morning from Miss Westwood for Dr. Carew. He was gone an hour or more. When he returned his face was full of sympathetic gravity.

"Aunt Julia's poor friend is in a sad condition," he said. "Dell, if you could go around to the young girl. Just two days ago the suit was decided. They are to have their legacy. It is only a very moderate independence to them, but a great relief. And they were so happy. Mrs. Westwood has been poorly for some time with weak lungs. In her youth, it seems, she had some hemorrhages. They were planning to go to California. And in the night a sudden rupture occurred. It is checked now ; but if it should return the end is certain. How mysterious it seems!"

Dell had become quite warm friends with them, and the better she knew Evelyn the more she wished Archie's fancy had run in that direction. She did not know that Ethel's efforts to detach him had broken a promising friendship. A music-teacher, a young woman paid for entertaining people at receptions or musicales, was to be strictly tabooed. Archie had a passionate love for music.

It was sad enough Lyndell found when she went on her errand of mercy. Bertram had sent a nurse from the hospital. Mrs. Westwood opened her eyes with a grateful, pleading kind of light, but neither stirred nor spoke.

"Mamma has been growing weaker; I could see that," exclaimed Evelyn. "But we were so happy. I wanted to come and tell you yesterday, but the lawyer was here twice, and there were papers to sign, and so much talking. And last evening we planned that I should come this morning and have your cousin tell me about that lovely place Dr. Carew is interested in, and whether two lonely women could find shelter there, and renewed health. And now—oh, what will the money be without mamma?"

Lyndell comforted her. She had learned many things in these years. And though she could not, dared not, hold out hope, she left the young girl much more tranquil.

"She begins to look like a ghost herself," said Dell to Alice. "The anxiety about the suit and the effort to get established with scholars has been a great drain on her. She is a really charming girl, not exactly beautiful, but with the sort of Madonna sweetness of Millicent. And her voice is unusually fine."

"What a pity they could not have gone out a little earlier! When these things miss by such a little, it seems the saddest tragedy, the greatest mystery."

When Bertram came in to dinner he had scarcely any hope. Mrs. Westwood was much weaker.

"And to think of the poor girl without a relative near her! She is an only child. Let us all believe in large families," and he gave a gravely sweet smile.

The city was brilliant with every kind of entertainment. Mr. Osborne brought home tickets for a grand concert, with some famous singers and a renowned violinist. Nora was delighted to be included. Dell watched her with a secret sympathy. So far she had heard only very ordinary performers. Her soft eyes kindled with delight, and her cheeks were in a glow.

"She suggests her father a good deal more than Millicent," Alice said afterward.

There was some shopping to be done, the treasures of the art museum to inspect, and so many things called up reminders of other times. They went to the Murrays', and shy little Densie was very much attracted by Nora, and promised to come and make her a visit at Auntie Dell's. Papa Carew made so much of her that Dell declared that she had been superseded.

"I must get into practice for little Milly," he replied laughingly.

And then the dreaded event occurred. Mrs. Westwood had gone almost forty-eight hours, and there had grown up something like a hope, weak as the patient was, when a fit of coughing had undone everything.

Miss Carew went to the poor, motherless girl. Bertram found his aunt of great assistance, for he felt now that Lyndell had sacred duties to her children that could not be overlooked. He attended to the business part for Miss Westwood, and saved her the most trying scenes. Mr. Westwood had died in a pretty country town in Connecticut, where the young couple had spent their few happy years, and Evelyn desired to have them buried together.

"But Evelyn never can go alone," declared Lyndell.

"It is not best for her to go at all. I will find some trusty person to send; she is worn out with fatigue and

grief. All she can endure will be the simple funeral.
And she must not remain there alone."

Bertram looked at his wife and then at his aunt.
This was one of his father's ways, and Dell gave a soft,
approving smile over it. She remembered how she had
been taken in that lovely, sheltering home and had her
wounds bound up.

" Yes, she must come here for a few days. And I
dare say Aunt Julia will ask her to Old Point."

Evelyn Westwood made many protests. She gave up
the burial journey with very few arguments, though
she shuddered at the thought of staying in the place
where her mother had been carried out for the last time.
She yielded to Dr. Carew's persuasion and accepted his
hospitality, but it was to remain in bed for the next
twenty-four hours, she was so thoroughly worn out.
And when she did come downstairs she looked like a pale
ghost of her former self.

It was as Dell had surmised. Aunt Julia wrote a sympathetic and comforting letter to Evelyn, inviting her
cordially to spend some weeks with her until her health
was re-established.

" You are all so good to me that I can never thank you
sufficiently," Evelyn exclaimed, deeply moved. " I shall
be very glad to accept Mrs. Stanwood's invitation. I
feel so utterly astray, so without ballast, as if there was
nothing more for me to do in this world, no further effort
to make."

" The world will look different when you are rested and
refreshed," rejoined Bertram with his encouraging smile.

Evelyn raised her tearful eyes. It seemed as if there
never could be any brightness again. She almost hated
the money that had caused them the struggle and anx-

iety, though there had been other heirs as well as her
mother connected with the fight.

Ten thousand dollars was not much of a fortune, to be
sure, but she could not help feeling the relief.  For years
there had only been a trifle between her and actual want
in case her health should fail.  Occasionally, during an
unprofitable summer, she would have to break into her
sacred fund, but it was always replaced when business
brightened up.  And oh, what a delight it would have
been to her mother to know the most pressing anxieties
were at an end !

Dell and Alice became warmly interested in her.
They talked over the little romance that had never even
had a shadow of existence, but was a vague "might
have been" in Aunt Julia's mind.  Evelyn certainly
would have made a sweet and devoted wife, as she had
been a tender and thoughtful daughter.

"I wonder if it *is* too late ?" questioned Alice.
"Archie is to make quite a visit home in the spring.
Aunt Julia is so fond of girls, she will want to keep her.
And then——"

"But Archie has not really accepted the divorce.  He
had no notification, and there was only the flimsy dissatisfaction, incompatibility of temper, to give it a high-
sounding name.  Of course she did not even try."

"And I dare say her sister's marriage roused all her
envy and longing—a worn-out, dissipated *roué* with
plenty of money.  I do not wonder that divorces are
common when marriages take place with no real affection."

"I think she would not have married Archie if there
had been anything else to do.  The March girls were
brought up to marry.  There was no other future placed

before them. I only wonder they did not marry younger and really better. They were quite attractive girls. But young men have begun to count the cost of such wives. I wonder if we shall ever go back to the simplicity of living," and Lyndell gave a little sigh.

"Still there are love matches."

"And some desperately imprudent ones. If a girl could be content to accept her husband's station! It is hard to be content and ambitious at the same time. And it takes wisdom as well as love to make a happy marriage. I suppose it *is* right that we should not be all-wise in youth," and she flushed half smilingly, remembering her attempts at profundity in the past. "That is the use of experience."

"And so much experience goes for absolutely nothing. I never can understand how men and women go through events that ought to leave a mark and are absolutely untouched, just as ready to commit the same blunders."

Bertram advised Miss Westwood about her investments. She gave up her rooms and packed her choicest belongings. Her piano was in Washington ; it had not been advisable to bring it North.

"And I do suppose I shall settle myself in that vicinity again. I am not rich enough to live without work," and she gave a sad little smile. "I should not know what to do with my days."

"You would soon get established here," said Dell in a tone of encouragement. "But you will enjoy Mrs. Stanwood so much."

Gifford and Mr. Drayton came up to the city to say good-by to Ethel, who was to sail, and to Alice, who was to return home. Gifford had not quite finished visiting, and he wanted a little stay at the Stanwoods', and another good-by to Sherburne House.

"I am afraid you will get charmed away," Alice exclaimed with some solicitude.

"Oh, no, you need not fear," and he gave a cordial smile. "It really seems more like home out there ; and now that mother is gone, one of the most important ties is broken. Poor mother and father ! How many mistaken views there are to life ! I think I shall be more in earnest among the real things. How much patience you have all had with me ! I begin to appreciate it as never before."

They went down to see Ethel off. She was shrouded in the deepest of mourning, and took it rather hard that Gifford had not accepted her offer.

"I *do* almost wonder," and Alice studied him inquiringly.

He came and kissed her. "You and Dell are the dearest of womankind to me. I realize that Ethel's pursuits and aims would not be judicious for me, nor agreeable. I have fretted sometimes about the limitations at home, but they look like safeguards to me now. And the life suits me infinitely better. I have come to the true meaning of manhood. I have been longing for some of the high places, but I know now I could not have filled them, and they would have been sources of temptation."

Alice Osborne smiled up through tears, and her heart overflowed with gratitude.

"Some time I should like to go abroad ; but I could not see the world through Ethel's eyes, nor go flying from city to city. Yet it was very good of her to ask me."

Then the Osbornes said good-by. Dell and Bertram counted on coming out when the babies were older, for Bertram was anxious to see the result of their schemes, and not allow them to develop into Utopian inefficacy. Harry and Gifford were to leave next, and Bertram had persuaded Miss Westwood to remain for their escort.

"Now for a quiet little time with ourselves," Dell exclaimed. "I seem always to be in some stir or confusion. We have hardly had a day for Nora."

But Nora had not suffered. She was delighted when she could drive with either doctor. Bertram had grown very fond of her. And now Mr. Drayton was planning for her entertainment. Lyndell felt curiously amused with his interest in the child, with the graceful kind of patience that brought everything to her comprehension. He and Bertram were more than friends—brothers. The little shadow that might have been a cloud was only a drift over the royal shining of true regard.

"Sometimes I almost envy Tessy, who seems to have so much time for her children." Dell was in the nursery this bright winter morning, giving herself up to delight in her babies. Aunt Neale sat by the window knitting some pretty sacques, with here a cast-off stitch and there a double one; that left an odd, fluted effect—one of the accomplishments of her long ago girlhood. The children were tumbling about on a soft rug, kicking and crowing, and Dell had been playing with them. Downstairs, Mr. Drayton was talking French with Nora and going over a translation. When that was through they were to have a skating frolic in the park.

"There are not so many social demands upon Tessy. And you remember Leonard is often away two or three days at a time. Miss Eliza is a delightful child enter-

tainer, and Aunt Aurelia is so fond of them. And with
all the little darkey children about there is so much
amusement.''

''And if I didn't have you! O babies, what should
we do !'' and she pressed a warm little body to hers and
nestled the face close against her glowing cheek, cover-
ing it with rapturous kisses.

Grandpapa had decided the boy's name, about which
there had been a kind of curious halt. Dell had named
her girl when she saw its soft, dark eyes. They left the
other choice with Aunt Neale, who hesitated to signify.
And they begun by saying '' the boy.'' Then grandpapa
had given him his own and the father's name.

'' So you will have them both if there never should be
another boy. Neale wanted them, but she thought of
your own father——,'' said grandpapa.

'' The new Edward Sherburne is to grow up in Sherburne House,'' returned Dell in a tone of pride. '' I
should have proposed it long ago if I had known which
name to put first.''

'' Randolph was my mother's family name. It is odd,
but for generations the Carews have had only one son.''

They would call him Bertie as a little boy. When he
was growing up the world would forget his father had
any name besides Doctor, so there would be little confusion.

Would they ever be large children—a girl like Nora
downstairs, a boy studying and playing and planning?
Dell could never show them the old apple-tree where she
had played. The homes of her childhood had been so
far apart, so strange. But they could see the old house
where papa was a little boy. There would be cousins at
Sherburne House and merry Christmases and birthdays,

and old lives lived over again, with just a touch of the modern changes. Did God know how glad she was to have them? In hours like this her heart seemed to run over with joy.

"I'm going now, Auntie Dell," and Nora stood in the doorway in her close, fur-trimmed coat and seal cap, with the bright, eager smile she remembered in the face of Emil von Lindorm. Oh, why did people die who were loved and wanted?

Bertie reached out both hands for the flying tresses, and uttered his longing baby exclamation. "And I have been writing a French letter to mamma. It was so funny—just as a real French girl would write. We laughed so over it. And we invited her in such a pretty, formal fashion. I am just longing for her to come; but I'm not a bit homesick. Adieu," and she kissed her finger tips.

"The child is having a delightful time," said Aunt Neale.

"Milly will be our next guest. I must write. She declared she would not come while we were so full of everything. But Milly is not quite like a visitor. Still, I shall enjoy having her all to myself."

Then the babies were to go out in the sunshine for their ride. She was a very proud and happy mother as she saw them started. Sometimes she was almost afraid of her happiness. Her husband's young mother had died. Milly had lost her love before they had more than quaffed the bubbles at the edge of the cup. But then Mamma Murray had her husband and all her children. Why, her life had been like a fairy story with not a single sorrow in it. And there was Aunt and Uncle Beaumanoir going down the shady side of life with children and grandchildren about them. She uttered a little prayer and thanksgiving in a breath.

"Come to my room," she said to Aunt Neale. "I have letters and letters to write."

Aunt Neale often came and sat with her in this fashion. It was pleasant to look down on the street, though you could only see the opposite side. There were nursemaids and babies—seldom two, she noted with a thrill of satisfaction. How cheerful and bright it all was!

Lyndell had not lost her interest in the great charities of the world. Her heart went out to the babies and the little children and the poor, toiling mothers, and in such moments her own happiness smote her. But she had given over the "vain disquisitions." One did not need to comprehend the infinite to love and to work. There would always be mysteries beyond unravelling. We were to know only in part, and she could be glad over her part.

Though she wrote to Millicent, she scarcely mentioned Mr. Drayton's name. It was hard work to curb her impetuous anticipation. He would win the child, and through her the mother.

How the happy, busy days sped along! Aunt Julia wrote the most thankful of letters that they had bestowed such care and attention upon her friend and shown such interest in the daughter. Evelyn had already improved greatly. The major and the two young men had gone to Charleston. Gifford had changed immeasurably, she thought; and there was no question now but that he would make a fine man. How little real satisfaction Edith had taken in her children! She was glad Floyd dropped in now and then, more than thankful that he had a prospect of a happy life before him.

" O dear !" cried Nora a few days later, " mamma
can't come as we wanted her to. And Mr. Drayton said
he would take us to see ' Lohengrin ;' he was going to
be sure of the tickets. And I have been reading about
Wagner and the operas, and it will be too bad ! Little
Dell has the measles, and Aunt Aurelia isn't very well.
Does mamma have to go and take care of every one ?"

Dell laughed at the child's disappointment and perplexity.

" You will have to take Aunt Neale," she said. " She
has never heard ' Lohengrin.' "

It was quite too bad. The Sherburne baby was really
very ill, and for a few days they had been alarmed about
Aunt Aurelia. If she had not mended they should have
sent for Dr. Carew. And now there was some important writing. Of course Nora ought to come home ; and
if there was any opportunity to send her through to
Uncle Leonard she would reach home safely.

" Nonsense !" declared Bertram. " She shall stay
until spring. And if her mother doesn't come then we
will adopt her."

Aunt Neale declared she was quite too old to go to an
opera, though she had committed that frivolity in Europe. Bertram would be out of the city, and Lyndell
thought she could not matronize her small niece under
the circumstances, so there was no help for it. For
though Reese Drayton felt proud of the sincere friendship that existed between himself and Dr. Carew's wife,
he did not mean that any idle tongue should make a
comment. But Miss Neale did enjoy it intensely.

Drayton watched the child's enthusiasm and sympathy, and was moved by her sorrow. But the story was
old to him, and he sat and dreamed of the other woman

who should have been there.   Were the reasons she had
given in her letter quite insuperable?   Was she to condemn herself to a lifelong seclusion from happiness because the dream of her youth had been so tragically
blighted?   If he could see her!   He had said he would
be patient, and now he found he was like any other
lover, that with a degree of certainty he could go on for
months uttering no importunity.   He was not so sure
now as he had been when he read her letter, and there
was no step he could take.   True, he had the *entrée* of
Sherburne House, but all his manliness protested against
an uninvited appearance at Beaumanoir.   And if she
would not come he was quite helpless.

A fortnight later Uncle Leonard had business in New
York, and was instructed to bring Nora home.

# CHAPTER IX

IT was good to have something rouse her from the lethargy into which she had fallen, Millicent von indorm thought. She never remembered a mood like this. She had been tired, dispirited, almost crushed by sorrow, but some inward strength had upheld her. If there was any certain despair or discouragement she could rout out the enemy. There was nothing tangible to attack. Perhaps she missed Nora. No, she was glad to have the child away, bright and happy. She ought to be going to school somewhere and making young friends. She had felt heretofore that she could not part with her. They had read and studied together. When they were in Baltimore Nora took lessons in French. Millicent had always kept up her German, and Nora had a child's enthusiasm about it. They would go to Germany together some time. She could not write. All the beauty and brightness had gone out of her brain, it seemed, leaving a leaden atmosphere behind.

Julius came over from Sherburne House. "Miss 'Relia's mighty poorly," he said; "an' Miss Dell's done caught measles, 'n little Mas'r Bertie have 'em shore. An' Mistis want you to come over soon as you ebber can."

"I'll go at once. Stop for me when you come back from town. You have had the doctor, of course?"

"Yes'm. He say yisterday it was de measles; but Miss 'Relia was took long toward mornin'."

Millicent went to announce the tidings to her mother. Fanny had gone down to the Armitage house to help with a little feast for the school children, and would not return before evening.

"If it is anything really serious I will send you word," Millicent said to her mother.

Baby Dell was restlessly sick and troublesome; and as Bertie had been with her all the time, he was likely to be taken. The two older children had gone through the uncomfortable experience.

"Aunt Aurelia had one of her old attacks," explained Tessy. "And as Leonard will not be home before Saturday, unless we send for him, I thought I would like to have some one——"

"Yes, I am glad to come," with a sweet smile.

"I wasn't anxious about the babies—I can care for them—but at first Aunt Aurelia was very bad. At daylight we sent for Dr. Underwood, and he was in again an hour ago. She is comfortable, but he is afraid of another attack."

"At her time of life it is a serious matter," returned Millicent. "Yes, I am glad you sent."

She laid aside her wraps and went upstairs presently. Aunt Aurelia lay in a dozing state, with Cassy keeping watch. Miss Carrick had gone to lie down; she had been up since four.

There was nothing Millicent could do. Aunt Aurelia was to be kept quiet and sleep all she could. Cassy was a faithful watcher. She went through to the room she always had at Sherburne House, that she had once helped furnish and arrange for her Cousin Dell when she was coming home from school. Here was the pretty desk, with all its appointments. She sat down and wrote a note to Nora, wondering a little if it was best to pass over Aunt Aurelia's attack so lightly. Of course now she could not go up to New York. Was it a relief?

She crossed over to Tessy's room with a curious lightness of heart. Perhaps there had been some sort of presentiment weighing upon her, and now the matter had culminated. It was not really alarming. Aunt Aurelia did have a bad spell now and then. They thought it quite wonderful she had stood all the excitements so well.

Tessy was in the nursery soothing the fretful child, who wanted to be rubbed, who wanted a drink and to be turned over in a cool place, she was so hot. And then mamma must sing.

The other children were out playing. They had a sort of nursery governess, a friendless young girl her own mother had sent her.

Then Aunt Milly must come and hold the hot little hand and brush her hair and bathe her face. After awhile Aunt Milly soothed her to sleep. She was scarlet and roughened with the disease, but this was likely to be the worst day.

It was almost dusk when Dr. Underwood came in again. Miss Aurelia was decidedly better. All real danger was over he thought. She would be very weak for several days. And Dell was quite bright and not so restless.

"Leonard has a very important case on hand, so I have not said anything particular about the children," Tessy remarked afterward. "It is so bad to be interrupted when you are making special efforts," and she smiled. "He will be home on Saturday."

"It is not worth while to alarm him since Aunt Aurelia is no worse."

And Millicent wondered how many wives would so consider their husbands' highest interest. It had been much better for Leonard to keep his Washington connection, and now he was making rapid strides financially as well as in his reputation. There were engrossing times, when he was away for a whole week, as his evenings were of importance. Tessy was too ambitious to have him sink into an indolent country gentleman and neglect his gifts and training.

Miss Carrick enjoyed Millicent extremely. She was so glad to be of use. Yes, it was simply that she had missed Nora and given way to a fit of loneliness. Now that she had some real work in hand she was buoyant again.

Aunt Aurelia improved, and on Saturday sat up a full hour. Baby Dell was better, but Bertie had taken his turn, though he bid fair to have the disease very lightly.

"And you have been all alone!" said Leonard with reproachful tenderness.

"With Milly, and Cousin Eliza, and May, and all the servants, and Dr. Underwood coming twice a day, and your mother to call on in an emergency. But do believe, if anything had looked like going wrong I should have telegraphed at once."

"I have perfect faith in you, my darling wife;" and he drew the sweet face to his shoulder, kissing it with rapture. "You have such good sense. I am glad nothing did go wrong, for I was in the midst of a tremendous effort. We shall not know until next week, but I am confident I have won the case. At all events, I had high praise for my argument."

"I am so glad!" and he could see the pride in the shining eyes.

He would not let Milly go home for Sunday. He would drive them both to church in the morning, and the rest of the family should come over to supper.

"And, Milly, in about ten days I must go up to New York. Suppose you take time now to have a visit with Dell?"

"I will see," she returned.

But the first of the week she went home to her neglected work with a curious kind of energy. Fanny offered to stay at Sherburne—indeed, seemed rather desirous of doing so. She was a great favorite with the children, and brought a whiff of March air with her that blew about a dozen different ways with the utmost inconsequence.

Dr. Underwood espied her on the porch one morning, and, as all the patients were improving, crossed over to her. She glanced up with a bright half laugh as he sat down beside her and took her hand.

"I am not a patient," she said saucily.

"Are you quite sure? I have been moved to inquire into your case, and—prescribe."

There was a curious little glint in his eyes, which were a kind of steely blue, almost black.

"Oh, you can prescribe; but I won't promise to follow directions unless they suit me. You won't find me a tractable patient, Dr. Underwood."

He nodded. "I should not expect that."

"Then why bother with me?"

"A physician sometimes chooses difficult and unpromising cases."

"Oh, am I as bad as that?" She laughed gayly,

then colored under his scrutiny. He looked so long and steadily that a sense of embarrassment crept along her pulses and made her nerves quiver.

"What do you mean about Mr. Armitage?" he asked abruptly.

"About—Mr. Armitage?" Her face was in a sudden scarlet glow.

"He is a good friend of mine. I have come to respect him very thoroughly for his simple honesty and truth and earnestness. I cannot stand by and see him led astray by a woman's wiles."

Fanny turned her eyes straight upon Dr. Underwood. She was so astonished that her face was almost a blank.

"Do you mean to marry him?"

Every feature assumed a steel-like haughtiness; but she did not change the direction of her eyes.

"You have no right to ask such a question. Only one man can expect it to be answered."

"You would certainly know by this time if you did not. You have been very amiable and encouraging to him. You have interested yourself in his plans and pursuits. To an honest man, who studies a woman's preference and feels confident she approves of him, it can mean but one thing. I don't know why a woman should not show an honest preference. It is a good thing for a man to go upon. But when she hangs out false lights for her own amusement, how is he to distinguish and keep himself from being dashed on the jagged rocks of experience?"

"Suppose I *did* mean to marry him?" exclaimed Fanny daringly.

"Then I beg your pardon for my rudeness in sincere fashion." Had his eyes some protest to make?

" You would not consider it wise ?" tentatively.

" It would be your lives, not mine. The young man will make a tender, devoted husband. It is supposed a woman out of imaginative girlhood considers whether she can accept the life and help him make it noble and fine and generous, and, in this instance, self-sacrificing. He has chosen this path in which to do his work. He might not make a great success in any other. In the present case Mr. Armitage has offered his life to the cause of Christianity. Anything that hinders will mar it and keep it from perfecting fruit—for, you see, it has blossomed already. Has a woman any right to take a life she does not like and turn it all awry to suit her own fancies ? There must be some wisdom besides that preference we call love."

She knew from the tone that he did not consider it wise ; that he doubted any such intentions on her part. As if it could matter to Dr. Underwood ! His *friend*, he had said.

He turned as if to go.

" I had *not* considered the matter," she said with a touch of sarcasm. " I supposed it time enough when one was really asked ; and I have not been asked."

" If you desire to be asked you are taking the proper course. I hope whatever is best will come to pass ; but I do not want his way planted with thorns."

Fanny sat still when he was gone, quite amazed. She thought she had flirted a very little with Dr. Underwood ; they had bright skirmishes now and then, and he piqued her about certain things. She never found him twice alike, and the freshness amused her. The young men of her early youth were nearly all married now, and there were few companionable men. Beaumanoir and

Sherburne House were dull. True, Leonard occasionally brought a friend down to stay over Sunday, and she and Milly were invited to help entertain. She was away a good deal, roaming over fresh pastures. And when she was at home she liked to be entertained with the two men.

Mr. Armitage had come oftenest in her way the last six months. He *did* admire her. She was rather proud that he should admire her more than beautiful Millicent. After all, she had made more conquests than Milly. She could not quite imagine her sister being a clergyman's wife, and just now she wondered why.

What had she meant? Well—nothing. The preference and admiration gratified her, that was all. The desire to be amused was uppermost.

And all through this time she had been thinking of Reese Drayton. But no thought had proved strong enough to lead her to give up the other pleasure. And she knew now, just as she had known long before, that he did not love her with the best a man could give. She had come home cross and disappointed at not having gained any power over him. His friendliness vexed her. She was quite certain she held the key.

So she had been amusing herself. What a pity the wrong people fell in love with one! Dr. Underwood was preferable, and one might be a physician's wife without the strenuous efforts of Dell Carew. But she could not recall one sentimental mood or moment with Dr. Underwood. And he had dared to question, to really advise her. A passion of anger she had not felt then flared up in her face.

That afternoon, in his riding around, Mr. Armitage called at Beaumanoir. He *was* disappointed at not seeing Fanny—that was evident.

"I do not know what we should have done without her at the children's feast," he said. "She is so bright and amusing. I think she could work in a much larger field if she allowed herself. She has not enough faith in her own abilities."

"She has been the spoiled one of the family," returned her mother with a touch of embarrassment. "It often happens with the youngest girl."

"Some natures can take a great deal of spoiling," continued the young man. "I suppose they are glad to have her at Sherburne House. She must quite add to the brightness."

Then they talked about Miss Sherburne's recovery, and he decided, as he was on the way, he would go over and call.

Millicent and her mother sat some time in silence with the same unquiet thought in both hearts.

"Milly," Mrs. Beaumanoir began at length, "I am anxious about Fanny. Do you suppose she is really in earnest?"

"He is, evidently. I had not suspected anything of the kind. Do you think it—suitable?" with a touch of hesitation.

"It seems to me Fanny is not fitted for such a life. And if she does not mean anything she ought not lead him on. He owes some duty to his mother; and to take a wife in with the two women who have a better right——"

They glanced at each other with troubled eyes. Neither could imagine Fanny sharing her kingdom. She was not one to give generously of her very own.

"I must talk to her about it. Only sometimes opposition brings about the very course you wish to avert."

"I am quite sure Fanny will not marry him," said Millicent decisively.

"Then she is doing very wrong."

Meanwhile, Mr. Armitage went over to Sherburne. He found the whole family out on the porch. Fanny had been reading aloud. Did he realize all he put in his wistful glance? And her quick flush seemed to answer his thought.

She always did so many small things to attract. A change of position, some curiosity she had just discovered, a dainty acceptance of attention as if it were quite her due—one saw her as the central figure. But to day she let the talk go on without her help; and it vexed her, because she thought of so many bright things to say. She could not shut out the consciousness that here was a regard waiting to be proffered, and she knew she did not want it. One might go on indifferently in society, but in this narrow sphere it would lead to trouble. Was she afraid of Dr. Underwood?

"How quiet you were!" exclaimed Tessy afterward.

"On my best behavior," and Fanny gave a short laugh. "Aunt Aurelia, you ought to compliment me; the call was to you and Cousin Eliza. Didn't I behave beautifully?"

"You let us have most of the talk. Yes, it was very respectful. But so many of the good old fashions have gone out. I do like Mr. Armitage very much, and yet it seemed to-day as if he had something on his mind. Didn't he say, Eliza, that no one was ill?"

"Yes. And, Fanny, you must have been imbued with quite a missionary spirit the day of the feast. I'm very glad, since Millicent could not go. It is time you began to take an interest in such matters."

When Fanny returned home there was a letter from Ned's wife, who was always wishing for her. " So I think I will go to Baltimore for a week," she said. "I am not especially needed any more than the fifth wheel."

While she was sauntering up and down the platform Dr. Underwood drove slowly by and nodded. She returned the haughtiest inclination.

" She doesn't go a day too soon. I hope she will stay a full month. Meanwhile, I will try and get this absurd fancy out of Armitage's mind. I never supposed she was in earnest. A girl like that wants a master. Give her her head and you will have your hands full."

Dr. Underwood had his wish. Society proved quite tempting, and Fanny sent for a trunk full of things and stayed a full month. Uncle Leonard brought home Nora, who was really loth to come, and was dreadfully disappointed that her mamma couldn't have a visit with her. It seemed to Millicent as if Mr. Drayton almost lived at the Carews again.

Tessy and the two younger babies and the two old ladies went down to Fortress Monroe for a change. Little Edward and Princess spent the fortnight at Beaumanoir, to Nora's great delight. Millicent had her days to herself and wrote steadily. And sometimes it seemed a long way to the end of the journey. Sherburne people were long-lived.

It was a delight to get Tessy back again, with her vials of freshness and eager interest, her bits of news about Aunt Julia and the little girl, and the two big nephews, who had been such a gratification to Uncle Stanwood. They were going up to New York presently, and Harry thought of taking a flying trip to the Pacific coast, as Gifford felt that he must return.

"And I am confident that Gifford has fallen in love with that Miss Westwood. She is such a fine musician that one could listen to her forever, and she has a decided influence over him. She brings out the best in him, and he is so improved I could hardly tell which I did like best, though Harry is charming."

"Aunt Julia would like to keep Miss Westwood, I know," returned Millicent.

"But she is growing a little restless, now that she seems thoroughly recruited. And a genius like hers ought not to be lost to the world. She is quite in favor of New York, I find, though she would hardly have time to get established before summer. And she is really in love with the Carews."

"Does Aunt Julia object to Gifford's fancy?"

Millicent recalled the disappointment that had been hers.

"She thinks it would be a splendid thing for Gifford. No, she doesn't really object," with a smile, "but it isn't a whole-hearted approval. Still, I suppose the young people will settle it in their own way. We generally do," and an arch light illumined Tessy's sweet face. "But, Milly, have you not been working too hard? You are thinner, and your eyes have a strained sort of expression."

"Some work came for me to do. No, I am not working really hard, and devote a good deal of time to Nora, who is rather homesick after all her city dissipations."

"You ought to go up yourself, Milly, or somewhere else for a change. You and Fanny ought to take turns, instead of her having three holidays to your one."

"But I have Nora to think about and educate. And

there is her future. Fanny is entirely care free. And there was my delightful Western trip."

Tessy would not suggest, even by implication. Had Milly a purpose in her renunciation?

" I must try to make up a little of Dell to you," she said with winsome sympathy. " We have been so gay that the fast comes rather distastefully after the feast ; but it may all be good for us."

Millicent walked home. She wanted to discipline her restless thoughts a little. They kept reaching out, making importunate demands. She must be satisfied with the life before her. Yet there were joys it would be hard to miss. As the years went on, could she keep a sympathetic hold on the things she loved, without personal influence?

# CHAPTER X.

REESE DRAYTON hunted up some of his old friends while he was waiting for the future to shape itself according to his wishes. After all, the world had not changed much. Mysteries were as far off from being unravelled as when he was in the city before, and speculative souls were just as eager for their solution. The younger people took them up as new questions—was there anything new? Yet the old was not half understood.

Curtis, his old college associate, as far as a Freshman and Senior could be, and a friend thereafter, had married a stylish society woman with a son of twelve and a pretty golden-haired seraph of eight or so, who was the step-father's enthusiastic delight. Their home was admirable, combining gayety and intellect. The questions of the day were not tabooed, social or political. There was sufficient art and æstheticism to attract those who soared in the higher realms of fancy.

He liked best the pretty, engaging home side—a quiet dinner with no other guests, or an evening devoted to Mrs. Curtis's playing and conversation. At the first the children were allowed to be present, and little Hazel had an hour's indulgence in the evening if no one dropped in. The pictures were so beguiling that he often made them his own. The child of his fancy was older, not so angelic-looking, quite a human child, with a quick but generous temper, intelligent and companionable ; the mother more beautiful.

He had enjoyed Nora von Lindorm very much. He found while at the Osbornes' that he really had a paternal side to his nature. He preferred the girl ; why, he could hardly tell—perhaps because Millicent's child was a girl.

The Carews were not much in society this winter. Dell felt that her babies were her first charge, and that she must keep her health and spirits for them. She understood as never before the solemn compact of marriage, with its marvellous and beautiful power, its compelling love, its sacred companionship. There were no more restless questions as to duty, when God had bestowed this high office upon her. But looking into her own children's faces, her heart warmed infinitely to those needing home and love. Her charities were increased, if her time was more circumscribed.

Bertram was not long in finding his place—partly the old one he had filled so well, but largely a new one, for which he was admirably fitted by his travel and new courses of study. And though if the days had been twice as long he could have found employment for every hour he kept some time sacred to family duties and enjoyments. He had thrown himself into the struggle with tremendous ardor at first, because he had been too proud to owe anything to his wife in pecuniary matters. Fortune had prospered him, but there had come the higher understanding of mine and thine, the divine point where manhood and womanhood met in sacred agreement. A little leisure and a little pleasure would be more to Lyndell now than straining every nerve to lay up for the future.

The elder doctor was soon imbued with the spirit of progression. No, he would not despise the simplicity of the past years—there had been a wisdom in it all—but he thanked God heartily and reverently for the breadth and interest of this new life. Reese Drayton often dropped in upon him, and from the younger man he learned still more of his son's work as it had been carried on in the Western home. Now and then they sent out some recruits—a family whose children could grow up in a clean, wholesome atmosphere, or some young country lad who had missed finding his place and his work in the great city.

Then Harry and Gifford came up. Society was at its gayest point, and the two young men were flooded with invitations.

"You will consider me a butterfly of fashion," laughed the brilliant young fellow. "But when you think how rarely holidays can be spent among kinsfolk and acquaintances you will hardly blame me—five months after five solid years of duty, and then years of expatriation again. I begin to envy you fellows who can stay at home and have flocks and herds and wives and children."

"But you officers do marry," subjoined Dell.

"Still the separations must be hard to bear. Your wife might travel round the world and meet you at different ports, but that isn't having a home. No, I am going to stay single awhile longer, and when I have done my country good service in this manner I'll try for a fat berth at some naval station."

"Let it be Brooklyn," said Bertram. "Let us get as many of the clan as we can in this great city."

"I should like nothing better."

Gifford managed to find one evening alone with Dell

for a confidence. She had heard nothing on the subject from Tessy, and the confession was a great surprise.

"I used to gauge any fancies—no, they were not really fancies, but possibilities, by you. I used to compare girls I met with you——" he began, flushing as Dell looked at him smilingly.

"That was a cousinly regard," she answered in a quick tone. It might have been something more.

"I don't mean that I ever thought—well, we have all made a sort of ideal of you; even Harry admits that he admired you very much back there at Naples. But we all supposed you would belong to Leonard."

Gifford could recall many suggestions of his mother's that Lyndell in a manner belonged in the family and was a fair mark for any of them.

"You have been my good angel more than once. Dell, a whole life of gratitude can never repay all you have done."

"But a noble, manly, honorable life can," Dell Carew exclaimed proudly.

"And it shall be that. It would have been in any case. Wisdom comes late to some—it did to me. And now I have another incentive to keep in the path of strictest rectitude. I know now that I can make myself a true man. And do you think, Dell, that I have the right to ask a sweet and good woman to marry me?"

Lyndell Carew was startled. It was a solemn question.

"You are not engaged, then?"

"I have not asked her. It has been only such a little while since I knew her. But she is so lonely, without a near relative in the world. We were talking it over a few evenings before I came away, as we were pacing the sands. I knew I loved her, that she was the one woman who could influence my life and train it to nobler uses. And—how can you tell? but you *do* know and feel when one sympathizes with your inmost soul. I could have fallen at her feet and declared my love, but I felt unworthy to disturb such a heavenly moment. We just clasped hands and went on. I think both understood. We are to correspond."

"Have you told her—anything of the past?"

"No. I could not then. Dell, ought I confess it all —that shameful, despicable weakness?"

He gave a passionate, indrawn breath like a sob. Lyndell was deeply moved. Was it necessary? Would not any woman who heard it be forewarned? Could she not fortify the life she accepted on stronger lines if she knew?

"I should tell her." Lyndell's voice was tremulous with the effort she made to keep to simple honor.

"I thought I ought. I hated to so desperately. I was pulled both ways. I said first I could not give up a hope like that."

"Better relinquish the hope, than having won her, to feel there was something between destroying perfect confidence. Be fair and honorable to her."

"I promise you." He took Dell's hand and pressed it to his lips. "I have given you a good deal of trouble and anxiety, Dell, and you have been heroically sweet and patient. I realized when poor mother died that life could be put to many false uses, and I took a vow then that, God helping me, I would make mine of some service to my fellow-beings. I can do it out there. And if *she* comes to help, it will be precious beyond compare. But you are right. I must meet the issue bravely."

"I think you will have the courage given you. I do believe we always have enough strength given us to do right if we would use it at our first conception of duty. But when we have dallied and weighed, and consulted inclination, we find so many plausible reasons on both sides, that we weaken."

"I am glad you do not altogether disapprove," Gifford replied with a smile of assurance. "You will see her again. She comes up to the city on business before long. Then you will be better able to judge——"

"Gifford"—Dell's breath came with a quick gasp of apprehension—"suppose she should decide the other way? With her attainments and her small fortune she can marry very well—if she is at all eager for marriage. All her earlier life has been devoted to her mother; but now she is really free."

Gifford turned from scarlet to a fierce kind of whiteness, shown also in the compressed lips and set eyes. Only a moment did the passionate temper dominate him; the color came back to his face, the stern lines relaxed.

"I suppose it is so." His voice was a little unsteady. "It is just the beginning of a blessed hope. You see, Harry made no pretence of admiring her; he was continually with Uncle Stanwood. He will not marry for years to come. And I *did* have her all to myself. Well, it would be very hard, but I shall not throw away any of the remaining years of my life; you may trust me for that, Lyndell. Life has grown too full of earnest purpose to sacrifice it again."

"O Gifford, I am glad to hear you say that!" and her eyes shone with a lustrous light.

"Oh, you may rest assured that I have learned something from experience, and begin to understand the dif-

ference between self-appreciation and self-pity, which is
a despicable weakness, in which I have revelled too much.
Even without this blessed aim I shall do my best to
make a success of life."

Dell was glad to talk the matter over with Bertram
that night. Unless matters detained him unusually late
they always had an exchange of domestic confidences.

" I wonder if it would be quite right ?" she inquired
hesitatingly. " Would Miss Westwood be likely to sacrifice herself ? I do not think I could stand by and see
a woman do that without raising a warning voice."

" The sooner women understand the folly of sacrific-
ing themselves to redeem any profligate, the better off
will be the whole world of humanity. No one seems to
consider the next generation. But in this case it is not
so much heredity as a rather weak will. Your uncle
was a man of irreproachable morals and extremely temperate. Gif was a fine boy. There was no especial
home influence, and he fell among a bad lot at college.
There are so few safeguards thrown about our young
men ! When integrity and virtue are set up as the highest aims and respected we shall have made a long stride.
I don't know what he might have done if he had set
himself resolutely about it, but he never did in those
young years. If his father had gone on prospering, it
would certainly have been Gifford's ruin."

" That is one bit of silver lining to the cloud. And I
doubt if Alice would have made such a happy marriage."

" I can forgive Gifford all that earlier escapade easier
than his second break from the best influences of his life.
I don't know how he would stand another desperate
strain."

" I do believe you need not fear for him. We discussed this point."

" He does need a strong, guiding influence of his very own. But they must begin on the basis of perfect truth. It isn't quite as if he had to reform from any evil ways, as if there had been years of bad practices. He belongs to that class who are ' overtaken in a fault.' And if we could never forgive, never assist in restoring our erring brother, we should be of small service to the world. There are so many weak people among the better classes. We sometimes forget that we are called upon to fight weakness as well as viciousness."

Dell looked at her husband as he stood there, proud and strong and earnest, and he read the love in her admiring eyes as he clasped her to his heart, kissing her with a lover's rapture.

" What puzzles me," she said after awhile, " are women's fancies and the kind of men they love."

He laughed softly with a sense of amusement.

" It is well for our sex they are not all as exigent as you."

" Do you think I am ?" with a half-regretful cadence.

" In your demands, yes. In your practice—well, rather shaky. I can recall a bit of heroic unwisdom on your part——" glancing tenderly into the lustrous eyes that indicated a rain of the spirit rather than real tears.

" But suppose I had fretted and worried you, and demanded a hundred frivolous attentions when you were so engrossed. I am glad I did not," triumphantly.

" I am thankful you have not the temperament to demand frivolous attention or to fret. But it is wise for a wife sometimes to enforce her full rights. We always get around to ourselves, do we not ? *We* are the most interesting people to each other out of the whole world. And then we laugh at lovers !"

"Whether it is a good choice for Miss Westwood—that is the question before us."

"She must not choose until she has heard Gifford's story. I think she *can* marry him safely if she loves him. I should not want to make the match, yet I should bid it Godspeed. You see, she will not marry him from the mere sake of being married or wanting a home."

Dell smiled at that. It was very satisfactory.

In certain ways it seemed now as if Gifford was the elder, as he did not plunge into pleasures with Harry's zest. Two days before their departure for the West, Archie Stanwood made his appearance and met with a hearty welcome.

"We need Len to complete the party," Bertram Carew said.

"Why, you have brought up the true Sherburne air with the doctor and Miss Neale. Dell, you are the happiest woman in all the world ; and you give out Bible measure, pressed down and running over," declared Archie.

How much she had had to do with all their lives ! Had she crowded Millicent out of anything ?

To see Harry's pride in his country's service brought Archie's keenest disappointment back to him. The true ambition of his soul was not money-getting, yet there were some compensations. Hearty and well as his father seemed, there was now and then a sign of fatal weakness, unsuspected by his mother. Some day he might be needed for her support and comfort. The younger boys had their bright, hopeful lives before them.

"And now what next ?" exclaimed Dell, when the

last good-bys were said and they had settled to quiet.
" We have had everybody but Milly."

Was there any reason for Milly staying away, when she
had been so eager about the new housekeeping and so
delighted with the babies ? She wrote to her urgently.

The babies grew apace and took on cunning ways. It
was one of the mysterious blessings of Providence that
there should be two, she thought. Dr. Carew simply
adored little Milly, and she was extravagantly fond of
him. And though Aunt Neale insisted upon the utmost
impartiality with herself, other eyes saw that Baby Bertram brought back the sweet delights and experiences of
her younger days. Sometimes Dell dreamed of a baby
of her very own—for it seemed as if these had been
given away.

She stood pondering over a note from Violet one
morning. Millicent had come up for a little change,
though Dr. Underwood had insisted upon a whole month
of recuperation at Fortress Monroe.

" She has been working very steadily, it seems,"
wrote Violet. " And yet Millicent has such a fine phy-
sique a little strain never seemed to tell on her before.
She is thinner ; but what troubles me most is the effort
she makes at being cheerful. Fanny had a flirtation
with Mr. Armitage that he took rather seriously, I believe, and that distressed Milly. And now, curiously
enough, it is with Dr. Underwood. What a queer com-
pound Fanny is ! Why isn't there some Petruchio to
marry her out of hand ? I think all that wears on
Milly. And Nora is rather restless. You spoiled her
among you all at New York. She talks incessantly of
Auntie Dell, and Aunt Neale, and Uncle Bert, and
Mr. Drayton. She is beginning with admirers quite too

young, going to operas and all that. She is very sweet and cheerful, but she seems some way to overpower Milly. Girls will grow up, and Nora has the start of all the other cousins. I quite frightened myself last night to think that some day she might have a lover and be married, just as her mother was the first to go out of our circle. Our children! Our babies growing into men and women! Doesn't it alarm you, Dell?"

What had happened to Millicent? To be sure, she dropped down a little now and then, but soon recovered. Was there any more subtle cause? Mr. Drayton had never referred to the more engrossing subject, though Dell knew well that he was loving the child for the mother's sake. Was Millicent going through a conscientious struggle concerning the right of a second love? But if she did not love there would be no struggle.

"The next," said Bertram that evening, "is Miss Westwood. You see, she desires to consult me on a very important subject. Read her letter. Gifford has told his story, evidently."

Dell perused it with interest. Yes, it was not mere money matters, but something evidently nearer her heart.

"And now read this from Violet."

"How odd! To-morrow night I must go through to Washington to be present at a very critical operation. I wish they could have brought the patient up to New York. There is scarcely a chance for his life, I believe; but they are willing to risk it on that. I will run out and see Milly. O Dell, you don't imagine her a love-sick girl, do you?" looking into his wife's eyes and laughing softly. "Have a little patience. Remember how I waited for you."

"But Milly is ultra-conscientious."

"And what were you when you made such a heroic renunciation to my father—nay, even to me?"

Lyndell blushed as if she was back to that day.

"I wish Milly might see it our way," Bertram said with grave tenderness. "Every week I like Drayton better. He seems coming to the full stature of a man. He has a great deal in his hands and can make his influence widely felt. I think he means to settle in the city; he has already made some investments in property. And he wants a home. If Millicent doesn't come into it, it will be an ideal bachelor's home. When I hear some of this pessimistic talk on degeneration I think of the really fine men I know, and the grand things that are being done. And there is marrying and being given in marriage continually. With all the worldliness love is not at a discount."

"If he could see her——"

"Let me try first, if you can trust me that far, Mrs. Carew."

Dell kissed in the midst of a saucy smile.

She wrote at once to Miss Westwood in a most cordial fashion. But she did wait impatiently for Bertram's verdict. He left on the midnight train, and could not return until the next night. The operation had been a signal success, but the recovery depended on the patient's strength.

"I went out to the Amorys', dined there, and had quite an opportunity to study Millicent. I ordered her to Fortress Monroe, as there is no pressing literary work on hand. She is extremely nervous—I never saw her in such a state—run down physically as well. It is evident something at Beaumanoir worries her, for she could not see just how to stay away. Then she is expecting some shock or struggle to come suddenly upon her, and she wears herself out preparing for it."

"Do you deal in occultism?" Dell's voice was bright and mirthful.

"It did not need much occultism to tell me that. I am quite sure Drayton has asked his question and refused to accept her answer. And she lives in dread of his asking it again."

"Oh!" cried Dell with an accent of disappointment.

"If she really was not interested it would be all clear sailing. That little witch of a Nora has added fuel to the flames continually. Drayton could not have had a better ally. Perhaps he set out to win the child. Women have not pre-empted all the artfulness."

She could smile again, and her face was one gleam of rapt attention.

"If I gave a guess, I should say she cared for him very much, and was afraid of loving him—solemnly, awesomely afraid. Whether it is a question of conscience or some outside influence or the proprieties, I cannot determine. She has promised to go to Aunt Julia's. Then I shall advise Drayton to take a tour to the same place. She will not fly home from any sudden whim, and he will possess himself of the eternal certainty."

"O Bertram, how wise you are!"

"I am always sorry to see happiness going astray in the world, and love compelled to stand outside of human hearts for some fancied scruple. There might be so much more with a little pains, and in a certain sense love is redemption. It opens the soul to all blessed influences. It is God's choicest gift. And now, my dear, let us wait in hope. We must think how to help this other girl decide her great question."

" But you believed—he might marry," said Dell hesitatingly.

" It depends a good deal upon her and her strength of mind and the honesty of his confession. It may be manly, it may be morbid and weak. And yet we are so bound together that we may hurt and hinder where we most desire to bless. My darling, it is a strange and sacred thing to live and to be answerable for other lives."

Did she always feel the importance of it ? Yet righteousness was the foundation stone of happiness, and sin that of misery. Every transgression of the law of God brought its punishment, for after all that human wisdom had devised, the laws were God's, of the everlasting, and no theory had been able to turn their working aside or to fully escape the consequences.

And if one believed this, could he or she go on lightly, carelessly ? Lyndell sighed a little. Perhaps only a few really believed it. Would it make the world a dreary place if one were trained to face the responsibility, even when another hand had created the difficulty ? But what of those who walked deliberately into temptation with the secret assurance the hand of some friend must needs be stretched out to save them !

# CHAPTER XI.

EVELYN WESTWOOD looked immeasurably bene-
fited by her stay at the delightful home of her mother's friend. Lyndell had associated her so with sorrow,
that although the black robe remained as a memento, the
sweet, cheerful face and almost buoyant voice surprised
her. But who could be dreary or intensely sorrowful
with such an inspiriting friend and mentor as Aunt
Julia ?

Perhaps life did not look as dark and lonely as at that
first season of bereavement. She had learned to talk of
her mother and bring her near, and the awesome dread
of death was overcome. The other country was nearer,
the time of meeting again did not seem so interminable.

Dell had been a little curious to know how Archie had
impressed her.

There was a certain friendly sympathy, a pity for his
wrecked youth, an interest in his little girl ; but his
sorrows had not touched that keen point of appreciation,
or she had been more strongly impressed by the other
influence. Dell tried to look at Gifford through her
eyes, for every characteristic of his nature seemed instinct with interest for Miss Westwood. Did she indeed
understand him ?

His written confession had not been so much of a surprise to her, for she had heard surmises and whispers

about his college episode. After all, it was no uncommon thing. And he had overlived it; there had followed years of the utmost probity and upright endeavor. And did Lyndell think it such an uncommon thing that he should go almost crazy over his losses and be hardly accountable for what he did? There might have been a passionate regret at not following Osborne's advice.

Dell smiled a little. Was it not love that could find such ready excuses for that moment of moral weakness?

He had offered his love, all his efforts in the years to come, efforts that he knew now would be productive of honest, earnest work and reward. He did not ask her to accept poverty and uncertainty; he spoke of his position with a little honor. And he as proudly referred her to her own friends, Dr. and Mrs. Carew.

"I am not a real young girl any more, you know; at six-and-twenty one has greater strength and judgment than at eighteen. Then I have no one dependent on me, no one who would be defrauded by any marriage I should make. I do not mean by this that I am ready to throw my own life away. And I will say, Dr. Carew, that I abhor drunkenness. I could not marry the kind of men I have seen nice society girls take. But I could help some one who was in real earnest after a better life. I should want to trust him as well, and feel assured that his endeavors were sincere. I think I could make Mr. Lepage very happy. He is so fond of music and all the refinements of life. His ideal home is very fascinating. I have never had a beautiful home—at best a few rooms to adorn. Toil has restricted my desires. To make mamma comfortable was my chief aim. Oh, why did this money come so late!"

Evelyn Westwood's voice broke a little. Bertram paced the floor softly, much moved.

"I want something of my very own, a real home; I want some one to care for again, to whom I can be truly useful, and help and strengthen. I want to give as well as to receive. It was the urgent need of sympathy in him that first attracted me. I could have decided the matter myself, but I knew he would not be satisfied unless I laid it before you. And you know him with the acquaintance of years, while mine has been brief."

"But you would have accepted him?" said Dr. Carew with a tender half smile.

She colored deeply. "I should have tried him. If he had fallen far short of my expectations I should always have remained his friend. But it might not have been wisdom to marry. This is what I should have done if I had known nothing about his relatives. But living in Washington, meeting some of you, and understanding the family position, I could not feel toward him as a stranger. It seems as if I had known him for years. Yet I never thought of his caring for me in that way until one evening—well, I was not certain then until his letter came."

"I am sure you could help him. I think his wife would have a great influence over him. A happy home would be an ark of safety to him. He has never been vicious, and his lapses have come from circumstances in which he may never be placed again. Only you must not sacrifice your life or any aim. You can do a good deal with your musical abilities."

"And make a lonely, unsatisfying home?"

"But you might meet some one else——"

"I can be content just here. I do not think there

will be any people in the world that I shall admire so
much as I do all of your family, except——'' She smiled
a little. '' I dare say Mrs. Longworth would disdain
me ; but we shall live the other side of the world, so
that will not matter.''

'' There are many people, women and men, saved by
a devoted love that ministers to what is best and highest, not merely selfish, absorbing personal regard, that
can correct no fault, even if it sees the fatal defect.
And life should be an effort at improvement, not merely
enjoyment, though that is not to be despised.   I am no
ascetic,'' smiling with vivacious brightness.

'' Thank you for all the interest.   You were such a
good friend in my trouble,'' and her soft eyes suffused
with emotion.   Then a vague sweetness played about
her mouth as she added with a shy sort of hesitation,
'' There will be at least a year's engagement.   Even if
we do not meet we shall learn enough about each other
to decide whether a marriage would be for the very best.''

When Evelyn had retired Dell glanced across to Bertram with an inquiry in her eyes that was half curiosity,
half doubt.

'' You are wondering if it is for the best ?   Yes, I
think it is.   And you see she is really in love with him.
It is not quite the ' blind necessity ' of the poet, but a
very human necessity with her.   She has had some one
to love and to care for since real womanhood began,
some one to work for, as most of their small means was
spent upon her musical education.   I am not sure but
six or eight years is long enough for any woman to
work.''

'' Bertram, according to the new creed, you have some
heresies about women.''

" Wishing them all homes and husbands ?" he laughed with a sense of amusement. " No, there are women who never should marry ; there are born business women ; there are women to whom household cares are irksome. But a home is an essential longing to them. I often wonder why two or three do not join forces and have a true home, and why women with large motherly instincts and considerable means, who are earnest in charitable work, do not take some pretty, attractive children in their homes and rear them into useful men and women. If each person who had the ability saved even one human soul, look at the measure of good that would be achieved. We pass people—children—on to others altogether too much. They find their way to institutions at length, and then we wash our hands of them and call it charity. That is straying from the text. But while we were talking to Miss Westwood I could not help thinking what a fine couple she and Archie would have made. Perhaps Gif really needs her more."

" And I wonder how she came to be so suddenly interested, when there was Harry to contrast him with ?"

" He showed her his need of her. And she has a passion for giving, for devotion. It was very honorable in him to refer her to us in that manly manner. I shall think the better of Gifford for it. She will make a blessed home. I do suppose a wife would have saved him from the last misfortune."

" There was Alice. And Bevis Osborne had been the best of brothers."

" There is a sort of jealous longing for some one of his very own to pin his faith to. These are the kind of men a woman saves or ruins. Do you suppose he could have made any kind of stand against Archie's fate ?"

" Oh, poor Archie !'' Dell cried with tenderness.

" Archie will make a superior man presently. His is a rather slow development, but the real force was underneath. And perhaps a commonplace happiness would not have brought out a single fine point except a sweet domesticity,'' said the doctor.

" But Miss Westwood is not commonplace, Bertram,'' with a kind of injured feeling in her tone.

" No. Well, you women are very good to us. And who can explain love ?''

Lyndell hardly understood the struggle within herself. She had loved Gifford a great deal by what it seemed now were spells of affection. She had experienced a sense of elation when she had helped to take his feet from the mire and set them in the right path. Yet he had not come up to her ideal possibility. He had shown himself weak, jealous, and unfriendly to those who should have been dearest to him. He had not been noble or generous to her, even. And her work had gone for nothing. Another hand would take it up now and do what the others had failed in.

Bertram bent over and kissed the perplexed crease between her eyes.

" My darling, it is the sick who need a physician, not those who are whole. And many need it all their lives long. I am not sure of restoring a man to health for all time ; some unforeseen mishap may bring back the disease to the weakened tissue, some lack of watchfulness undo the labor and thought of many anxious hours that I have spent. It is the work of a lifetime.''

She glanced up and smiled. No labor was ever lost in God's sight, and many hands often joined to bring about one result. Was it not all written in the Book ?

She came really to rejoice in Gifford's good fortune as she learned to know Evelyn Westwood better. During all these years of devotion to her mother, when she had the support of both to provide for, no thought of marriage had entered her mind. Perhaps some tender, devoted soul might have won her had any such crossed her path ; but in her position they were hardly likely to. Her voice had gained her some admiration, it was true, but she respected the line society had drawn so strictly, and she held herself above the ordinary, meaningless flirtations.

Already she had found the difference between the absolute dependence on the labor of the hands, and the fact of her being an heiress, even in a small way. To be sure, rumor multiplied her few thousands. Several of her patrons who had accorded her a little more than business appreciation had sent her notes of congratulation and cordial invitations for a visit. She had met two or three at Fortress Monroe. Aunt Julia had made her promise to return. The season was so far gone that it was useless to endeavor to take up her music teaching. There were two offers from summer hotels that she would have accepted eagerly last season for her mother's sake.

"You do need a vacation," Dr. Carew said. "And if you accept this year of probation," smiling a little, "it will be none too long to renew your strength and energies, that you may be better fitted for your new life."

.It was quite delightful to have a little leisure for the varied entertainments of the city. She had a feast of music. There was something of interest every day ; there were charming women devoted to the larger social questions and pursuits, and she found much to occupy her during her three weeks' stay. When Gifford's reply to her letter came, her whole heart went out in a great bewildering gladness. And Dell wondered if Gifford would be large enough of soul to appreciate this treasure that had come to him with so little effort.

She did not quite do him justice, though one side of her nature gave thanks, as a fine, appreciative soul always must for any good result. The man's inmost being had been awakened to the revelation. What paltry, puerile longings had filled his mind hitherto when set by the side of this pure affection! How all his weak resolves shamed him! He had been living with false ideals, and now the light of true manhood illumined his way. That Evelyn could forgive his mental weaknesses and stand ready to strengthen with her brave, sweet smile! He could say honestly that she was the first one who had touched the deeper chords of harmonious adjustment. He understood how he must have tormented Dell with his boyish demands for a friendship that should exclude almost every other object.

Reese Drayton had heard incidentally—or had Dr. Carew a purpose in remarking in a casual manner that Mrs. von Lindorm was not well enough for city dissipation and had gone to Fortress Monroe, and that they were both quite disappointed? For a week or so he had seen nothing of him.

"What has become of Mr. Drayton?" asked the elder doctor one evening. "I miss his entertaining chats. I am getting old and exigent, you see—spoiled with the multiplicity of amusements."

Bertram raised his brows a little. "I have not seen him myself," he returned carelessly.

Lyndell noted it. She had been so engaged with Miss

Westwood and household cares that she had hardly remarked the fact of his absence for the last ten days.

But he was in the next morning to ask Miss Westwood's services for a charity entertainment. He had been put on a committee without his knowledge or assent, he declared in a complainingly humorous tone.

Miss Westwood assented cordially. There were some plans to make, and Dell lent a willing interest.

"We were wondering to what cloister you had retired," Miss Westwood exclaimed as a bit of pleasantry. "I believe both doctors were complaining of your absence."

"Why, that is quite delightful," he rejoined with an eagerness of tone that was belied by his grave eyes. "I must make a note of that to use again when I think I have bored my friends."

"You never do bore us," Dell said quietly. She did not glance up. She felt half afraid.

When they had settled their arrangements he proposed that Miss Westwood should go with him to inspect a private view of pictures that were to be sold at auction a few evenings hence. Some were by well-known artists.

Had Millicent dismissed him with a refusal? If so he made no sign. He had to some extent dropped into his olden place, and he was often the younger doctor's companion in public. Since the confidence at Sherburne House he had exchanged no word with Dell on the subject of his heart's desire, only she knew he had not given up his dream.

It was true he had seen Millicent, and for two days she had been so delicately on guard that he was forced to respect her seclusion. But he had come upon her unawares and asked his question straightforwardly. The answer had not been given in a like manner—he understood that. She had evaded the issue of regard with a curious coldness. She would not argue, but intrenched herself behind the olden reason that she had no wish to marry, that there were reasons why it was quite impossible for her to consider the subject.

He was not unmanly enough to persist. " Then if there can be nothing more, will you at least grant me the privilege of friendship ?" he asked in a grave, earnest tone. " We are likely to be thrown together a good deal in the future, and it would be awkward to have this cause of embarrassment between us. Let us have it out and dismiss it. I have quite made up my mind to reside in New York for some years at least ; and your dearest cousin, your sincerest friends are there. I am afraid only a few weeks ago the thought of meeting me prevented your visit and disappointed Mrs. Carew."

In spite of her effort a soft pink quivered to the very edge of her dusky hair, and the finely cut lips compressed a trifle.

" There was illness, you know. We felt alarmed at first. And then I was too tired to enjoy the excitement. I explained it all to my cousin."

There was a faint hesitation in her tone, as if she was not quite certain this was her most cogent reason.

He had too much wisdom to use the vehement persuasions of a younger man. He cared for her too sincerely to compel her to find weak and elusive excuses.

" But you understand how it would be. We could not go on forever with this sense of discord between us, or endeavor to avert each other's presence. There would be some awkward questions if we set out to shun one another."

" Oh, I did not mean that !" She drew a long, quivering breath. He saw it stir her pulses and flutter about, as if a soft breeze had touched her. But she did not raise her eyes.

" Then we can be friends ?"

He kept his voice free from emotion and held out his hand, as if he was quite willing to accept that instead. How true and sincere was his regard—that had been offered to another !

Was it an instant or moments ? She saw his hand, slim, with rather long fingers, as if, should it close over another's, the clasp would be for all time. Of course they must be friends. She could not drag out these confidences for Lyndell's inspection, much as she loved her.

She laid her hand lightly, hesitatingly in his—just the merest touch. It was cold and tremulous. The clasp was warm and strong, and she knew the man loved her. She could not withdraw it. After one vain effort she was afraid to try. He led her on a few paces in silence. The organ roll of the ocean came up to them majestically, musically, and seemed to carry away something with it that neither of them had said, that could not be recalled.

" You see it is best so," he continued. " In some curious manner I have entered your circle—are not all the elected intimacies more or less curious ? You go around the whole world sometimes to find a friend, another stands beside you. I have no relatives, and your family life has interested me, does interest me, has awakened me, I might say, to some of the grander purposes of existence. I should like to be own brother to Bertram Carew. I admire his father—I reverence him when it comes to that. I cannot go away from these people unless it should be your wish."

"My wish! Oh, no; why should it be?" hurriedly.

"I cannot tell all your reasons." His voice was wonderfully sweet and low, yet she heard it like a clear tone of music above the symphony of the winds or the diapason of the waves. "We talk a good deal about occult understanding of each other's souls—perhaps in some other sphere we may; but here and now we hardly translate a sentence rightly, much less apprehend a thought."

She made no reply. He could hear the long breath surging upward. They went on in silence. Another turn would bring them in sight of the household. The family were out on the broad, low porch. Nora's voice ran gayly on to the end of some incident, and they all laughed.

Millicent stopped suddenly, and this time withdrew her hand.

"Good-night," she said. "Yes, we shall be friends——"

"Good-night." He turned and left her.

She did not look, and yet she saw the retreating figure, with its ease and grace, that had not yet taken on the lines of middle life. The voice lingered in her ears, in her brain; the warm, vigorous hand still seemed about hers, and she made a gesture as if to shake it off. Then she covered her face with both hands. One was still warm with the fervor of his clasp. There was a moment's longing as if she might let herself go.

"It *is* better." The struggle was over, she told herself.

Aunt Julia was not quite satisfied with her improve-

ment ; but Archie was going up to Sherburne House for
a brief visit, and Millicent thought she could not remain
any longer.

"I am sure I never saw you looking quite so poorly,
Millicent, as you did a fortnight ago. I am afraid
you take too many cares. You ought to go away
and have a good long summering. How delightful it
was when you were all children at Sherburne House !
And if Gifford should marry, there will be only Fanny
left."

"But, you see, we are all growing up to be the next
relay of children," said Nora.

"And there is Cecil, and Floyd, and Win——"

"And Floyd, foolish boy, is engaged. I ought not
to call him that when I think of the sweet girl who is
waiting for him. Early loves are sometimes better than
later ones."

"There will be no dearth of children at Sherburne,"
Millicent added with a smile. "But we do not need to
consider marriages just yet."

"Aunt Fanny is going to be an old maid ; but it will
take a great many years to get as old as Aunt Aurelia or
Cousin Carrick, won't it, mamma ?"

"My dear, you talk quite too much."

"After all, I'd rather be married like Aunt Violet
and Auntie Dell," continued the child, not heeding her
mother's admonition.

They had discussed Gifford's engagement. Miss
Westwood had written that the matter was settled.
Archie had been delighted, and sent a message of con-
gratulation to his cousin. He admired Miss Westwood
extremely—they had been cordial friends that winter in
Washington ; but if there had been any susceptibility

on Archie's part, it was quite evident Evelyn had never remarked it, and it had proved only a boyish fondness.

Millicent rejoiced unfeignedly. She and Archie were sympathetic friends. It seemed to her that he as well as Gifford had just come to a true appreciation of manhood. His mother had her son again, and he and his father had dropped into good comradeship. But for the child and the ambition of his early youth so rudely wrenched aside he could almost have forgotten that dreamlike experience. Had he been wise in yielding to his wife's demands ?

Millicent was anxious to get home. She should feel safe and resigned to her lot when once more within its sacred precincts. Resigned ! Even in her solitude the quick flush burned her face. This was not quite the virtue for right doing, for giving up what was really not hers. One could resign one's self to a misfortune, to the result of another's wrongdoing, but to keep from wrong herself required a more energetic endeavor than mere acceptance.

Archie gave his mother a tender good-by. "Some time in the future," he said in a longing sort of tone, " I hope to have a home to my own satisfaction. You and father must be in it. When a man has once set his whole soul on a home and domestic life, nothing else will satisfy him."

Millicent remembered another man who had set his heart on a home, who was tired of rambling about. Could Fanny create that haven of domestic bliss that should be neither inane nor frivolous ?

The Beaumanoir carriage was awaiting them at Ardmore. Mr. Beaumanoir smiled delightedly as he welcomed his daughter and nephew and yielded to Nora's rapturous kisses.

"You have improved so much. Aunt Julia must have some magic panacea."

"Hillo!" exclaimed a rather brusque, inspiriting voice, and Dr. Underwood's buggy gave a sudden turn around to them. Fanny sat beside him, gay, smiling, audacious.

"You see, we did get in time." She nodded to the doctor saucily. "I wanted a peep at you, so you wouldn't feel hurt and slighted when you reached home and found I had gone off pleasuring. O Milly, you've gained ninety-nine per cent! You see, there is something in the world far and away beyond your skill," turning to the doctor triumphantly.

"I think I recommended a change for Mrs. von Lindorm some weeks ago," he returned with a kind of quiet triumph in his tone as he greeted the others cordially.

"That is a new whim of Fanny's," remarked her father as they drove on. "At all events, the doctor is capable of holding his own."

They had all felt somewhat distressed about Mr. Armitage. Fanny was quite regardless of the feelings of others so long as she was enjoying the amusement.

Archie spent the remainder of the afternoon with his cousin looking over lists of books he meant to get in New York, and detailing some of his plans. He was very much interested in Millicent's successes.

"Only I *do* think you ought to be in a larger sphere," he said, looking so intently in the beautiful face that a flush overspread it. "So many of your best years are yet to come, for I do not think either youth nor that period past middle life can be as rich in effort and the accumulation of mental treasures. And you might wield such a fine and widespread influence."

" Oh, we are not quite benighted," she answered with a faint smile. " Leonard has a good many choice friends, who are delighted to partake of his quiet and attractive hospitality. Tessy is a really charming hostess. I often go over there."

" But Tessy has all these satisfactions for herself—her home, her husband, her children, and friends. You can only enjoy the overflow, as it were, and that vanishes and is gone. There are a hundred lovely hopes and ambitions to her life. What a man of weight Len is becoming !"

" And I have my daughter. In a few years, if I feel that I can be spared, we shall go abroad. But just now——"

" Milly, one can make a mistake even about so noble a thing as duty," he said warningly. " After all, we are not required to love our neighbor better than ourselves."

That was surely a disinterested warning.

# CHAPTER XII.

THEY were at supper when Fanny entered, bright and
animated, and in a moment the rather serious turn
of conversation was changed. Her incidents always had
a touch of the ridiculous. Even in a sick-room she
seemed to find some humorous side, or if the illness was
very severe she kept away. She had no taste for anxiety
or gloominess.

Archie went up to Sherburne House, and would continue his journey the next morning. Nora was tired
and sleepy, so she went to bed. Milly and her mother
had a tender confidence. Fanny was amusing two
young callers with some lively airs on the piano.

" Is it the doctor now ?" Millicent asked when the
talk had veered round to Fanny.

" O Milly, I don't know. I feel so troubled at times.
Fanny is so different from either of you girls. Some one
must always be dancing attendance on her ; and she has
that curious manner of making the present man believe he
appeals to her in a way no man ever did before. There's
Ralph Clayton downstairs. He is only two-and-twenty
—just the impressionable age—and of course Fanny
doesn't mean anything serious. I used to have an idea
that it was only beautiful and attractive women who
could flirt,'' and the mother sighed.

" Fanny often looks very arch and pretty. I think it is a certain gift of fascination."

" I wish she were safely married—the first daughter I have made such a wish about, although it is a comforting prospect to have your children settled in homes of their own. And at her age she is quite beyond control. I hoped she would tire of it and really settle down, but she is not the kind to accept the common duties and pleasures of life. She has no diffusion of interest. She follows one bent until she extracts all the amusement from it, and then she drops it and takes up another. If I thought the doctor was in earnest—but that would be of no avail unless he could compel Fanny's attention. Your father likes him so much."

" I was surprised to-day——"

" Fanny has been out with him several times in that pronounced manner, quite as if they were engaged. He can hardly be called a middle-aged man. And Fanny makes a point of her not being a young girl. To hear her talk, you would sometimes think she was forty ;" and there was a spice of indignation in Mrs. Beaumanoir's tone.

" She looked about twenty this afternoon."

" Ethel has had a bad influence over her. After all, it does seem best that girls should be married quite young and settle themselves to the duties of wives and mothers. I suppose that is an old-fashioned way of thinking. But Ethel has not settled very much."

Mrs. Beaumanoir gave a short, half laugh of disapprobation.

" Is it true, I wonder ? Violet wrote she had gone on to Russia with a party, and was coming home by the way of Japan."

"Yes. I do feel sorry for Mr. Longworth, only he has led that half-bachelor existence for so long that perhaps he doesn't miss the wifely interest. Violet said he grew wonderfully absorbed in little Bevis Osborne. What a pity there are not some children!"

"If they were all boys," returned Millicent.

Then they talked about Gifford's engagement, and Mrs. Beaumanoir was much interested in it.

The young men went their way. The lights were put out and the house subsided into the silence of sleep.

Millicent was asking herself a curious question. Had she come between what might have been a safe and sure love for Fanny, and was her recklessness the result of a disappointment she would never admit?

Dell and some of the Murray family, with the charming grandmother, were going away for the summer to a great, roomy farmhouse among the New Hampshire hills. Little Milly had somehow dropped down, but Bertie was simply magnificent. Bertram thought they all wanted the wide, fragrant, joyous out of doors. Aunt Neale would go, but the housekeeper would be left, and each doctor would make a stay as long as circumstances would permit. If Milly and Nora would join them. Mamma Murray was insisting that Tessy should take a good long holiday.

"I do think you ought," Millicent declared. "Aunt Julia is to come up to Sherburne for a month, and mamma never goes away, you know, except a week now and then at Violet's."

"But four children and a retinue of servants! And they all keep wonderfully well. Can there be a lovelier out of doors than here?" Tessy asked rather proudly.

" But the change would be beneficial. And you would be released from care awhile."

" There doesn't seem very much care with servants to come at your slightest beck," and Tessy laughed with a kind of gracious delight.

" Will you go ?"

" I must consider. Yes, I might come for awhile. And I would send Nora at once if you would take charge of her."

Fanny's example was making the child quite pert and emancipating her rather too rapidly. And as Millicent cuddled little Dell up to her neck, she sighed for Nora's lost babyhood.

Leonard at first scouted the suggestion.

" You ought to send Tessy for her own sake," said Aunt Aurelia. " She has never had one real long holiday since her married life began—just those flying trips to New York or Washington. Surely, Leonard, you can afford to reward such devotion," and her tone was more than persuasive.

" I do not believe she would go. And what would you do ? What would I do without the children ?" in a humorously complaining tone.

" We must not allow ourselves to get wrapped up in our own selfish longings, and think merely of our personal pleasure. Your mother will look after us. Aunt Julia will be up here a month, and Floyd will come for a vacation. And if you would go for a week or two I know she would consent."

" Dear Aunt Aurelia, how you have our welfare at heart !" and he bent over to kiss her.

She clasped her arms around his neck. " Son of my love," she said in a sweet, shaken voice, " put in the place of the one I ought to have considered. God has been good to me. And, Leonard, you would make Dell very happy."

That argument moved him. And though Tessy laughed gayly at first, and said her mother never had to go away from home, and all the children were happy and healthy, she was touched by her husband's solicitude and the probability of his coming for them.

" Why shouldn't you go, Milly ?" asked her sister when the subject was being discussed.

" I have some other plans. And you may like a journey somewhere."

" No, I am not going away," in a rather abrupt tone. " I've been about everywhere except to India, China, and Japan. I'll save that for my old age."

She examined Millicent so intently with her sharp glance that the elder flushed.

" You are growing thin again, Milly," pettishly. " I wish you wouldn't worry about me, but just let me go my way. It suits me."

" Are you quite certain it is the best way ? You trouble mother as well. And, Fanny, people will begin to gossip——"

" Oh, I don't mind the old frumps !" with an airy toss of her head.

" But you ought to mind. Dr. Underwood"—yes, she would say it—" after the unfortunate episode with Mr. Armitage——"

" I really did not mean that Mr. Armitage should think— Why, his common sense ought to have convinced him that I never would do for a clergyman's wife," and Fanny gave an ironical laugh. " I didn't quite let him ask me, though he made strenuous efforts.

Dr. Underwood should have gone at him instead of me."

" At you !" said Millicent in surprise.

" Yes. He gave me some good, fatherly advice. Oh, it *was* comical ! And then he took to thwarting the young man, for which I was immensely thankful."

" Oh, is that all it means ? Fanny, it will end by Dr. Underwood despising you," and Millicent flushed with the sense of disapprobation that Fanny did not even entertain.

" I don't know what it means. You see, we joined forces in a queer sort of way. Really, Millicent, I had no idea Mr. Armitage was in earnest. He had a charming sentimental side that amused me. I didn't suppose any one would come to me for sentiment. And then he was asking my assistance—it was positively flattering, Milly," and there was an arch innocence in her face as if she had found it a delightful thing to be flattered.

" Fanny ! And your real regard was somewhere else?" Millicent's indignation amazed Fanny.

" Somewhere else ! What do you mean, Milly ? Oh, it isn't—you are not thinking—do you mean that episode with Mr. Drayton ? Well, I should have been a fool if I had fixed my regard very deeply upon him, granting I possess such an article."

" But you once said——" the elder drew a long, quivering breath.

" Oh, goodness, Milly ! if you are going to quote things out of my past you won't get through until doomsday. What did I say ? That I was going to try for him——"

" That he had asked you to marry him, and you regretted your refusal."

"Well, you needn't faint away about it; you look like a ghost. He isn't the first man who has asked me in that lazy, perfunctory way, as if it was a duty to be gotten over with, and I really was not worth any great effort. I *did* like him. I like him now. And something Ethel said piqued me a little. It would have been a triumph of hope over experience. And how do you suppose we would have managed?"

"I hope you would have tried——" she had hard work to keep her voice steady and unconcerned.

"Bosh! He would have given me my own way everywhere. I could have thrown away his money and flirted," laughing ironically; "gone hither and thither, because he wouldn't have cared, and sometimes it would have been a rest for him to have me out of the way. A man in love does not do that."

"Well——" her voice sounded hollow to herself.

"It would have been as good as a great many of the marriages, and they seem to satisfy a large part of womankind. But I am not intellectual, I am not philanthropic; I like a good time with some one who will help me to have it, or else he must be strong enough to keep to his way of thinking, and his way must not be up among the clouds. My head swims in those high altitudes—the air is too rarefied. I should have grown so tired, that in sheer despair I might have done something dreadful. And, Milly, it will shock you and vex you to have me say it, but you really are his ideal. I don't see why you didn't both fall in love out there in those mighty ranch solitudes. I had it in mind when I persuaded you to go out—I truly did," she admitted gravely.

Millicent bent over to pick up the pretty golden pin she had been running in and out of the open work on the end of the bureau scarf, but she knew the fall had not been accidental, and she wanted to hide the scarlet flush.

"Love is a mighty queer business." Fanny laughed with a kind of alien gayety. "You put two people together who just suit, and they are blind in the superlative degree. Then the two people who ought not get together kindle with a look or a word, and there is a mighty tempest at first, and sullen storms at last. If he had really loved me no doubt I should have tried it and spoiled both lives. Honestly, Milly, do you think I could make Mr. Armitage truly happy?"

"Not unless you were very much changed," answered the elder with almost hesitating candor.

"I like myself better than I like Mr. Armitage's ideal wife. I want to suit some one *now*—not spend years getting fitted. And I like some stiff breezes. I should hate going along forever in smooth water. I want what I do to make a difference. I want some one to argue with, well—perhaps convince me. You get tired of always having your own way."

"But you can yield."

"You see, I am not heroic enough to give it up of my own accord. Mr. Longworth lets Ethel go away and stay—likely it will be a year before she returns. Mr. Drayton would have let me do the same thing; but he wouldn't with a woman he loved. I don't like tyrants, but I want a man to care what I do. Oh, I don't quite know what I do want! He must not be beggarly poor; he must not need to be prodded up all the time; he must not be turned about with every wind of doctrine; he must not live up in the clouds, but he need not be so very rich. Violet can keep up the family elegancies; you can be the caryatid to hold up the intellectual column, and Len the judicial, so I need not strain after anything. What did you ask me first—about the doctor?"

"Yes." There was a sense of deception about her, to herself, a sweet, stifling kind of hypocrisy.

"I don't know. Honestly and truly I am doing my utmost to make him fall in love with me."

"O Fanny!" in dismay.

"I believe in the new order of things—the female will be allowed to show her preference. You see, it wouldn't be safe if I was taking my first skim over the sea of uncertainty. I truly do not know how much heart I have. If you really are not entitled to ask yourself anything until a man speaks, why, then, you must wait until his lordship—what is it an Oriental despot does, drops his handkerchief at your feet? Then *I* must consider whether I want to pick it up. Meanwhile, we are trying to convince each other that every thought, and feeling, and view, and belief each has held is totally wrong. The arguments are entertaining. And you must admit there is not much in this sleepy place to satisfy one's thirst for knowledge."

Could anything make an impression on volatile Fanny—some grand love? Could she appreciate or comprehend the refinements of a truly noble love? Millicent glanced up wistfully.

Fanny colored and laughed, then with a hasty kiss danced out of the room with the vim of sixteen.

Millicent von Lindorm gave two or three long inspirations, as one does when a great strain has been removed. She leaned her forehead on the marble edge of the bureau top, and its coolness felt grateful. Yes, Fanny could not satisfy the kind of man Reese Drayton was now. The years had given him a larger hold on life, had brought him face to face with the finer realities. She tried not to be glad ; she could not feel sorry that one life had escaped the grinding exactions of inharmony.

It was true that Fanny had no power of living and loving outside of herself. Everything must appeal to her first. The delicate effacement of self was not a part of such natures.

Dr. Underwood dropped in a few days after this. Fanny had gone over to Sherburne. She had times of being curiously interested in the children, then for days she was indifferent. She had taken Nora, and the two ladies sat on the vine-shaded porch with their sewing. Mr. Beaumanoir had been reading a magazine article aloud.

" You look the picture of comfort," he exclaimed. " May a wayfarer stretch himself out in this beguiling retreat and breathe the refreshing air of ease and indolence ?—the last an attribute of mine, so you need not take offence," bowing to the two ladies.

Millicent rose and offered the doctor a willow easy-chair.

" No," with a graceful gesture of the hand that attracted her and won an unconscious smile. " I am going to sit here on the step opposite Mr. Beaumanoir, as if we were the two pillars of the house. Now, will you sew and talk ? I like those dainty feminine employments. One's hand going in and out seems like a fluttering bird."

" Fastened by a thread ?" Millicent held up her slim, white hand.

" That isn't such a delightful simile as I thought it was going to be. Did your superior wisdom spoil it ?"

" Oh, I hope not."

" Then mine must have blundered in trying to be extremely complimentary. The people who sew in a leisurely, enjoyable fashion have an unfailing tonic for their nerves."

" It *is* restful. One gets tired of doing nothing. Though it is getting to be a lost art except in country places like this, out of the reach of the dictates of fashion," commented Mrs. Beaumanoir.

" Do you suppose Dr. Carew really feels at home in the city ?" he asked a moment afterward with a little abruptness. " I had a compliment to-day. An old negro woman thought I was almost as good. Sometimes I have scruples of conscience, especially on a lovely day like this."

" Oh, he is so fond of his son. They ought to be together, as they are. Of course we miss the doctor and his sister, but it softened the blow by their going abroad."

" What a treat it must have been, with that remarkable young fellow, too ! If I thought he would not come back I should fix up a sort of hospital at Ardmore and send for an assistant—the son of a friend, graduated last year, and who has had rather hard lines. His father was my guardian and very good to me. And I heard some tidings to-day that will give me a little money."

" Dr. Carew will never come back to take up his practice," remarked Mr. Beaumanoir.

" Then I think I shall move in the matter. A place of that kind is needed, especially for children and accidents."

Millicent watched Dr. Underwood with new interest. He looked his years—thirty-five—and he was slipping into the easy ways of middle life. He had a strong, vigorous face, but large, dark, and rather sleepy eyes that gave one the impression of indifference. Now and then you surprised a sudden gleam in them that indicated a reserve of strength and temper, a will that could rise and assert itself, but that did not bristle up for trifles. The lips gave a half laugh very easily ; it might be a conventional trick or an assumed suavity, for they could shut with a decision from which there was no appeal. His hair and beard were dark and close cropped, and Millicent noted to-day that he had a finely shaped head.

They had taken very kindly to him at Sherburne House ; here they had hardly needed a physician, so the acquaintance had been a matter of neighborly friendliness. Several of the old families had grown very fond of him. He had not allowed his sympathies to be played upon as easily as his predecessor, and at first there had been some dissatisfaction among the poorer people. But he had proved himself ready in the hour of real need.

Supper was announced, and he went into the dining-room without much persuasion. Afterward the two men strolled around the plantation, enjoying their smoke in the open air. He had not seemed the least disconcerted because Fanny was not at home. Did he really care for her, Millicent wondered.

He had his horse brought around presently and said adieu to them. He had not been gone a quarter of an hour when Fanny drove up in her pony carriage. From that time until she went to bed Nora claimed her mother, and compelled her to listen to the doings and sayings at Sherburne House. And they were all going away with Auntie Dell.

" O mamma, why can't you go too ?" teased Nora. " Uncle Len said you must."

" I will think about it, dear," said the soft voice.

" It is so stupid to stay here all the time."

" O Nora, with mamma and grandpapa, who loves you so !"

" But he loves little Ned Sherburne just as well," almost pouted the child.

" And if you both go away, how lonely he will be."

" But there will be Aunt Fanny."

" It is bedtime now."

" I shall be glad when I am grown up and need not go to bed until I get good and tired."

" I often go to bed early."

" Come now," pleaded Nora.

She had half a mind to humor the child, but her mother whispered in passing, " Come to my room when you are through with Nora. I have something to tell you."

Nora had more than half a mind to be unamiable. Was she losing the motherly guidance over her ? Millicent sighed a little as she kissed her.

There was no light in her mother's room except from the hall, but the moon shone through the open window.

" Milly, dear, we can settle our minds quite at rest," her mother said with a cheerful accent, discernible even in her low tone. " Dr. Underwood has been talking to your father. He is in earnest about Fanny, and seems to feel confident that he can win her. And he has had quite a bit of good fortune. He was comparatively well off at one time, it seems ; but he invested a good deal of his money in some Western mines, that came to grief five or six years ago. Latterly, by some of the new methods of working, they have become very profitable again, so he feels that he is able to marry and do a little for Ardmore besides. And now, if Fanny *should* decide in his favor! It would be very pleasant to have her settle at Ardmore, and a great relief."

"I hope she will be happy," returned Millicent from her full heart.

"Well, Fanny is rather queer. But your father thinks Dr. Underwood has a good deal of spirit and firmness. I do suppose the younger children in a family get spoiled. There are so many more cares when you come to have half a dozen, and grandchildren," laughing a little. "But Cecil is a fine fellow. The boys do have to go away. You can't settle them on farms just around. Still, we have Len and must be thankful. I have been a very happy woman, my dear."

Millicent put her arm about her mother's neck and kissed her. Happier even than Aunt Julia, and oh, worlds happier than poor Aunt Edith. In the moonlight she saw the silver threads in her mother's dark, shining hair. How delightful it was to grow old with children and grandchildren, and a pleasant home, with the husband of one's youth, and the completed romance!

For a moment, as she glanced down the future, the loneliness of her lot oppressed her. She had hardly needed a home of her very own. There would be changes in the course of years, and she could not keep alive the interest in Beaumanoir that Aunt Aurelia had at Sherburne. She would have been more than woman if she had not thought of the love proffered her. But if Fanny went away, would not the old reason be still stronger? must she not be the one to stay and comfort?

Lyndell's next letter was full of eager persuasion. She was quite sure of Tessy joining them. What a grand summer they might have ! The men would come up by turns, so they would not feel lonely or deserted.

Millicent was very much engrossed. Tessy found so many things needing to be done, that but for the pleasure of spending weeks with her mother and her two really agreeable sisters-in-law, and Dell, she must have given out.

Major and Mrs. Stanwood came up. He had not been quite so robust of late, and needed a rest. Leonard was to take the party up to New York, and Bertram to their destination. Nora was beside herself with delight, and somehow hardly missed mamma in her excitement.

Violet and her children had gone to Sulphur Springs. Leonard, on his return to Washington, found Mr. Longworth quite ill with some sudden attack, that for a few hours had rather alarmed the physician, who had ordered him away as soon as he was able to travel.

Did Ethel give him a thought now and then, Millicent wondered.

Leonard came home from his visit full of enthusiasm. They wanted Millicent to complete their delight, and Nora sent eager persuasions.

" You ought to go, Milly," said her sister. " You stay at home too much. You do need a broader sphere, you can fill a larger place. And, Milly"—she turned quite away with a delicacy new to her—" I do not see why you should not accept any joy or delight that may come in your life. I shall always remain here——"

" O Fanny ! I hope—that you——"

" Don't hope too much." Fanny gave a little, strained laugh. " I am not at all sure it would be right to torment a man's life when he has no means of escaping you. Of course you mean Dr. Underwood. We have had one desperate disagreement. Only—as he is not romantic and is not looking for perfection, and has some quite commonplace tastes——"

"Oh, you don't do him justice," interrupted Millicent.

"He is likely to stay here all his life. So, you see, in any event I should be near mamma ; and, with such a host of grandchildren, she will not be neglected. It isn't any more your duty to stay at home than it would be mine or Violet's. And—see here, Millicent, I understand what it is to have a man love you quite apart from the glamour of society flirtation, when you can make him say almost anything to you, even if he repents the next morning. I can also understand that a man may fancy he owes you the duty of a proposal. But when he has met his ideal woman and paid his debt honorably, she has no true cause to despise him or think him weak. Dear, you had such a short dream of bliss, you have so many admirable qualities, that I shall always feel as if I had stood in your way, if you keep continually on the defensive. There, I had to have my say."

Fanny ran out of the room. Millicent covered her scarlet face with her hands. Could a woman love twice ? Was not the question answered with this great throb that stirred every pulse, and the still more delightful assurance that she was loved ?

# CHAPTER XIII.

THE soft afternoon light fell over the grassy slope, quite shaded at the west by the belt of tall trees. Out beyond, where sumachs were ripe and heavy, and the bittersweet showed clusters of shining, scarlet beads, the world was alight with the golden fires of a setting sun that touched every common shrub and blossom and made the stubble field a thing of royal beauty. Farther beyond were tents, made of the yellow corn in stacks, topped off with nodding plumes. The wind shook out a waft of fragrance now and then, and in the shaded places there was already a dewy sweetness.

Nearer the house the scene would have done for a pastoral, had an artist been at hand. The ladies had been sewing. The two houses turned out a goodly array, and an opening had been made in the partition fence, that they might step back and forth. The children were grouped on the Murrays' piazza, where the pretty grandmamma sat, who seemed to have grown smaller with advancing years, but who kept her softly rounded face with very few wrinkles in it, and her sweet smile that was like sunrise. Densie and Nora were entertaining the babies, and the eager laughter rippled over without interrupting the flow of the reader's fine voice. Mrs. James Murray had some exquisite lacework growing underneath her fingers, but Dell and Millicent were con-

cocting actual baby gowns, dainty enough for a dream.
Aunt Neale knit baby stockings of the finest, softest
wool. Reese Drayton sat on the step, leaning against
the square column, almost hidden by vines.

He had been reading from Miss Mulock's poems.
They had held their breath over "A Dream of the
Resurrection." It seemed to Dell she had never known
its sacredness before. Then there was a long pause.
He turned several leaves, and, without reading the title,
began "A Man's Wooing."

Millicent was out of range. Even if she had not been
he could not have raised his eyes. They were all to return the ensuing week. He had come up with Dr.
Carew, who was off somewhere with James Murray.
Millicent had spent a delightful fortnight. And during
these two days hardly a friendly advance had been made.
Was he waiting for some sign?

She listened to the man's story. It was one of her
favorite poems. In a way she knew it was being read to
her. Did the voice fall to a softened, entreating in-
tonation?

> "Come! if you come not I can wait,
>   My faith, like life, is long;
>   My will—not little; my hope much;
>   The patient are the strong."

The slim, white fingers trembled like a fluttering bird
among the laces she was holding and had forgotten to
sew. She listened to the next verse of manly persuasion and promise. Then—

> "And so before you it lies bare,—
>   Take it or let it be.
>   It is an honest heart, and yours
>   To all eternity."

The voice died away, leaving the sound of an exultant ring on the soft air. Drayton closed the book and dropped it beside him.

"What a brave lover!" said Aunt Neale. "Miss Mulock goes to one's heart, the meaning is so direct. She is of the older, clearer school, and suits the old-fashioned people. I am not fond of puzzling over meanings."

"You would not enjoy a Browning Club, then," said young Mrs. Murray with a smile. "Lawrence thought it the thing last winter, and insisted on his wife's joining one. I went with her several times. When a meaning is obscure and impresses a dozen people differently they cannot all be right."

"There is so much that is sorrowful in modern poetry," remarked Miss Carew. "You see, now, I do not have much to take up my time"—and the half smile brought a pink flush to her cheek—"so I have come back to my girlish love for poetry. And we have so much of it now in every paper and magazine."

The two men were winding down the wooded path. Drayton rose and went to meet them. The way was all shady now, and he strolled on without his hat. From the end of the porch Millicent watched the compact figure, that still bore itself with a youthful grace. For the fortnight she had managed to put him out of her mind. He had been up for one brief stay. Lyndell mentioned the fact that he had purchased a house and was having some alterations made.

"Then he is not going back to California?" Millicent commented.

"No. He has begun to enjoy New York very thoroughly. And it has come to be quite a fashion for a bachelor to have a home of his own," laughed Dell.

" He has so many valuable pictures and curiosities. His home will be really enchanting. I am quite longing to see it. He has made some delightful friends as well."

" But his interests at the West——"

" They will all go on. It is really an excellent thing for Gifford to have the responsibility."

Then they talked a little about Gifford's engagement.

" I am most thankful," declared Millicent. " It would have been a good thing if Gifford had fallen in love some years ago. There were plenty of nice girls around when I was at Alice's. People's love affairs are often a surprise, and you are sometimes astonished at the kind of men and women you see attracted toward one another."

" And the men and women you see staying single who would suit each other so admirably!" exclaimed Dell regretfully.

Millicent colored.

She could see that Mr. Drayton's second visit was a surprise to them all. Had it a purpose?

And now the last things were beginning. Dell and Millicent gathered some rare wild flowers and pressed them. There were cool evenings, and the thinnest of summer clothes could be packed. These two days Millicent had kept very busy ; but Reese Drayton really evinced no desire to put himself in the vanguard for any special privileges.

The masculine element did not come into the house until summoned to supper. The babies had their bath and their bread and milk, and Freda had taken them upstairs, where Aunt Neale would go presently to croon over them. Grandpapa sent word that he could not exist much longer without his Baby Millicent.

Dell and her cousin went next door to talk about the return. What a summer it had been ! At first Dell had almost felt jealous to see her dear Mamma Murray loving James's wife so well, rather, she thought, to the exclusion of Tessy ; but she soon found the motherly heart had not lost any of its blessed capacity.

Leonard was to come up on Saturday, and Tessy was all dainty eagerness. Aunt Julia had managed things beautifully, and had her two younger boys with her. But the wife's fond heart was yearning for her own household joys.

Millicent sat alone while they were upstairs. Mamma Murray was overlooking the somewhat prim and slow New England maid, who always rubbed the cups and saucers until they shone, and did her other work according to that pattern.

The men were arguing some sociological question on the other piazza. Drayton laughed now and then in his light fashion, and she could hear the half satirical modulations of his voice. How much in earnest could he be ? Yet he was Bertram Carew's fast friend ; and the old doctor had said he coveted him for another son. Did she do him justice? No, she had never been jealous of Fanny, but between the two thoughts, whether Fanny had not really loved him and why he had asked her without any love on his part, her mind was quite tossed to and fro.

He knew she was here, and yet he did not come. And presently the men strolled away to smoke in the clear, broad starlight.

She sat alone on the porch the next morning considering a ramble. Bertram had taken all the larger children for a drive. The mothers and grandmothers all seemed busy. Then there was an enticing new novel, the reviews of which had roused her curiosity. Could she not combine both pleasures, stroll over to the woods, and then sit in the shade and read ?

She rose suddenly as the sound of Drayton's voice came through one of the rooms, and, following her first impulse, walked rather hurriedly up the woodland path. Ah, how sweet the morning air was, with all the dew not yet distilled ! A few moments later there was a stride behind her, and every pulse started with a vague desire of flight, yet if anything she slackened her pace.

" Millicent," there was the little stress of haste in his breath as he stood beside her, " I told you my story yesterday. You have known it before. Is it still to be merely friendship ? Is that the only crown of the future ?"

She stood quite still then, though her face was turned away. Every pulse throbbed.

" The years go on so fast, and happiness is too sweet a thing to lay aside for a future that may never come. Can you not love me now and take my love, that I think began when I first saw you, when you came to be your cousin's ministering angel in her illness ?"

He watched the pink flush go down her neck until it lost itself in some waves of soft lace.

" The instant I knew I loved I wondered if I had a right to cherish the tender, delicate flower that sprang up in my rather arid soil. You and your cousin have such fine consciences, that a man must judge himself by them rather than by any preconceived notion of his own. Your cousins talked so much about you that I seemed to know you better—much better than you could know me."

Even then she remembered Bertram Carew had been deeply interested in him.

"I had been idling away the winter, pleasing myself without considering the consequences to any one. I was very much attracted to Mrs. Carew ; your sister made me useful in various ways, as a man should be who has nothing especial to employ himself about."

"Yes," in a quiet, dignified manner, listening but not looking.

"And then, in the summer when I met her with the Amory party, I wondered if I had said or done more than an honorable man should. I asked her to marry me." His tone was strong and frank.

"Without love ?"

Did her exquisite voice condemn him ?

"You have a right to know. Without love, but with a man's honor, that he desired to keep unblemished. I could not say that I loved her above all women, but I should have endeavored to make her happy in her own way. If I had the woman I loved I might sometimes ask her to make me happy in *my* way. A man's love has strands of selfishness in it. I wanted you to know this, that there might never be any misunderstanding. Then you came out to the Osbornes', and I learned the sweetness of loving a noble woman. At first I would not have dared to ask you to take my frivolous life and make it worthy of your acceptance. I have been trying to bring it up to a nobler plane. I shall never make it wholly worthy ; but I have ventured to proffer it. Can we not both join to shape it to some better purpose than the mere daily living that perishes and leaves no fruit behind ?"

"Oh," she cried, "you hold me too high. Listen ; I have loved once ; I have been very happy. I have my child——"

"Yes, I can never grudge the love of your youth, for

I have no youthful love to give in return. But it is a
man's loyal regard, that many experiences may have
refined to a more distinct demand and appreciation.
And I have tried to win the child. You will find me a
powerful rival, Millicent——"

He turned her suddenly, and took her face in a soft
clasp, so that she could not escape his eyes. " I think
you have been struggling against some feeling in my
favor. I hardly dare call it love——"

A transport of emotion swept imperiously through
her soul.

" You may call it love," she said just above her
breath, closing her eyes to escape the intensity of his
gaze. Could she be less than truthful?

He kissed the tremulous lips, the hot, flushed check,
and then he let the sweet face hide itself on his shoulder.
Her avowal filled him with rapture.

" There were some other questions of conscience," she
began after a long silence, when he had held her heart so
close that it had beat in unison with his. "After having
had one dream of happiness, I was not quite sure that I
had the right to another, especially if I had defrauded
some other human soul."

" Millicent," he exclaimed suddenly, " Fanny never
could have loved me any more than I could have loved
her. Our desires are as wide as the poles. And having
had years of desultory life, some of it spent in the whirl
of fashion, I was really tired of it. I want a home, domesticity. Not that I shall desire to seclude you, my
gifted darling. You have really been hidden away.
You must fill a larger place. I am not sure but I should
tire of a life of incessant sweetness. No human being
ought so to waste the strength of his soul. Every bloom

perfects some kind of fruit or seed. Shall it not be like
that divine poem,

> " ' We two together dare to look
> Upon the years to come,'

and make them bear a rich fruitage? I am glad I have
so much to give you and the child."

"And I wondered whether I ought to go away. My
parents are both growing old."

"But when they were gone—and the last journey
comes to all of us—could you endure growing old alone
there?"

"Oh, not alone!" She shivered a little. "I would
have Honora."

"Would you be willing to have her relinquish the
sweetness of youth and love?"

"Oh, no, no!" She could not defraud her child of a
blessed future.

"Think of all these years your parents have had you.
I do not believe your father will refuse me. If he does,
I shall sit at his gate and wait until he relents. He is
too generous and far-sighted to restrict any sweet soul
that has already given him so much devotion."

She felt it was true. He had grown used to sons and
daughters marrying. And was not the making of new
homes one of the duties of a God-given existence, where
even the one talent was to be put out at usury?

"My darling," he began presently, "I want you to
absolve me from absolute wrong in this matter of Fanny;
for we never even played at love. I liked her dash and
spirit, and her freedom from sentimentality, and I was
one of the throng to her, a little more her cavalier
while she was at the Carews, because I, too, was a friend

of the house. Just then I had no thought of marrying.
I had gone by the period of ardent desire, when pursuit
is fascinating."

" But if she had—loved you——"

Millicent's voice was low and faltering, and the secret
dismay at her own suggestion quivered over her face.

" Then, as I said, I should have accepted my fate with
a sense of having been honorable. I could not fight with
a woman. I could not even command her. Yet we
know there are a great many people in the world better
for a little wholesome restraint."

Fanny's own way had not always pleased herself, Millicent remembered. And yet she had striven for it from
childhood up.

A tender, comprehensive smile illumined Drayton's
face. She liked the subtle strength.

" Perhaps you have not remarked of your own experience how few marriages there are in which both sides
exercise a true election. There are so many motives for
marrying, even when the words are not spoken in the
glamour of some entrancing moment. There are men
longing for homes, willing to forego the high and rare
moments of bliss, and content themselves with something less, because, after all, life is a sort of every-day
affair, and comfort is a great thing to a man who must
spend his days in toiling for the means of existence.
And there are women who have no desire for aught beyond society's approval."

She recalled Aunt Edith and Ethel in her own circle.
Yet Fanny was different from both of these women.

" I am not a pessimist about marriages either," and
he turned an appreciative glance on her that flushed her
face with a delicious color. " I think I had grown—

well, perhaps, not quite faithless, but doubtful when I met the Osbornes and Colonel Ashton. Their family life was enough to convert the bitterest heretic : and I was not bitter at all,'' laughing, with a caressing sound in his voice. '' But I have a half suspicion that if Miss Sherburne had been fancy free that fateful summer I should have looked no farther. So you really had a rival. It would not have been a marriage of the highest type, either. I should have smothered her convictions and enthusiasms—she was so young—and her husband would have had a great influence over her.''

'' I can't imagine her being the wife of any man except Bertram Carew. And not to have had her would have broken the elder doctor's heart.''

'' And Lepage had one of those unreasoning, boyish fancies for her. I was afraid she would throw herself away heroically.''

'' Oh, you do not know what she did for him once. It was cousinly friendship, not love.''

'' Yes, I know all. There are a good many weak people in the world, not vicious in the beginning, but an easy prey to the viciousness of others. There are men who, once converted from the error of their ways, go straight on all their lives. The others need a missionary at their right hand continually. I never had any patience with them until—well, I have learned that of the Carews, with many another good lesson. I do not know as there is much to choose between the man who throws himself away and the man who stands by and raises no finger to prevent the sin or sacrifice. We do not appreciate the sacredness of life since we have come to consider it a mere scientific incident in an orderly world.''

" But science alone will not save men and women, nor rescue them from perishing. And if it was always the fittest, the best who survived, we might see some wisdom in it. Oh, I am glad you do not believe it all a blind chance !" and Millicent's face was full of grateful interest.

" We simply cannot penetrate all the mysteries. As little can we explain the mysteries of our lives, our own loves," smiling, " or why two natures should meet and kindle a sacred flame, the result perhaps of some long-ago incident, when they did not know of each other's existence. Think how long it is since I first met you. My darling, will you believe I have been trying to shape my life to nobler uses before I felt it was worth offering to you ?"

The answer was in her eyes. He clasped her to his heart in a long, rapturous embrace.

" But you see," he began some moments afterward, " I have not much time to waste. ' The years run fast,' " quoting from the poem of yesterday. " If I have not considered matrimony a paramount duty before, you will find me impatient to begin a new life. Millicent, will you consider this subject ? If you accept me as a lover, be merciful, and do not put me on a long probation. You will find many faults to train away afterward, so you had better begin soon, if you desire to enjoy your later years in the perfection of happiness."

" Oh," with a sudden, sighing breath, " I must think ! And there is Honora."

" Oh, I have trained your little daughter to habits of admiration and preference," laughingly. " I shall count on her as my strongest ally. I shall try to make up to her the loss she has never known," and his voice took on a softened inflection. " I am glad to have her, and doubly glad she is a daughter. I confess to a fondness for girls."

" If she had been a son I should surely have lost her. She would have been heir to a German estate, and I must have given her—him," with a smile and a catch in her breath, " to the care of an uncle, who would have brought up the heir according to his own methods. I should have had no voice in the matter."

She shivered now as she thought of her weeks of anxiety and her thankfulness to an overruling power.

" We shall soon have a pretty girl growing up, repeating the sweetness and the follies of youth."

" She has not the Sherburne birthright—beauty," said Millicent with a dissenting motion of the head.

" Then I can feast on the mother's birthright." Drayton's admiring glance called a flush to her cheek. " But she has piquancy and is quite German, with her abundant, light, flaxen hair, so different from the floods of gold one sees ; and her laughing, wondering eyes, that are blue one moment and an indescribable gray the next."

" You will spoil her. She has some unamiable qualities. I soon found she had rioted in indulgence last winter."

" But you deserved all the trouble. You should have come and helped in my efforts to train her. Were you staying away—on Fanny's account ?"

His tone sank to a whisper that thrilled her.

Millicent's face flushed scarlet.

" Let me confess," she cried with tremulous eagerness. " I did you an injustice. I thought you were not honest that day when you said there had been only two women who had ever moved you——"

" Oh, my dear, believe me when I say it here in the sight of God and you that I never uttered a word or made a sign to Lyndell Sherburne when I learned she was engaged——"

Had he any right to repeat the other experience ?

" It had nothing to do with Dell. It is weak and silly enough for a girl of sixteen."

He laughed with a great, rapturous relief.

" I won't ask how you became aware of my proposal to Fanny, since only two people knew it. Did it rankle in your tender, sincere heart ? Circumstances change the aspect of so many things for us and frequently blind our motives. I am not so sure now that I was right in clearing my conscience that way."

" I think—if you had loved her," excusingly.

" If we had loved each other," in a serious tone. " Love is the great apostle who harmonizes discordant elements. But when love is lacking ? Millicent, are you going to let this disturb you ?"

" Oh, no, no." She hid her face on his broad chest. She knew how evanescent Fanny's fancies had been.

" You take me with all my faults and shortcomings. You will find enough to employ many an anxious hour. I am a long way from perfection. Oh, what if you should regret——"

His clasp told her how much of his true soul had gone into this first real passion of his life. She had a glimpse of his heart, blown open like a flower into subtle bloom.

" All the delicious morning has gone," he said presently. " They will wonder what we have been about. Are we enough in love to betray ourselves ?"

# CHAPTER XIV.

MILLICENT VON LINDORM did not return until the ripe sweetness of October pervaded the air. Every week she had pleaded and insisted, but the fates had overruled. Her lover had written to her father, and there had come to her so tender a letter with his approval that it brought tears to her eyes. He spoke of the years of devotion she had given them, and how gladly they would have kept her always; how much they would miss her sweet, generous affection, and how hard it would be to relinquish Nora. But there was a new baby at Baltimore, and little Ned was far from being robust. He had been in school now for a year, but the doctor had insisted upon an immediate change for him, and he had come to Beaumanoir. So grandpapa would not be utterly alone.

And no matter at what cost to them, since no real sacrifice was needed, they felt that Millicent had won the right to a home and happiness of her very own. They both rejoiced in its satisfactory accomplishment, and would cordially proffer the welcome of a son to Reese Drayton.

Her mother's letter had in it a kind of pride—she could discern that in the gratulations. After all, was it not a matter of rejoicing for parents to see their children settled in happy homes? And was it not true that the

new life would be more comprehensive and satisfying ?
She would not shut out the exquisite knowledge from
her own soul.

There had been no little perplexity about Fanny's
affairs, which were as tortuous and uncertain as the current of a March wind. Dr. Underwood seemed to keep
the even tenor of his way and leave Fanny to come to
herself after any disagreement. " He evidently means
to marry her," wrote Mrs. Beaumanoir. " He will tire
out her small modicum of patience, while she makes no
impression on his."

Dell's delight had been as enthusiastic as that of a girl
of sixteen. The elder doctor had taken Millicent in his
fatherly arms and kissed her fair brow with a fervent
tenderness. She had always been a great favorite.

" We shall get hold of you all by degrees," and there
was a suspicious huskiness in his voice. " Heaven knows
how glad we shall be to have you. It will be another
son and daughter for my old age. Your father is well
supplied, and he will not grudge me the delight."

" O Dr. Carew, he could hardly grudge you anything !" she returned with deep feeling.

Bertram was overflowing with satisfaction. " It places
Milly in just the sphere she is so admirably calculated to
fill," he declared. " She can have one of the charming
homes, a restful inn for a wayfarer, where the weary
and dispirited can be ministered unto and encouraged to
take the next step, even if a great effort is required. I
do think we need to have the way made attractive and
enticing. So many souls feel crowded out of better,
finer things if they have not the splendid guest garment
and the golden key. They will bar out no worthy soul,
neither will they crowd their rooms for mere show, but

gather the best. They will keep an altar sacred to wedded love, where the holy fire will never even burn dimly.''

If Lyndell's broad, generous nature could have been made jealous it would have been stirred by this enthusiastic approval and the promise of a splendid future she could see almost fulfilled. True, she could surround herself with not only intellectual people, but her husband's position and her own intelligence were of enough importance to gather the cream of fashionable circles if she so willed. Her income would allow her many indulgences if she desired, but she had some plans for the future and her children.

Mr. Drayton's house had been put in complete and artistic order long before. Only part of it had been furnished, however—a reception-room, dining-room, and some chambers on two of the floors above. If there came a mistress, her taste must evolve the rest ; if not, it might be the work of years ; perhaps some places would be left sacred to solitude.

Dell and Bertram had been the first guests in the bachelor quarters, bidden to a dinner and an inspection of treasures new and old. '' Oh,'' she said, clasping her husband's arm tightly—it was a pleasant evening and they were walking home for the delight of each other's company—'' suppose Mr. Drayton's dream should come to nothing ! Millicent may have dozens of fine, insurmountable scruples. And to live there alone with all that space, and ease, and luxury while hundreds are starving— But I need only to look at myself. I am not spending my income. Oh, what is right? how much do we owe others ?''

'' My darling, are you going to worry over this point

all your life? You have learned by this time that it would be the wildest of folly to divide your goods with the average poor, who in a month's time would be in the same need. Until every one is intelligent, trained in good judgment and possesses a clear comprehension of his or her real necessities, it will hardly do to start out with the idea. And the apostles distributed as they had need. I think Drayton has done a good deal of this. And it is a wise use of wealth that is going to benefit the world. We want some apostles to the rich, to show them the true value of money."

"At least, I am glad this has come to Millicent. And sometimes I feel amused, remembering my first introduction to Mr. Drayton. I never thought of his being such a very rich man."

Lyndell laughed with a gay, silvery ripple.

"I have come to give thanks that there are rich men—men trained to the fine arts of life, as one may say. I cannot quite approve of one's best years being spent in a feverish pursuit of wealth, with no enjoyment; and the sinful havoc their untrained children make afterward. But the world can have no advancement without money; and when I talk of simplicity, I, for one, do not mean degenerating into barbarisms. Indeed, I think I have quite a luxurious side to my nature. When I get old and rich I shall no doubt surprise even you. If no one should come to enjoy the House Beautiful I hope Drayton will still take pleasure in it."

Millicent had numerous engagements on hand, and invitations poured in upon her, though society had not resumed its sway. But many of the friends, made through her literary pursuits, were not dependent on times and season for their enjoyments.

"I sometimes think how much I really owe Bertram for this greatest delight of my life," Millicent said with emotion. "He not only inspired me with courage, but took the first steps himself. I should not have known how, and might have blundered."

"Is it the very greatest ?" asked Dell archly.

Millicent flushed like a girl.

"I am not certain but that other blessings have come through him. He sent for me when you were ill that spring, you remember," and she smiled. "Dell, you have brought us so much good fortune. What an ungracious lot we were !"

"*You* were not," with eager decision.

Reese Drayton found that Millicent had interests quite outside of his attentions. There were luncheons and receptions, and at several Dr. Carew was invited as her escort. She did not wish her engagement to be a subject of gossip so soon.

"Soon ?" her lover ejaculated. "How long do you suppose I am to wait after throwing away so many precious years ? You and Dell have not been to inspect your new abode. I may blunder in a dozen matters unless your highness states your desires and disapprovals. You cannot come to-morrow, nor Friday, it seems. Then Saturday ? I certainly ought to have one day."

"You have a great many parts of days and evenings," she returned laughingly. "I have hardly time to reply to the notes that come in. It is so long since I have been in the city. And there are some new arrangements under consideration—will not spring do ?" with blushing hesitation.

"Spring will not do, my darling, nor the beginning of the new year."

" O Reese, I cannot ! It will seem so sudden. No one at Sherburne knows a word ; and when I go home it will appear improbable that I should have consented at all."

" I am going with you for fear you will repent. I shall call a family council and appoint a wedding day. Millicent, dear, you shall have the ceremony all your own way. I would not care if there were a thousand looking on, I should see only you."

" But I want it a quiet family affair." Then her lovely eyes seemed to peer into another world and grow humid. " Oh," she cried, " is it right ? Can I always give you what your soul desires ?" and she buried her face on his shoulder.

" You can give me the kind of love I am capable of creating ; for the solemnity of love is that it is almost as solitary as death. Each one can take only his share. What has gone before, what will come afterward is as nothing. The two souls most concerned must go through their own experience. If you love me, that is all I can ask now. My whole life shall be devoted to feeding the sacred flame."

She was silent for a moment or two. Yes, it was not to be a love transferred, let her remember that. The sweet love of her youth lay in the grand, gloomy old churchyard across the ocean. It could never be forgotten. It need not be thrust aside. This was a new beginning.

" You are very generous to me," she said with a soft, indrawn breath.

" I love you," he made answer. " It is a wiser affection than a boy's impetuous passion. I think now it has been saved up for you through all the years."

She felt humbled at the thought of such devotion having been laid twice at her feet. Was there some woman starving for the very blessedness? But one could not give away the overflow.

They sent Nora to drive with Dr. Carew on Saturday morning. Bertram had gone to the hospital and had promised to drop in for luncheon. It seemed strange, indeed, to go to this new home, and her pulses beat with unwonted emotion.

Mr. Drayton summoned the servant—a youngish, well-trained colored man. The cook had charge of the other departments, but only these two lived in the house.

The hall was spacious, with its tiled floor and antique chimneypiece, and one high, stained-glass window. A reception-room and library adjoined, and back of the winding staircase a large dining-room. These had the easy, luxurious air of a man's furnishing. One's steps were buried in the soft rugs, and the tone of the library was fascinating—an ideal spot, Millicent felt at the first glance. The book-shelves along one side were just high enough to reach with ease. Above them vases and bric-à-brac, picked up from all quarters of the globe. At the end a cabinet of gems and minerals, necklaces, curiosities from various old cities gone to ruins centuries ago. Of his pictures not a few had been gifts. An antique desk and easy-chairs that might lull one to dreams, tables with portfolios of engravings that took one on journeys round the world.

Millicent thought of her own simple study, that was Nora's school-room as well. She had seen grander places, it was true, but this had the air of daily using, that charmed her. It might have been this way for years, so slight an aspect of newness pervaded it. It

could be thrown open to the other room or quite seclud-
ed, as one desired.

The drawing-room was on the floor above, and took
the whole width of the house. At the back a large
apartment and a smaller one, all of them awaiting the
advent of a woman's taste and touch ; but the next floor
had been furnished for sleeping chambers.

Millicent did feel somewhat startled at first. Would
Fanny grow envious at the thought of losing this golden
opportunity ? For a moment she regretted the aspect of
so much possible luxury for herself. She should not
desire to queen it in Ethel's fashion, yet it was harmoniously beautiful, and it appealed to her æsthetic
side.

" And now, if you will give me any orders, or if you
will make a choice while you are in the city, you and
Mrs. Carew——"

" Oh, no, let it wait." A curious hesitation pervaded Millicent. " Surely there need be no haste."

" As you like," he said acquiescently. Why, she was
as shy as if she was beginning her life anew. The delicacy touched him.

" I think you hardly need any suggestions," she said
presently. " I shall be quite content with your judgment."

They heard Dr. Carew's voice in the hall. He came
up the steps with boyish litheness.

" Oh," he began laughingly, " I thought I would be
asked to pass my opinion on rugs and hangings and
furniture of all sorts, and I find a great, empty room.
You idle people ! It was just in this condition last
May."

" Oh, no, it has been frescoed and polished. It might

be called a health parlor. You physicians are always inveighing against so much 'stuff,' as you disdainfully call it."

"People have twice too much. It wearies them."

"And there is the summons to luncheon. Let us go and see if there is twice too much of that. You view me with a physician's eye."

They went down to the dining-room again. The rear of the opposite house was covered with a climbing ivy, now in shades of golden crimson, with here and there great patches of soft, dark red and some purplish berries. It gave a delightful country suggestion.

"Yes," Drayton exclaimed, "it has been a great pleasure to me through the summer. I used to sit out on my own little porch and smoke, and read, and build air castles. You would not believe so much pure pleasure could be extracted from a small city yard. But when we want a greater expanse we can go over to the park."

Millicent's color kept changing, and her eyes drooped in a fashion that in some women would have been coquetry. She could not dismiss the thought that she should soon be here as mistress. She knew the tide was too strong for her to make headway against it.

Bertram longed to tease her—he was in a mood of half mischief. Matters had gone unusually well with him to-day, and there had been but few desperate cases. The prospect before him gave him unalloyed satisfaction. He had longed to keep Drayton in the city, and he knew a happy marriage would promote that end.

They discussed a few plans, but Millicent would make no suggestions. She would be satisfied with whatever was done.

They returned to the library, which Drayton declared was only fit for an evening room.

"It lights up finely. The pictures have been chosen mostly for that. Only a millionaire can have a city house with windows all round. I like my den at the top of the house for that."

Millicent glanced over the books. There were some rare editions ; there were choice bindings with an indescribable fragrance that she always associated with luxury.

"And then we prate about God's free blessings of light and fresh air," exclaimed Bertram with a touch of indignation. "When money can barely procure it, poverty gets but a scant allowance."

Millicent experienced a stricture of conscience. Was she to have all this when hundreds of others were going without? One could not send them all to the waste places. They did not always want to go. Oh, what a large question life really was ! But she remembered that Bertram had once instanced the good Samaritan who had not waited for plans or arguments, but taken up the sufferer in his path, and hesitated not to repay another for kindliness.

They had a merry little chat about irrelevant matters. No one had the courage to touch upon the future. Then Bertram looked at his watch and declared he had a lecture and could not waste any more time. Lyndell said they would walk over a few blocks with him.

They found Nora in a most impatient mood.

"Where have you been all this while ? Luncheon was over an hour ago. And I am homesick from being alone," she declared vehemently.

"But there was Aunt Neale——"

"She's nursing little Milly. She cares the most for her, and asked me to go downstairs. And Grandpa Doctor had to go to the office. I'm homesick for folks," with gay insistence, twining her arms so fervently about her mother that she could hardly step.

"You are spoiled, Honora. How would you like to go away to school? You ought to have some girl friends of your own age."

"I don't like big girls very much. I never know just what to say to them, they have such queer ideas. But all the little ones are lovely and cunning, and Uncle Bert, and Mr. Drayton, and both of the Mr. Murrays, and grandpa here, and at home——"

"What an inventory!" laughed her mother. "No little girl ought to get lonesome with these friends."

"But when they are all off somewhere!"

Lyndell ran up to the nursery. Master Bertie was taking his nap. Baby Milly was a little feverish and fretful, being in a troublesome period of teething. Nothing seemed to have any effect upon Bertie. He was strong and riotous, slept and ate, laughed, and could discover more ways of mischief than ten ordinary babies. At times Aunt Neale's moral suasion was completely lost upon him.

"He makes me think of myself, when I first went to Sherburne," Dell would say. "And if he gets beyond us we shall have to turn him over to Mother Murray. She never could write out a system for bringing up babies, but she could do the work admirably."

"I do not believe we will need to call in the neighbors," Aunt Neale replied with a touch of dignity. "He is simply a strong, active, healthy baby."

"And irrepressible," with a sweet-humored laugh.

But little Milly did not escape so easily. She had a more delicate organization, and childish ailments went harder with her, though she was a healthy child.

"The disappointing thing," said Dell, "will be that in two or three years they will have outgrown their twinhood. But it was so with Alice and Ethel."

"They were beautiful little children," remarked Aunt Neale. "Mrs. Lepage was justly proud of all of them."

Mr. Drayton was detained that evening, and Nora went to bed bewailing the fact that she had not seen him all day. It was nearly ten when he dropped in for a little chat. Bertram and Dell were upstairs.

"Do you remember Milly's betrothal party?" he asked suddenly. "What a beautiful event it was! Aunt Lepage had a way of managing such affairs that was admirable. I am glad this is going to be quiet and different. What sort of retrospection is in your eyes, Dell?" studying the soft brown gleam.

"I was thinking—several of the young men seemed to feel disappointed that you were not in Mr. von Lindorm's place."

"I?" The color deepened in his cheek. "That couldn't have been," laughingly. "You see, I was being saved up for you. All that early youth was delightful. Millicent was a queen, and we were her loyal knights and true. Every boy all about adored her; but I do not know of one I should have wanted her to marry. As for me, I was studying away and had no time for sweethearts. And we would not have stood the ghost of a chance with Mr. Beaumanoir. You see, she was the first to grow up, and it seemed to be such a rare, sweet thing to have a beautiful girl who could be friends with us all—some one we never quarrelled about."

" Oh, I wonder—if Emil had lived——"

" Don't wonder, nor anything," he said with tender gravity. " It had the perfectness of an idyl, in the sorrow, as well as the joy. I don't know as one would want to wish that it had never happened."

" But I feel so sorry at times for Emil," Dell exclaimed with a burst of emotion.

" My darling, we cannot doubt the compensations in that divine life. We simply accept God's decisions. We cannot see the end from the beginning. I leave a great many puzzles with the all-wise Father, since I cannot solve them. I feel assured that Millicent will be very happy in her new life. You and she have been Reese Drayton's spiritual salvation—sociological as well, if such an argument may be admitted. The world needs such men, who are not so over-strenuous that they weary their friends and take up all manner of injudicious theories, but still never lose sight of the higher aim. We must make goodness fair to look upon, not have it go shrouded in a monk's cowl."

Millicent insisted upon going home. She felt somewhat bewildered by the responsibilities of her new station. Not that they would be ultra-fashionable people, but there were duties they could not well evade. She wanted to be quiet and think it all over.

There did not seem much prospect of solitary reflection. Mr. Drayton insisted upon accompanying her and arranging for a speedy marriage. Nora was wild with delight. No one had suggested the impending change to her until then. Millicent had once mentioned the school project.

" Oh," Drayton had returned with a glance of piquant amusement, " I am not going to spare my little

girl this winter. I find her an entertaining scholar.
And I cannot afford to give her the impression that my
first exercise of authority will be to separate her not only
from her mother, but all the joys of her present life. I
even desire her affection."

Millicent had no answer. She had not taken in that
aspect.

" She will soon be unmanageable."

" Human nature stands a good deal of spoiling when
the foundations are pure and trustworthy," he returned.

How long she had been away! Everything had a
strange appearance. Ardmore seemed listless and sleepy,
with the peculiar aspect of an unimproved town. But
the lovely old drive, with its wide-branching spruces and
hemlocks in their deeper autumnal green, the crimson
maples and silvery poplar and birches nodded a welcome
that quivered in the soft sunshine, as if pervaded by emotion.

Leonard and Tessy had come over to greet her. Violet was expected down in a day or two ; she had some
guests staying with her. And there was shy little Ned
Beaumanoir, with his formal ways and precise speech,
who kept close to grandmamma and was amazed at
Nora's enthusiastic demonstrations.

Everybody was well. Aunt Aurelia dropped down a
little now and then, but had sent oceans of love, and
was longing to see Milly and Nora.

" I shall have so much to tell her," declared Nora,
" that I want her strong and well, so that her head won't
ache."

Fanny was bright and piquant, and had greeted Mr.
Drayton without a tint of embarrassment. Millicent
thought she had grown prettier ; her eyes had a softened

light in spite of their merriment, and her complexion
was fine and clear.

The men had their chairs brought out on the lawn
after supper, and were joined by Dr. Underwood. Nora
charmed Ned away from grandmamma by a glowing description of Central Park and the animals, the museums,
and Auntie Dell, and the twins, and Grandpa Carew,
who was the sweetest and funniest and dearest grandpa
in the whole world.

" I think he can't be any better than mine," Ned returned with some pride.

" But Grandpa Beaumanoir belongs to me, too," said
Nora.

" Oh, no, he doesn't," was the grave rejoinder.
" You are too big. And your name isn't Beaumanoir.
And if you have a grandpa in New York, how can you
have so many ?"

While the children were chattering Tessy was detailing bits of news. There was a new baby at the Osborne
ranch.

" Where is Ethel ? Does any one hear ?"

" She has had a grand time in Japan, and went with
an English party to Honolulu. Mr. Longworth has
gone to California on some business, and will remain
until she reaches San Francisco. Leonard feels quite
anxious about him."

" Why ?" asked Millicent.

" You remember he had a rather serious attack in the
early summer. The doctor ordered him North to Rich-
field Springs. He was somewhat improved, but not well.
Leonard said he had changed greatly. He was so strong
and robust, you know. He has grown much thinner,
and is curiously pale. The doctor advised him to take a

year's rest. He has been putting a good deal of his business in Len's hands. And he has made a new will."

Tessy's voice dropped with the kind of awe one often uses in such cases.

" Every man ought to make a will," said Millicent. " Papa's was made long ago. It doesn't shorten life any. And I have made a will," with a bright, soft laugh.

" Oh, he had one, but it needed altering. I think Leonard was not quite satisfied with the new one. Oh, I can't bear to think of any one dying !"

" Is it as bad as that ?"

" They hope a good deal from the trip. And he may go on to Honolulu. I can't help thinking what if Ethel should never see him again ! Oh, I could not stay away from Leonard so long !'"

Julius drove up the avenue with the carriage, and the husband and wife so dear to each other went home. The children were in bed. After the good-nights Fanny followed Millicent to her room. The elder stood a little abashed. All the circumstances of this engagement had seemed in a manner contradictory.

Fanny placed both hands on Millicent's shoulders and looked steadily into her eyes. There was new tenderness in the lines about her mouth and more real fervor in her glance.

" It has come about all right, Milly, only I do hope you are going to let yourself love him."

" I love him," the elder answered with downcast eyes.

" Well, tell him so occasionally. Men can take an enormous amount of sweetening in their daily lives. And you are going to be happy. Milly, I am thankful nothing I ever did or said made any difference, for I know we shouldn't have loved each other a bit more than Ethel and Mr. Longworth. And I am not like Ethel, even if I am uneven tempered and frivolous."

"And you——" in a questioning tone.

"We have quarrelled ourselves in love. We have brought out our worst points, so we can never accuse each other of deception. We had some dreadful times, and for a fortnight we did not see each other ; then we passed by as proud as the priest and the Levite. He said he would never again ask me to marry him."

"O Fanny !" Millicent's tone was upbraiding.

"And I found that I did care for him ; that I liked him better than any one I had ever tried to love. I began to feel wretched. And then we met—Miss Armitage was quite ill and I was doing an errand of mercy for her. He was as stiff as you please."

"But what happened ?" in a breathless tone.

"Oh, then I asked him to marry me. I didn't want him to prove recreant to his vow ; and I was a little afraid he wouldn't anyhow. And he gave such a sweet, fascinating laugh, and picked me up and put me in his old buggy. We have been the dearest of the dear ever since. We are to be married at Christmas. O Milly, will you kindly betake yourself to the magical land of matrimony before that ? I want all the honor to my-self."

Would Fanny ever look seriously at anything ?

"Good-night. Dream on a date ; and if you can't decide I shall help Mr. Drayton. I hope he is an impatient lover. He has waited long enough."

# CHAPTER XV

MR. DRAYTON was glad of Fanny's impetuous assistance. Before he went away, early in the next week, the time had been shortened to a month. They would spend a few days in Washington and go directly home. The marriage would be at Beaumanoir at noon, with only the immediate family. She could not have gone to church. Mr. Drayton was glad to assent to this quiet arrangement. It was with no feeling of jealousy that he understood Millicent's half nervous state. He would have been shocked if she could have forgotten all the past.

Nora was a little puzzled at first, then wild with delight.

"And will Mr. Drayton's house be your very own? Can I take my books, and dolls, and my desk, and everything?" she inquired eagerly.

"I should take the dolls over to Miss Armitage for the Christmas tree. You are too old to play with them."

"But I only play with them when the children come. I guess I'll give Queenie to Princess, she loves her so. No, I really do not care about them. Do you suppose Princess could come up and see me just as she does here?"

"Oh, yes. You must be a good, obedient little

daughter, for you will have such a generous—friend."
She could not give him the new name at once.

"He is to be my papa. He told me so. It will be just the same as Uncle Len and Princie. And I want him to love me as much as Uncle Bert does."

"He does love you already."

Millicent sighed. She had once talked a good deal about her own father to the child, but the whole story was too sad. She wondered how she had ever lived through it.

"Will I have a pretty room like Auntie Dell's ?"

"Yes."

"And will papa keep a carriage like grandpa and Uncle Bertram ?"

"I am not sure. But there are cars to ride everywhere, you know."

"And such beautiful skating in the Park. O mamma, he used to take me nearly every day last winter ! It was splendid ! We'll teach Princess to skate. And the opera, mamma ! It was enough to make you cry when the lovely white swan sailed away. Aunt Neale did cry. And the music was just enchanting. I mean to ask Mr. Drayton if he will not take us again."

"You must not wish for too many things."

Nora was silent a few moments.

"Mamma, is he not a great deal richer than you are ?" in a tone of consideration.

"Yes, dear ; but it costs a great deal more to live in the city. There, run and pack up all your dolls and their clothes, and then we will go down and call on Miss Armitage."

She packed up some of Nora's outgrown clothes as well, and they started off.

Miss Armitage was delighted to see them.

" We shall all miss you so much," she declared ; " in a place like this there are so few real workers. O Mrs. von Lindorm, I am so glad—we all are—that your sister is to marry Dr. Underwood. He and Ralph are the best of friends. He is a really generous man, although he pretends not to have much faith in anything."

Miss Armitage spoke from her heart. She had been greatly startled at her brother's fancy for Fanny ; it was in every way so unsuitable. Millicent would make an admirable clergyman's wife, she had always thought.

" Yes, Fanny's engagement meets with general approbation," said Millicent smilingly.

Miss Armitage and her mother had accepted the other suspicion with a sense of regret that they did not even dare to confess to each other. Yet they had both been attracted by Fanny's brightness and a certain readiness to assist, a quickness to plan, but the real depth and earnestness of purpose was certainly not apparent. They were glad now they had not been tempted to remonstrate. Dr. Underwood was amused with her spirited frankness and her tempers, and in trying to snatch his friend from danger he had become interested himself. When he found he could really afford to marry he was not long in making up his mind. A sweet, sentimental woman was his abhorrence. He was fond of the spice of life.

The dolls came in most welcome. There was a great box full of them, of all sizes, and several rag babies, made by the old mammys. Queenie was the beautiful French doll Aunt Violet had brought home to Nora.

Tessy was delighted with Millicent's prospects, and Leonard gave her the tenderest approval. Aunt Aurelia could not withhold her loving wishes from her favorite, yet she did hate to lose her, Millicent seemed such a link with the outer world. She was proud of her successes and her daughterly devotion, but with the inertia of age she deprecated the change.

Millicent felt more than ever grateful to Tessy for her tenderness and exhaustless sympathy, her happy content in the present. Who could have filled the place with such wisdom? Not Lyndell, with her ambitions and desires reaching out for full satisfaction in the present. Could she have done it herself? It was the divinely touched temperament satisfied with the manna for to-day, sure of the double portion for the Sabbath.

There were so many things she was counting on for the future of husband and children. Princess had a lovely, bird-like voice, and every day she found time to develop it a little, to teach her some pretty thing to surprise papa. Edward was reading quite well, and yet no one could remember that any especial persuasion had been used. They were merry, naughty sometimes, yet always ready to please mamma.

She never fretted at the narrowness of the pasture, but found the sweetest clover blooms and the tallest grasses. There was no dulness, no wearisome sameness to her, for every day was a new day, with its sunrise and blithesome shining. When the little ones were gathered in bed, and Cassy had come with the last tidings of Aunt Aurelia's comfort, she settled herself for an hour or two of reading.

"How do you ever find time for anything, with such a little flock?" the young wives and mothers asked. "Mrs. Beaumanoir looks just like a young girl," a neighbor would remark.

Leonard was proud of this youthfulness.

"Mamma didn't grow old," she would reply to his query. "And she really had to work harder. Along first there was not even a servant; and oh, when we had gone out of the little house it seemed so odd to her to give orders to some one else. I think she felt almost afraid of offending the servants," and Tessy would laugh. "But she is quite a grand lady now."

May Dennis, the young girl her mother had rescued from bitterest poverty, when her father had died and left three children younger than herself, was being trained in many serviceable ways that might presently fit her for some other station. She had looked forward to the occupation of a teacher, but with no real inspiration in her soul. When the factory was her only refuge, Mrs. Murray had found the weak and ailing mother and provided her with a country home, where she could have her youngest child, and the duties were not arduous. The two boys had been placed in training schools, and May, under Tessy's wise supervision, was growing into a sensible, useful womanhood, with qualifications that would presently fit her for a governess to young children. She sometimes read aloud when Tessy was sewing, and her adoration for the pretty mistress of Sherburne knew no bounds.

Nora's plans were a source of much amusement to them all. But oh, how quickly the weeks flew by! Millicent had ordered most of her trousseau in the city, and it was to be sent to her new home. Consequently there was no hurry or bustle. She had days at Sherburne House, hours of daughterly confidence with her mother, and long talks with her father. She was not going so far away this time, that might account for the cheerful acceptance of the coming separation. She was thankful now that she had not been such an utter necessity to them. And Fanny's courtship divided the attention. She accepted Dr. Underwood's delightful cordiality, and found much interest and amusement in the lovers. The doctor had begun building his house, though it would not be ready for occupancy before spring. Fanny was adopting housewifely ways that sat oddly upon her. In these different interests the time flew rapidly, and before she was really ready her wedding morning dawned auspiciously.

Violet declared it altogether too quiet. The children were full of delight. Nora, Princess, and Pearl were to be maids of honor and carry baskets of flowers. Even the babies were to be at Aunt Milly's wedding, and Mr. Beaumanoir felt proud of the flock of grandchildren. The house somehow seemed to get quite crowded with the few invitations sent out. It was beautifully ornamented with autumn leaves and vines and clustering flowers in rich, bright colors. All the cousins within call were glad to show their regard for their favorite.

Paul Amory held her for a moment in a clasp that was convulsive with tenderness.

"Heaven only knows, my dear Millicent, how delighted and grateful I am that God has filled your cup of happiness once more. I shall be much more content and joyful in the bliss that has come to me, knowing that the oil of joy has been poured over the heartache we have shared for so many years. No one else could quite understand the bitter pang. Perhaps I ought not recall it at this festive moment; but there have been many hours when my heart has been secretly heavy about you, and I have prayed that you might be comforted. You will take it as from the hand of God, and accept it with great gladness. Will you not?"

"I will, I do," Millicent said tremulously as she felt the more than brotherly kiss on her forehead.

The party entered the large room, Millicent on her father's arm, the bridal gown of pale lavender, with its soft laces and clustering stars of jasmine, her only ornament. Reese Drayton took her from his hand, and the solemn words were uttered that made her his wife; the benediction was pronounced over the kneeling couple, and for some seconds no one stirred.

Then Reese Drayton raised his wife and kissed the quivering lips. Her eyes had the mistiness of unshed tears; for his sake she would not let them come to the surface. Her father held her to his heart.

"My dear daughter," he said, "Heaven bless you even as you have blessed so many with the richness of your care and devotion. You will know her better as the years go on," and again he put her hand in Drayton's, "for she is the choice blossom of my flock, where all have been tenderly treasured in a father's heart. Give her the happiness she deserves, and I can say without hesitation that your reward will be tenfold."

Reese Drayton pressed the elder man's hand in heartfelt recognition and bowed his head with solemn reverence.

There was a stir and changing of groups, the bright young voices of children, congratulations, a sudden lightness, where laughter was not amiss, with which the morning's tense strain was broken. Again Millicent was sharing a sacred joy with her brothers and sisters as they received into their number the new member.

"Fanny, you ought to have made it a double wedding," said Cousin Eliza.

"As if I could not have a wedding by myself!" with a saucy lightness.

"Ask me or I shall forbid the banns," declared the doctor. "And as we shall be undertaking it for the first time, we do require the undivided attention. I shall make myself look as youthful as possible, even at the risk of having the audience think you have married the wrong man."

They all thronged about Millicent, who looked like some fair queen. The three young cousins, Cecil, Floyd, and Winthrop, were very enthusiastic. The children clung to her gown. Honora took her new papa's hand.

"I am your little girl, to have and to hold from this day forward," she said imperiously.

"And to be endowed with my worldly goods," he made answer.

"Oh, just the same as mamma?"

"Well—perhaps not *quite* the same. It will take more for her gowns."

"Do you mean to buy—everything?"

"Nora, you are too exacting," laughed Uncle Leonard; "you want the bill of particulars."

She clung to her new father's hand and smiled up in his face with radiant delight.

There was a simple wedding feast—breakfast it would have been called in fashionable circles. Some of the old servants were present who remembered the other wedding, brilliant with youth and joyful anticipations, and hallowed with a kind of Easter glory. How far and wide the group of cousins were scattered now!

The children running about added a touch of gayety and brightness. Little Ned Beaumanoir's mother said now and then, "Oh, how wild you have grown! Do be

a little gentleman.'' But she did feel that the soft pink
in his cheeks improved him, and his little chin was less
sharp. Neither had he lost his pretty manners, though
he was more eager and childlike.

" You see, he is so much with all the little cousins,''
said grandmamma in a tone of tender excuse.

" I like to see him hold his own with Len's children,''
Ned's father commented proudly.

" And what a host there are—four ! How can Tessy
half attend to them ? It has taken the most of my time
to look after Ned and train him and keep his clothes in
order. Children's fashions keep changing as well as those
of older folks. You would hardly believe how I have
given up society. And with another baby I know I
never shall go anywhere.''

Mrs. Edward sighed. She had been a conventionally
fashionable girl, she had made a punctilious wife, and
she considered herself a devoted mother. She hardly
felt it was right to come to Millicent's wedding. No
well-regulated baby ought to have any decided change
before it was a year old. The air was different ; there
were draughts and strange faces and strange noises and
jolting about which must be bad for a child's nerves.
She was always horrified when she found Tessy had been
up to Washington for two or three days or a week.

Ned, however, had overruled her in this matter by
promising to return in the evening.

There were some toasts to Millicent and her husband,
and then the good wishes went on. Dr. Underwood was
as cordial as if he were already a son of the house, and
seemed to enjoy the pointed allusions to Fanny, who
was almost as much a heroine of the occasion.

Some time afterward, while the elder people were still

lingering about the table and talking in a reminiscent strain of other weddings, Lyndell caught Reese Drayton's hand and drew him out to the end of the hall.

"You are not going to take Nora with you?" she exclaimed with disapproving eagerness. "I—we——"

Drayton gave an embarrassed laugh. "I promised her. We are going home, you know."

"Millicent left it to you, and you had not the courage to say no."

"Oh, how could you guess so exactly?" in a tone of surprise. Then he flushed at betraying himself unawares.

"But you do not really want her?"

"I love the child; yes, I really do. I am glad she is Millicent's. Oh, my dear friend, my cousin now, I am glad we have come to a relation that cannot be misunderstood, that I may tell you how much I admire you, and what you have been to me in many ways—one greater than all in the influence you have exerted in helping me to make myself worthier of such a peerless woman as Millicent. I feel that I have accepted a more than ordinary trust. I shall divide the mother's interest, I shall absorb much of her love, and I want to be just where the child is concerned. She is a bright, fond, eager child with a sensitive soul. I want all her years with me to be happy years, that she will be glad to remember."

"And have you and Milly no right or claim to these first few days of wedded life?"

"O Dell!"—it seemed so sweet and natural to use her pretty, household name—"do not appeal to my selfishness."

"It is a rightful aspiration. There will never be a

time with this exquisite freshness of joy. It is for you two alone. I know how Millicent has felt for the last two months in her high-minded earnestness and her fervent wish not to take from Nora anything that is Nora's right. Through her indulgence the child has claimed more and more with the endearing thoughtlessness of childhood. Do you suppose, does any one think, Millicent will cease to be the tenderest of mothers in becoming your wife?"

All his soul seemed to shine in his eyes. "Oh, no, no!" with a depth of emotion that touched her keenly. "But—I promised. I should not like to break my word the first day of assumed fatherhood."

"Still, true and kind and generous as you will be, these few days would prove a greater delight without her."

Reese Drayton was silent.

"Dr. Underwood would have made short work of her request and been quite right about it," subjoined Dell with a smile he felt rather than saw. "I like him famously. Fanny cannot twist him around her finger. Well, will you absolve me from interfering unwisely between parent and child if I can convince the midget that mamma as a new wife has certain inalienable rights guaranteed to her by the Constitution?"

"Oh, my dear cousin, I must not put such a burden on you in this cowardly fashion!"

"You do not even proffer it to me. There, some one is calling you."

Dell vanished up the broad stairway as she heard the children's voices.

"I am to have a beautiful room furnished just to my liking. I can go out and choose everything." Honora made an impressive pause, as she stood in the centre of Millicent's room. Princess was hugging the great wax doll in her festive attire to her heart. Little Sherburne and Ned were listening wide-eyed, and Pearl patted the doll's arm. "And, Princess, he said I might give you my desk and have a handsome new one, but—you won't mind, will you?" with a beseeching smile—"mamma gave it to me for a birthday, and had my name put on a little silver plate just here," and she crossed the room to point it out. "I was ten years old, and I said I would rather not give it away. Then he said, 'We'll buy Princess something beautiful for Christmas.' He's just splendid. And now I have a father like all the rest of you, and we are going to live in his house, and you can all come to see me."

"Papa will buy me a desk," said Princess in her dainty, comforting voice, "and I'd rather have the Christmas present."

"Let's go and see the twins again," exclaimed Pearl; "Bertie does such lots of funny things."

They all started, Princess holding her doll tightly. Auntie Dell waylaid Nora and drew her back, then closed the door.

"Dear," she began, "I want to ask something of you —that you will stay all night and go home with us to-morrow."

She looked eagerly into the child's eyes as if she had quite set her heart upon it.

"O Auntie Dell, I'm going to Washington with mamma and my new papa! Of course I know he isn't my very own papa, but he loves me, and I have loved him—oh, a long, long while!"

"Yes, Nora, dear, I hope you will love him, and that

you will let him counsel you and listen to his advice
cheerfully. Love isn't all indulgence. And sometimes
when you love a person very much you are willing to do
a great deal for him or her—we must make it collective
and say them," laughingly.

Nora opened her blue eyes with the wondering expression that made them seem almost round.

"What do you want me to do, Auntie Dell ? What
can I do for them ? I don't think little folks can do
very much for the big ones."

"You can give them a very great pleasure by not
going to Washington with them. Then papa can devote
all his time to mamma, and she need not be thinking
what her little girl would like and wondering if she felt
a little neglected ; for, you see, now they have promised
to think about each other, to do ever so many pleasant
things for each other."

Nora gave several long, swelling inspirations and let
her eyes drop to the floor.

"But you see, Auntie Dell, they wouldn't have to mind
about me. I could read, or—or do something. And
we are going to papa's new house. Mamma says it is
almost as beautiful as Aunt Ethel's. O Auntie Dell, I
really couldn't !"

Her chest began to show the throbs of emotion, and
she winked her eyes as if tears were not far away.

"Listen, dear." Auntie Dell placed her arm around
the child and drew her unwillingly to her knee as she
seated herself. "If you go home with us you can have
a little visit with the babies and be there to receive them.
They are coming to us first. And then you can all go
together to the new home."

"But mamma wouldn't mind. I am the only little

girl she has. And she explained it all to me." Nora's voice fell to a serious impressiveness. "She doesn't love me any less because of—of papa. She said you couldn't love Bertie any less because of little Milly. And we are to be together, and my room will be right next to hers, and there won't be much more difference than here with grandpa ; for sometimes she goes to ride with him when they can't take me, and she reads to him, and—it will only be another home."

"She has sometimes stayed at home with you and given up pleasures because it was something you were not old enough to enjoy. She has done a great many sweet and lovely things for you, such as mothers are continually doing for little girls. And when the little girls are older they might give back a little. Do you not think so ? O Nora, love is doing as well as saying ' I love you.' "

"But it can't make any difference to mamma," replied the child with a gentle obstinacy.

"It will make a good deal of difference. She could have a lovely little holiday, and papa would be doing everything for her pleasure. Otherwise he will keep saying, ' Would Nora like this ? Would it not tire her to take this walk ? She would not feel interested in such a thing, so we will not do it.' They would give up their own pleasures for you."

"They need not." Her tone was a little hard, and Dell saw some tears bead the brown lashes, much darker than her hair.

"Well, then, dear, if you do not think you could give them such a sweet gift as a brief holiday I suppose they must give up to you."

Lyndell rose, though she still kept her arm around

Nora. There were two or three long sobs and the child buried her face in Dell's gown.

"My dear, you must not be unhappy about it if you can't give up."

"O Auntie Dell, I could, but I don't want to! She is my own dear mamma. And Mr. Drayton is so lovely I want to go."

"You are a little girl, and there will be many years for them to love you and make you happy. Mamma is much older, and there are not so many years for her. Some of those that are past have been full of sorrow. And if she could recall a bright week you had given her, when she had nothing to do but just accept all the delights and pleasures Mr. Drayton could find for her—and she will save them all up and tell them over to you. Well, which shall it be? They must go presently."

"O Auntie Dell, it breaks my heart to think they will be happier without me."

"Not happier, childie, but more comfortable, with no one's pleasure but their own to consult."

"And you will be sure to take me up to New York?" as if she was almost afraid to trust.

"To-morrow, dear. And on their return their little daughter will be there to give them a joyful welcome— their first greeting."

"I think—I will stay," she returned reluctantly, from persuasion, Lyndell saw, and not conviction. But she stooped and kissed her fondly, while the tears flowed afresh.

"There, my child, you must not make the sacrifice harder for yourself."

"O Auntie Dell, I am glad you know it is a sacrifice and a great disappointment!"

"Yes, I appreciate it. But, you know, he who gives cheerfully gives twice in value." Then she kissed her tenderly, bathed her face and brushed her hair. "Mamma is coming to change her gown. See if you can't find papa and tell him."

Lyndell thought it wise she should not see her mother at this crisis. She saw her started on the stairway, then she went to her cousin's room.

"I was coming to find you," exclaimed Millicent with a nervousness quite unlike her usual mood. "Will you assist me a little? I don't want Fanny's chatter. She is really in love, is she not? I have always liked Dr. Underwood. No, Susan," to the maid, "I shall not need you just yet. You can come presently and fold my gown. Everybody has been charming. I was so glad Aunt Aurelia could come."

"Yes; Mr. Drayton can never complain of his reception to the fourth generation," and Lyndell laughed with a soft brightness, a joy in itself. It inspirited her cousin.

"We shall be quite a party going up."

"I have persuaded one member to decline."

"One—who?" wonderingly.

"Nora. O Milly, how could you consider such a step for a moment?"

"We are really going home, you know. To have left her here——" Millicent paused and flushed.

"You knew I would take charge of her gladly."

"It was so hard to refuse her, Dell," and Milly put her arms around her cousin's neck. "When I think of the love and companionship she can never have—and for the last two months so many old recollections have swept through my soul, I have wondered what was wisest and best——"

"It is done now. O Milly, I want you to be very happy, and not cultivate a morbid conscience. The child must not come the first, or you will positively spoil Mr. Drayton's life."

"I sent him to her. I did not think he would assent so readily—I really did not. I was weak," and the new wife blushed with a sense of delinquency. "I hated to seem to push her out of our joy, when I was not quite certain that I had the right to be joyful, to take so much. There is more even than I imagined of love and prosperity."

"You have a right to the first sweet draught of happiness. It is too sacred to divide or fritter about on a child too young to understand. She will have an abundance. No fear but that you will both love her enough and indulge her ruinously. O Milly, isn't it queer that I should be absolutely scolding you?" and a soft light of amusement flooded Lyndell's face.

"A very tender scolding, my dear cousin; and you were altogether right. I hardly see how you persuaded her. She seems to consider Mr. Drayton the bound subject of her rather imperious will. She was spoiled last year, and I am sure you helped. She is outgrowing her little girlhood. It gave me a pang when I first realized that. If he had not been fond of her——"

The tears stood in Millicent's eyes.

"She is bright and attractive; but you must not allow her to demand the affection that will belong to another by the most sacred right."

Millicent had changed her gown, that now lay on the bed a shimmering wraith. Her gray cloth had a band

of fur at the edge of the skirt and around the jacket,
and a soft, wide collar that seemed to embrace her neck.
She looked charming and youthful.

There was a light tap at the door. Lyndell answered
the summons.

"Is Millicent getting ready?" Mr. Drayton asked.
" But, O Dell, how can I thank you——" and his eyes
gleamed with a grateful, delighted expression. " These
precious days—quite to ourselves."

" I never considered you lacking in courage before,"
and a sense of amusement lighted the smiling face.

" It was for *her* sake. If she wished it——"

" Nonsense ! it was Nora who wished it. You will
have to take a comprehensive glance at the real duties
of fatherhood. You have won the flower of the Sherburne cousins ; but I shall train Millicent Carew to be
the flower of the Sherburne children. So you must look
to your laurels. You may come in."

Millicent turned from the mirror, where she had been
adjusting the few last touches. Reese Drayton took her
in his arms and held her in a wordless embrace, so sacred
that Dell turned her eyes away. A new and exquisite
life opened before them, and her heart went out in silent
thanksgiving.

There was a pleasant stir afterward, and young Mrs.
Beaumanoir's fussiness kept it from any aspect of sadness.
There was always so much coming and going at Beaumanoir that now, when the wedding gown was no longer
a feature, it seemed like quite an ordinary party.

The Drayton carriage held only the two. Nora ran
away as soon as she had said her good-by in the hall, to
have her cry in mamma's deserted room. Mrs. Ned, with
her maid and her baby, her budgets and her husband,

were at last safely deposited. She could hardly resign herself to leaving little Edward behind, only the doctor's injunctions had been too strict to disobey. But he held tightly to his grandpa's hand lest he might be spirited away by some untoward fate.

The Amorys were to remain for a day or two, and Violet was to help Fanny plan, then she was to impress Dell into the shopping raid. Christmas was not so far off.

The Sherburne host went next, and the friends that had been bidden in neighborly fashion. Bertram had gone with the bridal party, but his father remained to escort the others. Dell took charge of Nora, who indulged in the bitterness of a separation that looked to her eternal. It was hard to comprehend that some one else must have the first right to her own dear mamma.

# CHAPTER XVI.

THE Carews took little Princess Beaumanoir home
with them. She was quite sure she should not be
homesick with Auntie Dell and Nora. And there was
Grandmamma Murray and the other cousins she had
grown fond of during the summer.

Nora was a source of secret amusement to Lyndell.
She had a child's sense of having made a sacrifice and
wanted to be considered heroic. Auntie Dell let her cry
for her mamma the first few nights, and comforted her
in a sweet, cheerful fashion, remembering how she had
been unwisely repressed about the Murrays. But there
were so many delights. Grandpa Doctor took them out
every day. The Park was so marvellous, and Nora began
to feel that she was really hostess to her little cousin.
The Museum of Natural History was an unfailing entertainment. Aunt Neale and the babies were such a delight. They were merry and sweet and naughty—at
least Bertie was a regular mischief.

Then Aunt Neale could remember when mamma was
a little girl and Grandpa Sherburne was alive. It seemed
very strange that Auntie Dell was another little girl,
living in London and knowing nothing about her
cousins. And Nora forgot to cry, she was so happy
and full of merriment. After the second day a note
came from mamma, followed by one every morning,

and she had to write in return, which was quite an important matter.

The wedding journey lengthened itself into a fortnight.

" I should like it to be a whole year going from place to place in this charming, leisurely fashion. Millicent, I shall grow young and foolish, and—jealous. How shall I ever share you with any one ? I have half a mind to take you to the ends of the earth," declared her husband.

The intensity of the love sometimes gave her a pang, but it was a blessed thing to be so dear to any one again.

" We can't be spared to go to the ends of the earth," in a soft, tremulous tone that unwittingly confessed her delight.

He liked to watch the lines that hovered about her face, relaxing it from her olden gravity. How beautiful she was ! He had not thought much about it at first, but now he was proud with a man's pride in his own possession.

" Yes, there is the poor little tot. But she has had you all these years—felt sure of you, and knew you would relinquish anything for her pleasure. And I have been certain only a few days," with a sweet sort of regret.

" Why not since in the summer ?"

" Because a hundred things might have happened. You have been very hard to win ;" and he glanced tenderly into the dark eyes so full of emotion.

" And yet I loved you," with a soft little sigh.
" Whether——"

" There shall be no more questions, Miss Tender Conscience. We have accepted the future together. We have nothing to do with the past. You don't uproot a tree when it is done fruiting for the season. It stands, and out of the leafless, desolate loneliness, when the branches sough and moan in the winter blasts and everything is bleak and brown, comes another season of bud and bloom and fruit. Is a human soul less in God's sight than a tree?"

There was plenty in her to bloom again.

He was very proud of her gifts as well as her beauty. Out on the Pacific coast he had heard her pathetic story from her cousin's lips. She was glad now some one had told it to him.

She, too, would have been glad of a long holiday. But the house must be put in order. She understood why he had left some rooms especially for her oversight. Fanny would soon be up. Oh, would this luxury give Fanny a longing, jealous feeling? She would be satisfied with much less, with no more real grandeur than she had been accustomed to all her life.

"It's queer," exclaimed Nora; "mamma says they will be home *some* day soon; but she doesn't say which day. And Mrs. Murray has asked us to luncheon. Of course we must go. It is Princess's own aunt. And Densie is so sweet."

"Yes," said Auntie Dell, with a little prick of conscience. *Her* letter said the travellers would be in by noon; but they were not to wait luncheon for them in case of delay.

"Mrs. Murray isn't quite as lovely as Aunt Tessy, but she is real delightful. And Densie is just the dearest girl! She is so glad I am coming to live in the city. She knows such a host of girls. And she goes to school only in the morning. I shall ask mamma if I cannot go to the same school. I have chosen her for one of my friends."

" A lovely friend she will make you," said Auntie Dell as she tied the sash ribbon and settled the shoulder bows.

" If mamma *should* come"—and Nora looked in the doorway, nodding the plumes of her pretty gray fur hat— " you will keep her, Auntie Dell, won't you ?"

" Oh, yes," replied Auntie Dell. Childhood was not inconsolable, and she was thankful it was so. Nora had ·been very happy.

But she had bidden Bertram to be sure and come home by one.

Ah, how lovely Millicent looked in her new wifehood ! Old Dr. Carew told her she was not a day over twenty if a woman was no older than she looked. There was such a restful aspect in every softened feature, such an acknowledgment of happiness in the limpid eyes, a fulness and content in the voice that it was a delight to hear.

" And my little girl——" with a quick breath.

" She is a big girl chaperoning her smaller cousin at a luncheon. She gave me strict orders to keep you if you should come. You did not say positively to her ;" and Lyndell gave an arch smile.

" She takes disappointments so hard that I did not want her to have one the first day."

And yet the mother's heart experienced a pang, a secret assurance as well, that the child would choose ways of pleasure outside the mother's life.

Certainly Reese Drayton was very happy and very much in evidence as a husband. What a pity if these delightful qualities had always gone to waste ! Yet his friends had not considered him a marrying man.

If Dr. Randolph Carew had entertained a few little fears about the marriage of his favorite, he laid them gladly aside now. A woman like Millicent ought to be the centre of a happy home. She could adorn a wider space than daughterhood in her father's house, and he gave thanks that this had come to her. There had been so many outside interests to his own life, and a sister devoted to him personally, a home in its fullest sense. Yet how he had counted on the marriage of his son! To see him the happy head of a family had been the most fervent hope of his life. There were other men quite as deserving, the doctor admitted in his secret soul.

"Shall we go over to the house?" asked Reese Drayton after luncheon.

"I promised to take Nora," answered Nora's mother, who could not be altogether the wife, as she had been the past ten days after she had really settled to the fact.

"We can wait a little. I will go down to the office with the doctor and be back at three."

"But you will not remain to-night," Dell said, more as assertion than question.

He smiled over at his wife. "I am impatient to take Millicent home to her own home," with a lingering inflection. And Dell remembered that she had not had a true home of her own, even at Lückenwalde.

"You may go with the doctor. Of course the children will be home then."

"But you have nothing really settled——" and Dell glanced from one to the other.

"Oh, yes, Katy Black is an excellent housekeeper. And I have written. She will have dinner for us. To-morrow we will have a great deal to do. Yes, we had better go presently."

The babies had their dinner at noon and were not too old for their daily nap. Miss Neale took hers at the same time. Then she was bright and fresh for the evening. And the two were left together for a conference.

Dell put her arms around her cousin.

"You are very, very happy," she said with an exultant ring of joy.

"So happy that I feel half conscience-smitten at times," looking up out of lovely, contented eyes. "And yet your hero is far from being perfect, Dell," with a satisfied smile that it should be so.

"None of us assured him perfection;" and Dell laughed with a saucy brightness. "If he were, half your life work would be done. You would forget him and turn all your attention to Nora. I understand better each day that taking your husband at the moment of marriage is only a little step in the journey. There is keeping him afterward in the high, comprehensive sense, and learning what wifely love means. I suppose it comes to all true women with years and experience. I do not think I have discovered any new secret. Your father and mother have learned it, Aunt Julia and Uncle Stanwood."

"I think mamma and papa are more truly lovers now than they were ten years ago. Then the children occupied them so much. Dell, we are all different. I suppose that is true living, to put something in to-day that was not there yesterday; to let experience as well as patience have her perfect work, and not keep trying to fit the incidents of to-day into the experience of last year, when events and duties were very different. Oh, I hope God will give me the grace of wisdom."

"He does not give it all at once. Perhaps free will

means that we are let to try our own way until we get it
fitted into His.''

'' Dell, you seem to have learned so much.''

Millicent glanced up wistfully.

'' You have been living a good deal in an ideal world.''

'' Do you mean that writing tends to idealism ?''

'' In a certain sense no doubt.  So do many other
things.  In intellectual life you have to study and compare and give your knowledge a reasonable air at least ;
but you can live in an ideal world without ever writing
a page, without comparing one dream with plain, every-
day facts.''

'' Do you think I have been unreasonable ?''

'' Oh, no.  But sometimes needlessly self-sacrificing.
Anything that tends to exalt a person or even a project
above its just due is useless and often wrong, and leads
to harm.''

Millicent smiled with a sweet, tender gravity.

'' I think I understand.  I have wanted, nay, I did
feel at times that I was absolutely necessary at home.
I supposed Fanny would marry some time.  But I was
given up with the tenderest consideration.  I think
mamma felt that I had not had a true, full life, and she
was glad to have the future promise me happiness again.
And I meant to live for Nora.  I am afraid I have made
her a little selfish in the manner of her demanding.  Did
you have any trouble ?''

'' Oh, no.  She was brimful of enjoyment, and most
consequential when she had to answer your letter every
day.  She missed you very much at early evening, and
begged me dozens of times to assure her that you would
love her just the same.  I could trust you for that,''
smilingly.  '' She was not troubled during her last win-

ter's visit, though she often wished then that she could
see mamma."

" Oh, my precious, darling girl !"

" I am afraid you will both join to spoil her.  O
Milly ! do not lay up trouble for yourself."

The nurse came in for the babies to say good-by to
mamma.  Freda still had them in charge.  But now
they walked or ran and had a joyous time generally in
the Park.  Bertie was growing very rapidly, a bright little fellow with brown hair and very deep blue eyes that
in moments of temper were black.  Milly was quite a
contrast, with soft, dark eyes and dainty, golden rings
of hair.

The clock struck three.

" Oh !" exclaimed Millicent, " I ought to send for
Nora.  I suppose she doesn't think.  That little Deusie
is so enchanting."

" I will send at once."

Mary soon returned.  Mr. Murray had taken all the
children out driving.  Mrs. Murray was sure they would
soon return.  And then Mr. Drayton walked in.

" Ought we to wait ?" he asked doubtfully.

" Oh, yes."  Millicent's voice was full of entreaty.

It was four when the truants appeared.  Nora sprang
to her mother's arms, quite oblivious of any other person.  She had talked a good deal to Princess about her
new papa, but just at the instant there was a half resent-
ful feeling.  He had kept mamma away for a whole fortnight.  And it was not until Mr. Drayton had taken
Princess on his knee and was asking her if she had been
homesick, and praising her, that Nora turned suddenly.

He held out his disengaged hand without putting down
Princess.  She hesitated half bashfully, half pridefully.

" My dear Nora !"

His voice was attractively sweet, and his eyes willed her hither. He drew her to him and kissed her, smiled into the rather grave face that looked askance at Princess.

" Are you not glad to see me ? We have been waiting and waiting, and would not go home without you, although it is getting late."

The autumn afternoon had grown cloudy, and it seemed quite near night.

Nora appeared to hesitate, then she flung her arms about his neck with a vehemence that crowded Princess quite to one side. The child made a motion to get down, but Mr. Drayton restrained her.

" I am glad you brought mamma home," in a certain decisive tone.

" Would you rather *I* had stayed away ?" There was a teasing laugh in his eyes. " But you couldn't have gone to the new home until I came. I have the key."

" Well, she could have stayed here with me. Couldn't she, Auntie Dell ?" almost defiantly.

" Yes," returned Auntie Dell, amused at the little show of jealousy. " And you can stay if you like."

" Oh, you will have Princess. And maybe I can come to-morrow. Is it very far ?"

" No ; you will soon learn the way," said her new papa, giving her an affectionate squeeze.

Millicent rose. Nora sprang to her side with a passionate grasp.

" Now? Are you going right away, mamma? I will put on my hat and coat again ;" and she clung to her as they went out of the room together.

" You must come and visit Nora," he said to Princess. "We shall be out all day to-morrow ; but you might come to dinner and remain all night."

"No, wait until the next day," said Lyndell. "You will both be busy and tired."

"And Miss Nora is to go choosing her own belongings, I believe."

"You will have your hands full." Dell glanced over at Mr. Drayton with eyes full of meaning.

"We have always been the best of friends."

"This is a new beginning."

He nodded to assure her that he understood.

She came back bright and eager and impatient to be off. Her good-bys were rather joyous.

"And you have not said a word to Auntie Dell for the pleasant time she has given you." Her mother glanced at her with soft reproach.

"O Auntie Dell ! it's been lovely. Will you say good-by to Grandpa Doctor and Uncle Bertram ? And Princess—maybe I will come to-morrow if mamma has time."

The children kissed each other. Princess glanced a little wistfully after her cousin.

"Did you have a nice time at Aunt Helen's ?" asked Dell when the guests had gone.

"Oh, it was delightful. Aunt Helen gave us the pretty tea-table by ourselves. And the next-door little girl came in. Her name was Florence ; and O Auntie Dell ! she's just beautiful, with eyes like stars. Nora poured the chocolate because Bessie was so small. We had such lovely grapes and figs and nuts afterward. And the dishes were Bessie's very own. They came on Christmas from her auntie who lives in Scotland. And she has such a beautiful doll's house. Then Uncle

James took us out to the Park, and we saw the funny monkeys and things, and then we went way up the river. Uncle James had to see some one about money, and that was why we stayed so long. Oh, dear, I do like Nora's new papa," with impressive earnestness.

" And he is very fond of little girls."

" I don't mean that he is any nicer than *my* papa ; but when a little girl hasn't had any papa for ever so long she must feel glad. Will Nora live here always ?"

" Yes, dear."

" I think we'll miss her a good deal. She knows so many pretty plays. I'm sorry with one side of me, but I am glad she has such a nice papa and a beautiful house. Will it be ever so much better than Sherburne ?"

" Oh, no, my child. Sherburne is a grand old place. And we cannot have any fields or gardens or great lawns and plantations in the city. No ; Sherburne is much more beautiful."

Princess gave a happy sigh of content and glanced up with a smile. Then she thought she would like to go and play with the babies. She was such a bright, cheerful child, Dell enjoyed her very much.

As they were sitting over their dessert that evening Bertram exclaimed suddenly, " O Dell ! I had a letter from Leonard with some bad news. I had just time to glance at it, and I thought I wouldn't spoil our dinner talk."

" Tessy !" Dell's cheek was white with apprehension.

" Everybody at Sherburne and Beaumanoir is well and happy. It is about Ethel. Mr. Longworth died quite suddenly."

" Oh ! and Ethel did not see him ?"

"Yes; she was with him three days, but they were not days of comfort. He had improved a good deal, they thought. He has never been considered seriously ill, you know. But it seems now it was one of those insidious complaints with some complications. He was waiting for the steamer from Hawaii—expected in that night or the next morning. After leaving the wharf, he walked about the city awhile, and then went to his hotel. At the dinner-table he was stricken with what seemed apoplexy, and though he lived three days, never recovered consciousness. Ethel came in the next morning; and now she is on her way home."

"Oh, poor Ethel! What a sad homecoming!"

"And what a long absence! I am glad she reached San Francisco before he died, and had those three days. It was a very worldly marriage, of course; but it seems as if any woman's heart must have upbraided her in that awesome silence when the man she had promised to love lay in that death-in-life state with no hope."

"And she had been away more than a year! Oh, do you remember how very much little Bevis Osborne interested him? And no one of his own kin to take his wealth!"

"You couldn't *all* be perfection," said the elder doctor with the gruffness of emotion. "And there is Milly as an offset to it all, with her devotion. Ethel followed in her mother's footsteps. And Alice is a queen of wives and mothers."

"It seems a great waste of life—two lives really capable of something finer," replied Bertram. "I think Mr. Longworth had begun to feel the insufficiency of it. I am not sure but he longed more for Ethel at the last than she did for him. Leonard thought he was rather disappointed at her electing to take such a long tour. And there is her lovely house! She hated mourning and sorrow when her mother died, and now she cannot escape it. She is too well bred for that."

Dell heard more of the particulars in Tessy's letter. Leonard was to make all the sad arrangements and meet them. Ethel had put everything in his hands. And Mr. Longworth had made a will some six months previous that Leonard was afraid she would not like. He had tried to persuade him to change some of its provisions, though he considered it a very just will, under the circumstances.

Millicent was a good deal shocked. She hoped the sorrow might touch Ethel's heart.

There were a few very busy days selecting furniture. There was a little question which room should be Millicent's. Mr. Drayton had chosen the room on the parlor floor, and the smaller one could be Nora's for the present. Upon the next story she could have a pretty sitting-room as well.

"And there is the library and the reception-room down-stairs. Why not make real home rooms of them? We do not want so many show places. And this pretty hall is so spacious for a city house."

Nora had a dozen minds as to her color. Her mother's preference was blue; and after some persuasion the child assented, though rose color was a powerful rival. It was a new experience to be large enough to make a real choice; and oh, the beautiful things that looked fresh from fairyland!

She was so tired and excited that she could not even keep her promise to Princess, and was ready to go to bed soon after dinner. Millicent had been rather startled by her evidences of self-will and her suddenly developed sense of authority. Her friend had allowed it in his endeavor to win her regard, and he was naturally generous with children when from any cause they were the objects of his attention. He had assented to her request that she should "go home with them," as she phrased it, fearing that a denial might pain her mother. And so, as if to make amends, all day long he had not once checked her freedom nor denied her most extravagant wish.

Now and then her mother had uttered a gentle remonstrance. A stepmother's place was difficult to fill, she knew—she had not thought much of the other side of the question.

Nora said her prayers in a tired, sleepy fashion, and kissed her mother. "I have been brimful of delight," she declared. "I just can't say another word but good-night."

It would not be an opportune moment for the counsel she longed to give; so she went slowly downstairs. Mr. Drayton had drawn out his reclining-chair and put a dainty plush rocker next to it.

"Milly!" as he heard her soft footfall on the tiling and held out both hands.

The rich, deep tints were illumined by the fire and the opalescent glass of the globe that softened the burner within. It was like a beautiful picture. She had enjoyed it in the houses of friends with no feeling of envy. But to have it of her very own !

She was so moved with gratefulness that she bent over and kissed him. He drew her down beside him, the chair was so wide.

"O Reese ! it is a fairy dream come true," and her eyes were lustrous with emotion. "I have put heroines in such rooms, I have given them devoted lovers——"

" Then my devotion will not weary you if you thought it a good thing for imaginary people. I warn you that you will have a good deal of it."

She had it before, she remembered—she had so much while hundreds of women were going heart-hungry.

" There's a theory, you know—the world is full of theories," laughingly—" that each individual has about so much power of every kind. It may be frittered away, it may congeal or decrease for want of use, but one must be past middle life before the last happens. And curiously enough I have been a man's man. I had my father through all those early years. I feel now that he was rather cynical where women were concerned. He rarely spoke of my mother. Not having any sisters, you see, I did not learn much about the gentler sex except in the way of society. All of my journeyings about have been with men. That Californian episode was the first real family party I ever undertook. A pretty, devoted wife and mother, a baby and a Chinese nurse, a charming grandmamma, and a frank, delightful young girl who could talk by the hour without once making big eyes at you ! Of course Dr. Carew was back of it all. I heard your pathetic story out there, and enough fascinating family history to pique my curiosity about Sherburne and Beaumanoir. And family living was delightfully new to me. So all the possibilities that have lain dormant are coming to light, and if they should overwhelm you——"

" I am not young enough to be swept off my feet, and I am old enough to appreciate the devotion you proffer me. O Reese ! I want to make you a happy home and

have you believe in the higher virtues, not merely assent
to them because they are in my creed."

> " ' And she who most believes in man
> Makes him what she believes,' "

he quoted.

" It may be so with a wise, judicious belief."

" Yes ; people often confuse admiration with belief.
When the admiration is gone there is nothing left. I
want you to believe in me, to be sure that I am endeavoring to do the best for you and Nora," and he glanced
out of entreating eyes.

" Oh," she cried quickly, " it is about Nora that I
want to talk."

" Well," with a tone of gravity, soft and inquiring.

" You—we are both spoiling her. We shall make her
a disagreeable girl if we go on this way."

" You shall instruct me. My darling, I am afraid I
know very little about fatherhood except indulgence.
Seriously, I want to do what will please you. I don't
need to think about money with such a famous mentor
as you ;" and he laughed with a sense of delight.

" Compared with real wealth, we have been only in
comparative circumstances. I thought them quite luxurious as a girl ; but in fifteen or twenty years there has
been a great advancement in the larger cities, perhaps
all over the world. Papa's income has not increased to
any noticeable extent, but the children are all cared for
and prospering. The Von Lindorm estate was entailed,
and though it had a certain aspect of grandeur, there was
not a great deal of money. The elder brother was as
generous to me as circumstances would permit. I have
been able to add a little to my store——"

" There was nothing said about your endowing me
with your worldly goods as I remember." He paused
to kiss the sweet, tremulous lips. " Now, what is it all
about ? There must be no mine or thine. What you
have may be Nora's if you like, but I have taken the
child as well as the mother ; and I love her. Only do
not ask me to love her the best."

" You have given her so much that she demands the
best, and soon she will demand the gratification of
numerous whims, and perhaps be unamiable on refusal.
You must consider what you would think wise for a
child of your very own ; and you must demand her respect for your authority. Suppose you had to refuse
her something ?"

He shrugged his shoulders.

" She must go to school and take her place with other
girls. I do not want her to feel that she is to be grander
because she lives in a beautiful home, or to be imperious
because she has a rich father—children learn the hom-
age paid to money so readily. The only one I know who
never cared, and who remained utterly unspoiled with
the gifts of fortune, was my Cousin Lyndell. I should
like Nora to have a little of her principle ; and she is
not rich because you are."

" But children get over these things. Why, I thought
it quite fun to-day to have her go around ordering articles with the air of a princess."

" I should have had her room a good deal plainer.
There ought to be something for the older girl to have.
And, O Reese ! you will not buy her the diamond ?"

" I have better sense than that. Trust me."

" I am glad of that. There are so many cousins to
grow up, and she is so much the eldest that she ought to

be an example. I had thought of sending her away to school. But we did not go until we were sixteen. She needs a mother's supervision through these years of formation."

"Oh, do not send her away! There are splendid schools here in the city—and I will try. Only I am afraid I should be indulgent to girls on principle. I might be stricter with a boy. And perhaps it wouldn't be a bad scheme to give her an allowance."

"If she did not coax money out of you before the month was half gone, or persuade you to buy whatever she wanted."

"You will have to take charge of us both for awhile. Perhaps I need some training. Now, you are to devote the rest of the evening to me. Milly, it is selfish, but I enjoy having you alone."

"I do not want to forget that I am first."

"Thank you, my dear wife." His very tone had a caress in it.

# CHAPTER XVII.

## FROM DIFFERENT POINTS OF VIEW.

WHEN Millicent had read her letter from Leonard that came in the morning's mail she passed it over to Mr. Drayton. "I must go down to Dell's," she remarked. "How very sad! No one can do anything for Ethel but proffer her sympathy. Leonard will be her best counsellor."

"O mamma! don't go this morning," pleaded Nora.

"Why not?" smilingly. "And I thought you wanted to see Princess."

"But the rugs and the curtains and the furniture are to come," she replied eagerly.

"Well, you need not go. Mrs. Black will look after you."

"Will papa go?" glancing up at him, then at her mother.

"Yes, I am going for a little walk with mamma," he answered gravely over his paper.

"And am I to be left alone?" with a breath of indignation, turning her eyes beseechingly on Mr. Drayton.

"But you would not have me let mamma go out alone in a strange city!"

"She used to go alone at Beaumanoir, and New York isn't so *very* strange."

"Well, I have promised to take care of her, and a gentleman always keeps his promises."

Mr. Drayton went around to Millicent's side and passed his arm over her shoulder. Nora sprang to him and captured his other hand, pressing it against her soft, rosy cheek.

" You had better go with us," he said relentingly. " I doubt if the furniture comes before afternoon."

Nora was divided in her soul. She wanted her own will, and she was impatient to see her room furnished. But if nothing came——

" I think I will go," she answered presently.

" Shall we ride ?"

" Oh, no," returned Millicent with a smile. " I want to keep in good habits of walking."

" But the cars are so delightful, mamma."

Neither paid heed to the remark. Drayton remembered how last winter he had taken Nora over route after route just for the pure fun of riding. She lagged a little behind, and her pretty mouth drooped in dissatisfied curves. The two were talking, they paid but little attention to her, and she did not like it. She came around to her mother's side presently with an irrelevant question.

" Don't, dear," said her mother with the least bit of reproof.

Nora's heart swelled. She had been first for so long that it was not pleasant to find herself of little consequence. She walked rather stiffly and said not another word.

But Princess was so delighted to see her that she was merry in a moment. And she had so much to tell. Her beautiful brass bedstead, her lace cover and shams, her bureau with its long glass, and her pretty dressing-table with its broad mirror, her lovely bookcase without the glass doors that were always such a bother, and the splendid rug that was like walking on velvet, with a centre of flowers that looked as if set in a dish of blue, and beyond blue and gray arabesques and curious corners that seemed to have no settled design. Then a pretty rattan couch, and cushions and cushions, and willow chairs tied with blue ribbons, and pictures that she had chosen her own self.

For once the babies did their cunning tricks unheeded. Nora was so full of her own wonderful belongings and what mamma was to have that she could talk of nothing else.

The ladies discussed the sad occurrence quite at liberty. Mr. Drayton was to go down-town on some business. Nora pleaded that Princess should go back with them.

They found the rugs had come and been laid. The children danced over them with delight, and when this amusement failed they inspected the house. The two guest chambers on the next floor were handsomely furnished. Then there was papa's room with a kind of Oriental air, and many curiosities there had been no room for in the library. Nora made her tour of observation unchecked, and displayed a wide knowledge of her new papa's belongings.

He had not come home yet, so they had their luncheon with mamma. Millicent realized with a pang that Nora was no longer a little girl. She recalled the fact that she had developed wonderfully in her last winter's visit, but she had gone back somewhat to the childhood of the younger cousins. And Fanny's queer, daring, independent ways had not been a good pattern for her. Had she, Millicent, really been remiss?

Then the boxes and trunks came from Beaumanoir, and Davis began to unpack them. Millicent had most of her pictures hung in her room. Several of them had been gifts from admirers gained by her pen, and a few choice copies she had brought from abroad were reserved for the drawing-room. Then some of the furniture arrived, and Mr. Drayton, who had just come in, superintended the placing of it, as well as the arrangement of the curtains and *portières*. The children enjoyed it all with eager interest and delight.

But alas! nightfall came, and Nora had watched in vain for her furniture. It had grown quite cloudy, and now a drizzle of rain set in.

"We must keep Princess all night. I will send Davis down with a message," said Mr. Drayton.

"But Auntie Dell said I must come home."

"Not in the rain. I did not think it was so late. She will not expect you."

"It is not so late," returned Millicent, "but dark and cloudy."

"Will Auntie Dell——" Princess hesitated and glanced up questioningly.

"If Auntie Dell thinks you had better come, I will take you," replied Mr. Drayton.

The children had been very much engrossed and full of interest. But now Nora stood by the window in a disconsolate mood.

"Mamma, do you not think the furniture will come?" she asked presently.

"Not in this rain," was the quiet answer.

"O dear! why couldn't the man have sent it earlier? I did so want Princess to see it. And now we cannot sleep there."

"Will it matter so very much when you are asleep?" asked Mr. Drayton teasingly.

"Yes, it will!" pettishly. "And when the man promised—he surely said, 'I will send it to-morrow'—he ought to keep his word. Mamma, isn't that telling a falsehood?"

"He meant to do it no doubt. But, you see, he sent the drawing-room furniture first. I should not want mine to come in the rain, would you? If it had remained clear the day would have been an hour longer."

"And all my books are piled up in the hall!"

"I wouldn't worry about it to-night. You and Princess come and sing, and we will imagine ourselves back at Sherburne."

"I'd rather be here than at Sherburne," said Nora. "I like the city; don't you?" to Princess.

"I like mamma and papa and the children best," answered the soft, sweet voice. "Little Dell is so cunning and lovely. I couldn't live anywhere without them."

"Well, I have *my* mamma here."

"Who is coming to sing for me?" asked papa.

Princess bounded to the library. Nora followed reluctantly. Millicent ran her fingers lightly over the keys, and in a moment they were singing a familiar song. Nora's discomfort vanished.

"What a beautiful voice the child has!" Mr. Drayton said as they passed out to dinner. "I do not suppose Leonard would be quite willing to let us adopt her?" laughingly.

"Aunt Aurelia wouldn't;" and Milly looked up with shining eyes.

The word came that Princess might stay all night, and

the little girl was much pleased. Mr. Drayton devoted the early part of the evening to their amusement. Nora's jealousy cropped out now and then, but, on the whole, they had a delightful time.

All the next day it rained. Millicent was busy enough. Just at dusk Uncle Bertram came for the little girl in his carriage, and then Nora was unwilling to have her go.

When the room really was completed, the books in their case, some of the Christmas and birthday gifts settled in their new niches, Nora's delight knew no bounds. She said in a quivering kind of voice, " It is too truly beautiful to use, mamma."

" I am glad my little girl is satisfied. And now you must repay papa by being a sweet, grateful, and obedient daughter to him, and trying to make him happy. You see, only half the work is done when he tries to make you happy. There are two sides to most of the events of our lives, and each side has its duties."

Nora ran upstairs to find him in his " den."

" O papa ! I want to thank you for all the delight you have given me," she cried, clasping her arms about his neck. " I love you very much ; and I am so glad to be your little girl, your only little girl."

How would she feel if others came to share the home ? But she would have so much wider interests when she went to school and made girl friends. She did have an unmistakably jealous tendency.

Leonard brought Fanny up a week later to do the last of her bridal shopping. Princess was so glad to see him she wanted to sit on his knee every moment. Ethel was home in her grand house, the funeral had taken place, and Mr. Longworth's will had been read. It was not satisfactory.

Leonard did not say that Ethel had been positively angry at first.

There was one large bequest to charity. A child's hospital that had struggled along under adverse circumstances was given enough money to build a commodious wing to be called by the donor's name, and a yearly endowment, a sum set aside for this purpose. There were some gifts to friends. Edward Sherburne, little Bevis Osborne, Paul Amory's son, and Edward Beaumanoir were handsomely remembered. The house was to be Mrs. Longworth's if she cared to reside in it, and a generous income while she lived, but at her death the property was to go mostly to Longworth relatives.

"It is a fair enough will, since there are no children. Mr. Longworth felt that Ethel was young and would likely marry again, and he frankly admitted that he did not care to have his money enrich a second husband and possible children. She had half a mind to attempt to break the will at first. While her income will keep her in luxury, it is hardly large enough to satisfy the cupidity of any one with mercenary desires, especially some impecunious nobleman;" and Leonard laughed lightly. "Ethel is very much in love with life abroad. And Mr. Longworth was an ardent American. I found a great many things in him to admire. But the will has been so carefully considered that I do not think she would gain anything by a contest. She is sure of a good income, even if she should live to old age. In that case she would have quite as much as her dower rights—perhaps more."

Fanny had gone at once to Millicent's. She had spent

a night with Ethel, and been the recipient of complaints and descriptions of the elegant time she had abroad and the friends she had made.

" I do think I shall go back—perhaps to live," she said. " And, Fanny, it is much pleasanter to have a companion. You might accompany me. After six months or so I should go into society a little. You could have a pleasant time, and you might marry well. You keep your looks remarkably," surveying her with critical eyes.

" I don't need to go abroad husband-hunting. My wedding day is appointed already. I have waited until I was good and ready, and found a man I liked, who will keep me from stagnation. I am obliged to you, Ethel, for considering my welfare."

There was a touch of sarcasm in Fanny's tone, and her eyes were brimming with amusement. Yes, she did look very young, and she had grown prettier, surely.

" And who have you found to marry, pray tell ?"

" Oh, finding some one has been the easiest part of it. The trouble generally has been liking them after they were found. A country doctor who does not have to depend altogether on his patients, but who will never be rich, I am aware. He suits me ; and, after years of experience, I shall doubtless suit him. I do not care so much for the gay world as I once imagined I did."

" O Fanny ! what a foolish woman ! And you allowed Millicent to capture that Mr. Drayton after all !"

" He was desperately in love with her. I am glad they are happy. And I think mother ought to have one daughter within call. We shall live at Ardmore or in the vicinity. And Dr. Underwood is quite as desperately in love with me."

"Oh! Dr. Underwood! You might almost as well have married old Dr. Carew!"

"Oh, no; I wanted some one a little nearer my own age." Fanny's good humor was imperturbable.

"You had better reconsider," Ethel said the next morning. "I have quite decided to go abroad. There is always something new going on. I have had about all there is of Washington and the rest of the country. I've been bored to death; and I can't think of being moped here in the house a whole season. But it is a comforting thing to have some one of your own to talk to when you want to pick people to pieces. If Gifford wasn't so stupid he would make a good companion. But a woman is more enjoyable. And when one is done with sentiment, and all that sort of thing——"

"I am not," interrupted Fanny. "I'm foolishly in love, and within six weeks of my wedding day. The idea of throwing it all up for the mere sake of quizzing people and picking them to pieces! You would have to find something better to offer me."

"Fanny, you are a fool! But you always were," said her stately cousin.

That very evening she had been welcomed in Millicent's lovely home. Just for a moment it gave her a pang of envy. The man with the smiling, contented face, finer and stronger than when she first saw it, held her hand in a brotherly clasp and spoke in a brotherly voice. No, he never could have loved her, and presently she might have grown into a careless, discontented wife, flirting with attractive men, trying every new pleasure and finding them vanity and vexation of spirit. After all, she would have enough.

Mr. Drayton took Nora upstairs to play a game of

checkers that the sisters might have the talk quite to themselves. Ethel was a more engrossing subject than wedding gowns.

"She isn't a bit happy or content, and she has had almost everything. To think how good and indulgent Mr. Longworth was to her, and she talks about him as if he might have been her grandfather. I am glad now she hasn't all the money. And to imagine I would be glad to go abroad with her, and just throw up all my own plans!"

"Do you suppose she really meant it?" Millicent was amazed.

"Oh, yes; Ethel is a snob. She loves titles and grand people and great houses full of servants and style, and has grown to be very un-American. She aspires to leadership. And when she has gained one eminence she goes on to the next. The thing attained is as nothing. She had a circle of literary and artistic people—you must have enjoyed that, Milly."

"Oh, I did!" Millicent's eyes were suffused with a radiant light. "I came near to envying her then, or her splendid opportunities."

"I am glad you are to have them; yes, very glad, Milly," and Fanny's tone was informed with a feeling so deep that it touched her sister. "They are a part of your life, and you would always go hungering for them, even if you accepted cheerfully the more ordinary feasts. And I am glad I did not spoil the grand feast for you."

Both girls colored deeply at the remembrance.

"I know now that I did not love him, and I never blinded myself to the fact that he was not in love with me. It would have been Ethel's life over again, only I do not think I could play so successfully at intellectual-

ity. Then she started in to outshine everybody, to dress
and give entertainments that should rouse envy, to snub
people in her superb fashion. And now that has lost its
charm. She's like Solomon—she has had it all, and it is
weariness of spirit. Now she wants to be amused, admired, flattered, and she is awfully disappointed at not
being an immensely rich widow. She is angry with
Leonard because he allowed such a will to be made, and
he told her he had hard work to persuade Mr. Longworth not to lessen her income in case she married.
And since she has not been really happy with all
this——"

"I am very glad it has not influenced your life, as it
seemed to indicate at one time."

Fanny laughed brightly.

"There was Tessy when the pendulum swung back,"
she made answer. "She is about the happiest woman
I know. And the children will be growing up to give
her a glad young life over again. Somehow I have come
to want a living of my own, a home, children, a continu-
ous interest. I have outgrown the fun and flirting ; I
am hopelessly commonplace, but I do like a great deal
of love," laughingly.

"O Fanny ! I hope you will be very happy !" cried
Millicent, much moved.

"And isn't happiness an agreement—*you* may call it
a divine harmony—between the person and the things
he has, whether they are surroundings, daily incidents,
the one you elect to live with, or the pleasures you enjoy
most ? Do we change, Milly ? Is it growing older ? I
want a little restfulness now and then, but I can't abide
loneliness. And I like people with different ideas and
opinions that you can argue with—I don't mind a bit of

a tiff now and then, when you can kiss and make up. I would rather marry Dr. Underwood and live at Ardmore —and we are going to have a beautiful house after all— than to spend five years with Ethel's whims amid all the luxury."

Millicent smiled. Fanny had kept her childhood's characteristics wonderfully. She would never be a woman of large brain and lofty soul, but she might be a very happy one for all that. And now she centred all the interest in herself. Dell and Milly must consider her shopping. The wedding gown would be made and sent on to her, she would be married in church on Christmas morning, and all the friends and relatives were bidden to a Christmas dinner. There were pretty articles to look up for the house, hangings and carpets and rugs and curtains, and endless discussions about economy, that were very amusing on Fanny's part, since she was sure to end by some extravagance.

Leonard would make only a brief visit, and that had to have all of one day devoted to important business. But Princess was so delighted to get her own papa once more that Nora and her lovely room were quite thrown into the shade. And she was more than ready to go back to mamma and the children.

Tessy was training her young girl into a capable nursery governess. Once she had almost lost her. The farmer for whom her mother was keeping house came to like her so well that he won her in marriage by promising to bring her two boys home and provide for them. Even a grown-up daughter would prove no incumbrance.

May went to make her mother a visit. The rather coarse living contrasted too strongly with the refinements of Sherburne House. Everything was hearty and strong and commonplace. The boys were overjoyed after the routine of institution life.

"Here are five people provided for through Mrs. Murray's kindly thoughtfulness," said Bertram Carew. "The little girl who couldn't have lived through privations and the stifling air of a poor, foul tenement will grow up well and strong, the boys will in all probability make useful members of society. This Mr. Hardham seems a very sensible sort of man. And Tessy will train the young girl so that she will be able to earn a good living if she should not want her in time to come. Five people are not many out of the great maëlstrom of poverty; but if every well-to-do family did as much the result would be tremendous."

"But Mamma Murray always finds such nice poor people, the kind you can do something for and with," returned Lyndell.

"Or is it that her good sense discriminates? I have observed that she seldom puts a person in the wrong place. It is a rare art. A great deal of the useless endeavor comes from the lack of this knowledge. I remember now that May Dennis looked like a refined and rather ambitious girl, even if she was a factory worker and a child of the tenements."

"And she kept her a month before sending her to Tessy. Mamma Murray is a born missionary. She does a good deal of the work herself—she always did."

May Dennis had been very glad to come back to the charming household at Sherburne. She was studying all the time to keep in advance of her little charges. With her eldest boy Tessy lent her assistance. She was hardly ready for a full-fledged governess, and she thought him not quite old enough to send away to school. Leonard had objected to his going in to Ardmore, as there was no first-class school. He was a bright, eager, but very manageable child, and Aunt Aurelia's delight.

"I shall be very glad to come again," exclaimed Princess with her good-by. "And it has been just lovely, Auntie Dell, with Nora and everybody. But I do want to see my own mamma."

Fanny vibrated between the two houses, and her comments were amusing. Lyndell was surprised at the utter absence of envy at any mention of Millicent's good fortune. Almost every comparison except that of money was to Dr. Underwood's advantage.

"One could never imagine Fanny being so much in love," commented Dell mirthfully.

Miss Westwood had come up to the city with a friend who was to be married and go out to Denver, where her lover had business interests. They were both persuading her to join them and be their guest until her own marriage. Gifford's letters were very cheerful, with a little strand of impatience. Alice confessed she was counting on his marriage as well. He was building a house for his bonny bird, and she, Alice, had the warmest of welcomes ready for her.

"You have all been such kindly friends that I hate to go away," Miss Westwood said; "but it is not as if I had a home of my own that I wanted to associate with my marriage, and I shall have an unsettled feeling until I am really your cousin's wife," with a delicate inflection as she smiled. "I know you will all wish me the same success and happiness there as here."

Half of her portion had been invested in some long-time bonds paying excellent dividends that Bertram advised her not to change. The remainder was at her disposal any time.

"Perhaps it would be as well to let that accumulate. I shall not be extravagant, even if I do set the old adage at naught."

They sent her off with the most cordial wishes.

"I doubt if Gifford serves his year of probation," Dr. Carew commented.

"I think he will," answered Mr. Drayton. "I feel very much encouraged with the accounts of the Osbornes. Now, when we have Fanny off our hands——" smiling over to Millicent.

"We shall have nothing to do but enjoy ourselves and grow selfish," declared Dell. "I wonder how people feel who have no strong interest in anything beyond their own wants?"

"Not as happy as one might imagine."

Fanny reduced herself to bankruptcy, and returned home to be welcomed by her lover in a most ardent manner.

"I was beginning to think the spice had pretty much gone out of life," he declared with a humorous shrug of the shoulders. "Fanny, as a letter writer you are not a brilliant success. On your next journey I shall go along to jog your memory."

"I really had no time to write letters. Next time I go away it will not be to discuss and purchase wedding paraphernalia."

"I should hope not," said Dr. Underwood with a mirthful light in his eyes.

Tessy listened with delighted attention to the real new styles, and Millicent's lovely home, and Nora's amusing half jealousy, first of her mother and then of her new father ; and all of the Carew doings in such a jumbled fashion that only one of the initiated could disentangle the various threads. And though Fanny had never been an especial favorite with Aunt Aurelia, she did like Dr. Underwood extremely, and was very generous to the prospective bride.

Nothing occurred to mar the plans or the harmony. They were all to meet together again, except Ethel, who sent a handsome gift and regrets. She had just received an offer to lease her house, furnished, to a new senator, and as there was nothing to keep her in Washington, which had grown very tiresome to her, she should go abroad early in the new year.

Fanny made a very pretty bride. Nora, Pearl, and Princess were lovely maids for the occasion, and strewed her path with roses as she walked slowly up the old church aisle where so many of the family had been given in marriage.

# CHAPTER XVIII.

THE bright Christmas Sunday was drawing to a close.
A grayish lavender cloud had spread itself over the
western sky and there had been no sunset. The air was
still, and there seemed a hush everywhere with the curious, pervasive softness that often ushers in a snow-storm.

Dell had been to morning service with the twins and
Aunt Neale. Bertram had come in at noon with a word
of anxiety and swallowed a hasty luncheon. There had
been many little housewifely things to occupy her, and
Sunday afternoon, while grandmamma was taking her
rest, she told the children stories. They were too old
for naps now, but they had an early supper and went to
bed with the chickens. Princess had shown Bertie last
summer how the chickens went to bed before it was
dark. Mamma often called them her little chickens.
Bertie had outgrown his sister by a full year already,
but she was always well and sweet-tempered, and grandpapa thought there never would be such a baby again.

Next summer she would be large enough to go riding
alone with him. But it puzzled her small brain to know
when next summer would come.

They were having their supper now, with Freda, who
was like a second mother to them. Lyndell had her new
baby on her knee as she sat by the window in a curiously
expectant mood. For though it was six months old it

still seemed new to her, with its big, wondering brown eyes, with the velvety softness of her own. Its hair was a kind of bronze gold, little rings already around its neck and at the edge of the white forehead. Baby Milly's straight, soft, golden hair would not curl.

This was her very own baby, she had told Bertram months before, and she was glad to have it a girl. "There were babies enough now to go round," she said laughingly to her husband.

He had smiled down into her sweet eyes, informed with all motherliness. "I have wondered sometimes how you could be so generous," in a soft, full tone that went to her heart like a rich reward. "You have tolerated a good many rivals. There was the year of the book."

"And the long, delightful holiday afterward. I was paid fourfold." There was delight in her tone.

"And they took possession of the other babies," smiling with rare tenderness.

"After all, I was their mother. But I hope no one will really want this little darling. I have her name chosen—just simply Honor—Honor Carew."

"That is beautiful. And we shall never call her Nora. We are getting a confusion of names in the family, and yet it is comforting to perpetuate names endeared by the tenderest association."

Honor was healthy and sweet-natured and grew surprisingly. Little Millicent had a rare, delicate charm. Honor was brilliant with a laughing face that dimpled with the least movement.

Lyndell had always tried to keep this between time for her baby and herself. It was one of her happy hours. But now she seemed rather absent and listened to the steps coming from the corner, her breath dropping a little as they passed by. Then she would clasp her baby and kiss it with rapture and lean toward the window again.

Yes, that was the step, firm and manful, with the elasticity of youth. It mounted the stoop, it was in the hall, it sprang up two steps at a time, and two fond arms were about her while the joyous kiss told the story.

"It is all right," she said in a tone of emotion. "Oh, thank Heaven!"

"Yes, it is all right. A little girl. I was afraid Drayton would be disappointed—men *do* like sons. But he is wild about girls, it seems, and he could hardly speak for delight. A Sunday baby, 'full of grace.' A Christmas gift also. Milly will do well, though I will confess now I had some fears. Yes, thank Heaven!"

He took his own little girl and held her up high while she laughed aloud.

"Let me go and tell Aunt Neale. She is happy once more with her Sunday-school class. I can recall several blessed Sundays when she had in a little black crew and told them Bible stories, and the child Dell listened."

"Dell, how good you are! I wonder sometimes if I could have been as generous to yours——"

"Yes, you would if you could imagine yourself living with Aunt Aurelia and Cousin Eliza. But you know your father fell in love with me and adopted me before I scarcely knew about you. And I took the love without the least conscientious scruple."

"There, run away with your news. Then run back. No more going out to-night unless it is for life or death."

Dell vanished for a few moments. He caressed the baby; he had loved it for its mother's brown eyes before it could give an answering smile. He could understand the joy of the other father.

"Bertram," re-entering the room and smiling at her husband, "how do you suppose Nora will take it?"

"There will be a tempest; but it is a fixed fact."

"Nora is not like father or mother in that respect. Millicent is too grand for jealousy. Emil was the soul of generosity."

"There is Len and all the rest of them. And were you never jealous?"

"I went into tempests," and Dell laughed.

"The party was a perfect godsend. Do you not suppose wise little Tessy planned it with wisdom aforethought? Think of the frolic they will have to-morrow night. Sherburne children again! And little Ned Sherburne is nine years old. And pretty Pearl Amory. Aunt Julia is to be up with her little Sunbeam. And there will be changes in that household if Archie comes on. I hope with Shakespeare that 'The bargain may not catch cold and starve.' What a mercy that creature married again!"

They had received an English paper with a marked notice. Mrs. Trainor had married an Austrian count. Archie's divorced wife had married an Englishman in some country town, and that was all they knew.

Archie's company had been for some time considering an offer from a syndicate. A new vein of very fine copper had been discovered, and now the parties were not only insistent, but had offered a much higher price. Archie was extremely gratified with the prospect.

"I hope she has married to her satisfaction this time. At all events, I do not believe we shall hear anything more about her. But how could she give up her child and not know whether it was dead or alive?"

Lyndell stooped to kiss her baby and her husband encircled her with his other arm.

"What were we talking about? Oh, the Sherburne children! I want ours to come in with the clan. Think what it would be for Tessy to have a silver wedding and gather everybody in the old house!"

"But Edward Sherburne is to come of age first, and the boys always celebrate that event. And now he is past nine. How delightful it is to see the children growing up! I wonder if the most blessed thing in life is not a happy mother."

"You forget the happy wife," Bertram Carew said almost jealously.

"I can't fancy her being a happy mother unless she has been and is a happy wife. A part of Millicent's motherhood has never been developed because she missed the shared joy, which is so much more comprehensive than the joy alone."

Dr. Carew gave a soft sigh. He had already seen a great deal of the wrong side of motherhood.

Lyndell pressed her baby to her heart and then rested its soft, young face on her shoulder, where her own cheek could touch its exquisite freshness. To-night she wanted to cuddle it; she did sometimes, and broke her own rules; but baby did not get spoiled with all the love.

She was thinking as her husband sat beside her of the swift, happy months since Millicent's marriage. There had been some friction at first. Mr. Drayton's ease-loving temperament was like sailing on a tideless summer sea. One could so easily give up and drift, and oh, it was so easy to drift now when all things were pleasant!

But Millicent felt they both owed the world something, because to them had been given more than one talent.

He was very proud of her genius, but for awhile he would have been quite content if she had made no further effort. There were drives and walks ; even Central Park was lovely in the winter. One could imagine such a thing as getting lost amid its clustering woods and winding paths. There were books to read in the quiet mornings or disengaged evenings, old books, new books, absolute studies in the new events and discoveries. They opened their house to society, of course. They did not storm at fashionable doors or sit down watchfully in the hope of slipping in at some unguarded moment, but waited to choose for themselves.

The fact that Reese Drayton had never done anything but travel and lounge and spend money was an open sesame in some circles. He laughed about it.

Millicent understood the fine gradations ; she had been brought up among them without making wealth the great question. " We could not have so much culture if there were no leisure," she said. " And, with all your democratic tendencies, you are——"

" Well ?" laughingly as she paused and flushed.

" Not exactly aristocratic, but——"

" Exclusive ? Will that help you out ?"

" It is not quite that either," with a rather perplexed expression.

" A refined sort of laziness—an indifference to the welfare of my fellow-creatures or their advancement. I do like ease and luxury, yet I have done a good deal of roughing, as travellers always do, and enjoyed it. Yet I find it has not spoiled me for civilized life any more than years of bachelorhood have spoiled me for being the most exacting of husbands," and a glint of mirth shone in his eyes.

" I hope I know you are not quite indifferent."

" But I like some one to do my work. And Carew is such a splendid almoner! Then Mr. Moore and Dr. Wolff are managing that Western experiment so successfully. I haven't cared much for money except to spend it, and yet I have been told I am shrewd at bargain-making. You see, I have so many sides to my nature. It is the embarrassment of riches. Now, what do you want me to do? What I want to do is to have years of honeymoon."

" I want us to give a little out of our abundance. I want us to make some hard lives a little easier."

" You and Dell are so strenuous. Is it doing good? Though I think motherhood has changed Mrs. Carew. Oh, 1 wish we could have had you that winter so long ago. She was trying on so many things; she was so deep in charities; she wore herself out. You shall never do it."

" She would not do it now. You are to prove all things and hold fast that which is good. And how can you prove unless you try?" glancing up earnestly.

" The old world will go on in the same way. It has been so from the beginning."

" It does some grander things now. And let me mention this: you were talking with that young Mr. Travers Floyd Stanwood brought in, about the real fruits of Buddhism in India—you remember. He had been listening to the lovely side of it, and you did correct some false ideas. You gave him several facts to think about. Floyd was quite delighted. If you would take the trouble to talk about things you really do know when some one wants a little help. You can bring two people together who need each other, you are in the station to do it. Years ago Bertram Carew opened the doors of literary life to me—he knew so much more about the world. I might have blundered and become discouraged."

" Oh, the world would have found you out."

" The world doesn't find out some people until it is too late, it seems, not in one respect, but in a good many—from uplifting at the first fall to starvation. It seems cruel that in a world of abundance any one should starve to death. Yet they do. Mrs. Murray finds them before they starve. And in a world of intelligence it is a pity one should go hungering for knowledge, saddest of all that one should perish for the want of a friendly hand held out to him. Let us hold out the friendly hand. We will turn the sick and the starving over to Dr. Carew."

She looked so lovely and inspired that he would have consented to anything.

They set apart one evening for the work of society, while there were many for pleasure. Floyd Stanwood, just ordained, a very eager young deacon, found some young men who were charmed at once with such a host and hostess. There were youngish women busy all day, to whom the pictures, books, music, and fascinating atmosphere was a treat. They did not expect to be invited to grand society functions, but they enjoyed this without heartburning.

Lyndell tried to get in, and the doctor whenever he could. The evenings were so enjoyable. " O Milly," she said one morning, " do you remember a foolish young dream I once had, that you should come to Sher-

burne House, and we two have a beautiful home for young
girls who were in need of love and home and the sweetness of a little prosperity ?    I wanted to influence people.    I wanted to form other lives on a great, high
plane, lest my own should go to waste.    What impossible things girls dream !'' and she smiled retrospectively.

"But you *did* influence Leonard and Gifford.    And
you saved Anita Garcia and put her where she could do
some splendid work in the world.    But for that episode
with Leonard, that seemed so dreadful at the time, and
your generous care, she might never have found her
beautiful voice.''

Dell had flushed with pleasure.    The years had not
been wasted, even those extravagant desires of youth.

"And now it has come about that we can work and
plan together, with the added benefit of discipline and
experience.    I am so glad to have you here.''

It had been a very happy year.    Gifford's marriage
and new home had proved a source of unalloyed delight
to Alice, and she was most enthusiastic about her new
sister-in-law.    Fanny's marriage was a success, a decided
pleasure to her mother, although she would be Fanny to
the end of the chapter.    But the doctor admired her
pungency and liked spirit in a woman.    Arranging her
new house had raised a deep personal interest.    She
told Tessy and Aunt Aurelia that she found she had
many domestic tastes.    Cousin Carrick came for a three
days' visit, and admitted that she never suspected there
was so much in Fanny.    There had been slight ailments,
and some of the older people had passed away, Mrs.
Kirby among them.    Mr. Armitage had received an excellent call, but his mother felt that she could not undertake a change, with her failing health, and Dr. Under-

wood sent him an Easter gift that made his salary equal to the new proffer. The people were so friendly, Mrs. Armitage thought, that she was afraid they would never find the like again.

The only drawback to Millicent's perfect felicity had been Nora's changes and development. She was affectionate and gay tempered, made friends easily, but was often indifferent to them afterward. New girls, new circumstances and pleasures were her delight. She had been sent to an excellent private school the Curtises had recommended, and she proved herself a good scholar. She was quick to see that her new papa's wealth enhanced her standing. When he came for her to go for a drive or to take a walk she was extremely proud of him.

" But, after all, he isn't your own father," said one of her mates one day. " And unless he chose to will you some money you would not get a penny. Then there may be ever so many children. And it seems queer to have your name Von Lindorm. It doesn't sound as if you were any relation to him."

" Mamma," cried Nora that day, rushing in flushed and excited, " why isn't my name Drayton as well as yours ?"

" Oh, my child, be a little more ladylike. You are too old for such boyish roughness."

" Well—why ?" persisted the child.

" You have your own father's name. It ought to be very dear to you, Honora."

" But I never knew my own papa. And I wish he had not been a German. Then, mamma, if you wouldn't call me Honora with such a solemn accent."

" You were named for Auntie Dell and a very dear friend, at whose wedding I met your papa."

Nora drummed with her foot on the carpet. "And can't I ever be called after this papa's name? I do love him."

Millicent felt unable to reason with the child. She had striven to impress her own father's memory upon her young mind. Would they both forget him? Oh, that would be cruel!

"My dear child, I think you are too young to decide. There are many things about your own father of which you may be very proud by and by."

Should she tell her of the title? That would appeal to her childish pride. Yet it looked snobbish.

"The girls think it so queer."

"Ask Uncle Bertram and Auntie Dell what they think of it. And now go to your lessons, and we will talk it over some other time. I have several letters to write."

Nora often went up to papa's den to study. She had a little corner to herself, cut off by the screen.

Papa was often out in the afternoon, but to-day he was stretched luxuriously in his reclining chair, with a silken cushion at the back of his head and a book in his hand.

"O papa, dear, dearest papa!"—and the child's voice was seductively sweet—"I have such a great favor to ask of you. You will break my heart if you refuse to grant it."

She almost smothered him with kisses from her soft, fragrant lips.

"Let me see," when he had released himself from her exuberant clasp, "didn't mamma put you on an allowance?"

"Oh, it is not to go anywhere, nor to have you buy me anything—for I haven't spent all my own money—

nor to stay up late, nor to——" what other forbidden thing could she recall ?

" Well, you may venture to tell me, I think. Though I distrust the Greeks when they bring gifts. And such oceans of kisses——"

" Then I will not give you any more." She stood up straight with an effort to be stern, but a smile was lurking everywhere. How piquant and winsome she was without being handsome like her mother ! He was very fond of teasing her and watching the changes in her mobile face.

" I shall pine under such a system of cruelty. Oh, was it a problem or a Latin exercise ? Come, be good friends and kiss me once, and I shall relent a good deal. I feel myself weakening."

" It was not any trifling thing," she answered serious-ly. " Papa, *do* you love me ?"

" My little dear !" He clasped her in his arms and drew her down to him.

" Then, papa, why didn't you have my name changed when you had mamma's ?"

He was surprised and touched to the heart. " My child, I don't just know. I never thought of it."

" But if I am your child I ought to be Nora Drayton."

" Why, yes. Of course you shall be. What put it into your head ?"

" The girls at school think it queer that I should have a different name."

" Oh !" He was a little disappointed at the trivial reason.

" It is your name ; and if you choose to give it to me, just as you gave it to mamma, then it will be mine al-

ways. And O papa, I shall be so glad!" with a soft, lit
tle sigh as she kissed him again.

"A wife always takes her husband's name—that is
the law of the land. And if I adopted you legally—that
is, by process of law—you would have all the rights and
privileges of an own child. I think myself it would be
better. Yes, my dear, I am glad to grant you that
favor."

"Oh, a hundred thousand thanks!"

"Now, dear, I am going down to see mamma and talk
it over with her."

He rose smilingly. Nora went to her corner quite
elated, and began to study. When papa took a thing in
hand it was sure to succeed. Yet her conscience was not
quite clear. She had schemed to get papa to agree by
asking him first. He hated to deny her anything, for
she was not an aggressive child.

Millicent was stamping the last of her letters, and
looked up with a cordial smile.

He sat down beside her and took up her pearl paper-
knife. "Milly," he began, "there is a point I want to
discuss with you that I wonder I have not thought of
before. It is about Nora's name. Have you any real
objection to her being called Drayton?"

"Oh, has she been besieging you? Reese, we must
form a league of defence. She is shrewd enough to
know that she can coax most things out of you. And
have you promised?"

"I see no good reason for objecting," he returned
gravely. "Curtis has legally adopted his wife's son and
daughter, and is very proud of them."

"I do not know that any adoption would make you
care more for Nora. You are very generous, Reese;

but when she is older she may be proud of her father's name. I gave myself away—ought I to give his child to another?''

" Milly dear, if you feel this way about it——''

" She might be sorry some day that she had relinquished it. I can see that her heart is quite set upon it now ; but the principle of extorting anything out of you that I have not consented to is bad, and will make us both trouble,'' she said in a serious tone.

The child's eager kisses were still warm on his lips. He looked out of pleading eyes, yet there was a sense of amusement in his heart. " Let it go this time, Milly dear. Let her use the name, since her heart is set upon it, and we will discuss the real adoption later on. I have made a will—I did it a month after we were married—and you will understand——''

" O Reese, don't !'' she said with a little cry.

" There, dear, let us dismiss it for the present. Only don't scold the little witch.''

The next day Nora found a pretty story-book on her desk that she had been wishing for. On the fly-leaf was written, " Nora V. L. Drayton, from her papa.''

" O mamma, papa said I might have his name ! And see how he has written it ! Doesn't it look lovely ?''

" Yes, dear.'' Her mother kissed her and smiled.

If she had been less winsome Reese Drayton could have been firmer with her ; but her adoration did touch his weak side, and it was quite weak toward the child of the woman he loved. She was proving herself a rather brilliant scholar. Her mother had given her a wide range for her thoughts and fostered her natural intelligence. She had been so much her companion that it was difficult to reduce her to the status of a child. And being older than the other cousins, she had always taken the lead.

Violet had gone to Beaumanoir for a visit. Tessy had decided that Edward Sherburne should have a Christmas Eve party on Saturday night ; but Ned Beaumanoir was coming from Baltimore, and she had written for Nora to come early in the week before and make a good long visit—as long as mamma could spare her—for Grandma Beaumanoir was longing to see her, and Aunt Fanny had the cunningest baby in the world, with a head full of curls.

There was not much to do at school that last week, so Nora went off in a tremor of delight. Uncle James Murray took her and Densie to Washington, and Uncle Leonard to Sherburne. They felt themselves quite large girls.

Lyndell and Millicent had enjoyed a lovely year of friendship. She dreamed it over there in the Sunday evening silence, listening to her husband's tender confidences, with her baby's soft breath of slumber against her cheek, and experiencing a thrill of delight for Millicent's sake.

The dinner bell rang. There was a soft, noiseless fall of snow outside—a Christmas bridal veil.

# CHAPTER XIX.

THE new year had begun when Dr. Carew went down to the station at Jersey City to meet the children. Densie Murray he deposited at her own door. They had had such a delightful time.

"O Uncle Bertram, are you not going to take me home?" cried Nora as they stopped at the Carew house.

"Auntie Dell has something to tell you," smiling cordially.

"Oh, what can it be? And mamma?"

"Mamma wanted us to tell you. Come upstairs in Auntie Dell's room."

They went together. Lyndell clasped her little guest in a fond embrace.

"Nora," exclaimed Auntie Dell, when the greetings were over, "a little sister came to you on Christmas Day. Mamma and papa think it one of the choicest of God's gifts, and they hope you have a warm welcome for it— that you will love it for their sakes."

Nora glanced from one to the other in amazement. Her chest swelled with a quivering inspiration, her eyes lost their laughing brightness, her pretty lips hardened with a protest. She stood straight and stiff.

"Nora dear, we are all very glad and happy," Auntie Dell began in a persuasive tone.

"I can't be glad; O Auntie Dell, I can't!" and she

stamped her foot on the floor. "They won't love me first and best now. Perhaps mamma—but for papa to have a little girl of his very own, and I am not his very own! Oh, why didn't God send her somewhere else?"

"Nora!" Uncle Bertram's tone was grave, rebuking.

"I can't tell a falsehood about it. I am not glad. Oh, I wish I had not gone away! It was such a lovely Christmas, and now it is all spoiled. I shall never like Christmas again—never!"

"My child, that is very wrong—wicked." Dr. Carew took both dimpled hands in his, but she jerked them away with unwonted passion. He took her arms then in a firm but gentle clasp and drew her to him as he sat down. Her eyes were shining with temper and tearless, but she made no further struggle. "Nora dear, you will break mamma's heart by such conduct," after a pause.

"Will anybody care if my heart is broken?"

"Yes, we all should; but you are not going to be so selfish as to insist they shall have no one to love but you. God, you see, would not allow you to grow up in this selfish manner, and He has sent some one to share the regard."

"Nora," said Auntie Dell, "do you think because I love little Honor very dearly that I have ceased to care for the twins?"

Nora studied her aunt in silence. Her lip lost a little of its firmness and quivered.

"But that's different," she subjoined at length. "I've had mamma such a long while, and she has had no little girl but me. When papa came I did not so much mind, because, you see, he loved me too. I think if it had been a little boy I wouldn't have cared quite so much ; but—and he is so fond of little girls. He loved Princess so much that sometimes I did not like it," she admitted with a peculiar honesty.

" But this is all very wrong and naughty. Nora, if I were papa I would not love you again until you loved my little girl."

" I don't suppose he will love me any more," she said in heart-breaking accents. " He will have his own little girl to love." Then she hid her face on Uncle Bertram's shoulder and gave a long, dry sob.

Dr. Carew kissed her cheek and pressed her close with infinite tenderness. It hardly seemed possible for a gay, laughing child to carry jealousy so far. He was sorry for her, provoked as well.

" I am going to see mamma," he began in a low, even tone. " Will you go with me ?"

" Must I go ?" raising her head.

" No ; you can stay here for days until you have thought it all over and have become convinced of the self-ishness in not wanting any other person or thing loved."

" O Uncle Bert, it isn't that ! Mamma loves you, and Auntie Dell, and the children, and the Sherburne children. I don't mind that—I love you all, too—but it is having some one come in your place and crowding you out."

" You will not be crowded out."

Nora was silent. He rose, and she stood there alone in a deserted attitude that gave him a pang. He felt moved to a relenting mood.

" At least you will send a message. You will make mamma very unhappy, perhaps keep her from sleeping to-night, and that will give her headache to-morrow. And you have loved her so."

"I love her now. You can tell her that. But I don't want to see——"

"And papa?"

"He isn't my real father, you know."

"Yet he has been so good and generous to you, and you will not make any return."

Dr. Carew crossed the room slowly. Then he kissed his wife and went out of the apartment. Nora took his seat and turned her face toward the window. Dell saw two big tears course slowly down her cheeks. She took up some sewing, and was puzzled what course to pursue, for she had not expected as much frank obstinacy as this, although she had experienced a misgiving that Nora would not welcome the tidings. Her reign had been so complete that she could not stand aside with the grace of love. Yet she pitied the child profoundly.

The early evening dusk was beginning to settle about the room. The children's voices sounded from the nursery—Bertie's joyous and laughing, little Milly's fine and clear, then Aunt Neale's. Nora listened and made a sudden movement, then checked herself with a touch of stiffness.

"Auntie Dell, may I go in and see the children?"

"Yes, dear," she answered unhesitatingly; but as Nora was passing she caught her hand, then rose and clasped the little girl in her arms. "We are all so sorry not to have you take the tidings with gladness, my child. You will be loved just the same. It will be you only who are hard and cold and unjust. Can't you soften a little? What will you do when you say your prayers to-night? Do you want God to forgive any naughtiness of yours in just this manner by standing aloof?"

"Auntie Dell," after a pause, "it isn't any question of forgiveness, I think. The beautiful house is Mr. Drayton's. All the lovely appointments and the money are his. I suppose in a certain way mamma belongs to him just as Aunt Tessy does to Uncle Leonard or you to Uncle Bert. And he gives mamma everything."

"Doesn't he give you everything as well?"

"Not quite everything," hesitatingly. "They both give me—that is——"

"They give you what is best for a little girl. You will have everything just the same."

"I don't care for the things so much. But I shall be at school and studying, and they will have *her* just every moment, all day long. She may be as sweet as little Honor, that you love so much. And she is all his. Of course I shall be crowded out. Perhaps now mamma will send me away to school. I think I would rather go. I can't be glad when no gladness will come. If you can't love anybody——"

Dell had said almost the same thing about Aunt Aurelia in her childhood. The bitterness of that experience flashed over her. The suffering had been very real. Childhood was narrow from its lack of experience.

"Go see the children and Aunt Neale."

In a moment Nora was the centre of attraction. Between the kisses and the clasping arms she was trying to tell Aunt Neale about everybody, and giving her a message Mrs. Armitage had sent, and the Christmas feast for the little colored children, as well as the lovely party at Sherburne. Freda came in to take the children to their supper, and Nora must go to see their new plates and bowls.

"I wish you wouldn't go home!" exclaimed Bertie.

" It will take you all day to-morrow to see my Christmas things."

" Perhaps I shall not."

To please them she ate a little. They had another play. Then Uncle Bert came in and romped with them until the dinner-bell rang, and they kissed Nora good-night.

" You saw Milly ?" Dell had questioned.

" Yes ; I simply said we thought it wiser that Nora should remain all night, that she, Milly, would be better able to take the meeting in the morning. She is quite nervous about it. I did not say a word concerning the tempest with her, but simply that Nora was surprised, but I gave the whole story to Drayton. He has indulged Nora foolishly, and now he must suffer for it. He has loved her too much."

" Do people ever love each other too much ?"

" Well, unwisely, then. Yes, I think you can love a child too much. There should be some new affection for the coming years."

" Bertram, I remember that I had a jealous tempest about Milly. I had come to love her very much, made her a certainty in my life, twined my girlish hopes about her. And when she told me of her engagement I went almost as wild as Nora. I really could have swept Baron von Lindorm off the face of the earth."

Bertram laughed and kissed his wife with a sense of amusement.

" And I was jealous of her later on," flushing, while her eyes grew dewy with emotion, " only then I was heroic," laughing softly.

" I do not mind the tempest as much as that passionless certainty. I wanted to shake her. The confidence vexed me."

" I think I have lived through that also. Perhaps it
is Sherburne obstinacy. When Mr. Wittingham took
me home to Sherburne the first time I was just as sure
that I could not love anything or anybody. I would not
even let his consideration soften me."

" But you were going among strangers, and this is
her own mother. She is so fond of children, too. She
is so quick to comprehend their desires, so ready to
amuse. Well, children are queer bundles of perversi-
ties."

Nora came down, holding tight to Aunt Neale's hand,
and took the place beside her. Grandpa bent over and
gave her a kiss and began at once to ask questions about
Sherburne. Nora's voice was not quite steady at first,
and she stole furtive glances at Uncle Bertram, wondering in her secret soul what mamma had said. But he
too seemed interested, and she gained courage as she
went on. She had played checkers with Grandpa Beaumanoir and beaten him.

" Hi ! hi !" exclaimed Dr. Carew, " we will have a
bout after supper. I think Grandpa Beaumanoir could
not have been trying his very best."

" He made one mistake and I took his king ; and then
I just swept along. Papa says I am a very good player,"
and there was a touch of triumph in her tone, but the
next instant she flushed and bit her lip. She had been
so fond of repeating papa's commendations.

" Well, you will have hard work to beat me, I warn
you."

" Uncle Beaumanoir taught me to play checkers,"
said Dell, " out on the great porch at Sherburne. Ned
and I had come to words about the game. I had a good
deal of temper in those days."

" And is Aunt Fanny's baby splendid ?"

" It has beautiful curly hair. And Uncle Cecil came down, and Uncle Win, who is just lovely. And little Ray is growing very pretty. O Auntie Dell, Aunt Julia says she looks a good deal as you did when you were a little girl !"

Auntie Dell laughed at that.

Grandpa found the checker-board when they went up-stairs, and they had a good deal of amusement, first one and then the other being victor.

" But I want you to play your very best," Nora declared. " I am not such a baby that I can't stand being beaten."

But when she had the best four out of seven games Aunt Neale suggested that it must be bedtime for little girls who had travelled all day, and grandpa said he would stroll down to the office and see how young Dr. Copeland was getting along. Aunt Neale went to the nursery to have a good-night with Auntie Dell. Uncle Bertram had been engrossed with a book ; but Nora could not rid herself of the sensation that a watchful eye was on her.

" Come, dear," said Aunt Neale's soft voice. She could not go around behind Uncle Bert, and she must say good-night. He raised his eyes, and somehow they impelled her.

" Uncle Bert"—her voice had a great tremble in it— " you said I was wicked. I did not mean to be wicked. I don't hate anybody, not one single person," with a bit of emphasis, " but you can't make yourself love all in a moment."

" No, my dear ; but there are days and weeks. And if one does not wilfully decide not to love, tenderness may creep into one's heart. But if you shut the doors very tight and keep out every kindly feeling you will make yourself miserable, and all for nothing—for mamma's heart is just the same. Do you suppose after having loved you all these years she could forget you in a brief fortnight?"

Nora's passion was mostly over, but the hurt and distrust remained. She could not argue about it. "Goodnight," she said with a kiss.

He caught her in his arms. "Do you not want to see mamma?" he asked rather upbraidingly.

"I suppose I shall go home to-morrow," she said, swallowing over a great lump in her throat that threatened to dissolve in tears.

"Papa is coming for you in the morning."

She made no reply, but gently disengaged herself, and the face that had been so bright fifteen minutes ago was sad enough now.

Lyndell joined him presently. His book was lying across his knee with his finger in to keep the place. She asked a question with her brown eyes. How beautiful they were with womanly tenderness!

"I wish I were as wise as father," he said with a sigh. "His experience was of a different kind, and some of it came with suffering. He ministered to souls as well as bodies. He does still. He is as good as a clergyman."

"I suppose the years and experience help."

"A child ought not puzzle one so. Yet I was almost afraid to promise for Drayton, though he promised readily enough for himself," and Bertram's face softened with a vague, sweet smile. "But he is simply overwhelmed with love for his own child. I wonder if I was so utterly carried away with joy?"

" Oh, yes, I think you were," and her eyes shone with mirthfulness.

" I couldn't send the poor little thing to bed with a sermon. She will no doubt cry herself to sleep many a night before she accepts the situation ; yet I am very thankful. An only child is not to be envied—hardly desired. I did not miss any companionship, for Beaumanoir was like a home to me ; but when I went away to school and college my heart used to ache for father. How I did wish there were other children—girls who would comfort him ! He was so fond of Millicent. Dell, you will never know how grateful I am that you love him and Aunt Neale. It has always made my heart ache to see old people crowded out. And you really were his child before you were my wife."

Lyndell leaned over and kissed her husband.

" Nora made one little apology, and I let it go at that. I *was* shocked this afternoon ; but a child with a large, generous soul is like a perfectly proportioned boat—it may be tossed about in a gale, but it rights itself. She has been first so long—the first grandchild, the first in all our affections. Yes, it will come hard to her to find herself superseded in a measure. And I dare say Drayton will want to indulge Nora more than ever because he has taken some of the devotion away from her."

" What did Milly say ?"

" I think she felt disappointed. Well, she has had a delightful fortnight, and is able to stand some strain. I said it was late, and we thought she would be better without the excitement. I couldn't and wouldn't answer her eyes."

Dell gave a little sigh and picked up some sewing. It was a great pleasure to her now, yet she could recall the terrible punishment it was to her in childhood. She realized now that a great deal of Aunt Aurelia's training had been unwise, but she also understood how the mistakes had arisen. And she often prayed for wisdom to guide her own little ones aright.

Nora was cuddled awhile in Aunt Neale's tender arms. She knew something had gone wrong, but she respected the child's reticence.

Nora shut her lips tightly when she was first left alone. "She would not care," she said to herself. And then she saw papa with the white bundle of lace and muslin in his arms, as she had seen Uncle Leonard and Uncle Bert, and the soft sound of a baby's voice, the kisses, while she sat one side neglected. A little sob broke through her stoicism, and she cried herself to sleep, as she had the first night Mr. Drayton had taken mamma away. And he was not her own real papa!

But the world was bright the next morning, and Kitty, the maid, came in to brush her hair and dress her, and everybody seemed gay and joyous. Grandpa teased her a little, and said he was going to win back the games he had lost last evening, for it stood to reason that with all his years of playing he knew more than a little girl. Uncle Bert kissed her as he went out, and then she had to see Bertie's Christmas stores, which seemed to be an accumulation of all the gifts that had been showered upon him since he was born.

Then "Miss Nora was wanted in the drawing-room." If she might run away somewhere! if she could have stayed at Beaumanoir! She went down reluctantly with her eyes on the fast diminishing steps of the stairs, and then some one clasped her in his arms so tightly that it was useless to try to get away.

"My dear little girl!" exclaimed papa in his tenderest tone. Then to his surprise he kissed amid some tears. They entered the drawing-room, and he drew her to a seat on the sofa. "We are longing to have you back," he said; "we have missed you very much. I found the old den lonesome; and mamma wants to see you."

"But you have had—her. And you can't care so much for me. I can never be your little girl again," she said resentfully.

"But you will be my big girl, my daughter. You will have a double portion of love, because you were mamma's first; and if I had not loved you I am quite sure she would never have loved me, and then I love you for yourself. O my child, you need not fear being crowded out! You are dearer to me than ever before."

Only a very obdurate heart could have resisted the tone and the reassuring words. She was glad to feel his arms about her; she let her head rest on his shoulder. Yes, he was hers. After all, a little baby just had to lie still and be tended and couldn't say a word, nor go out, so she could have papa awhile longer. She wouldn't give him up, since he loved her still.

Yet she was silent, and heretofore she had been so ready to chatter. He felt the difference. Still he was glad not to have her in a temper. Of course it was hard at first.

"Well," he began presently, "will you go home with me now? There has been some fine skating at the Park. For a few days after Christmas there was fine sleigh-riding. I did not go because I had no little girl to take. I have been spoiled, and could not go alone."

She smiled then. Had he missed her?

" And you had a lovely time with the children ?"

" It was splendid ! Aunt Tessy taught me a new song. Princess sings so beautifully—just like a bird. And, oh, dear, little Ned Beaumanoir is so queer and so awful particular ; and Ray Stanwood is so bright and sweet, and she is taller than Princess."

She was talking herself into her usual good humor. Perhaps Uncle Bert had announced the tidings without due care.

" Well, will you hunt up your wraps ? Where is Auntie Dell ?"

" I will call her," exclaimed Nora, flying upstairs.

Lyndell was very glad to hear the cheerful voice and find a smiling face.

Kitty helped her on with her coat, and she said good-by to Aunt Neale and the babies. Then a few moments later they were out in the sunny street.

" Shall we ride ?" he asked.

" Oh, no, I don't care to." She was in no hurry to get home. The old feeling was coming back. This miserable little baby had changed everything, even the home.

Here they were at the door. Davis let them in with a bow and wished Missy a " Happy New Year." She lingered a moment in the hall ; there was a great bunch of carnations in the jardinière that made all the air fragrant. How beautiful everything looked !

She unfastened her coat going up the stairs. Mamma's door was open, and she sat there in a reclining chair in a soft, white gown with gay cushions piled about her. She held out her hand and smiled. It was not quite the picture she had expected. The arms were not full of the new love, and she flew to them.

" O my darling !" exclaimed her mother.

She was curiously changed, Nora thought at the second glance. Her eyes were so large and soft and dark, and her skin was so very white that you could trace the fine veins underneath. Her gown was tied with soft red ribbons, and the bright cushions at her back threw her up like a bit of sculpture.

" O mamma, how beautiful you are !" the child exclaimed in a sort of surprised way.

" And glad to see my little daughter—a big daughter now. Nora, you grow every moment."

" It must be because I've run so much. Sherburne and I ran races. Ned couldn't beat a tortoise. And every night we danced, mamma. Aunt Tessy plays such bewitching things that your feet just can't keep still. It has been lovely !"

" I am very glad, my daughter. See, dear, this is Miss James."

The nurse was a sweet-faced woman of thirty or thereabout. She had the daintiest little cap, and a soft, white fichu crossed Quakerwise on her bosom. Her smile was quite fascinating.

" I did not think she was so large," said Miss James. " And now we have a little sister for you that has your mother's dark eyes, and will resemble her, I fancy."

Millicent felt the figure she held stiffen in a way of protest. " I don't want any one but just you," she said in a whisper, kissing her mother eagerly.

Millicent went on questioning her about her visit. Presently she said, " Your Christmas gifts are in your room. Do you not want to see them ?"

" And I brought ever so many from Beaumanoir. They are in the trunk."

She turned suddenly. In the corner stood a pretty bassinet with a lace cover and rose-colored ribbons. She remembered she had wanted rose-color in her room ; but she had fallen in love with the blue rug. She made a swift movement away.

They had been using her room ; but yesterday it had been restored to its former order at a little inconvenience. Millicent felt that she ought to turn it into a nursery, but to send Nora on the next floor alone was not to be thought of. The bed lay spread out with gifts. There was a picture of some kittens at play that Nora had admired so much—"for you can almost hear the laugh in it," she had said—a white India silk gown, a box of gloves, assorted tints, a beautiful dressing-case, and a tiny box from papa. It was not the diamond she had coveted, but an exquisite ring of pearls around a fire opal, and two pins with heads to match. Books there were without number.

" O mamma," she cried in delight, " you will have to give me another room to hold all my beautiful things, this is getting so full. And there isn't a vacant corner in my case for one single book. Oh, how good you are !"

She flew to her mother and kissed her rapturously.

" Yet you have not even said a word about papa's Christmas gift and mine," said her mother softly.

Nora's face settled into lines of dissatisfaction. She stood quite stiff beside her mother.

" O mamma, yesterday, when Uncle Bert told me, I didn't want to think papa had any little girl besides me ; and now"—her voice began to tremble—" I shouldn't mind quite so much if she did not belong to you. I've had you always——"

" You will have me just the same."

" No, mamma, it can't be the same ; babies need so much care, and I suppose their mothers can't help loving them.   And if she has eyes like you—papa thinks your eyes so lovely——"

Nora gave a swift, choking sob.

" Well, your eyes are like papa's, only merrier.   And, my dear, he is so good and tender to you, you ought to make him some return."

" I will love him."   Then she ran into her room and drew the *portière*.

" She takes it very hard," said the nurse.

# CHAPTER XX

SCHOOL began, and a fortnight passed before any girl learned that Nora Drayton had a rival in a small sister. By that time she had learned to tolerate the fact with a good deal of equanimity. It had not made as much difference as she feared. The regular nurse had gone, and her place had been supplied by a tidy, cheerful maid, who looked really pretty in her dainty cap and white apron. She had a pleasant, smiling face, and was neat and deft. Mamma came downstairs to meals and spent evenings in the library. Nora seemed to have papa as much as usual, and he took a greater interest in her lessons, was ready to talk French or German with her, and to go skating, of which he was very fond.

She had at first glanced indifferently at the child as it lay on the nurse's knee, staring around. It *did* have her mother's eyes, and its hair was dark. And if it should be beautiful like mamma ! For Nora was simply pretty with youth and health, rather merry, blue eyes, and an abundance of light hair that would not curl, although a few tendrilly locks drooped about her forehead and never grew long.

But there was no eager enthusiasm, which was a great disappointment to both parents.

"I am not as fond of babies as I used to be," she said to her mother one day in a vaguely excusing tone ;

" there seems such a host of them now. They are more entertaining when they can talk and run about. And I have so many lessons. Mamma, I suppose I could go away to school next year ?"

" You are rather young, I think, when there are so many excellent schools at hand," said mamma with no show of special opposition. She was trying to be very patient.

Oh, how Nora studied and practised her music ! She was beginning to paint flowers and to take an interest in botany. Then she wrote letters to Grandma Beaumanoir, to little Cousin Sherburne and Bevis Osborne. There were several " girls' teas," from five to seven, when they played hostess and visitors, and mamma gave her one in the reception-room, which was the admiration of her schoolmates, because Mr. Drayton asked them in the library to view his curiosities, and mamma played for them. She went to dancing school also, and once a month the girls could invite their friends. Nora was very proud of her stylish papa. She could not give him up—he should not love baby best ; but she knew he loved it very much. She detected a curious new softness in his tone ; and sometimes when she spoke he was a little absent, as if he was thinking of something else. Then he did not sit up in the " den" as much as formerly. She used to hear him reading to mamma, and from the tones she knew they were both talking to the baby. She began to notice and to laugh, though she was graver than little Honor Carew.

" You don't come any more," Bertie said complainingly, " and you don't play."

" I am getting such a big girl and have so many things to do. Big girls do not play."

"Then I don't like big girls. Densie Murray plays and makes us laugh, and we run and do everything."

They would soon love Densie better than they would her! She choked up a little. Well, she could not be a child even for their sakes.

She was shooting up into a tall girl. She wanted her gowns made down to her shoe tops, and took on some young womanly ways.

Millicent sighed a little.

One could not really find fault with her. She was respectful, obedient for the most part, and rarely teased for any indulgence now. Mr. Drayton would have been very glad to have her, and she could have coaxed many a favor out of him, but she was quite too proud. She *did* suggest Dell in her childhood, only she was making new girl friends continually. They were pleased at being asked to the Drayton house, since so many of the "best" people had the *entrée*.

But baby grew, and did not seem to pine for her sister's favor. She had her morning ride in her handsome carriage with dainty white blankets, her play with mamma, her dinner and nap, and ride again, unless the weather was very unpromising, and by six she was in her bed and seldom disturbed any one in the evening. When there was no company mamma insisted that Nora should spend an hour after eight in the library in social life.

Uncle Floyd was quite fond of her, and now Uncle Cecil was in the city. Uncle Floyd had a parish in view on Long Island, and was to be married in May, having kept tryst all these years with his sweetheart. Then Uncle Archie had settled business matters quite to his satisfaction, and had the proffer of a governmental position in New York. His father's health had failed a good deal, and there was some talk of his being retired on half pay.

"It seems providential," he said to Lyndell, "that it should come about this way. We can have a pretty home in some of the suburbs, and I can be the mainstay of their declining years. I shall have my little girl, and go shares with her and mother. She has never missed any love or care since she has been old enough to know what it really meant. I have had such a long exile that I shall be glad of a home of my own."

Uncle Archie took a great liking to Nora. "You will soon have a young lady on your hands," he said to Millicent.

"Oh, I hope not. I wish there were some cousins nearer her age. You see, she is quite advanced in her studies, and it takes her into the classes of girls two years older than she is. And she is so tall. She has grown by the moment the past six months. I did not get out from under the wing of a governess until I was sixteen, when I went to school; and though I was tall, I felt like an immature girl. She is as self-possessed as a young lady. I have lost my little girl."

"But you have another in her place. What a lovely child she is!" and Archie's eyes kindled with tenderness.

Had she put the baby too much in Nora's place, and was the elder daughter slipping out of her heart? No, not that; for there were times when she had grown sore with longing love, when the aloofness on Nora's part had been like a stab to her. It was hard for the child to see another in her own mother's arms; but she had grown out of them.

She had come to notice her little sister rather more,

and she made no protest about anything. She answered cheerfully when any one asked about the baby. She did take a secret pride in hearing the girls comment on her beauty when they saw her in her pretty carriage as the nurse passed them in the street. Her mother did not appeal to Nora's affection, and baby evinced curious shyness. She never wanted to go to strangers. She soon became fond of Auntie Dell, and stretched out her hands at once to Uncle Bert, who cuddled her up in a most beguiling manner.

"I am rather glad," Reese Drayton declared when Bertram Carew had been in one morning nursing her in such a charming fashion that her eyes followed him, and she held out her dainty hands, ready to be carried off without question. "I don't want her to love many people like that. Oh, my precious darling!"

She smiled then as her father caught her in his arms and almost smothered her with kisses, adding, "I like her to be exclusive."

"She doesn't make advances first, certainly. I have almost wished she did where Nora was concerned," said her mother. "O Reese, what shall we do with her? You have been so generous and tender. I have wondered at you sometimes."

"Part of it may be good breeding." He laughed and flushed a little too. "I promised her that morning, when she seemed to think she would be dropped out altogether, that I should give her the same love, that she would be just as dear to me. Why, it would be detestable if I had loved her merely for the sake of winning her mother and thrown her aside when I had achieved my purpose."

"She could go away to school another year."

"Oh, I should miss her too much! I admire her little piquancies. She sometimes suggests Mrs. Carew in an intangible manner, and it does amuse me—just that illusive resemblance, gone in a moment, that recalls the other young girl. But I wish she wouldn't grow up so fast."

"That is a Sherburne trick."

"If she was cross about it or unamiable it would be different. She is so particular about keeping the strict line of propriety, it makes me smile sometimes when I want to shake her," and a half smile crossed his face.

"I am glad you do want to shake her," Milly said with a touch of humor. "And instead you take her off somewhere, and she is proud of her escort. You see, she really has not begun to suffer any of the pangs of rivalry."

"I like to watch the changes—the ideas a girl has one week, and with what supreme wisdom she discards them the next; how her opinions take shape, and her judgment matures, and all the little inconsistencies that make her charming and keep you in a state of surprise."

"If she were only ten!" sighed the mother.

"We will not think about the school yet. She is too young. And if all the Sherburne children could be together next summer!"

"Oh, dear, there is Floyd's marriage, and all the Stanwoods are coming up! I do hope it may be very happy. I ought to go home and see mamma before warm weather sets in."

"I should like to buy a big farm, or acres of seaside, where we could go every summer. Why couldn't we all join?"

"And yet home is so delightful with its many comforts," Millicent said, with a lingering cadence as she glanced about.

"I have talked this baby asleep," said the baby's father. "Score one against me for a clergyman, though I might set the congregation at ease."

He laid her carefully down in her pretty white bed without waking her, though he kissed the sweet lips.

"Mamma," Nora said a few days later, "I would like to propose something—a change—and if you only would approve! It would be a great deal nicer all around."

Millicent glanced up with questioning eyes.

"It is this, mamma : I have my room so full of everything, and you are crowded in here. When I was at Helen Meade's yesterday we were up in her room. She has the hall room for a pretty library, with books and her desk, and then her chamber seems roomy and clear. It is just like ours upstairs——"

"Would you like to be up there alone?"

"Why, it would be just over you, and not very far. I could call. I am not afraid," with a little laugh. "And if any of the girls came to stay—then, mamma, Auntie Dell said you ought to have this for a nursery."

"It would be very nice. I was thinking we might all go upstairs and keep these for guest chambers."

"But I should not feel lonesome."

"If you really like it——"

"O mamma, I do !" She came and kissed her mother, quite like old times.

Millicent wondered if it was a plan to take herself farther away. Oh, that was ungracious !

Mr. Drayton fell in with the idea readily. When they went to survey the smaller room he suggested widening the doorway and making it more of an alcove, then shelving all across one end. There would still be abundant room for her bookcase and her desk.

" Oh, that would be splendid !" she cried enthusiastically, her eyes shining in appreciation.

" We will have it done at once, before Aunt Julia gets here."

" O papa !" she caught his hand.

" My little girl, don't you know that I desire to make you happy ?"

There were tears in Nora's eyes. She could make papa very happy on one point, but she had never tried. It was not enough to avoid doing evil ; one had to learn to do well ; and she did not desire to.

She was all excitement the week the alterations were going on. After the shelves were set the room was papered in the same tints of the other—a very pale bluish green. She could have new colors, but her lovely rug harmonized very well. She had a fine time putting her belongings in order—taking all day Saturday except the hour for her music lesson.

" And now I have an array of empty shelves," she said laughingly. " It is like the monkey and the bread and the cheese."

" In the course of years they will come out even," rejoined her father. " I think I have some vacant spaces yet. Now you have a house to grow into."

" I hope I won't fill it all myself," she returned gayly. " I don't want to be immense."

But oh, how pretty and spacious it was ! Yet it did seem a little strange when she went to bed. Jane and Mrs. Black were upstairs, and mamma and papa just below her. Had she gone away from her mother ? Yet her mother had first gone away from her, she said with a swelling heart.

The very next week Aunt Julia, Uncle Stanwood, and little Ray came. Ray was such a sweet, bright child, and adored her grandmother. Dell was thankful that Aunt Julia had a little girl of her very own after the years of loss and longing.

Floyd's marriage was at noon in church. Elsie Bevans had come up from the country rectory, and was married from the home of her aunt and grandmother, with whom she had spent a good deal of her time for the last three years. They were going on a little journey, and when they returned would take possession of the quaint old rectory at Edgeport, that was quite a seaside resort in summer and not really unpleasant in winter. Aunt Julia and Archie were to go down for a few days to make some additions and help put the place in order.

Uncle Stanwood remained with the Carews. He was a good deal worn out and had a weak heart, but with care it might do its work for many years. Winthrop would graduate this summer, and now the real work of their life was done. They could lean on Archie through the declining years.

Nora was studying hard for promotion. She was not quite sure that she wanted to go to boarding-school; there were so many splendid things in the city and so much more freedom. And now that she had her beautiful room and her books and her friends to drop in and envy her—yes, they really did ! There were some richer girls, but not one of them had a father who had leisure to be so devoted. Now that the weather was pleasant he occasionally called at school and took her to drive, though she declared she had to study her lessons by the way. And of course he took mamma and the baby out separately. It was nicer than for them all to go together, she thought.

Aunt Julia came back with quite a glowing account of Floyd's new home. The people were cordial and kind, the real settlers being rather old-fashioned, plain people. Between them and the bay there was perhaps a mile, and this was largely devoted to summer cottages, with two or three hotels. Young Mrs. Floyd was very sweet and cordial to her mother-in-law, and both were sorry it was too far off for Archie to select a home where he could go in to the city every day.

"Why not the city itself—uptown?" suggested Dr. Carew.

"I want some space, some ground. You know, we have never been very much restricted, even when we lived in a fort. And some out-of-doors life will be better for father. There are so many pretty towns up the Hudson, on both sides of the river. When I find a place just to my liking I shall buy. I have made money enough for that, and a little over," smiling cheerfully.

Archie and Lyndell talked about the time little Ray had been left motherless with her.

"I suppose the real good will be in these years to come. Unless *she* had married again I should never have felt quite safe, though I made up my mind she should never take the child away from my mother, no matter what happened. Sometimes I feel a little curious to know how matters are with her ; but I suppose, after her experience with poverty, she married well at least. I hope she is satisfied."

"What will you tell Ray presently ?"

"That puzzles me. Ray isn't a curious child. I

wonder if it is wise to allow her to take it for granted
that her mother is dead? My mother has always said,
'she had no mamma,' which is too sadly true. I think
she has come to consider her mother dead."

"I believe it is one of the things best left to the
future," returned Dell thoughtfully. "I used to try to
arrange the world a good deal—it is the province of
youth"—smiling, "and now I wait to see God's plan
for events."

"We think Floyd delightfully married. His wife's
heart is in his work and happiness, and religion with
her is daily living. We are apt to make it too much
Sunday work. Through these years of prosperity which
have come unexpectedly to me, after all, I have tried to
keep in mind what I could best do for others, my own
life having been swept away. And now this duty has
come to me. With care father may live years. Winthrop is entitled to his own young life."

"Oh," cried Dell, "the first time I saw you all stands
out like a picture. Floyd was a little boy, Win not
much more than a baby—and I was so fond of little children. Am I growing old?"

"You certainly do not look superannuated yet, and
they are very young men. It was that Christmas at
Sherburne and you had been ill. Mamma was desperately gone on you. And if my little sister had lived she
would have been just your age. I suppose that was one
reason you seemed so near to her—that and not having
any parents of your own. But you have been very near
and dear to us all."

She smiled, yet the quick tears flooded her eyes as she
remembered the time when she thought the whole world
had been swept away and herself stranded on rocky soli-

tudes. But that had been only a little space, seen through cloud and storm. How the sun had shone afterward! And all these little things had their influence. She had been helped as much by the things she had waited for as those she had snatched at impatiently. There was no great mystery about life; it was plain, every-day living, forgetting and going back and then going on again. It was all one could do.

How pleasant the little breaks were! One and another going and coming and keeping alive the flame of family love. She and Millicent talked it over afterward.

"I hope Archie will not go very far from New York," Millicent said. "He is in the right state now for manly, friendly development. His retirement from the world has laid a foundation for higher knowledges, and he could enjoy society so much."

"We can none of us regret the step his wife took, and yet it does seem a pity when a man is so formed for domestic life that he cannot have what is best and sweetest. I am glad the child is so little like her mother. One can feel sure after Aunt Julia's judicious training that she will not be a reed to pierce through his heart."

"Can one be sure about children?" Millicent sighed just under her breath.

"Oh, children are not perfect. Neither are grown people," with a bright, cheerful laugh. "Yet we have all made out very well in spite of the numerous faults some of us had. And we shall do our best with our own little ones. That is all God asks of us. Are you borrowing trouble for this lovely angel?"

"Oh, no," Millicent smiled then.

"I am so glad you have her, and that you find a little time for other things. How delightful these rooms are!"

Dell sat holding Millicent's baby, and she glanced around with an appreciative air.

" Yes, I am glad of the larger space, and Nora rejoices in her added domain. Her study is really pretty. She is painting quite well, and has added two very pretty plaques for its adornment. She has one quite artistic friend who goes into an art school next year. Only her friends make her seem too old for her years.''

" Or you make her too young. Yet I am glad matters go on smoothly. Perhaps the change was inevitable. I cared for babies always ; she seems to have outgrown them—I see it with my children. She is not half as enthusiastic as she used to be, but she is very proud of little Baby Hope.''

Pride was not love the mother of the two children knew. Nora seemed aiming at companionship with her father. The little withholding had disappeared. She was not quite as demonstrative in some ways ; she took attentions more as her right. Millicent realized that she saw less of her elder daughter. She smiled to herself, but it seemed as if Nora rather relegated her to the position of the baby's mother instead of her own. The curious pang of jealousy seemed to have died of its own lack of sustenance.

These pleasant mornings the nurse took her little charge out early. Nora had a half hour's music practice before she went to school, and often evaded an adieu to the baby in the morning, though with no really defined intention. The school session with a short intermission continued until two. There was music twice a week, a painting lesson, and now a botanizing expedition.

Millicent had two or three morning hours exclusively to herself. Mr. Drayton would not hear to her giving up her literary pursuits. When they drove in the afternoon she generally took her baby, and in the early evening it was in bed. But she remembered when Nora felt almost as if a day was lost if she had not seen the Sherburne children.

Nora had decided within her own heart that the baby would not be a very powerful rival for two or three years. She might be at school, she would be a grown-up girl, if not a young lady. She would take her full share of papa now. And she said proudly, when some girl tried to pique her into a show of jealousy, that the advent of the baby had made no difference at all. She purposely kept from witnessing the caressing tenderness its father bestowed upon it.

May came in warm for the season, yet the house was so airy no one suffered, though people began to discuss summer resorts, and plans for the benefit of the poor children of the crowded streets were being considered on every hand. Millicent had them at heart almost as much as Lyndell, whose little ones kept in a riotous state of health.

"Doesn't the baby look pale, Jane?" Mrs. Drayton said one morning.

Her eyes seemed so large and dark, and the dusky little fringe of hair was a foil to the clear, fine complexion that did not abound in roseate tints. Yet she had been exceptionally well, a little restless for the last few days, but sleeping quite as usual.

"She is always so white," returned Jane admiringly. "I notice it when I have her in the Park. She's as fair as any child with golden hair. And oh, Mrs. Drayton, she is so much prettier than the average children that people turn around to look at her."

"You are very devoted, Jane," said the mother

with a smile, glad the child was not old enough to be harmed with admiration.

" She's such a little darling ! You seldom come across such a good child. Perhaps it is because you use so much regularity ; but she'll be getting teeth and all that presently, and it stands to reason she won't be so generally well. Though it isn't quite as if you did not know about babies, and Miss Nora is such a fine, splendid . young girl. But this baby is more like you."

" Keep in the shade this morning," Millicent said, smiling a good-by to the faithful nurse.

Mr. Drayton had a business friend in to luncheon, and they sat a long while over the fruit, discussing some Western investments. Then it was Mrs. Drayton's last " afternoon" for the season, and for some cause it seemed unusually entertaining. Mr. Drayton came in, and everybody lingered as if loth to go. They had an engagement for the evening that they could not well relinquish.

" The baby frets a little," Millicent said as she was dressing. It was rather unusual.

" She woke up out of her nap. Miss Nora is practising that duet with her friend. I think it rather startled her."

" We shall not be gone more than an hour or so."

Millicent stooped to kiss her baby. Nora, she remembered, had had various little illnesses. Was it because the baby had been so generally well that now she felt disturbed ?

How brilliantly the girls were playing ! Should she check them a little ?

" Come," said her husband, holding out his hand as she reached the foot of the stairs. " Good-evening, young ladies."

Nora darted out and kissed them both. "I shall be deep in lessons when you return." she said, "or else deep in bed."

"We shall not stay late."

How soft and refined her mother's voice was! She was beginning to remark some of the elegancies of speech and tone that she had once told her mother were "fussy."

Miss Golding was to give a musicale with her scholars at the close of the term, two or three weeks hence. Nora Drayton and Myra Copeland had been selected among the players. Myra's brother was in Dr. Carew's office, and she was quite a favorite among Nora's friends.

Every now and then the baby woke with a start. The music stopped at length, and Davis took Miss Copeland home. Nora ran up to her room and began to study.

"How queer the baby should cry so much!" she thought. It disturbed her. But she was abed and asleep when her mother returned. The baby too was sleeping peacefully.

"If I tell her about it she will feel worried," Jane said to herself. She had come to have a good deal of care for her kindly mistress.

But from midnight to morning baby was very uneasy. Just at daylight she fell asleep again and Millicent with her, and Mr. Drayton would not have the tired mother roused.

"What is the matter with mamma?" asked Nora, not finding her in the breakfast-room, as she crossed over and placed her dimpled hands on her father's shoulders.

"The baby disturbed her, and I want her to have another nap. Can't we get along alone?" smilingly.

"O papa, can I pour your coffee? Why, it is just charming."

She went around to her mother's place. The table

was small and cozy. Davis waited on them in his perfect fashion. Papa talked to her as if she were quite
grown up, telling her some of the incidents of last
evening. She enjoyed it all wonderfully.

" Can you do without the practice this morning?"
he asked.

She would have done without a greater thing for that
tone and smile.

" Oh, yes ; and I ought to study every moment."

She was so rosy and bright, so round and dimpled.
Study and city life left no mark on her perfect health.
Would baby ever be like that ? he wondered. But Millicent had a rare sort of delicacy, and yet she was always
well.

When Nora came down in her graceful, wide-brimmed
hat and her books in her silk bag she paused for a mo
ment. The *portière* was drawn at her mother's door.
She raised the corner.

Jane shook her head and placed her finger on her lips,
and the child tripped lightly down the broad stairway
without even giving the baby a second thought.

At noon Bertram Carew came and looked a little grave.

Mr. Drayton was watching for Nora, who, flushed and
eager, ran up the steps.

" Where is mamma ? It's botany afternoon, and we
are going to the Park. And do you suppose I could take
tea afterward with Beatrice White ? We are planning a
kind of picnic—all our class—and the girls are to meet
there to arrange it."

" Yes, my dear, I will explain to her," taking Nora's
books as if the matter was settled.

" Oh, you delightful papa !" She kissed him and
was off.

# CHAPTER XXI

"DELL," Dr. Carew said quite late that evening, "could you go and stay all night with Milly? You are her dearest friend. Honor will not suffer for any care with Freda at hand."

"O Bertram, you do not mean——" All the bright color went out of Dell's face.

He drew a long breath and compressed his lips, as if to admit the danger would make it true.

"Is the baby as ill as that? O Bertram, and we have never had a really anxious moment! Dear Millicent! Are you sure——"

"I am sure of nothing. It is one of those inexplicable cases. I shall fight for it as if it were my own, but it is a very serious matter, and it will go hard with Millicent."

"Why, how long has it been ill? It seemed well enough two days ago."

Dell was so surprised that her very throat constricted.

"It has been dropping down about thirty hours. I was there this morning, and did not apprehend anything very serious; but still the case was grave. I have been twice since—indeed, only left them an hour ago. I shall stay all night. I have been arranging everything with father. I will explain to Aunt Neale while you see Freda."

He glanced at his own little flock and kissed their rosy

faces, for even Milly was outgrowing the delicacy that had marked the two earlier years of her life. And he breathed a prayer for the other mother and father.

Dell was soon ready. They walked on in silence. She was so stunned that she could only cling to her husband's arm. How happy they had all been in their children— Tessy, Alice, Violet, and herself! Was the first sorrow to fall upon Millicent as that other sorrow had fallen, swiftly, with hardly a warning? She implored Heaven to avert it.

When Mr. Drayton heard the voices he came out on the landing and gave each a hand as they ascended the stairs. Millicent was sitting by the small white bed, and raised her pale, apprehensive face, that smiled with a gratitude that was voiceless from emotion. Dell bent over and kissed her.

The baby lay with its eyes half open, a little star of dark shadowed by the dusky lashes that were already plentiful. The dark hair made tiny rings about her forehead, and the face looked like an exquisite bit of sculpture. Now and then a shadow as of pain would creep over it, and a hardly perceptible cry would pass the lips without any decided motion.

"Millicent"—and Dr. Carew took her hand with a gentle authority—"I want you to lie down here. You will be utterly spent."

"Oh, no, no!" in a tone of entreaty.

"Yes," firmly, raising her to her feet. "Dell will take your place. There is nothing you can do, and you will be here if any change occurs. See, I shall not send you away. I know what it is to you."

Drayton took her other arm, and thus impelled, she crossed to the bed. He arranged the pillows and kissed her lips, almost as colorless as the baby's. Then he fanned her gently, but she lay with wide-open eyes and brain strained to its utmost tension.

Some time after he motioned Dr. Carew to his place.

"I must write a note and send to the Whites'. Nora is there. She had better remain all night, for her mother's sake."

"Oh, yes," replied Bertram; "we want as little excitement as possible."

Millicent moved her eyes assentingly. Perhaps Nora would return to-morrow to be the only daughter of the house, to have all the love again.

Drayton wrote to Mrs. White, begging her to keep Nora for the night, and to the child, making no alarming explanation. Nora had entertained some of her schoolmates with an all-night visit, but her mother had objected to her staying away. Beatrice had two brothers older than herself, gay, jolly young fellows, and, with the aid of another friend, they had been passing a merry evening.

"Oh," she cried, "let me see Davis! Is the baby very ill? What did he say?"

"He just left the notes and went away. Babies are often ill," returned Mrs. White. "If it was really serious they would have sent for you."

The young people went on with their amusement. When the other visitor went home, Arthur White accompanied her. Beatrice and Nora retired—for it was past ten—and they chattered for awhile after they were in bed, until Nora was so sleepy she forgot to listen. When she woke in the morning she was rather confused at her surroundings. Then the incident of last evening came back to her. While Beatrice was still asleep she rose and brushed out her hair, braiding it deftly.

"Good-by," with a kiss ; "I must go home. Oh, I hope baby is no worse !"

"Don't go," returned Beatrice sleepily. "I will get ready and go down to breakfast with you."

"Oh, no matter, I really can't wait. We had a splendid time last night. I wish I had some big brothers or cousins. I will see you again at school."

Mrs. White tried to make her take some breakfast ; but the glamour of the lights, music, and fun was gone. How warm the morning seemed ! or was it that she hurried along so swiftly ? The hall door was open, the vestibule speckless. She touched the button, every pulse in a tremor ; but she had been bidden to stay.

Davis opened the door with a grave inclination of the head. She entered the hall and then stood still in alarm. Mr. Drayton was coming downstairs pale and sorrowful-eyed, weariness and grief in every line of his face.

"O papa !" She held out both hands as she uttered a cry of dismay.

He turned her into the reception-room, and, clasping her in his arms, kissed her with dreariness instead of pleasure, though the arms were tight about her as if he would never let her go.

"O papa !" she cried in a broken voice. "The baby——"

"We have been watching all night. There is no hope, I think. Dr. Carew and Aunt Dell are still here. O Nora, you will be our own little girl again—you will have no need——"

"Papa, do not say it ! You will break my heart,"

she interrupted passionately. " Your little girl ! For
I am only half yours ; and oh, I don't deserve to be even
that ! Poor, sweet mamma ! Uncle Bert said once that
I was wicked because I could not be glad ; but now,
papa, I shall be sorry my whole life long. Oh, what can
I do ? Can't Uncle Bert save her, when he helps the
sick people in the hospitals and everywhere ?"

" He has done his best. Poor, sweet little girl !
Mamma will want all your comfort, my dear. We
couldn't tell you last night——"

She was sobbing now. The little sister she had not
loved, that she had not made really welcome, that she
had hardly ever caressed, and whose infantile beauty had
been a source of half envy, another cause for hardening
her heart. And she knew, she always had the inner
conviction, that little Hope had the best right.

" O papa, you ought to send me away somewhere—to
school, perhaps—where I could not see you or mamma or
any one I had loved, just to be solitary and without love
or any one to care for me——"

" I am afraid we should punish ourselves quite as
much as you. Mamma could not stay alone in her sorrow. I hoped you would grow to love her, Nora. I
know it was hard. Child, you could not understand
that your mother's heart was not really divided."

" It wasn't so much mamma. You see, she *did* belong to me, and no one could take her quite away. But
you were not my very own," and the tenderness with
which she clung to him moved him in his sorrow. " I
didn't want you to love any one better than you loved
me."

The jealous eagerness went to his heart. Had she
cared so much ? He had considered it a rather amusing

childish ebullition at first, and then he had wondered at
her steadfast indifference to the pretty child.

"I shall always love you. Even at your naughtiest
you are very dear to me. And she would have been so
sweet that I think you could not have helped loving her.
I am quite sure affection would have come in time."

"And I can never love her now? Oh, if I prayed in
the deepest earnest, if I promised to love her and let you
love her with all your heart and not be jealous. do you
think God would send her back? Oh, can't some one
save her?"

Nora's sobs shook her with regret and a sense of abhorrence with herself. Little Hope's father, not her
very own! It was wicked to want to take him away
from his own little girl. What could she do to give
him all back again?

Some one came down the stairs and stood in the doorway. The two men glanced at each other, the father
with breathless pain.

"I don't really dare to give you hope, Drayton," said
the comforting voice, "but the symptoms *are* better.
She has taken some nourishment, and has fallen into a
natural sleep. I will be back presently. Dell can watch
her."

Nora did not raise her head. She felt awe-stricken at
the sound of Uncle Bertram's voice and scarcely heeded
what he did say.

"Come, child, and have some breakfast."

"No, I don't want any." Then Nora made a sudden
rush up to her own room and threw herself on the bed.
What a cruel, selfish girl she had been all this while!

Drayton went up a few minutes afterward. Millicent,
utterly spent, had fallen into a doze of exhaustion.

Dell's eyes were bright, hopeful. And only then he realized what Dr. Carew had been saying. He came and leaned over his child. There was the same deathlike pallor, but now the blue-veined lids were closed and the breathing regular.

"I cannot help hoping," Lyndell said softly, and he pressed her hand in wordless gratitude.

Before Bertram's return the baby had stirred and uttered a natural little cry, that was like music and roused the sleeping mother. Dell gave her a spoonful of nourishment, then another, and she lay still in perfect content.

"O Dell," Millicent said weakly, "I think I should have died without you!" She came around and leaned her head on her husband's shoulder. The big girl might reasonably have been jealous then, for her mother had no thought about her. It was the first time she had faced death when human love could still plead. The other sorrow had stolen upon her as a thief in the night.

Bertram came in with Aunt Neale and took his wife home, though she hardly felt her fatigue.

"Do you know, this has recalled Leonard's long illness," Dell said, "and how you fought for him. What a long night!"

"That *was* fighting. This was a good deal waiting and feeling your own impotence. A baby is such a delicate little thing—at least so we think, except when we see the children of the slums come through everything. The baby was stronger than it looked, and its strength was the blind chance I was counting on. I feel now as if it might come through, though we cannot be quite sure until the next twenty-four hours have passed. I must look up a nurse, for Millicent must sleep to-night or she will be ill. How hard Drayton would have taken it ! I am glad for his sake——"

"It would have been strange if the first baby to go out of all the household had been Millicent's. Would any of us have given one of ours in its stead, I wonder?"

"God does not ask us to do that," he answered reverently.

He sent Dell to bed presently, and at noon Aunt Neale was relieved.

Millicent and Mr. Drayton had watched through the morning with a more intense interest, if possible, than through the night. There were little changes now. The lips would have a shadow of color, the breathing greater depth, the moments of slumber more restful. The little cry did not have the tremulous gasp in it that marked it at the infrequent intervals through the night— not that strange, eerie sound.

"She is beginning to improve," said Aunt Neale in her soft, cheery tone. "I have watched this way a good many times when life was not so precious perhaps. Yet her own is dear to any true mother," and a heavenly smile illumined the face. They could trust her verdict. Aunt Neale was almost as good as a doctor.

They stood there in a speechless thanksgiving for which there were no words. Jane brought up a cup of bouillon, and Millicent drank it passively. She sat beside the little bed. Drayton paced up and down with noiseless steps.

He paused and leaned over Millicent. "Nora is up-stairs," he said. "I had almost forgotten. She came home quite early full of distress——"

"Oh, I must go to her !" Millicent's heart was

moved with intense sympathy. She had supposed in a vague way that Nora would go to school with Beatrice.

Nora lay on the bed in a dull, passionless state, having exhausted herself with weeping. She did not even stretch out her hands. Had she any real right to mamma when she had been so selfish and indifferent?

"Nora dear, Aunt Neale thinks there may be a little hope." She bent over and kissed the warm, throbbing face, so instinct with healthy life that even despair could not quench it. "My darling, do you think you could be less dear than if you were all?"

"O mamma!" There was a child's despair in her voice.

"You were my only comfort in a time of great sorrow. Perhaps I ought not to have taken so much joy again, but you loved him, and he loved you. You would always be the sweet elder daughter if there were half a dozen."

She clasped her mother's neck and drew her down beside her, shivering as she kissed the cool forehead.

"I want her to live," she said with fervor. "I have prayed and prayed! And, mamma, I *will* learn to love her. She is beautiful and sweet, and God sent her to papa for his own little girl. If He had taken her away!" and a convulsive tremor shook the child.

"She would have been God's then altogether until we could have gone to her. But I truly think He means to spare her to us. You have had no breakfast, Nora. I thought you would go to school with Beatrice."

"Oh, no, mamma, I couldn't. Beatrice is so glad to be the only girl—she doesn't mind the boys. But Pearl and Princess are happy with little sisters."

"I think you can learn to be happy. Would you

rather have this life and home or that back at Beaumanoir ?"

" Oh, this, a hundred times more, mamma."

" I have sometimes thought it might not have been a
wise step where you were concerned——"

" Please do not think so any more," Nora entreated
tearfully. " Why, we have been so very happy, and
Papa Drayton is splendid ! The girls envy me. And
now you will see—if Baby Hope gets well. O mamma,
how pale you are ! If you should die——"

Millicent knew then she had not lost her daughter's
exuberant regard. With years and experience the finer
love would develop.

" I am very tired and worn."

" Please go back to papa and baby. And perhaps I
had better go for a few recitations, though I am afraid
they have all gone out of my mind."

" I would not try to-day. Come down to luncheon
presently—for the morning is most gone. Poor papa is
very weary as well."

Nora kissed her mother and let her go. Then she
brushed her hair afresh and took off her crumpled frock
and glanced over her lessons. She would be allowed to
recite to-morrow and keep her standing. But at first
she could not concentrate her attention and the words
blurred together.

Aunt Neale came up and comforted her with her wise
sweetness, that had been manna to many a young soul,
and had brought peace of mind to her own mother in
troublous times. Then she heard Uncle Bertram's inspiriting voice, and she knew matters must be on the
mend, but she would not go down until afterward.

They were all strangely quiet at luncheon. No one

wanted to recall the great stress, and neither was the hope sure and steadfast.

Nora could not keep the tears from her eyes when she caught sight of her mamma's strained and pallid face. "It is painting afternoon," she said as they strolled through to the reception-room, where a lovely breeze was sweeping out the curtains like a flock of sailboats.

"I think you had better go, if you can pluck up enough courage. Nurse has ordered me to bed," and Millicent gave a wan little smile.

"Yes, mamma," Nora answered with unwonted meekness.

She heard her papa upstairs in his "den." She was so in the habit of running thither. She had really monopolized him hitherto. Would it be hard to let him belong to some one else ? Should she begin bravely and at once ?

"Nora, child"—the voice floated down to her soft and entreating—"are you going out ?"

"To the painting class. Mamma thought I might."

"Wait a moment. I must have a little walk, and we will go together."

This attention was one of the things Nora had been so proud of. She raised her eyes in grateful love as he came down in the hall and kissed her, and just glanced into the nursery, where the placid watcher held up her finger.

They could not say much to each other, for both hearts were full. But his smile of farewell was a bit of exquisite joy she carried in the studio with her.

"O Nora Drayton, is it true your little sister is very ill ? You were not at school——"

The quick tears flooded Nora's eyes as she answered

with a great effort, " They think she has improved a little."

" It isn't scarlet fever nor diphtheria——"

" Oh, no ; something to do with teething, I believe."

She was very quiet and attentive, and walked slowly homeward by herself, for she did not want to talk. Papa was in the library with a gentleman, so she went on upstairs. Mamma was lying on her bed. The nurse came to the door.

" The baby is better," she said, " and your mother is asleep."

Then Nora went at her two days' tasks. She was proud of her standing at school. She liked to be first in a great many things.

When Uncle Bert came in, just before dinner, he said the baby was out of present danger. Nora squeezed his hand with such adoring gratitude he was really moved, and he kissed the rosy, tremulous lips with full and free forgiveness.

Several days passed before the baby began to notice much. But the proof of her good constitution was in her rapid recovery when she was once started. And when she smiled two little white teeth showed. She had fallen away noticeably, and her dimples had a kind of languid effect.

The nurse stayed a week, which gave Millicent a chance to recruit. But she looked curiously changed to Nora, delicate and high-bred. And baby had just that appearance.

" I don't resemble mamma a bit, do I ?" and Nora turned from the mirror over the hall chimneypiece, where she had been settling her hat to the proper girlish droop.

Mr. Drayton smiled. He was gathering up some papers. After he had walked to school with Nora he was going downtown.

"Not much; but I see Auntie Dell in you, and a gleam of Aunt Violet——"

"Oh, I shall never be handsome like either of them."

"Auntie Dell insists she wasn't a pretty little girl. Grandpa Carew admits that she was not, and she says he taught her how to be beautiful."

"But she has such lovely eyes—brown velvet eyes," and Nora's voice had a caressing sound. "Mamma's are dark, but they have a limpidness like a shaded river. And mine are so queer—blue and gray and dark sometimes. I suppose I *do* look like my own papa."

It was a trial to say it when little Hope was going to look so much like mamma.

"And the pictures indicate that he must have been handsome. He was that, and charming as well, Uncle Bert declares. Nora, I wonder if this would comfort you any?" and the old, mirthful gleam illumined Mr. Drayton's face. "You know this Mr. Mallory, who has been here several times, and dined with us last night? While we were smoking upstairs he said, 'Drayton, I suppose this tall girl was by your first marriage; she looks so much more like you than Mrs. Drayton; and I heard some one say this was a second marriage.'"

"O papa!" She clasped her arms around his neck and laughed. "Then I can't look much like any one——"

"And if you have an insuperable objection to beauty it may comfort you to know that no one ever complimented me on my good looks in my youth."

"But, papa, you are very fine-looking. Uncle Leonard is the handsomest man I know, and I love him, but I would not change."

"Thank you, my dear. The first time you see Auntie Dell you ask her for the text Grandpa Doctor gave her about Socrates, which she insists made her a handsome woman."

"But she had the lovely eyes."

"Yet they might have worn a very different expression. And our dear old doctor insists that it is one's duty to make goodness beautiful and beauty so full of goodness that it shall bless the world. When we are as wise as mamma we will write a book on the manifold uses of beauty, by two people of wide experience. Come, or you will be late."

Nora laughed as she tripped down the wide stone steps. She felt very happy. Papa had not made a bit of difference, though she had told him with the sweetest seriousness that she should never be jealous of his little girl again. She had tried to notice it more. It was a rather grave baby, not like Honor nor Aunt Tessy's laughing babies. And she had a misgiving that she was outgrowing babies and play. There were so many lessons.

Mr. Drayton had spoken of taking Millicent and the baby away.

"I doubt if she has any trouble under another month or two," said Dr. Carew. "Your house is light and airy, and there is every convenience. But I would like you to try the seaside through the hottest months. Archie has hit on a place through Floyd—a big old place, two houses joined together for a hotel, far enough from the bay that the children cannot stray off and get drowned. I want Aunt Julia and Uncle Dick to go somewhere in the mountains and have a new honeymoon. Lyndell will take care of Ray. Aunt Julia has been too devoted all these years. Violet and Amory will join us, and perhaps Tessy for a month."

"Why, you will have quite a settlement of the clan."

"Yes," with a bright laugh. "Nora's school closes —when?"

"About the middle of June."

"Get off before the heat of July. Though I do not think you or Millicent need worry about the baby. Still I pray you may never have such hours of anxiety again."

"It was a good thing when the Lord put two such men as you and your father in the world," Drayton said, clasping his hand with fervor.

Lyndell, who seemed to have the best opportunity, went down to Edgeport with Winthrop and reconnoitred. The house was partly furnished, had been rented early in the season, but the lessee had failed to meet the terms. There was a great stretch of scrubby pines back of it, cleared up and answering the purposes of a shady resort. For the next half mile the ground sloped gradually down to the great bay, and there was the mighty ocean beyond. Dell's heart was moved with the memory of a bygone summer.

They soon settled their plans. Nora's school exercises went off satisfactorily and promotion awaited her.

"I think I do not want to go away from you this year," she said to her mother. "And I like the girls, and Miss Whiting, who thinks I may do some quite praiseworthy things in painting. I am to do some sketches while we are away. O mamma, do you know that in a very little while I shall be fourteen? It frightens me, I seem so old. I have changed in the last three

months. I have different thoughts ; I see things clearer ; and then I shrink back and want to be a little girl."

" You need not grow up too fast. I want you to have
a long, lovely girlhood. I did. And there will be as
many cousins for you—only Leonard was older than I,
and the boys were bigger, and we were all together."

" Mamma," very softly, as she hid her blushing face
in the little niche between her mother's cheek and shoulder, " I am beginning to be glad about Hope ; for I
shall outgrow being papa's little girl, and there will be
another. When I am twenty she will be only a little
more than six years old. And if I should marry and go
away, how lonely you would be !"

Marry ! Millicent started at the thought.

" And I am finding that it does not change the love.
It is queer about love, isn't it? that you can give so
much and have so much left. And if one had it all,
would it be any sweeter or better ?"

" No, dear ; it is one of the things made to distribute.
As God loves us we are to love the brethren, and that, I
think, means all those brought into near relationships
first ; for if we cannot love our brother, whom we have
seen, how shall we love God, whom we have not seen ?"

" There are so many strange things about it. And I
am trying to feel pleased when baby is admired. I was
proud at first, but I think I wasn't really happy over it.
And to have her look so much like you, with your beautiful eyes——"

Yes, it had been hard for a little girl who had never
had a rival. It was almost like giving her mother away.
Grace and generosity seldom came in one enlightening
flash, but were the fruit of time and experience.

Millicent drew her closer and kissed her. Perhaps they

had both made too much of a little girl of her at first. Even mothers learned wisdom by degrees.

And Nora had to acquire grace by degrees. Coming home one afternoon, full of eagerness with something she wanted to relate to her father, she found him slowly pacing the hall with little Hope in his arms. He was so big and strong and protecting, and she looked like a blossom gathered out of a garden of wonders. She was in short frocks, and her dainty pink shoes were outlined against his coat, her pretty cap, with its pale pink bow, just leaving visible a tiny fringe of dark hair, and her soft, dark eyes seemed to hold some mysterious depths. He had one tiny hand pressed to his lips.

During the earlier months Millicent had kept the baby in a quiet, reposeful atmosphere, and its father had hung over the crib and watched it in secret joy. Now it had begun to notice and laugh and have preferences, and he was quite fascinated with its intelligence. Millicent could not resist his claims.

They were waiting for the carriage to come. Mamma was improving the time with a few last things that mothers often find to do.

Nora stood quite still and flushed with a sensation of resentment. There was such an exultant joy of possession in papa's face that it was like a stab. She rushed into the reception-room and threw down her books, while her breath came in gasps. Then she remembered. It was his little girl.

"Papa, are you going out?" She entered the hall again; she tried to look up in unconcern, but the flush and the eyes betrayed her and touched him with sympathy.

"We are going to drive in the Park awhile. Will you

be through with lessons and everything? We shall be home shortly after five, and then you and I might take our turn."

" O papa !"—and there was unconscious repentance in her tone—" yes, I shall be very glad to."

He stooped a little and kissed her. Baby Hope looked over his shoulder and smiled and showed her two white teeth, and then put out her hand.

Nora kissed it—not a real heartsome kiss, to be sure, but she felt better for the effort.

The carriage came, and mamma floated lightly down the stairs.

" Now, if we had known you would be home so soon, papa could have had a larger carriage."

" Never mind," she said cheerfully.

" I am going to take her afterward," rejoined Mr. Drayton.

Her mother smiled tenderly on her.

" I have a long music practice," explained Nora—and now she smiled in return—" and you are always advising me to do my work first. I suppose it is best, if it is not always pleasantest."

Millicent carried away the remembrance of the bright girlish face.

# CHAPTER XXII.

THE musicale was a success. It was from four to six in the afternoon, and every pupil could ask two friends as well as her parents. Nora was quite delighted to have Auntie Dell and Win, who was staying in the city, for her guests besides her parents. She played her part of the duet admirably, and she experienced a secret pride at having two such lovely women for her share. She had found out the text about Socrates, and she should always recall it when she looked at Auntie Dell.

Then there was nothing to do but to get away. Mr. Drayton had sent down a load of cheap summer furniture. Mrs. James Murray had found a splendid housekeeper with a big boy who would be glad of a summering. They would use the large dining-room as if it really were a hotel, and each family have their own apartments. There were two spacious porches, and some near-by trees where hammocks could be swung.

Honor Carew was almost a year old, and could run about like a kitten. The Amorys came up with a nurse and the three children, the youngest, little golden-haired Alice, lovely, but not quite as pretty as Pearl, perhaps. And all of August there would be Aunt Tessy and Uncle Leonard and four more children, with little Ned Beaumanoir, who was such a bookworm that every now and then his busy brain had to take a rest.

Archie had started his mother and father on a long tour to the mountains and lakes. Ray soon fraternized with the children, she was such a merry, social body. All the mothers were tender to the motherless girl ; but she was so sweet she would have won her way on her own merit.

A merry life it was—playing in the sand, running about with no regard to fashion, sitting around with the real leisure of life and no conscientious urgings to climb or walk or discover new points or capture curiosities for city exhibition. There was boating and bathing, there were whole day excursions on the water, and on Sunday the old church, with Floyd an attractive and earnest young rector, who through the week was a delightful cousin. Mrs. Floyd they all liked very much.

"It is something like the old summer at Gardiner's Bay," said Violet, "only it is us and our children—and then we were the children."

"Oh," exclaimed Cecil, "do you remember, Dell, when we went out on the bay with the little fellow in his father's boat, that we loosened some way?"

"Jack Marcy? Yes." Lyndell Carew laughed with almost girlish gayety, and yet the memory of it was tragic. "Florence was with us, and she cried, I remember."

"And what did Auntie Dell do?" asked a chorus of eager voices.

"It is quite a story," declared Uncle Cecil. "And Auntie Dell wasn't a very big girl—how old were you?"

"Fourteen ; but I was large for my age."

"And I am fourteen," said Nora, coming around and putting her arm over Auntie Dell's shoulder. "I want to know what you did that was heroic. Perhaps I can be heroic some day."

"It was only a little presence of mind ; and if I had been kindly and careful beforehand I should have been spared all the anxiety. I was told to do something in a manner that offended my pride——"

"But it was not your real duty," interposed Violet. "Children ought to be trained in just ideas. Ethel and Alice were left with the children, and Florence was their own sister."

"I have the floor," declared Cecil gayly. "And I was one of the heroes. The other lad was about my size. We worked his father's boat loose and went sailing off in high feather ; but when we had gone far enough we could not make the boat turn around, and if Auntie Dell had not seen us and been brave enough to come out after us we should have floated off and been drowned, no doubt."

"But how did she do it?" asked Sherburne. "Could she row?"

"She took us in her boat——"

"The wind and tide were against me," interrupted Dell. "I could not row very much, so we just had to float until I could hail some one. It darkened up like a shower, too, but it was only wind. And presently a fisherman saw us and lashed us to his boat and towed us in. We were a good ways from home, and a young man took us in a wagon——"

"Neither of you do the story justice," declared Uncle Archie. "Aunt Julia will tell it over to you some time. Everybody was afraid the little ones were drowned. The night came on, and they waited and waited. Aunt Edith and Aunt Laura were away, and Aunt Julia was alone with Ethel and Alice, who were little girls as well. Everybody was wild with fear. And so you can imagine the joy when the wagon stopped and the children were handed out."

"And was Uncle Cecil a little boy like me?" asked Sherburne, catching Uncle Archie's hand.

"I wasn't as old," said Cecil. "And we children were all wild about Auntie Dell, who used to tell us the most fascinating stories—Uncle Floyd and Uncle Win and myself."

"I think Auntie Dell ought to tell us stories now," rejoined Sherburne. "Papa told us once how she went to England and found ever such a lot of cousins and had a splendid time. And all Sherburne House and the ground for miles and miles around was hers, and she gave it to papa for all of us—didn't she, mamma?"

"Yes," said Tessy, raising her eyes to Dell.

"And that is why I was named Sherburne, and why little sister is named Dell. And Princess isn't a real name. When she gets a big lady she will be called Aurelia."

"I like Princess best," exclaimed the little girl, holding her head royally.

When the young children were in bed that evening Nora found Auntie Dell alone on the porch. The men were sitting on some camp-stools and leaning against tree trunks, smoking and talking. It had been a long while since so many of them were together.

"Auntie Dell," the young girl said, "what a splendid life you had when you were little, didn't you?" and there was a sigh of half envy.

Lyndell put her arm around the young girl as she answered, "It was eventful, if you mean that. There were some great joys in it and some bitter sorrows. I

think now I should not wish it for any one, while I feel
very well satisfied.''

'' And to give up Sherburne House——''

'' Oh,'' returned Auntie Dell, '' that was not as heroic
as it seems. You see,'' with a bright, tender smile, '' I
wanted to come to New York and live with my husband,
just as your mamma did ; and some one was needed to
look after the estate and Aunt Aurelia, and Uncle Leonard
loved the old place. You know I was not born there,
and I had been changed about so much.''

'' I should like to do something grand,'' said Nora
longingly—'' give up something——''

'' My dear, I think you have been doing something for
the last three months. Giving up one's self is the noblest
of all.''

'' It was very hard at first ; but I felt so sorry, so
heart-broken when papa was likely to lose his little girl.
And suddenly I grew so much larger and older and saw
how generous papa had been to me, and that little Hope
had a better right to all the care and love. I could not
understand how he could love two children.''

'' And Uncle Leonard loves four children, and Uncle
Bert loves three.''

'' But, you see, the children were their very own, and
there was no one with a half claim,'' said Nora in some
perplexity.

'' And you had had so much separate love from your
mamma and everybody you had been spoiled.'' Aunt
Dell kissed her laughingly. '' But I think you have
learned now ; and it is one of life's most important lessons. I have been jealous, too. I have made myself
quite miserable ; and then I learned how grand it was to
have a love to give away, how happy it made those

around you. I am glad you are giving some to Hope, who is such a sweet little darling, and will be a pleasure and delight when you are grown and having other interests.''

Yes, she was trying not to claim the first and best of everything quite as if it were her right, and to feel comfortable when little Hope was praised for her winsomeness. She was so bright and playful now! Princess and Ray just adored her.

It was such a delightful summering to have so many of them together. The four men were like brothers in good fellowship, and the three younger ones were full of hope and ambition and ready to take up life in earnest. Cecil was going out on a government expedition, Winthrop had a city position under consideration, and his home would be with Archie. Aunt Julia would have two of her boys for some years to come.

'' But I don't wonder mothers think the little childhood of their children the happiest time of life,'' said Tessy one day before the final dispersion. '' One wouldn't keep them little forever, and yet how sweet they are before one has to really think of their future or have them go out to school or in the great world. What a pretty lot they are !''

They were all playing about except the two babies, for Honor had grown rapidly. Dell experienced a pang at losing the babyhood she had enjoyed so much. Hope had thriven wonderfully, and cut her next two teeth with only a few days' discomfort.

'' I do wonder when we shall all be together again? When Alice makes her next visit perhaps. It will be a good many years before we can have a wedding at Sherburne now that Fanny has gone. It is as good as a play to see her. She is ridiculously domestic, always going to mamma for recipes she never uses ; and if that wonderful baby sneezes out of regulation order the town is alarmed. As she is named for mamma, of course *she* thinks there never was such a baby. I am glad some one has a name that suits the Laura, for Amory would have made a wretched combination. But what a marrying off there will be twelve or fifteen years hence ! And think of us girls being way along in middle life ! Well, we have had a delightful summer."

Tessy was to spend some time in New York with her mother, and Violet was prevailed upon to make Millicent a visit. Archie had chosen his home within easy railroad communication—a pretty cottage with a plot of ground overlooking the Hudson. Uncle Stanwood was a good deal improved by his summering, but the united entreaties prevailed upon him to relinquish active army life.

" You would not be able to stand it very long—another year perhaps—and some sudden strain might end it in a moment. You have done conscientious service many years, and surely you can accept retirement," Bertram Carew said with some decision. " You and Aunt Julia ought to have a few years of rest and pleasure and comfort."

" We have had the pleasure and comfort all along ; we even extracted some out of the hardships. I should feel better if my boy was going to fill my place——"

That would be Uncle Dick's great disappointment.

" But he is doing his duty nobly in that station to which God, through sorrow and misfortune, has called him. And I hope so to train my boy that in the years to come he will think consideration to his parents one of his first duties. Why should it not be so ? Why should we fill the child's mind with ambition for himself solely ?"

" You will set him an excellent example."

" My father made sacrifices for me. He did a good deal of giving up when it would have been a pleasure to keep ; and even now he has relinquished some tender associations that we may have these rich and delightful years together."

A gravely sweet smile illumined the speaker's face.

" I suppose I ought to consider my boy's desire," Major Stanwood said in a half-convinced tone. " Military life has always been dear to me, but it is less so to him."

" You will find him in the front rank if his country should need him. And I am not sure but that an honest, upright, faithful man serves his country as truly in times of peace, even if he does not gain much glory."

Aunt Julia, woman like, was delighted with the prospect of a home with the true home-like feeling, where she could have two of her boys with her and Floyd not far away. To be sure, when word came of Harry Lepage's promotion for some meritorious work Uncle Dick winced a little, although he was too manly not to rejoice.

Alice and Gifford were well and happy. Grandon Park was enlarging its borders and had added some thriving industries. The other good work Mr. Moore and Dr. Wolff had in hand did not languish. They were helping people who might have become outcasts and criminals in cities to become useful citizens. There were no wonderful theories, but the old divine law of work, with fair remuneration and temptations kept out of the way of the weaker brethren until health and energy returned and they could battle successfully.

Millicent and Dell were making admirable and intelligent centres. Millicent took up her work again with a broader purpose. There was so much in her life. True, the self-indulgent side of Reese Drayton might have narrowed it if she had not been wise as well as watchful. She never for a moment forgot she was his wife—she was too utterly happy—but she would not allow him to drop down into the sensuous ease he really enjoyed and lose sight of the higher duties. He was so ready to give money and have that the end of it. Bertram Carew had some qualities it would be hard for Reese Drayton to acquire, and yet both were manly men. Perhaps the shaping on Drayton's part had been the ease of prosperity. Bertram had toiled energetically for his. Marrying an heiress had not weakened his fine fibre. Dell's early training had led her to place less value on the showy side of money.

Nora had chosen to continue her school life in the city, to her mother's entire approval. There were so many points, she found, in which a mother's oversight was needed. And there was the continual struggle against selfishness—which, after all, was its true name, though a weaker mother might have excused it as the intensity of an ardent nature. Little Hope grew charming, with pretty baby intelligence, and she was unusually lovely. But Pearl Amory had not been spoiled by beauty or love. Her father idolized her and was proud of her beauty, and no evil had followed.

"If she should die!" Millicent thought with terror. She was not the robust baby Nora had been. Yet Nora, she remembered, was grave and wondering and sometimes filled her heart with dread.

"You were fortunate in having two to divide your love," she said to Lyndell.

"And then one for myself. I have a secret, exultant

consciousness that Honor loves me the best of any one
on earth," and Dell smiled radiantly.

" And are you not afraid?"

" I am not going to live in the shadow of death or ter-
ror. I think God means us to enjoy every good thing
He gives us. If He sends me sorrow I must bear it ; if
He sends me joy, why shall I not take it thankfully?"

" I think of Reese mostly."

" Of Reese, who has had so many good things all his
life!" Lyndell laughed with a joyous, amused sound.
" Milly, you cannot play Providence to him. Where is
your trust ? Do you save it all for books and comforting bits of advice that go out to others?"

" I think I am convicted," and a sweet light of not
only conviction but acceptance shone in her eyes.

" We do carry a good many useless burdens. We do
judge a great many things ' before the time.' And there
is only the one day's work given us. To do that is to
plant the seeds for to-morrow. And you who are teaching so many——"

" Had better apply my own doctrine. Yes, I think I
shall. And I will try not to feel anxious because Hope
is beautiful and is loved or be afraid to love her myself."

Millicent found many new cares with Nora, who had
come to the trying years. What other girls said and
did and had was her standard. Her mother wisely drew
the line at evening dissipations. There were two or
three pleasure clubs that met evenings, some with the
aspect and motive of beneficence. It seemed very hard
to refuse her.

" You are too young to judge. And if you attend to
your studies you will have no time for such pursuits,"
she said gently.

Nora thought it very hard. Millicent's life had been so simple compared to this—a governess until she was sixteen, and the regulation pleasures of a small country round until she had somewhat matured and was able to see the wisdom of restrictions.

They spent the holidays at Beaumanoir. Her mother was delighted to have her at home once more ; and it was amusing, for Mrs. Beaumanoir had never, been engrossed with her youngest daughter until now. Fanny's house, her husband and baby were unfailing themes of admiration. The house was well appointed and well managed ; perhaps the surprise was that Fanny proved herself so capable. The baby was sweet and intelligent, rather imperious in her demands, and after an experience of Dr. Underwood's fatherhood Milly felt she could say nothing further to Reese. And Fanny actually pointed out some traits of superiority in her baby.

Aunt Aurelia was just a little more feeble. She never came down to breakfast. Tessy arranged the little room where Dell had once been so miserable and from which she had so daringly escaped into a dainty tea-room. The glass cabinet held some of the choicest china and silver. There were portraits of the children, and pretty gifts they had sent from time to time, a cozy table that accommodated four, and some easy-chairs ; and one of the greatest treats the children could have was to be invited to take tea with Aunt Aurelia and Aunt Eliza.

Millicent found it quite delightful herself when she and her husband completed the quartette.

" You are very happy," said Aunt Aurelia as she studied the contented face. " And your mother has been a happy woman. I hope you may have just as good fortune with your children. Her six have been prosperous and brought no especial anxiety. I am glad Fanny is settled near by. We are all very fond of Dr. Underwood, and though we used to think Fanny rather flighty, she makes a nice wife—a good, plain, every-day wife. And your father is one man out of a thousand, Millicent.''

Millicent's eyes smiled gratefully at the praise.

'' And now tell me about Dell and the babies and Aunt Neale. I enjoy the letters so much ; but I shall also enjoy looking at her through your eyes.''

The picture lost nothing in Millicent's loving heart and voice. Dell's felicitous home life, her delightful motherhood, the place she filled in society, the affection she gave to the doctor and Aunt Neale, were all charmingly depicted.

'' It could never have been here of course,'' said Aunt Aurelia. '' I think no one but Tessy could fill this place with such perfect grace of contentment, and make a man as happy as she makes Leonard. O Milly, I feel that God has forgiven my blind obstinacy and mistakes, and the thorns have been taken out of my path as well as Lyndell's. I *did* want to control her life and shape it to suit myself ; and the Lord showed me a more excellent way—His way. And here I rest in serene content with no wish ungratified.''

Tessy was deeply interested in her own family, and fond of hearing the little details of household life. James was prospering and had a charming little family. Lawrence had studied medicine and was well established. Con was still abroad with some party of explorers, writing brilliant letters from almost any quarter of the globe. It was a great trial to his mother that he did not come home and settle down. The two young sons were doing

well, and little Densie was a second edition of Tessy, with
all the advantages of wealth.

"And you are truly happy?" Millicent said with perhaps a faint misgiving. Did not the routine grow wearisome at times, she wondered.

"When I have so much?" Tessy looked up bright-
eyed and satisfied. "I am like my mother in that;
home is the most delightful place to me, and the children are an unfailing source of joy. When they are
grown larger Leonard and I mean to take a long holiday.
We are saving up some of our pleasures, so that the cup
of life will be sweet to the last drop."

"And what a companionable girl you are making of
Miss Dennis. You educate her as well as the children."

"She is ambitious and quick to learn. And now
Sherburne goes to Mr. Armitage three mornings in the
week, and she has begun Latin with him. It is a help to
the child. I suppose in another year we must send him
away to school; yet we want him to be so grounded in
home virtue and affection that the risk will be less. We
have a music teacher for them all, and the rest I find
May does very well. Mother wants me to send Princess
up to her for a year, when she is a little older."

"We should all be glad to have her," declared Millicent cordially.

"We do not mean to make much change while Aunt
Aurelia lives. Next year she will be eighty. We want
her to live so we can celebrate that birthday. She and
Cousin Carrick are each the last of their family."

"It seems a long while to live. And I am almost
frightened when I look at my own mother. How swiftly the years go by!"

Tessy thought Millicent's baby extremely beautiful.

Nora had remained with Auntie Dell on account of two parties in holiday week, and a dinner that was to be given at a day nursery by a society of young girls. Millicent knew she could trust her with her cousin.

They had to stop a few days in Washington. Baby Hope seemed to improve with the journey, and caught many cunning ways from the other babies. Her father considered her a perfect marvel; but he found Paul Amory quite as enthusiastic.

It was delightful to be at home once more and to take up daily life with a true and fervent interest, eager for the best, not only for herself and the stranger within her gates, but some far outside longing for the beauty and inspiration, and stretching out pleading hands for a little of the abundance. A strange, sweet, sacred thing it was to live when one believed all these things were of the Lord, and that the children who were not of this fold were all to be gathered in by the divine mandate and human love.

# CHAPTER XXIII.

## A GROWN-UP GIRL.

THERE are many happy years in some lives that flow on like a smooth stream winter and summer—the temperate zones of existence. The ordinary wants are satisfied, and the soul has accepted its limitations.

It was so with Lyndell Carew—a wife in the completest sense, who made her home a joy to her husband, a happy mother enjoying her children before the real questions of what should be done with them pressed upon her. There were four now—a baby boy had been added.

She and Millicent had one of the true satisfactory friendships that did not stop with their own selves. Other women drawn into the circle of their sweet, wise influence grew in spirit, in harmony with what was wisest and best for them, sometimes not the ardent dream of youthful enthusiasm, but the disappointment was sweetened graciously. Young aspiring geniuses came to Millicent, confusing desire and ambition for possibility of achievement, and were set in the right paths with such tender wisdom that they turned to her later on with the strength of honest conviction and took up new lines cheerfully.

"It is the hardest thing," she said one day to Dell, "to convince a person who has a great love for some one course in life that he or she cannot reach the highest

point of success in it, while the faculty that is passed by
with a secret disdain would develop the best that was in
them."

" I understand," returned Dell with a laugh. " I
had boundless ambitions myself. I wanted to gain a
wide influence, to have power over those with whom I
came in contact."

" I am sure you do." Millicent glanced up in surprise at the brilliant face.

" Yet it is on the foundation of the commonplace. I
do not understand even now why Ethel, of all us girls,
should have been given a real artistic genius and made
no use of it. I *did* covet that. Then I was almost jealous of your genius. And once I wondered if I had remained single, with all the money at my command, if I
could not have established some beneficent charity that
would have brought me in the front rank of women."

" But you would never have given up Bertram !"
Millicent stared at her in a dazed fashion.

" Women have given up lovers, nay, even husbands.
You see, the love *was* too seductively sweet to me," and
a rare smile illumined her face. " I believe now that I
was created for a wife and a mother, and some of my
choicest lessons were learned from Mamma Murray.
There is my husband and four children and two old
people—seven souls to care for and make happy. For
now we have come to esteeming happiness a good thing,
not a snare for weakness. There are hundreds of women
in the land doing the same work, and they will be the
salvation of the world if the duty is well done. Seven
souls ! And ten righteous souls could have averted the
flood. And I am happy in doing the common daily
things."

Content and joy irradiated the lovely face.

"I am wondering what I shall do with Nora," Millicent said after a pause. "She will graduate in June. She is fitted for college. Last year she was wild to go, and straining every nerve for fear. Now she really does not care. She paints very well, but she has not the divine inspiration. She writes a superior essay for her years, and has critical judgment. She is very proud of her mother's genius, but she does not aspire to it, and has no jealous feeling. The idea of medicine shocks her. She has no fancy for any specialty, no ambition to fill any decided place in the world."

"Then let her keep that of her own—a sweet young girl—and make girlhood lovely. That was what you did."

"And was very happy in it." A soft flush lighted up the lovely face. "Perhaps I am over-strenuous. I can't make myself feel old enough for the mother of such a girl. The babies keep me at the verge of youth."

Hope had passed through several anxious periods in her babyhood, though she always recuperated rapidly, and was somewhat above the average in size, while her childish beauty increased rather than diminished. The likeness to her mother was wonderful, and gratified her father beyond measure. She was between three and four now, and the little boy not yet a year old.

Nora had not made the slightest protest at his advent. And though Mr. Drayton was proud and glad to have his boy, the joy that had overwhelmed him at the birth of little Hope was toned down and reasonable.

There had been a few changes in the four years. Aunt Aurelia had rounded out her fourscore years, and once again the family had gathered under the hospitable roof of Sherburne House. The Osbornes had lost Colonel Ashton, and now the whole party were on their way to England, where they expected to spend at least a year. There were three bright, intelligent children. Lady Ashton had aged a good deal, but was still charming.

Gifford was to take sole charge while they were gone. His marriage had been extremely happy and successful, and he was settling to an earnest and wise manhood.

The prettiest show at Sherburne was the children, and there were a host of them—Edward Beaumanoir's two boys, Floyd Stanwood's one, and Leonard's pretty flock. The doctor and Miss Carew timed their yearly visit for this occasion, and neighbors and friends came from near by and far away.

Miss Sherburne was much moved by the ovation. It was a delightful reunion in the old house, where there had been so many good times. Mr. Beaumanoir had grown very grandfatherly, and Sherburne and little Ned were crowding each other for favors. As for Nora, she seemed quite grown up.

Dell remembered afterward, and it was a sweet memory to recall, how tender Aunt Aurelia had been to her, how interested in the children and all her happenings.

"I am glad you have Aunt Neale," she said. "No elderly person ought to live alone. They need the comfort of love more than they did in their youth. Eliza and I have had such an abundance."

Whether Ethel meant that her tidings should arrive at the opportune moment and add a grace to the occasion, or whether the event was of so much importance she announced it at once, it certainly came at the right time. She had achieved her ambition. She was

to marry a title and an estate with a record centuries old
—rather impoverished, to be sure—and she did grudge
the Longworth millions that were so tied up and diverted to others that she could not have the handling of
them. Florence was living in Paris among the fashionable colony. Neither of them could be happier than
Alice, Lyndell knew.

Some weeks afterward, when they had settled to their
own living in separate homes, the word came with a
shock that Aunt Aurelia had passed away. She had not
come downstairs for several days, though she was very
cheerful, and Dr. Underwood firmly believed she would
recover from her temporary weakness as she had times
before. Cassy left her at midnight sleeping quietly.
Before daylight she rose from her couch and crossed the
room. There was a faint, sighing breath, as if one was
satisfied to lay down the burden of life, and then all was
silence, so peacefully did Aurelia Sherburne fall into her
last slumber. There was no pain or sorrow to remember, and her face had the smile of everlasting peace.

Owing to some profitable investments, Aunt Aurelia
had died quite a rich woman. Miss Carrick was left a
comfortable annuity. She was the last of her family
now, her brother having died. All the younger generation had been remembered, but there was a special bequest to Lyndell and Tessy, and a loving letter, that Dell
wept over and cherished as one of her priceless posses-
sions.

Afterward Leonard Beaumanoir and his wife took a
journey abroad. Grandmamma was to look after the little flock. It was Aunt Aurelia's wish, her gift for the
loving service of years.

And then life went on again. Children were growing

up and trying their wings in the fascinating atmosphere
of knowledge, to be fitted for the men and women of the
coming years—Pearl Amory with her mother's inherit-
ance of beauty, Princess with a rare voice and birdlike
grace, Ray Stanwood carefully shielded from any bitter
knowledge, loving and beloved, and a merry host of
younger ones.

But Nora Drayton felt entirely grown up when she
graduated with honors one bright June day and had the
valedictory. She had many friends among the young
people and was deluged with flowers.

"There are enough to make the whole house fragrant," she said laughingly as they were handed out of
the carriage. "Everybody has been very generous to
me. I suppose most boys—young men," flushing a little, "*would* rather shower favors on some other girl
than their sister. And it is funny, too. Their sisters
really love them, while the other girl can't care for all
of them."

"I should think not," replied Mr. Drayton. "I
suspect you have more than your share."

"But you see how beautifully they will come in to-
morrow. Papa, you won't have to buy me as much as a
rosebud."

He shook his head as if he were amused and yet did
not altogether approve.

She looked very pretty standing there in the hall in
her gown of soft India silk and airy chiffon. Her great
mass of hair, still light, and of a rare color, was wound
about the top of her head, with some stray ends making
a mistiness at the edge of her broad forehead, that saved
her face by not being high. Her complexion was fair,
bright with youth and health, flushing easily. Her nose

was not of the Greek type, and her mouth rather wide, but her teeth were perfect and her lips full of curves, that laughed and almost danced in her merry moods. The girls could not agree about her. Those who adored her declared she was a beautiful girl ; those who did not thought her rather plain, and their brothers accused them of jealousy.

"You did splendidly," her father said, glancing at her admiringly. She was so gay and sunny, full of the whims and unreason of youth, and going from her most frivolous moods to the second thoughts of coming maturity that she always interested him.

Her mother came and kissed her. She thought she could never get used to her big girl, who was companionable one moment and flying off at a tangent the next.

"You spoke admirably," she said. "You have a fine voice, and"—with a tender smile—"you have had flattery enough for one evening."

"And I am going to bed to get some beauty sleep, although I am not a bit sleepy. I did not suppose the hall would be so crowded. I was a little nervous the first moment, but that soon passed over. Good-night, mamma dear ; good-night, papa," her voice melting to gentle sweetness.

"Davis"—when the white billows had floated upstairs—"take care of the flowers and keep them as fresh as possible." Then he fingered two or three of the cards and glanced at the names. One basket that was very beautiful had no card. "Troubles are beginning," and he smiled over at his wife. "Well, there is a dozen years at least for Hope."

Nora's room had been rearranged several times since the day she had moved upstairs. It was exquisite now in pale pink. She found her father most indulgent to her wants and whims. She did feel pricked in her conscience sometimes when she had suggested to him first what would make her perfectly happy when she knew her mother would not quite approve. She went straight over to the mirror and viewed herself from head to foot. Her eyes were shining, and their long bronze lashes made a glitter about them ; her cheeks were in a blossomy pink and her mouth was full of smiles. It always was a smiling mouth except when she was displeased.

" What difference does it make if one can *look* pretty," and she took a few graceful steps up and down. " No girl had as many flowers to-night. I'm so glad Tracy didn't put his card on his basket. Bee would just have been mad. She thought Roland extravagant ; and what would she have said to those beautiful orchids of Tracy's ?"

Lina came in then to help her disrobe and put her things away. When little Hope was hardly two years old the trusty nurse Jane had married, and in the reign of incompetency that followed she had sent home for a nurse and a maid of her mother's training. Lina was a slim, good-looking colored girl with the rather caressing ,Southern ways, and she soon adored Miss Nora, waiting on her and keeping her room tidy, looking after her clothes and yielding to the general tendency to spoil young missy. Maria, the nurse, was a much older woman, and Millicent had found her invaluable, though it was Lina who took Hope out for her walks and was proud enough of her beauty. Millicent sometimes wished she was not so strikingly pretty.

" She will have it all her life and get used to it. Has it been such a cross to you ?" asked Mr. Drayton, smiling, with a tender light in his eyes.

" Violet was handsome. I did not have it all. And mine wasn't showy girlish beauty."

" We won't worry now. By the time Hope is grown up beauty may be quite a common possession," said little Hope's father.

But the girl with no especial beauty except the winsomeness of youth was just as much elated to-night.

" Did you get *all* the flowers, missy? The hall's just full," and Lina looked up out of soft eyes of delight.

" Oh, not quite all," laughingly.

" You're just pretty enough to be married, missy."

" But I'll be married in satin and lace, and I shall have some diamonds then. Three of the girls have diamond rings. Papa's queer about that, and mamma thinks a girl oughtn't wear a diamond until she is engaged. Everything else was splendid but that. And Miss Jay, whose aunt gave her a ring, had only one skimpy bouquet. The flowers made more show," and Nora laughed gayly.

The dining-room was a mass of bloom and fragrance the next day. Fifteen girls came to luncheon. They were all more or less intimate with Nora. Ah, how they chattered and laughed and made plans and wished ! Several of them were going to college. Myra Copeland's brother was to send her to Germany to study music, and Elsie Prentice was going to Paris with two other girls to study art.

Beatrice White had just squeezed through in the severer studies.

" I'm going to be married as soon as I get a good chance," she announced, " but it must be some one with plenty of money, and who won't grumble as papa does. Mamma has a fight about everything. She wanted to go to Long Branch, and at first he made an awful fuss, but he gave in at the end."

" Make your husband give you an allowance. Mamma has one. And then papa gives her so much for each of us when summer comes on. She sends the little ones in the country to a cousin's, who is glad to keep them for a trifle. And she is to take Julia and me to Narragansett Pier. I do wish Julia would get married, and then I could have a clear deck. Where are you going, Nora Drayton ?"

" And what do you mean to do ? Come, we have all been telling."

" I haven't any plans but just to have a good time. Mamma would like me to go to college, but I do not think studying is fun by any means. There are a few things I would like to go on with."

" You are just the luckiest girl I know, Nora Drayton. And who sent those lovely orchids—or was the basket from your father ? It was some one who did not mind how he spent money."

Nora's cheeks were like a rose.

" Oh, it was your father. Girls, that doesn't count."

Nora colored still more deeply. Perhaps she had better let it go at that. She certainly could not confess the donor.

For young girls who had aims there was a good deal of chaffing. They had been serious enough the past fortnight.

The luncheon was very nice and not too ornate for a young girls' party, and the serving was exquisite. As the crowd said afterward, everything was perfect at the Draytons'. Then they went up to Nora's room and inspected her belongings, and said they had had a most delightful time.

She counted the orchids afterward. Twelve large exquisite flowers ! And she wished Tracy White had not spent so much money for them.

Circumstances more than anything else had made the two girls friends. Mrs. White furthered the intimacy. Roland thought a good deal of Nora. She was an ambitious mother, and wanted her sons to marry well. Roland was in a lace importing house, Tracy, the younger, in a bank. Mr. White did a brokerage and commission business, sometimes being very fortunate, and at others finding it hard to meet expenses. Now that the children were grown he thought it ought to be easier, but somehow it was not. He had a feeling that his sons ought to offer some assistance in the household expenses. They helped their mother out occasionally.

Mr. Drayton wondered a little about the orchids. Once he led the conversation around to them, but Nora veered off instantly, and he could not tell whether it was girlish inconsequence or indifference.

" Papa, where are we going this summer ? The girls are planning such lovely journeys."

" Where ? Mamma has been considering. Some place that will be nice for the babies."

" But I am not a baby. I should like a real pleasure," with a pretty, half-pouting smile.

" We might go somewhere when we had mamma settled. The seaside agrees so with Hope. Uncle Floyd wants us to come down there. I think Auntie Dell will go for a month."

" I should like a real pleasure. Papa, do you realize that I am a young lady ?"

She turned her eager, smiling face upon him as she stretched up her utmost. And he forgot all about the orchids.

They fell to discussing the real wonders—Niagara, which she had never seen ; the Lakes and Canada. And in the midst of the talk Millicent came upstairs with a face startled, yet full of interest.

" There is a gentleman in the reception-room. It seems so curious. It almost took my breath away. I never dreamed——" She looked at Nora in vague amaze.

" What has Nora to do with it ?" It sounded like a possible lover, and Drayton stared.

" It is Nora's uncle"—she held up the card—" Baron Zahn von Lindorm."

" Oh, let me see !" cried Nora. " Mamma, is it true ? A real baron ?"

" They were all barons." Her mother gave a little smile. " This is the youngest brother, and we all liked him so much." Millicent smiled up at her husband, who had heard the old romance about Lyndell Sherburne. " Come, you must both come down. He started away quite suddenly, having just found the auspicious moment. They only came in this morning. His wife and his eldest son is with him. They are at the hotel."

They went downstairs. Millicent had heard now and then from him, and he was always coming to America. She had quite lost faith in the announcement. He had apologized handsomely in his frankly cordial way for taking her so by surprise, and he was all eagerness to see his brother Emil's daughter, and Mrs. Carew, who had charmed them almost as much while in Germany as when she was Dell Sherburne.

But he had hardly counted on a grown-up girl. A

stout, fine, fresh-looking man of six or eight-and-thirty, unmistakably German, with the bluest of eyes and cheeks rosy as a girl's, a full face with an almost red mustache, and curly reddish-brown hair, with a very thin place on the top, showing the pink scalp. He took Nora in his arms and kissed her on both cheeks, then studied her attentively, smilingly.

"She is not much like her mother," he said. "Ah, how the years go! And my son is fifteen. But you look well and happy, child ; and your mother has grown more beautiful."

Then they talked over plans. The baron had come to inspect some machines for iron-work and to visit one of the Northwestern States, where a company had been making large investments in land with a view to settling a colony if it was found practicable, and he was to see what would be needed.

No one thought about the orchids after that. The next day Uncle Zahn brought his wife and son to luncheon. The boy was rather diffident, and would not venture on English. Nora was very glad she had kept up her German. Aunt Amalie was pleasant, a little awkward at first, but when she went up in the nursery that all vanished. Two such lovely children were enough to rouse any one, she declared.

That afternoon they were to go out to Pennsylvania to a great iron centre and finish their visiting when they came back. And then Baron Zahn wanted to see the Carews.

"Why, it is like a bit out of a story," laughed Nora. "Mamma, I hope I shall go to Germany some day. They are so different, so enthusiastic, and really charming."

" You would have a delightful time at Trachenburg,"
returned her mother. " It is a grand old place. And
six new cousins ! And your Uncle Franz has five children. His eldest son has the old Luckenwalde estate."

Nora would have enjoyed talking about her new relatives all the evening, but Tracy and Beatrice White came
in. She was going to Long Branch next week. They
would only spend a fortnight, and then later on go
somewhere else. She had some cousins going to Bar
Harbor, and she meant to move heaven and earth to
spend some time with them.

Then Nora surprised her about her new German
uncle.

" A real baron and living in a castle !" she ejaculated.

" But mamma lived in a castle and I was born in one,"
declared Nora laughingly.

Beatrice had never heard that before. Nora had not
been enthusiastic about her German relatives—perhaps
because she had loved Papa Drayton so well.

Nora and Tracy had been looking over the photo-
graphs of Luckenwalde.

" You had the orchids ?" he said in a whisper. " I
told you I should send the handsomest thing I could
find."

" Oh, I wish you had not !" Nora felt her cheeks
burn.

" But you *knew* they were mine. Roll would have
been awful mad, because they were so much finer than
his, so I did not put out any sign," with a conscious sort
of smile.

They stayed quite late, and Beatrice bade her friend a

very affectionate good-by.  To think Mrs. Drayton had been Baroness von Lindorm !

" You must go to bed at once," said Millicent, " you were up so late last night."

Nora went with the uncomfortable consciousness of having a secret it would be awkward to tell.

# CHAPTER XXIV.

NORA thought her good time had certainly begun. When Uncle Zahn returned there was all New York and its suburbs to see. Auntie Dell was glad to welcome the visitors, and they had delightful little excursions. Then Uncle Zahn with his wife and son were going up to West Point for a day, thence to Albany and to several noted resorts in the State, ending with Niagara. From that point they would travel West. And now, why could they not take Nora? It was inconvenient for Mr. Drayton to accompany them, as just now he did not like to leave Millicent with the children ; but he could take the night train out to Niagara and bid the travellers good-by. They would return by the way of the Lakes and Canada.

Roland White came in one evening with a note from his sister. She had forgotten a little picture that Gertrude Harrison had taken to copy. Would Nora get it and keep it until her return ?

" I don't see why she couldn't have sent Roland," she said to her mother ; "and I am to call any afternoon after four. I am so busy, too. Still I ought to say good-by to Miss Harrison, so I suppose I must go."

She had a nice little call, but Miss Harrison had returned the picture the day before. And then as she was walking down the street she met Roland, who begged her to go over in the Park for a stroll.

"I really haven't an hour to spend," she said with her bright smile. "I am going away for a week to have a grand time. Papa is coming to Niagara for me. I am just wild with delight."

Mrs. White had said in the presence of her boys, but not in a specially advisory manner, "There is a girl worth trying for. She is well connected, and her own father must have had quite a fortune. Mr. Drayton will no doubt be very generous to her—and there is no end to his money. If I was a young man I should look out for such a chance."

Roland White kept thinking it over. He liked Nora, she was so bright and winsome. And if she had a fortune of her own—and a father-in-law like that might do something handsome for one in a business way. He did not mean to marry a poor girl. He could just manage to exist on his salary, and certainly it was not enough for two. When winter came and the fun of society began he would look out for her. He walked home with her. What a style she had for so young a girl! She did not ask him in as he half hoped. "I wish my vacation was next week instead of August," he said to his brother; "I'd go out to Niagara and have a few days with Nora Drayton."

Tracy considered. He had meant to join a party at Lake George—well, he could go with them on Saturday, and the next Thursday start for Niagara. Roland shouldn't have everything his own way, even if he was two years the eldest; but he kept his own counsel.

Aunt Amalie was delighted to have Nora for a companion. Her father let her go rather reluctantly since

Millicent felt that she could not refuse. And oh, how delightful it was to be really grown up ! She patronized her Cousin Waldemar, and he would even have been happy if she had ordered him about. Uncle Zahn was much interested in the military aspect of West Point, and met some of the officers. Then there was a day and a night at Saratoga, a journey through a beautiful section of the country, with two or three stops, and their first view of Niagara was in a magnificent sunset.

The next morning, almost as soon as they started out, she espied Tracy White. He seemed quite surprised and extremely delighted, and proved a very entertaining guide and companion. Baron von Lindorm invited him to dine with them at their hotel, and as it was full moon they had a charming evening rambling about, and Cousin Waldemar felt quite *de trop* with them. Nora was so utterly delightful.

Tracy bade them good-by that last evening. The real freedom would be ended when Mr. Drayton arrived. Besides, now it had the appearance of a casual meeting.

" Oh, I wish you could stay !" Nora said frankly.

The next morning Mr. Drayton came, and Nora was rather sorrowful at parting with her relatives. She put down the visit to Germany as one of the lovely things to come.

The Draytons took in Watkins Glen on their way home, and spent a day or two in some of the smaller towns. Arrangements had been made to go to the seaside at once. Nora was so full of delight that nothing could seem dull. When mamma and Auntie Dell discussed the future, she declared she was not sighing for wisdom, but meant to have a good time for a year or so.

" Why should she not ?" said Uncle Bertram. " Life

will never be full of such roseate tints when youth is gone."

" She is so young to begin with society," sighed her mother.

" Do not put her in the forefront then. Let her take a little by degrees."

It seemed rather odd on their return to the city not to go to school. Millicent took up a course of literature with her ; papa read the German poets. Little Hope was very cunning, and had become so fascinated with her big sister that her admiration was quite irresistible.

Miss Beatrice White had a coming-out " tea" early in the season. She was a stylish young lady. Nora was not quite sure that she liked her well enough for a friend, but Myra Copeland was gone, and the two girls she had admired most were in college. Helen Meade was studying art with a girl's enthusiasm. Not that time hung heavy on Nora's hands—no day was ever long enough for the things she planned—but Beatrice seemed to have chosen her. It was flattering to be consulted on almost every matter when Beatrice was right in the whirl and had fashion and propriety at her tongue's end. Her preferences, too, had a sincere sound.

" I know you will tell me just *what* you think, you are so candid and honest. I can rely upon you," Beatrice would declare. But she said the same thing to half a dozen girls, and their opinions had no weight un- less they coincided with her own. She was not really insincere, and she admired Mr. Drayton without stint, while she felt a little afraid of Nora's serene, clear-eyed mother.

The Whites' house was made very attractive. Mrs. White began to think her sons might as well marry successfully as her daughter. She was very cordial to several young ladies, who considered it great generosity on her part. "For you know most mothers are so afraid of their sons," said a pretty society bud.

Nora had liked both young men in a girlish fashion—almost as she had liked Uncle Cecil and Uncle Win. Yet she vaguely mistrusted the little change. Roland began to appropriate her when she was out anywhere. Tracy decoyed her into corners and had appealing bits of talk. And he often said, "Don't mention this to Roll." He had begged her to say nothing about his being at Niagara.

"Why?" she asked with wide-open eyes. "Papa knew it."

"That doesn't matter a bit. Roll thinks he as good as owns you. He wanted to get away that week and couldn't, and he would be awful mad if he thought I had outgeneraled him. For peace sake one sometimes keeps things to one's self."

Nora was puzzled. "No one owns me," she said spiritedly. "I like you both—we have been friends so long."

"I only stipulate you shall not like him best," with a low laugh any other girl would have understood.

"I do not think I ever should," she returned in a serious tone, but it was incautious if honest.

When they called on her she did not mind so much : Mr. or Mrs. Drayton was present. On such occasions Tracy always appeared the most agreeable. She had a feeling that Roland was rather annoyed. And Mr. Drayton did keep close watch of his daughter. Nora enjoyed the sense of protection.

But the young people and the invitations increased so

that Millicent felt Nora was occupying a rather anomalous position. Girls' luncheons did not accomplish the object. So Nora was given a "small and early" dance. The babies were moved on the top floor. A band of music was stationed in the hall, and the supper was dainty and delicate.

Nora was in a maze of delight. It seemed to her the most delightful event imaginable. Auntie Dell came around for an hour or two, and Uncle Cecil happened to be in the city.

"Oh," said Beatrice White, "how did you chance to know that Mr. Mallory? I have met him several times, and he is just charming—the right sort," with a smile and a little toss of the chin that was piquant. "His uncle is a big man."

"Mr. Robert Mallory comes occasionally. He and papa have business about investments. I like him. He suggests my Uncle Leonard in some ways, only he is a good deal older."

"Well, you may have the uncle if you will give me a fair show for the nephew. Mr. Robert Mallory has been a widower so long that everybody has forgotten he had a wife. His sister keeps house ; she is old, too. And Mr. Adrian Mallory is the hope of the house. He has been abroad and almost everywhere."

"I knew he was abroad last year," said Nora. "It was about a railroad in Russia." She would air her little knowledge.

He had called once with his uncle. While the elder men had played chess he had told her about the Kremlin. But she took a new interest in him now, and she was glad he seemed to find some attractive girls. He danced once with her. She did allow Roland White two dances, but her father had begged her not to dance more than twice with the same person.

There was often just enough for a quadrille around at the Whites', and Roland claimed her then rather more than was enjoyable. She was too good-tempered to spoil the set.

Oh, how happy and pretty she was this night! Her eyes shone with rapture, the swift smiles made a dazzle and dimpled her face. She was such a charming hostess as well, for she wanted every one to have a good time.

" It has been splendid," said Tracy, " but I like best the evenings at our house, when old Roll is out of the way and we can talk by ourselves."

She was too inexperienced to know "just by ourselves" might have a danger. It had a friendly sound. Tracy nearly always had some interesting book to talk about. Roland affected athletics and games of various kinds, or the winners and the betting. Playing was much too hard for him unless it was a game of billiards.

When Millicent longed to restrict her daughter's pleasures she recalled the delightful times of her own youth. True, at Ardmore and the surrounding neighborhood everybody was known.

She spoke one day of Roland White sending flowers so often.

" Young men of that stamp are not counting on marriage," Mr. Drayton said reassuringly. " They spend all their salaries on themselves and their pleasures, and unless they have an opportunity to marry an heiress keep out of the danger. I doubt if the young fellow has a hundred dollars ahead—hardly enough to purchase a betrothal ring," and he smiled with a touch of satire. "Nora's safety lies in the fact that she is not rich enough to tempt an adventurer."

The holidays came on apace. There were bazaars and entertainments for charity ; there were dinners and feasts for poor children ; there were day nurseries and kindergartens that had to depend on outside help, and were very thankful to have enthusiastic young girls lend a hand. Auntie Dell found work that interested Nora, and between this and pleasure she was bright and happy and developing into a charming girl, coming nearer to her mother in true companionship. Millicent experienced a great pleasure in having a grown-up daughter. She went more into society herself and began to study young people with a new interest.

Christmas nearly overwhelmed her with favors. Young men were quite sure flowers with Christmas wishes would be accepted. Roland White sent a box of elegant roses. Tracy had lilies-of-the-valley and various flowers forced out of season—expensive of course. And Mr. Robert Mallory sent her an elegant set of books they had talked about only a few evenings before.

"If a young man had many friends, Christmas and Easter and birthdays and all the occasions would ruin him," said Mr. Drayton. "I wish they were less expensive, or that fashion should decree that it was vulgar. O Nora, did you ever discover the donor of the orchids ?"

A bright glow flushed up in her face, and her eyes drooped in embarrassment.

"Who was it, my dear ?"

The tone was kindly, not curious.

"It was Tracy White, papa. He said when I graduated he should send me the handsomest flowers he could find. They had no card, you remember. But he admitted it afterward."

The quick color came and went. It seemed almost as if Nora had something more to say, but she did not utter it.

"My dear girl"—and Drayton put his arm over her shoulder in a tender clasp—"I cannot quite approve of such expensive gifts from a young man except to his betrothed ; and I hope you have"—what should he say?—"no sentimental fancy that is not likely to be realized."

"O papa!" She hid her blushing face a moment. A pang of apprehension shot through him. "I like them in a certain way. I *do* like Tracy the best ; but I sometimes feel afraid. I wish we were not meeting everywhere. I can't quite explain it to you——"

"Has he troubled you with love-making?"

She hardly imagined papa's voice could be so stern, and for a moment she was startled.

"No, not that." Then she raised her head and met his eyes. Some secret knowledge came to her. "O papa, I am afraid it *is* that," and now little gleams of light flashed over her. "I never thought. We have been such good friends——"

"You are not interested?"

"Not that way. Oh, I do not want any bothers about lovers. I just like a nice good time, and you are lover enough for me."

He kissed her out of gratitude. "We must find some way, then, to drop gradually out of the friendship. I do not cordially admire either of the young men, though I think their training may be answerable for the extravagance and selfishness. Mr. White is far from being a rich man. His sons spend money with a free hand,

dress in the best style, and choose expensive amusements.  They ought to lift a part of the burden from
their father ; instead, I dare say, they spend every penny
of their salary upon themselves and lavish gifts on others.
It is *not* right.  I do not like you to encourage any
young man to waste his money.''

" But, papa, I never have.  And I really scolded about
the orchids.  I wish he had not sent these.  Oh, what
shall I do ?  It would be rude to send them back.''

" For the sake of Christmas-tide you must keep
them ; but when you thank him, will you have the courage to tell him such gifts are forbidden in the future ?''

" Yes, I shall be glad to.''

" It is sometimes this desire to be generous, as young
men call it, that leads them to spend more than is truly
theirs—to borrow, or, what is worse, take what does not
belong to them.  You are very young yet, my darling ;
and we do not mean that you shall tempt any young
man to lavish his money on you.  What pleasures you
need your parents will provide.  When you are older
you will have more judgment ; but I hope you will
never tempt any young man to go beyond his means to
gratify your whims.''

" You are so good, papa—you always were.  You
spoiled me, mamma said.  Oh, you wasted your money
on me when I was a little girl, and mamma thought it
very reprehensible.  And then I wasn't glad for you to
have a little girl of your very own ; but it wasn't for the
money's sake.  I am very glad now—you believe that ?''

" I certainly do.''  She was sweet and wholesome.
He wanted the very best to happen to her.

A fortnight earlier Miss Beatrice had arranged a theatre party with Roland's help.  A married friend was to

chaperone them. He would have Nora quite to himself.
The difficulty of seeing her alone piqued him and ren-
dered pursuit more fascinating. He fancied he was
really in love with her. He liked her better than any
girl he knew for her very freshness and freedom from
wiles.

Beatrice meant to capture Mrs. Drayton by a *tour de
force ;* but there was an honest engagement for that
very evening. They were to hear a celebrated ballad
singer. Aunt Elsie and Uncle Floyd were to be up to
buy Christmas gifts. Mr. Drayton had taken tickets for
them all.

Roland White berated his luck in ugly terms to his
sister. To waste all that money and have no good of it !

"Nora Drayton hasn't an ounce of wit. She is not a
bit in love with you or she would help. And there are
plenty of other girls who would jump at you," consoled
Beatrice.

"Girls without a penny, and who want the whole
world," sneeringly.

"Roland, there is Elsie King, who has her own
money, and who would give her two eyes for you."

"And who is snub-nosed and wears eights in gloves
and has horrid taste and a brother in a soap concern !
And she is twenty-five if she is a day. No, thank you.
I want a good connection when I marry. That German
uncle is the kind."

"Well, I am awful sorry it is coming out this way.
Why don't you make some sort of stand and go there
boldly. But Nora *is* kind of bread-and-butterish. I
cultivate her mostly for the style," and Beatrice wrinkled up her nose, of which she was justly proud.

"We must both be careful," Mr. Drayton said to his

wife. "The young men are attractive—we will give them their just due. I can see that Nora is not thinking of lovers, but of the good time that a girl ought to have. How wise we shall be by the time Hope is grown!"

"I am glad that is a long way off," said little Hope's mother with a relieved inspiration.

Nora acknowledged her Christmas flowers to both young men with a formal note of thanks worded exactly alike.

"It looks as if I had copied it out of a 'ready letter writer,'" she said laughingly to her mother. "And I think Beatrice doesn't care quite as much for me—she has come to have so many other friends."

For a fortnight Nora did not see either of the brothers. There was skating in the Park, but she went up in the early afternoon with papa, and there was nearly all of one week spent with Aunt Julia. Uncle Archie was very fond of Nora.

Tracy White happened to see a notice of a reception at the literary club of which the Draytons were members. Mr. Drayton was on the committee.

He had another gift for Nora. He meant to speak first, if it was a possible thing. Roland had been rather "grumpy" since Christmas. He was a good deal in debt. He envied the young men who could go to their fathers for a "lift." And this evening he had come home with a severe cold.

Tracy hung around with an eye to the house until he began to feel desperate. Then a hack came, and Mr. Drayton helped in his wife. Tracy wondered why they did not keep a carriage of their own. They rolled away, and he gave them good measure before he ascended the stoop. Davis wondered a little as he ushered him into the reception-room. No orders had been left.

Nora was curled up in an arm-chair with a book. She stepped out with a little effort and laughed at the awkwardness. She wore a soft white woollen gown with a Roman sash, whose long ends nearly touched the floor. A wide ruff of lace was about her neck, and if Tracy had not loved her before he would have fallen in love on the spot.

She held out one hand, but he took both.

" It has been such a long while since I have seen you except across the church on Sunday. And you don't know how glad I am. How lovely you look !"

Nora was desperately embarrassed. Of course he couldn't know mamma was out.

He led her to the sofa. The pleasant old friendship, the remembrance of evenings when he had helped Beatrice and her with lessons or untangled a knotty point in mathematics, the dances and the jolly times together, swept over her, and she could not be coldly dignified. If there was some one else present !

" I have wanted so to see you. I have thought of you day and night since Christmas. And I had another beautiful gift for you——"

" Oh, you must not give me anything more," she interrupted. " The flowers were too extravagant——"

" I don't know what you will say to this." He laughed in a low, happy fashion that somehow disarmed her and roused her curiosity at the same time. Then he clasped her hand and seemed to select the slim forefinger, and Nora had very pretty hands.

" Oh," he began, " I have so much to say. I want matters on a different basis. I want to come here and feel welcome. I don't blame your father a bit for being particular about young men ; but we are well connected, and I've never run about town like some young fellows. And though my position isn't very grand now—a chap of twenty-two can't expect everything—I've loved you right along, and those two days at Niagara were just splendid. We should be the happiest of the happy. And see here, my darling"—he drew a little box from his pocket and opened it, and a glimmer of light flashed across the apartment—" I have been saving up money and waiting to get this ; and I bought it a week ago for this blessed little finger. Just let me put it on, and to-morrow I will ask your father——"

Nora uttered a quick cry and sprang up. " Oh, no, no !" she exclaimed. " You must not ! I cannot take it——"

The ring rolled to the floor, and lay there a quiver of living light.

" Nora, you do not mean it. Why, when we have been such friends ! It is too sudden, perhaps ; but it doesn't seem sudden to me. I have been thinking about it for weeks. One can so rarely see you alone ; and you have not been at the house of an evening I can't tell when. And the many little things I have said that you seemed to understand—or do you love Roland best ?"

" I don't love anybody. O Tracy, take the ring away ! I can't wear it. I didn't think friendship meant that. I do not want to be engaged to anybody," and Nora's eyes were full of tears.

" Then I will wait for you. When you come to think it over, and all the nice times we have had, and that I shall never love any one so much again——"

Nora was bewildered. If she could fly to mamma ! If she could make him understand !

" Roll loves you, I suppose," reluctantly, "but he wouldn't try to make you happy half as much as I should. And some other girl could comfort him ; but no one will ever be as dear to me."

He believed it with all the ardor of twenty-two. He had given her his boy's heart, but he did not know then it could be taken back and given away joyfully later on.

" I am so sorry if it is my fault. Oh, why couldn't you have fallen in love with some of the other girls that used to come !" She drew a long sigh and turned her face away, lest she might be tempted by his sorrow. But she did not even want to love him, though she liked him very much. " We must not talk any more about it," she said with a great effort, " mamma would be displeased."

" But I should tell them the first thing. I hate underhand work. I knew that if Roll suspected me of coming there would be war. It was my precious secret, and I was just waiting until I had the ring and a chance offered——"

" You must not send me anything more. Papa and I had a talk about the flowers. You must not think of me in that way, and—and—you must not come any more."

How could she be so cruel with that sweet face ! He looked utterly amazed.

" I am so sorry," she said brokenly, but she stood up straight and firm. A curious self-possession was coming to her, and she was too honest to dally or hold out the smallest hope.

The young man picked up his despised ring. How very handsome it was !

" And all our nice times are ended ? You will never dance with me again, and I suppose we must just say cold little bits to each other when we meet. But I am glad you are not going to love Roland—I couldn't stand that.''

She wondered why she should feel so friendly toward him. But it was best not to confess it.

"Good-by," he said. She was even holding her hands behind her, and that vexed him.

"Good-by. Oh, I am so sorry you loved me that way." Her steady eyes dismissed him.

When the hall door shut she threw herself on the sofa and cried as if her heart was broken. Oh, would he feel very wretched?

And there the two found her when they came home from the reception, which had been delightful, and with many tears she told her story, and was praised for her firmness.

"Really, I did not think trouble would begin so soon," said Reese Drayton to his wife. "That he should hit this evening when she was alone! Then to have two of them! And it is only the foolishness of youth."

# CHAPTER XXV.

"I WOULD just like to go to Beaumanoir and Sherburne House and stay there a month," Nora declared the next morning. "I can't help meeting Beatrice and Roland, and there is the dance at the Remsens' on Monday evening. I have accepted it. It is mean to go away just to save one's self."

"I could not take you. I have some very important business on hand," said her father. "I might go on Monday."

It was settled that evening. Mr. Mallory had to send his nephew to Washington the next day. They could telegraph to Uncle Leonard, who would care for Nora until he could take her home.

"You do not seem to be afraid to transfer her to another young man," remarked Millicent with a touch of uneasiness.

"I am not afraid of this young man," was the quiet reply.

"I hoped there would be no lovers for a year at least."

Nora was up early and in blithe spirits. Her father crossed the ferry and took her to the train. She was seated in the drawing-room coach when Mr. Mallory entered—a quiet, gentlemanly, refined young man of six-

and-twenty, who was companionable without being offi-
cious, who read his paper and made sundry calculations
in a note-book, and saw that she was comfortable.

She had an interesting story, but in the afternoon she
tired of reading. Now and then they talked a little, but
she was not in a light-hearted mood. At the journey's
end Uncle Leonard was awaiting her, and Aunt Violet
was delighted to have her for the next two days. And
at first it was comforting to be out of the perplexity.

Miss Beatrice was surprised when she dropped in one
morning to talk over the subject of party gowns. Mrs.
Drayton admitted that Nora's departure was rather sudden, but vouchsafed no explanations.

Mr. Mallory went to the Remsens' dance. His uncle
insisted he should not be moped up altogether with old
people and forget that he was young.

Beatrice was delighted, and in a delicately flattering
manner laid claim to him. She spoke of Nora's defec-
tion. Wasn't there something mysterious about it?"

"I dined there Friday evening," he said with his
grave courtesy, "but no one made any comment."

"She is going to miss some of the loveliest entertainments during the next fortnight," Beatrice remarked
sympathetically. "And *I* miss her. I am very fond of
her. We were at school three years, and she ran in and
out of our house like a sister."

Secretly she was glad Nora had not been home the
night he was at dinner.

Adrian Mallory was very much interested in Mrs.
Drayton. She and her husband were such an admirable
couple. Genius did not spoil her, it seemed. Then he
met Beatrice at a musicale, and she was charmed with
his attention. Fond as she was of pleasure, she did not

mean to be talked about with non-eligibles in her first season.

Three weeks later, when Nora returned, he had become quite a frequent visitor at the Draytons', and of course he was not going to give up the pleasure because there was a young girl in the house. She was so bright and natural, so ready to oblige her parents, and her adoration of them was pleasant to watch. His uncle had grown very fond of her he remarked.

"I ought to have married some one myself who had a girl like that," he remarked jocosely one evening as they were smoking together. "Adrian, it's time you were looking about. Don't pattern after two queer old people like your aunt and myself."

"I have not found you very queer," returned Adrian cordially.

Nora went to call on Beatrice one morning, who teased her a little about her sudden disappearance when pleasures were at their height.

"You are quite sure you were not sent away?" she remarked with sudden sharpness.

"Who should send me?" Yet Nora colored vividly. "I wanted to go." Then she began to talk on another subject.

When Roland called and was informed that Miss Drayton was particularly engaged, and when he found one evening that Nora shunned him unmistakably, Beatrice began to suspect something had gone wrong and questioned both boys. Tracy had been rather cross and reticent of late, but he kept his secret in spite of her endeavors.

"I am sure there are plenty of girls with more real spirit than Nora Drayton," declared Roland loftily.

"Her folks are very fussy. They hardly dare trust her out of sight."

It was the latter part of Lent, and Nora had readings and lectures that were very entertaining, and sewing classes, so she did not join in much gayety. Beatrice kept straight on, but she did feel rather piqued over the distance that seemed to grow up between her and Nora. She did not mind giving up a girl who no longer interested her, but she hated to be given up. And there was a prestige about the Draytons. Then the Mallorys had grown really intimate ; and she thought the pick of all the young men she had met through the winter was Adrian Mallory, although he seemed rather indifferent to society, which accepted him with great eagerness. Women had given up trying to captivate the elder gentleman.

Nora found her good times overshadowed by a vague distrust. There had been little faults in Beatrice that she had deprecated to herself, but with her loyalty she would not complain of—comments on other girls when she was so fair and sweet to them personally. It did not make the matter less reprehensible because she said, "I wouldn't dare whisper such a thing to any one but you, Nora." Then Beatrice was not always truthful. "Oh, did I say that ?" she would sometimes ask, lifting her brows with a suggestion of incredulity that would make Nora wonder if she had heard aright.

She began to enjoy the evenings at home very much. Papa's friends were not all old and gray, and mamma knew some charming women. Little Hope was so sweet and affectionate, and had so many fascinating ways.

"And to think I didn't love you at all in the beginning—did not want you, indeed!" she would cry with a spasm of remorse.

" Would I have had to live with Auntie Dell, then ?" Hope would ask with wondering eyes.

" Of course you would, you little darling. Auntie Dell takes in everybody, and she would be just delighted to get you."

There were weddings after Easter and a rush of gayety. Beatrice White was secretly mortified that she had not married in her first season. There were three men she liked very much, and who had all the requisites, but they had not yielded to her charms. She had at one time fancied Mr. Mallory would not be a difficult conquest. A friend had told her mother that Mr. Robert Mallory was very anxious to see his nephew married. But he was such a constant visitor at the Draytons'. Did he care for Nora?

And then she had such a splendid chance to " settle" Nora. Mr. Mallory was walking home with her from an entertainment given for charitable purposes. He was to say good-by for several weeks, as he had to go to the Pacific coast on some business for his uncle. Very adroitly Beatrice made mention of Nora.

" I have found the Drayton household a very charming one," he said. " I am indebted to them for a great deal of pleasure."

" Nora is just lovely. I have always coveted her for a sister, and I hope now my wishes will be gratified. It fills me with delight."

Mr. Mallory gave a perceptible start. " Do you mean——" then he checked his question.

" Oh, the boys have been in love with her since her early schoolgirl days. We two were such warm friends.

That sounds very young, doesn't it ?'' with a soft, sweet laugh. '' I am puzzled to know which will get her. I suppose the one she loves best, but I do not care so long as she comes to us. If she had fancied some one else this winter we must have given up our hopes, of course, but she hasn't. No doubt the engagement will be announced in the early autumn.''

'' It would be a great gratification to have your hopes fulfilled,'' he returned quietly.

'' Yes ; I think I can give a guess as to the one *she* prefers, but that is my secret and hers.''

'' Yes,'' with his good-night.

'' He certainly has *not* asked her,'' Beatrice decided. '' And he will not ask her before he goes away. He is rather straitlaced about flirtations and all that, and if he thinks she *does* care— I wish he were going to be away all summer, especially if we go abroad. And Miss Nora, I have paid you out for your snubs.'' Beatrice enjoyed the thrill of exultation.

Adrian Mallory was certainly not in love with anybody. He had been a fine student in college, and enjoyed a year of desultory delight afterward. He had not much fancy for business, neither had he any desire for a profession. A leisurely, studious life with some travel and intellectual friends was his ideal. But his uncle had begged him to come, and here were two elderly people delighted to have him. Their fondness touched him. He could be of great assistance to his uncle—he soon saw that—and add to his happiness. And he found in the heart of the great city the intelligence, cultivation, and enjoyment he had associated with the haunts of learning.

The past winter he had tried society to gratify his

kindly relative, who had taken fatherly possession of
him, and he had been rather amused at the trend of the
elder's thoughts concerning the future. Adrian's wife
would be the petted and worshipped member of the
household if she happened to be a girl who would not
object to the position. He knew there were many girls
who would most decidedly. And he also knew the girl
his uncle had chosen, though no one had been mentioned.

He was thinking of Nora Drayton as he walked slowly
homeward. The Whites were ordinary young men with
a full share of good looks and attractiveness. He thought
the younger was the more promising. He knew, and he
could not tell just how, either, that such a marriage
would be a disappointment to the Draytons. Mrs. Drayton still hoped her daughter would want to go to college
and take up some of the higher methods, and he knew
also that Miss Drayton was not what would be called an
intellectual girl, though very bright and intelligent.
But this marriage ! The Whites did seem to adore her.

He was so engrossed all the next day and evening that
he did not make his call until the following morning.
Mr. and Mrs. Drayton had gone driving in the Park with
the children. Nora looked so fresh and bright and joyous. Papa would regret not saying farewell to him, and
how long did he mean to stay away ?

" Oh, it is only a matter of six weeks or so, unless I
should have to go up to Washington. It is so difficult
to get exact knowledge unless you do go yourself ; and
uncle will have a large interest in this matter if he takes
any at all."

" You are just like a son to him," Nora said with
shining eyes.

" And he is a father to me." Mr. Mallory's tone was gravely sweet, and he valued her compliment.

Then they touched upon the winter and the pleasures and how everybody was planning to go to the ends of the earth. When he said good-by he held her hand a moment. Did she really care for those frivolous, unambitious young men? He wished he were her brother to counsel her.

" I suppose when I return, or in the autumn——"

No, he could not be so ill bred as to suggest there might be any cause for congratulation even to satisfy his vague curiosity. She flushed, and he experienced a momentary awkwardness. Then he gave a gentle gesture of the hand and opened the door.

Nora ran upstairs singing. She was very light-hearted this morning.

Girls were going off again to mountains and seasides and summer schools. Plans were being made for poor children's outings and babies' summer homes and worn-out working girls. Auntie Dell and mamma were very much engrossed. Nora looked after the two little ones, Hope, and stout, sturdy Carew, who scarcely looked a bit like mamma. She told Auntie Dell she believed she was coming back to her old love for babies.

Beatrice White and her mother went abroad. Beatrice wrote a little good-by note ; she had been " just too awfully busy for anything," or she would have dropped in. They had hurried to go in this steamer because so many of the best people were crossing over in it. She should have a magnificent time she knew. She wondered Nora didn't go over to Germany to see her uncle's people—for not to go abroad was to be out of the swim. And this was *sub rosa*—she must not breathe a word of it until

the announcement was made. Did she remember Miss
Georgia Crosby? Roland was engaged to her. Her
fortune was up in the hundreds of thousands somewhere,
and they were all delighted.

The two Crosby girls had suddenly flashed upon society,
heirs to a fortune from some queer old person—uncle it
was said- and no one seemed to know much about them.
They lived at a hotel and had a middle-aged widow for
companion, and were not especially refined or intelligent, but they knew how to make the best of their
money.

Nora was really glad. " One changes so much," she
said to her mother. " You wonder how you could have
liked certain people ; you see faults and littlenesses that
you feel half ashamed of, and you find a good deal of
the admiration is sheer flattery. Uncle Zahn's visit put
me up on a pinnacle with a good many people. And he
is such a plain, every-day sort of man, not as elegant as
some of the ordinary men who have lived in the city all
their lives. It is delightful to grow wiser and broader
and more sensible."

Nora had a pleasant summer, part of it among the wild
magnificence of nature, part with the luxury and charm
of fashion and society. And it ran away quickly. She
had not decided to do anything, but she had become a
great delight to her mother.

She had carried about with her a little picture, which
she would have shown to no mortal eyes if she could
have transcribed it, and a voice had said, " When I return, or in the autumn."

It was just enough to keep a young girl wondering.
Adrian Mallory had returned, and now it was autumn
and they were home again. All the city was astir.

Cards were out for Miss Crosby's marriage, sent principally to friends of the Whites. Mrs. White was quite grand and impressive. Beatrice was to be one of the bridesmaids. A church wedding, a reception at a hotel, a Southern tour. The elder Miss Crosby had taken apartments with the companion. Mr. Roland White had done very well for himself, and he wondered now that he had ever thought of Nora Drayton.

She met Tracy a few days after—she was walking in the Park with little Hope, while the nurse had to have eyes all over to keep track of naughty, winsome Carew.

"Oh, I am just delighted to see you," he cried with his face in a glow of pleasure. I have begged Bee to call, but there has been such a fuss about this marriage. And Bee is so grand with all her foreign ways you can hardly come near her. Of course, if it suited old Roll it's all right. He was tired of digging straight along and just keeping his head above water—sometimes hardly that. I think there wasn't oceans of love on his side, but she has a fine-looking husband. I do hope she won't turn stingy. He wanted to go abroad for a year or so, but she said America was good enough for her. Praiseworthy and patriotic, wasn't it?" with a short, doubtful laugh.

"I hope they will be happy. And Beatrice had a delightful time?"

"Well, she didn't capture a lover. She's going after that Mr. Mallory now—the young man, though she would just as leave take the old one if she could get him—he has the money. That is all people think about nowadays. And that is one reason why it is nice to be very young; money doesn't count so much."

She had never had occasion to think especially about money.

He talked on until they left the entrance and met the car.

"Nora," in a hurried tone, "will you not let me call on you?"

"If"—there was such a pleading look in his eyes that it melted her, yet her tone was a little cold as she added, "as a friend only."

And she was very sorry she had given the permission, though her mother did not blame her or see what better she could have done. But the first evening he came Mr. Mallory called, who retired to the library with her father. She was disappointed and not quite cordial, but the young man was glad to renew the friendship on any terms.

"I suppose it *is* true," Adrian Mallory said to himself. He had taken his uncle out to drive in the Park and had seen them together. And now—"I am glad it is the younger one," he added.

The elder Mr. Mallory had been quite ill with some neuralgic and nervous trouble, and Adrian had been devoted to him.

This autumn little Princess Beaumanoir had come up to go to school. Nora found her very bright and companionable, and she also decided that it was not wisdom to see much of Tracy White alone—he dropped into sentiment too easily.

Something else wore upon her a little. She could not quite tell what it was herself, but she was too healthy toned and too conscientious to indulge in sentimental dreams over what might have been a possibility. She was so young—only eighteen—and the world was growing richer all the time; perhaps, too, she was more appreciative of the delightful home.

Beatrice White was very gay when her new sister-in-

law returned. She passed Nora with a careless nod, and
once apologized very pointedly for not calling. She
had so many friends it was impossible to get all around.

There were new friends for Nora and new blossoming
out of her discipline and her joys. She was only in the
first unfolding of life, and now her mother counted on a
long and happy girlhood for her before the real womanhood set in. And there were all the younger cousins,
who would soon be growing up to the girlhood she would
leave behind.

Young men came of course. Teas and luncheons
and dances began, and pretty gowns were an object.
She was glad Miss White's set had drifted out of her
orbit now. Other girls came in, some who were skim-
ming over the crested waves, some who were looking
deeper for the pearls. There were moments when she
experienced an almost infinite pity for Tracy White.
Some strong, loving woman might help him up to the
heights to which he aspired and seemed powerless to gain.

In December the Amorys came up to spend a month
or two in the city. Pearl was growing up in her golden
beauty, and little Alice was pretty, if not so striking.
The bright, manly boy who stood between interested
Nora greatly.

" I am going to have a Christmas party and a tree for
the children. We must send for Sherburne and Ned,
and Bertie is big enough, and Ray," Nora announced.

There was one tree from five to six o'clock, where a
mission school would be gathered. They could have
theirs at eight, immediately after dinner.

Auntie Dell came with three of her babies, but the
twins were big children ; Uncle Archie and Ray, who
was ten. Ned Beaumanoir was tall and slim and rather

pale, but a manly fellow, not quite as rosy and jolly as Leonard's children.

Mr. Mallory and his nephew were the only guests outside of the family. He was improved—quite well, he declared ; the rest was only the infirmities of age.

What a gay time they had ! If exclamation points had been pins, even they must have sought refuge from the shower. Such surprises, such laughter ; and when they all talked at once it was being in a foreign land— you could not understand anything.

When the gifts had been distributed the children sang some carols. Then they had a simple tea and a little dancing, and they all declared it was splendid.

Adrian Mallory wondered whether he had ever seen *this* Nora Drayton before—this tall, sweet girl with her crown of fair hair, her eyes shining with tenderness and lovely thought, the soft color coming and going, the mouth sweet and smiling, as if the right touch might move it to ardent affection. What a charm she had with the children ! How beautiful she looked bending over his uncle whispering some mysterious mirthfulness in his ear.

" I had half a mind to put my arms around her and kiss her," he said afterward. " If I could find a woman like Mrs. Drayton with such a daughter I'd marry her to-morrow. I don't wonder foolish old men marry young girls since they can't adopt them. I don't see where *your* eyes are, Adrian."

" They have been with Miss Nora Drayton all the evening," and the young fellow blushed like a girl.

" Well, well ! Don't take too long to consider. I shall die of old age presently."

Adrian Mallory began to go to the Draytons' again in

a friendly fashion. They talked books and new discoveries, Mrs. Drayton played while Nora sang, or they went over to the hotel and spent evenings with the Amorys. There were some fine plays and some operas, and then it came to the settled times when Nora was at home and there were no other guests, when they drew nearer and nearer in mysterious sympathy and sweetness until the one look and the one clasp of the hand told the story. And then it was spring.

"Do you know, I thought you were engaged to that young White. I heard so."

There was a curious something in Mr. Mallory's voice, not quite jealousy, but apprehension.

"Who could have said it?" Yet Nora's face was one flush of scarlet indignation.

"Were you—ever?" in hesitating inquiry.

"No. I should like to tell you. You have the right to hear."

The long lashes drooped over her eyes, and her voice softened unconsciously.

"Yes, tell me;" but now his tone was entreating.

"We had been very friendly. I used to think they were something like brothers. I liked Tracy the best, he was not so imperious."

"And he loved you." There was a certainty in his tone.

"I suppose he did." She told the story of the ill-fated diamond in a tremulous, pitiful fashion.

"It was after that I heard. And one day, late in September, I saw you both in the Park. Little Hope was with you."

"Oh, I remember."

" He seemed pleading earnestly. And when I called he was here. So I thought——"

" Oh, was that why——"

Her eyes were limpid, her mouth dewy and tremulous, and she hid her blushing face on his shoulder.

" That was why I did not come. But if I had been as much in love then as I am now I should have routed the young fellow utterly. I should have gone armed with your father's authority, which it seems he was not wise enough to obtain. And you are sure you did not love him? He is a nice-looking young fellow."

" If I had I should have taken his diamond," she replied saucily.

" And I haven't even a diamond."

She nestled closer. To be loved in this fashion was worth all the diamonds in the world. It is well there is one supreme moment to life.

They had a small family dinner afterward, and Miss Philippa Mallory, who rarely went out, came and kissed her niece elect and told her how glad they all were to have her.

They did not announce the engagement at once. Nora felt curiously shy with a real lover. Her mother wanted a long engagement. Mr. Mallory insisted upon a short one.

" There is that directors' meeting in London in May, and one of us will have to go over," he said to Adrian. " Why not you, and make it a wedding journey ? And if you liked to go on to St. Petersburg while you were about it——"

The next news was that the Osbornes were on their way home. Their year had lengthened out unconscionably.

"Mamma," said Nora one day, "I should like to be married in the old church at Ardmore, and have the oldest friends of all—Aunt Fanny's wedding was so pretty. We could have all the little girls for maids. Even Hope could be one. O mamma, I never could go away if you didn't have Hope and Carew and papa. Stories couldn't be quite enough to fill your life."

"No," replied her mother softly. Ah, there would be a good many years before she would be required to give away another daughter!

"There would be seven little girls—a mystical number—and Densie Murray, who will be married in the fall. Adrian thinks it would be beautiful. A special memory like that would be lovely for the girls."

Auntie Dell said that was the most felicitous idea of all. If Aunt Aurelia could only be there to see!

They settled upon that finally. It would be the middle of May, just giving Mr. Mallory time for his meeting. The Osbornes were delighted, and went at once to Sherburne House.

Beatrice White was very much surprised. She was balancing the claims of a rich widower and a young man with a long pedigree and not much sense. Roland had fallen gracefully into the position of a rich woman's husband, although it was rumored Mrs. Roland White had a good deal of temper.

Again Sherburne House and Beaumanoir were full of brightness and happy family life. The whole world was attired in bridal array. The air was fragrant with all manner of bloom, and the odorous breath of pine and spruce in their new growth. Birds carolled joyful lays. Like a happening in some other world, Millicent thought of her early wedding day. As she had been the first of the cousins to kneel at the altar in marriage robes, so now her daughter was the first of the new generation. She prayed fervently that the choicest of blessings might be hers.

And Nora was so bright and happy that she inspirited every one. Grandmamma declared that she was full of happiness to the brim ; but Nora said it ran over.

Adrian Mallory was surprised and fascinated with this new world of relatives, all eager for each other's happiness and well-being. He had been an only child, and his aunt and uncle were the last of their generation. He had led a rather solitary life at college so far as friendships were concerned, and now he felt as if he were in a new and magical world. Was there anything quite like love to broaden one's sympathies ? He had been glad to know Dr. Carew ; but Leonard Beaumanoir and Dr. Underwood were most agreeable men to meet. He hardly knew which was the heroine among the cousins, but they all insisted it was Lyndell Sherburne.

" Do you suppose we can live up to the family traditions ?" Mallory asked laughingly of Nora. " I am beginning to feel alarmed."

Everybody crowded around the old church to see " Miss Milly's daughter," who was a baby only a few years ago, and did not seem old enough to get married. But it was a sight long to be remembered in its beautiful simplicity. The old church was a bower of bloom, made so by loving hands. The host of pretty, graceful children that walked up the aisle, two by two, and parted to let Nora and her still noble and dignified grandfather walk between them, the nearest and dearest who stood around, while Adrian Mallory took her from the hands of her kindred, feeling with great solemnity that with the blessed words the marriage feast had begun and the lifetime sweetness was provided in those sacred words " As long as you both do live."

She was so smiling and joyous herself that it was really infectious. Old friends and neighbors pressed round with glad and hopeful words. She had to stand and be congratulated, looking really beautiful in her clouds of white, and the smiling cherubs all about her. This was friendship and love of the purest type Adrian Mallory felt.

They were to go up to the city and have twenty-four hours with Uncle Robert and Aunt Philippa before they sailed. And it was not going away for years, but just a pretty wedding journey.

It was the children in wedding gowns who had the party all the afternoon. Princess and Pearl and Ray were the leaders, and they marched about in stately grandeur, prefiguring future joys. When they were tired out with the day's dissipation and had gone to bed, the mothers and fathers came out on the old porch, where so many conferences had been held. A silvery moon nearly full was shining through the trees, whose leaves still throbbed and rustled to mysterious music.

" The best I can wish her," said Aunt Julia, " is the happiness of an ordinary, commonplace life. I suppose that is really content with what one has."

" We call it commonplace, as if there were something finer and better than the happiness of every-day living, that constitutes so much of our lives," returned Bertram Carew. " We talk of the ideal, but can we shape that vague imagining to the real love for God and our neighbor ? Are there not thousands of little things to the one grand endeavor ? hundreds of ordinary days to the one of supreme joy? And as they are lived, so shall our experience be clearer and more satisfying. Can we not believe

> " ' That all the good the world has had
> Remains to make our own life glad,
> Our common daily life divine,
> And every land a Palestine' ? "